VORTEX

By Troy Denning

Waterdeep
Dragonwall
The Parched Sea
The Verdant Passage
The Crimson Legion
The Amber Enchantress
The Obsidian Oracle
The Cerulean Storm
The Ogre's Pact
The Giant Among Us
The Titan of Twilight
The Veiled Dragon
Pages of Pain
Crucible: The Trial of Cyric the Mad
The Oath of Stonekeep
Faces of Deception
Beyond the High Road
Death of the Dragon (with Ed Greenwood)
The Summoning
The Siege
The Sorcerer

Star Wars: The New Jedi Order: Star by Star
Star Wars: Tatooine Ghost
Star Wars: Dark Nest I: The Joiner King
Star Wars: Dark Nest II: The Unseen Queen
Star Wars: Dark Nest III: The Swarm War
Star Wars: Legacy of the Force: Tempest
Star Wars: Legacy of the Force: Inferno
Star Wars: Legacy of the Force: Invincible
Star Wars: Fate of the Jedi: Abyss
Star Wars: Fate of the Jedi: Vortex

Books published by The Random House Publishing Group are available at quantity discounts on bulk purchases for premium, educational, fund-raising, and special sales use. For details, please call 1-800-733-3000.

FATE OF THE JEDI

VORTEX

TROY DENNING

BALLANTINE BOOKS • NEW YORK

Sale of this book without a front cover may be unauthorized. If this book is coverless, it may have been reported to the publisher as "unsold or destroyed" and neither the author nor the publisher may have received payment for it.

Star Wars: Fate of the Jedi: Vortex is a work of fiction. Names, places, and incidents either are products of the author's imagination or are used fictitiously.

2012 Del Rey Mass Market Edition

Copyright © 2010 by Lucasfilm Ltd. & ® or ™ where indicated. All Rights Reserved. Used Under Authorization.

Excerpt from *Star Wars: Fate of the Jedi: Conviction* copyright © 2011 by Lucasfilm Ltd. & ® or ™ where indicated. All Rights Reserved. Used Under Authorization.

Published in the United States by Del Rey, an imprint of The Random House Publishing Group, a division of Random House, Inc., New York.

DEL REY is a registered trademark and the Del Rey colophon is a trademark of Random House, Inc.

This book contains an excerpt from *Star Wars: Fate of the Jedi: Conviction* by Aaron Allston. This excerpt has been set for this edition only and may not reflect the final content of the final editon.

ISBN 978-0-345-50921-5
eISBN 978-0-345-51957-3

Printed in the United States of America

www.starwars.com
www.fateofthejedi.com
www.delreybooks.com

9 8 7 6 5 4 3 2

Del Rey mass market edition: April 2012

For Kevin McConnell
As he sets out on a grand new adventure of his own

Acknowledgments

Many people contributed to this book in ways large and small. I would like to say thank you to them all, especially the following: to Andria Hayday for her invaluable suggestions and creative support; to James Luceno, Leland Chee, Pablo Hidalgo, Erich Schoeneweiss, Keith Clayton, Christine Cabello, Scott Shannon, Frank Parisi, and Carol Roeder for their fine contributions during our brainstorming sessions; to editors extraordinaire Shelly Shapiro and Sue Rostoni for *everything,* from their patience and great ideas to the best dinner conversation and mojito recipe in the system; to my fellow Fate of the Jedi writers, Aaron Allston and Christie Golden, for being such a blast to work with; to Laura Jorstad for her usual attention to fine detail; to David Pomerico for making the trains run on time; to all of the people at Lucasfilm and Del Rey who make writing *Star Wars* such a pleasure; and, finally, to George Lucas for sharing the galaxy far, far away with us all.

THE STAR WARS NOVELS TIMELINE

OLD REPUBLIC
5000–33 YEARS BEFORE
STAR WARS: A New Hope

Lost Tribe of the Sith*
- Precipice
- Skyborn
- Paragon
- Savior
- Purgatory
- Sentinel

3954 *YEARS BEFORE STAR WARS: A New Hope*

The Old Republic: Revan

3650 *YEARS BEFORE STAR WARS: A New Hope*

The Old Republic: Deceived

Lost Tribe of the Sith*
- Pantheon
- Secrets

Red Harvest

The Old Republic: Fatal Alliance

1032 *YEARS BEFORE STAR WARS: A New Hope*

Knight Errant

Darth Bane: Path of Destruction
Darth Bane: Rule of Two
Darth Bane: Dynasty of Evil

RISE OF THE EMPIRE
1000–0 YEARS BEFORE
STAR WARS: A New Hope

67 *YEARS BEFORE STAR WARS: A New Hope*

Darth Plagueis

33 *YEARS BEFORE STAR WARS: A New Hope*

Darth Maul: Saboteur*
Cloak of Deception
Darth Maul: Shadow Hunter

32 *YEARS BEFORE STAR WARS: A New Hope*

STAR WARS: EPISODE I
THE PHANTOM MENACE

Rogue Planet
Outbound Flight
The Approaching Storm

22 *YEARS BEFORE STAR WARS: A New Hope*

STAR WARS: EPISODE II
ATTACK OF THE CLONES

22-19 *YEARS BEFORE STAR WARS: A New Hope*

The Clone Wars
The Clone Wars: Wild Space
The Clone Wars: No Prisoners

Clone Wars Gambit
- Stealth
- Siege

Republic Commando
- Hard Contact
- Triple Zero
- True Colors
- Order 66

Shatterpoint
The Cestus Deception
The Hive*
MedStar I: Battle Surgeons
MedStar II: Jedi Healer
Jedi Trial
Yoda: Dark Rendezvous
Labyrinth of Evil

19 *YEARS BEFORE STAR WARS: A New Hope*

STAR WARS: EPISODE III
REVENGE OF THE SITH

Dark Lord: The Rise of Darth Vader

Imperial Commando
- 501st

Coruscant Nights
- Jedi Twilight
- Street of Shadows
- Patterns of Force

The Han Solo Trilogy
- The Paradise Snare
- The Hutt Gambit
- Rebel Dawn

The Adventures of Lando Calrissian
The Force Unleashed
The Han Solo Adventures
Death Troopers
The Force Unleashed II

*An eBook novella
**Forthcoming

REBELLION
0–5 YEARS AFTER
STAR WARS: A New Hope

Death Star
Shadow Games

0

STAR WARS: EPISODE IV
A NEW HOPE

Tales from the Mos Eisley Cantina
Tales from the Empire
Tales from the New Republic
Allegiance
Choices of One
Galaxies: The Ruins of Dantooine
Splinter of the Mind's Eye

3 *YEARS AFTER STAR WARS: A New Hope*

STAR WARS: EPISODE V
THE EMPIRE STRIKES BACK

Tales of the Bounty Hunters
Shadows of the Empire

4 *YEARS AFTER STAR WARS: A New Hope*

STAR WARS: EPISODE VI
THE RETURN OF THE JEDI

Tales from Jabba's Palace

The Bounty Hunter Wars
The Mandalorian Armor
Slave Ship
Hard Merchandise

The Truce at Bakura
Luke Skywalker and the Shadows of Mindor

NEW REPUBLIC
5–25 YEARS AFTER
STAR WARS: A New Hope

X-Wing
Rogue Squadron
Wedge's Gamble
The Krytos Trap
The Bacta War
Wraith Squadron
Iron Fist
Solo Command

The Courtship of Princess Leia
A Forest Apart*
Tatooine Ghost

The Thrawn Trilogy
Heir to the Empire
Dark Force Rising
The Last Command

X-Wing: Isard's Revenge

The Jedi Academy Trilogy
Jedi Search
Dark Apprentice
Champions of the Force

I, Jedi
Children of the Jedi
Darksaber
Planet of Twilight
X-Wing: Starfighters of Adumar
The Crystal Star

The Black Fleet Crisis Trilogy
Before the Storm
Shield of Lies
Tyrant's Test

The New Rebellion

The Corellian Trilogy
Ambush at Corellia
Assault at Selonia
Showdown at Centerpoint

The Hand of Thrawn Duology
Specter of the Past
Vision of the Future

Fool's Bargain*
Survivor's Quest

*An eBook novella
**Forthcoming

THE STAR WARS NOVELS TIMELINE

NEW JEDI ORDER
25–40 YEARS AFTER
STAR WARS: A New Hope

Boba Fett: A Practical Man*

The New Jedi Order
Vector Prime
Dark Tide I: Onslaught
Dark Tide II: Ruin
Agents of Chaos I: Hero's Trial
Agents of Chaos II: Jedi Eclipse
Balance Point
Recovery*
Edge of Victory I: Conquest
Edge of Victory II: Rebirth
Star by Star
Dark Journey
Enemy Lines I: Rebel Dream
Enemy Lines II: Rebel Stand
Traitor
Destiny's Way
Ylesia*
Force Heretic I: Remnant
Force Heretic II: Refugee
Force Heretic III: Reunion
The Final Prophecy
The Unifying Force

35 *YEARS AFTER STAR WARS: A New Hope*

The Dark Nest Trilogy
The Joiner King
The Unseen Queen
The Swarm War

LEGACY
40+ YEARS AFTER
STAR WARS: A New Hope

Legacy of the Force
Betrayal
Bloodlines
Tempest
Exile
Sacrifice
Inferno
Fury
Revelation
Invincible

Crosscurrent
Riptide

Millennium Falcon

43 *YEARS AFTER STAR WARS: A New Hope*

Fate of the Jedi
Outcast
Omen
Abyss
Backlash
Allies
Vortex
Conviction
Ascension
Apocalypse

*An eBook novella
**Forthcoming

Dramatis Personae

Abeloth; female entity
Allana Solo; child (human female)
Ben Skywalker; Jedi Knight (human male)
C-3PO; protocol droid (masculine droid)
Eramuth Bwua'tu; attorney (Bothan male)
Gavar Khai; Sith Knight (human male)
Han Solo; captain, *Millennium Falcon* (human male)
Jagged Fel; Head of State, Galactic Empire (human male)
Jaina Solo; Jedi Knight (human female)
Kenth Hamner; acting Jedi Grand Master (human male)
Lando Calrissian; entrepreneur (human male)
Leia Organa Solo; Jedi Knight (human female)
Luke Skywalker; Jedi Grand Master (human male)
Natasi Daala; Chief of State, Galactic Alliance (human female)
R2-D2; astromech droid (masculine droid)
Saba Sebatyne; Jedi Master (Barabel female)
Sarasu Taalon; Sith Lord (Keshiri male)
Tahiri Veila; defendant and former Jedi Knight (human female)
Vestara Khai; Sith apprentice (human female)

A long time ago in a galaxy far, far away. . . .

Chapter One

BEYOND THE FORWARD VIEWPORT HUNG THE GOSSAMER veil of Ashteri's Cloud, a vast drift of ionized tuderium gas floating along one edge of the Kessel sector. Speckled with the blue haloes of a thousand distant stars, its milky filaments were a sure sign that the *Rockhound* had finally escaped the sunless gloom of the Deep Maw. And after the jaw-clenching horror of jumping blind through a labyrinth of uncharted hyperspace lanes and hungry black holes, even that pale light was a welcome relief to Jaina Solo.

Or rather, it *would* have been, had the cloud been in the right place.

The *Rockhound* was bound for Coruscant, not Kessel, and *that* meant Ashteri's Cloud should have been forty degrees to port as they exited the Maw. It *should* have been a barely discernible smudge of light, shifted so far into the red that it looked like no more than a tiny flicker of flame, and Jaina could not quite grasp how they had gone astray.

She glanced over at the pilot's station—a mobile lev-chair surrounded by brass control panels and drop-down display screens—but found no answers in Lando Calrissian's furrowed brow. Dressed immaculately in a white shimmersilk tunic, lavender trousers, and a hip cape, he was perched on the edge of his huge nerf-leather seat, with his chin propped on his knuckles and his gaze fixed on the alabaster radiance outside.

In the three decades Jaina had known Lando, it was one of the rare moments when his life of long-odds gambles and all-or-nothing stakes actually seemed to have taken a toll on his con-artist good looks. It was also a testament to the strain and fear of the past few days—and, perhaps, to the hectic pace. Lando was as impeccably groomed as always, but even he had not found time to touch up the dye that kept his mustache and curly hair their usual deep, rich black.

After a few moments, he finally sighed and leaned back into his chair. "Go ahead, say it."

"Say what?" Jaina asked, wondering exactly what Lando expected her to say. After all, *he* was the one who had made the bad jump. "It's not my fault?"

A glimmer of irritation shot through Lando's weary eyes, but then he seemed to realize Jaina was only trying to lighten the mood. He chuckled and flashed her one of his nova-bright grins. "You're as bad as your old man. Can't you see this is no time to joke?"

Jaina cocked a brow. "So you *didn't* decide to swing past Kessel to say hello to the wife and son?"

"Good idea," Lando said, shaking his head. "But . . . *no*."

"Well, then . . ." Jaina activated the auxiliary pilot's station and waited as the long-range sensors spooled up. An old asteroid tug designed to be controlled by a single operator and a huge robotic crew, the *Rockhound* had no true co-pilot's station, and *that* meant the wait was going to be longer than Jaina would have liked. "What are we doing here?"

Lando's expression grew serious. "Good question." He turned toward the back of the *Rockhound*'s spacious flight deck, where the vessel's ancient bridge droid stood in front of an equally ancient nav computer. A Cybot Galactica model RN8, the droid had a transparent head-globe, currently filled with the floating twinkles of a central processing unit running at high speed. Also inside the globe were three sapphire-blue photoreceptors, spaced at even intervals to give her full-perimeter vision. Her bronze body casing was etched with constellations, comets, and other celestial artwork. "I *know* I told Ornate to set a course for Coruscant."

RN8's head-globe spun just enough to fix one of her photoreceptors on Lando's face. "Yes, you did." Her voice was silky, deep, and chiding. "And then you countermanded that order with one directing us to our current destination."

Lando scowled. "You need to do a better job maintaining your auditory systems," he said. "You're hearing things."

The twinkles inside RN8's head-globe dimmed as she redirected power to her diagnostic systems. Jaina turned her own attention back to the auxiliary display and saw that the long-range sensors had finally come online. Unfortunately, they were no help. The only thing that had changed inside its bronze frame was the color of the screen and a single symbol denoting the *Rockhound*'s own location in the exact center.

RN8's silky voice sounded from the back of the flight deck. "My auditory sensors are in optimum condition, Captain—as are my data storage and retrieval systems." Her words began to roll across the deck in a *very* familiar male baritone. "Redi*rect* to *des*tina*tion* Ashteri's Cloud, arri*val* time seven*teen* hours fif*teen, Galac*tic *Stan*dard."

Lando's jaw dropped, and he sputtered, "Tha . . . that's not *me*!"

"Not quite," Jaina agreed. The emphasis was placed on the wrong syllable in several words; otherwise, the voice was identical. "But it's close enough to fool a droid."

Lando's eyes clouded with confusion. "Are you telling me what I *think* you're telling me?"

"Yes," Jaina said, glancing at her blank sensor display. "I don't quite know how, but someone impersonated you."

"Through the Force?"

Jaina shrugged and shot a meaningful glance toward a dark corner. While she knew of half a dozen Force powers that could have been used to defeat RN8's voice-recognition software, not one of those techniques had a range measured in light-years. She carefully began to expand her Force awareness, concentrating on the remote corners of the huge ship, and thirty standard seconds later was astonished to find nothing unusual. There were no lurking beings, no blank zones that might suggest an artificial void in the Force, not even any small vermin that might be a Force-wielder disguising his presence.

After a moment, she turned back to Lando. "They *must* be using the Force. There's no one aboard but us and the droids."

"I was afraid you'd say that." Lando paused for a moment, then asked, "Luke's friends?"

"I hate to jump to conclusions, but . . . who else?" Jaina replied. "First, Lost Tribe or not, they're *Sith*. Second, they already tried to double-cross us once."

"Which makes them as crazy as a rancor on the dancing deck," Lando said. "Abeloth was locked in a *black-hole prison* for twenty-five thousand years. What kind of maniacs would think it was a good idea to bust her out?"

"They're *Sith*," Jaina reminded him. "All that matters to them is power, and Abeloth had power like a nova has light—until Luke killed her."

Lando frowned in thought. "And if they're crazy enough to think they could take Abeloth home with them, they're probably crazy enough to think they could take the guy who killed her."

"Exactly," Jaina said. "Until a few weeks ago, no one even knew the Lost Tribe *existed.* That's changed, but they'll still want to keep what they can secret."

"So they'll try to take out Luke and Ben," Lando agreed. "And us, too. Contain the leak."

"That's my guess," Jaina said. "Sith like secrecy, and secrecy means stopping us *now.* Once we're out of the Maw, they'll expect us to access the HoloNet and report."

Lando looked up and exhaled in frustration. "I *told* Luke he couldn't trust anyone who puts *High Lord* before his name." He had been even more forceful than Jaina in trying to argue Luke out of a second bargain with the Lost Tribe—a bargain that had left the Skywalkers and three Sith behind to explore Abeloth's savage homeworld together. "Maybe we should go back."

Jaina thought for only an instant, then shook her head. "No, Luke knew the bargain wouldn't last when he agreed to it," she said. "Sarasu Taalon has already betrayed his word once."

Lando scowled. "That doesn't mean Luke and Ben are safe."

"No," Jaina agreed. "But it *does* mean he's risking their lives to increase *our* chances of reporting to the Jedi Council. *That's* our mission."

"Technically, Luke doesn't get to *assign* missions right now," Lando pressed. "You wouldn't be violating orders if we—"

"Luke Skywalker is *still* the most powerful Jedi in the galaxy. I think we should assume he has a plan," Jaina said. A sudden tingle of danger sense raced down her spine, prompting her to hit the quick-release on her crash harness. "Besides, we need to start worrying about saving our *own* skins."

Lando began to look worried. "What are you saying?" he asked. "That you're sensing something?"

Jaina shook her head. "Not yet." She rose. "But I *will* be. Why do you suppose they sent us someplace easy to find?"

Lando scowled. "Oh . . ." He glanced up at a display, tapped some keys—no doubt trying to call up a tactical report—then slammed his fist against the edge of the brass console. "Are they *jamming* us?"

"That's difficult to know with the ship's sensor systems offline for degaussing," RN8 replied.

"*Offline?*" Lando shrieked. "Who authorized *that*?"

"*You* did, ninety-seven seconds ago," RN8 replied. "Would you like me to play it back?"

"No! Countermand it and bring all systems back up." Lando turned to Jaina and asked, "Any feel for how long we have until the shooting starts?"

Jaina closed her eyes and opened herself to the Force. She felt a mass of belligerent presences approaching from the direction of the Maw. She turned to RN8.

"How long until the sensor systems reboot?"

"Approximately three minutes and fifty-seven seconds," the droid reported. "I'm afraid Captain Calrissian also ordered a complete data consolidation."

Jaina winced and turned back to Lando. "In that case, I'd say we have less than three minutes and fifty-two seconds. There's someone hostile coming up behind us." She started toward the hatchway at the back of the cavernous bridge, her boots ringing on the old durasteel deck. "Why don't you see if you can put a stop to those false orders?"

"Sure, I'll just tell my crew to stop listening to me." Lando's voice was sarcastic. "Being droids, they'll know what I mean."

"You might try activating their standard verification routines," Jaina suggested.

"I *might,* if droid crews this old *had* standard verification routines." Lando turned and scowled at Jaina as she continued across the deck. "And you're going *where?*"

"You know where," Jaina said.

"To your StealthX?" Lando replied. "The one with only three engines? The one that lost its targeting array?"

"Yeah, that one," Jaina confirmed. "We need a set of eyes out there—and someone to fly cover."

"No way," Lando said. "If I let you go out to fight Sith in that thing, your dad will be feeding pieces of me to Amelia's nexu for the next ten years."

Jaina stopped and turned toward him, propping one hand on her hip. "Lando, did you just say *let*? Did you really say *no way* to me?"

Lando rolled his eyes, unintimidated. "You know I didn't mean it like that. But have you gone spacesick? With only three engines, that starfighter is going to be about as maneuverable as an escape pod!"

"Maybe, but it still beats sitting around like a blind bantha in this thing. Thanks for worrying, though." She shot Lando a sour smile. "It's so sweet when you old guys do that."

"Old?" Lando cried. After a moment, he seemed to recognize the mocking tone in Jaina's voice, and his chin dropped. "I deserved that, didn't I?"

"You *think*?" Jaina laughed to show there were no hard feelings, then added, "And you know what Tendra would do to *me* if I came back without Chance's father. So let's *both* be careful."

"Okay, deal." Lando waved her toward the hatchway. "Go. Blow things up. Have fun."

"Thanks." Jaina's tone grew more serious, and she added, "And I mean for *everything,* Lando. You didn't have to be here, and I'm grateful for the risks you're taking to help us. It means a lot to me—and to the whole Order."

Lando's Force aura grew cold, and he looked away in sudden discomfort. "Jaina, is there something you're not telling me?"

"About this situation?" Jaina asked, frowning at his strange reaction. "I don't think so. Why?"

Lando exhaled in relief. "Jaina, my dear, perhaps no one has mentioned this to you before . . ." His voice grew more solemn. "But when a Jedi starts talking about how much you mean to her, the future begins to look *very* scary."

"Oh . . . sorry." Jaina's cheeks warmed with embarrassment. "I didn't mean anything like *that.* Really. I was just trying to—"

"It's okay." Lando's voice was still a little shaky. "And if you *did* mean something—"

"I *didn't,*" Jaina interrupted.

"I know," Lando said, raising a hand to stop her. "But if things start to go bad out there, just get back to Coruscant and report. I can take care of myself. Understand?"

"Sure, Lando, I understand." Jaina started toward the hatchway, silently adding, *But no way am I leaving you behind.*

"Good—and try to stick close. We won't be hanging around long." A low whir sounded from Lando's chair as he turned it to face RN8. "Ornate, prepare an emergency jump to our last coordinates."

"I'm afraid that's impossible, Captain Calrissian," the droid replied. "You gave standing orders to empty the nav computer's memory after each jump."

"*What?*" Lando's anger was edging toward panic now. "How many other orders—no, forget it. Just countermand my previous commands."

"*All* of them?"

"Yes!" Lando snapped. "No, wait . . ."

Jaina reached the hatchway and, not waiting to hear the rest of Lando's order, raced down the rivet-studded corridor beyond. She still had no idea what the Sith were planning, but she *was* going to stop them—and not only because the Jedi Council needed to know everything she and Lando could tell them about the Lost Tribe of the Sith. Over the years, Lando had been as loyal a friend to the Jedi Order as he had to her parents, time after time risking his life, fortune, and freedom to help them resolve whatever crisis happened to be threatening the peace of the galaxy at the moment. He always claimed he was just repaying a favor, or protecting an investment, or maintaining a good business environment, but Jaina knew better. He was looking out for his friends, doing everything he could to help them survive—no matter what mess they had gotten themselves into.

Jaina reached the forward hangar bay. As the hatch opened in front of her, she was surprised to find a bank of floodlights already illuminating her battered StealthX. At first, she assumed Lando had ordered the hangar droid to ready the *Rockhound*'s fighter complement for launch.

Then she saw what was missing from her starfighter.

There were no weapons barrels extending from the wingtips. In fact—on the side facing her, at least—the cannons themselves were gone. She was so shocked that she found herself waiting for the rest of the hangar lights to activate, having forgotten for the moment that the *Rockhound* did not have automatic illumination. The whir of a pneumatic wrench sounded from the far side of the StealthX, and beneath the starfighter's belly she noticed a cluster of telescoping droid legs straddling the actuator housing of a Taim & Bak KX12 laser cannon.

"What the . . . ?"

Jaina snapped the lightsaber off her belt, then crossed

twenty meters of tarnished deck in three quick Force bounds and sprang onto the fuselage of her StealthX. She could hardly believe what she saw. At the far end of the wing stood a spider-shaped BY2B maintenance droid, her thick cargo pedipalps clamped around the starfighter's last laser cannon while her delicate tool arms released the mounting clips.

"ByTwoBee!" Jaina yelled. "What are you doing?"

The pneumatic wrench whined to a stop, and three of the droid's photoreceptors swiveled toward Jaina's face.

"I'm sorry, Jedi Solo. I thought you would know." Like all droids aboard the *Rockhound,* BY2B's voice was female and sultry. "I'm removing this laser cannon."

"I can see that," Jaina replied. "Why?"

"So I can take it to the maintenance shop," BY2B replied. "Captain Calrissian requested it. Since your starfighter is unflyable anyway, he thought it would be a good time to rebuild the weapons systems."

Jaina's heart sank, but she wasted no time trying to convince BY2B she had been fooled. "When Lando issued this order, did you actually *see* him?"

"Oh, I rarely *see* the captain. I'm not one of his favorites." BY2B swung her photoreceptors toward the hangar entrance, and a trio of red beams shot out to illuminate a grimy speaker hanging next to the hatchway. "The order came over the intercom."

"Of course it did." Jaina pointed her lightsaber at the nearly dismounted laser cannon. "Any chance you can reattach that and get it working in the next minute and a half?"

"No chance at all, Jedi Solo. Reattaching the power feeds alone would take ten times that long."

"How'd I know you were going to say that?" Jaina growled. She turned away and hopped down onto the deck. "All right—finish removing it and prep the craft for launch."

"I'm sorry, that's impossible," BY2B replied. "Even if we had the necessary parts, I'm not qualified to make repairs. The specifications for this craft weren't included in my last service update."

"I flew it *in* here, didn't I?" Jaina retorted. "Just tell me you haven't been mucking around with the torpedo launchers, too."

"This craft has *torpedo launchers*?" BY2B asked. "I didn't see any."

Jaina rolled her eyes, wondering exactly when the droid's last service update had been, then rushed over to a small locker area at the edge of the hangar. She activated the lighting, flipped the toggle switch on the ancient intercom unit in the wall, and stepped into the StealthX flight suit she had left hanging at launch-ready.

A moment later Lando's voice crackled out of the tiny speaker. "Yes, *Jai*na? What can *I* do for *you*?"

Jaina frowned. The voice certainly *sounded* like Lando's. "How about a status report?" she asked, pushing her arms through the suit sleeves. "My StealthX is really messed up. No use taking it out."

"*My* that is *too* bad," Lando's voice said. "But don't be *con*cerned. Ar-en-eight has *near*ly sorted out the sys*tem* problems."

"Great." Jaina sealed the flight suit's front closure and stepped into her boots. "I'll head aft and check out the hyperdrive."

"Oh." Lando's voice seemed surprised. "That won't be *nec*essary. Ar-en-eight is running diag*nos*tics now. I'm sure the Em-Nine-O and his crew can *han*dle any *nec*essary re*pairs*."

And *his* crew. If there had been any doubt before, now Jaina *knew* she was talking to an imposter. Not long ago, Lando had confided to Jaina that the only way he had survived all those solitary prospecting trips early in his career was to close his eyes whenever one of the *Rockhound* droids spoke and imagine she was a beautiful woman. He would never have referred to M-9EO as a male.

Jaina grabbed her helmet and gloves out of the locker, then said, "Okay. If you've got everything under control, I'm going to stop by my bunk and grab some shut-eye before my shift comes up."

"Yes, why don't *you* do that?" The voice sounded almost relieved. "I'll *wake* you if anything comes *up*."

"Sounds good. See you in four standard hours."

Jaina flicked off the intercom switch, then started back toward her StealthX, securing her helmet and glove seals as she walked. Gullible, no Force presence, and a terrible liar—the Voice definitely belonged to a stowaway droid, probably one sent by the Sith. That made enough sense that Jaina felt vaguely guilty for not anticipating the tactic in time to prevent the sabotage. The only thing she *didn't* understand was why the Sith hadn't just rigged the fusion core to blow. A *living* stowaway, they might have valued enough to work out an escape plan—but a *droid*? She could not imagine that any Sith deserving of the name would give a second thought to sacrificing a droid.

Jaina reached her StealthX and found BY2B standing behind the far wing, holding the last laser cannon in her heavy cargo arms. Jaina made a quick visual inspection of the bedraggled starfighter, then asked, "Is she ready to fly?"

"*Ready* would be an overstatement," BY2B answered. "But the craft is capable of launching. I *do* hope you checked your flight suit for vacuum hardiness."

"No need—it's not *me* that will be going EV." Jaina ascended the short access ladder and climbed into the cockpit. As she buckled herself in, she asked, "ByTwoBee, have you seen any new droids around here lately?"

"No," the droid said. "Not since departing Klatooine."

"*Klatooine?*" Jaina's stomach began to grow cold and heavy. "Then you *did* see a new droid before we left for the Maw?"

"Indeed, I did," BY2B replied. "A Rebaxan MSE-Six."

"A *mouse* droid?" Jaina gasped. "And you didn't report it?"

"Of course not," BY2B said. "Captain Calrissian had warned me just a few minutes earlier to expect a courier shuttle carrying a new utility droid."

Jaina groaned and hit the preignition engine heaters, then asked, "And I suppose he told you this over your internal comlink?"

"Yes, as a matter of fact," BY2B replied. "How did you know?"

"Because that *wasn't* Lando you heard," Jaina said, speaking through clenched teeth. "It was a sabotage droid programmed with an impersonation protocol."

"*Sabotage?*" BY2B sounded skeptical. "Why would anyone bother? We don't even have an asteroid in tow."

"It's not an *asteroid* they're after." Jaina unfastened her flight suit just far enough to retrieve her comlink from her chest pocket, opened a secure channel to Lando, and demanded, "What was the last meal I ate before boarding the *Exquisite Death*?"

"You expect me to remember what you had for lunch thirteen years ago?" Lando replied, taking the verification query in stride. "But you didn't have time to finish it. I remember that much."

"Good enough," Jaina said, satisfied that she was talking to the man and not the mouse. The meal to which she was referring had taken place aboard Lando's yacht, the *Lady Luck,* shortly before he had tricked a

Yuuzhan Vong boarding party into taking her and the rest of a Jedi strike team aboard their ship. "Did you buy an MSE-Six while we were back on Klatooine?"

"No . . . why?"

"Because ByTwoBee saw one come aboard," Jaina replied. "Apparently, you told her to expect it."

"*I* told her?" Lando fell silent while he digested Jaina's meaning, then said, "*Blast*! Those aren't Sith out there—they're pirates!"

Jaina was skeptical. "What makes you think so?"

"Slipping a stowaway aboard is an old pirate trick," Lando explained. "Only this time, they were creative, impersonating the captain instead of just blowing an air lock."

"Maybe," Jaina said, still not convinced. An alert tweetle sounded inside the cockpit, announcing that the StealthX was ready to launch. "Time to go. You handle the mouse, and I'll take care of . . . whoever sent it."

"Affirmative," Lando said. "I'll have ByTwoBee organize a hunt. Can you lend her your comlink?"

"Sure." Jaina passed the comlink out to the droid. "Lando has a job for you."

The droid extended one of her delicate tool arms to accept the comlink. "How do I know this is the *real* Captain Calrissian?"

"You'll have to trust me on that." Jaina closed her flight suit again, then added, "That's an order, by the way."

"Well . . ." A soft hydraulic hiss sounded beneath BY2B as she allowed her telescoping legs to compress. "If it's an *order.*"

Jaina lowered the canopy and fired the engines, then slipped through the containment field and swung toward the stern, hanging tight beneath the asteroid tug to avoid silhouetting herself against the milky glow of Ashteri's Cloud. With the *Rockhound*'s sensor suite temporarily disabled, any worthy captain would maneuver around behind the huge tug, then launch a first salvo from as close as possible, straight down the thrust nozzles.

Even at full acceleration, clearing the *Rockhound* took longer than Jaina would have liked. The asteroid tug was nearly two kilometers long, with a white, carbon-scorched belly pocked by rows of bantha-sized tractor beam projection wells. Around the perimeter dangled dozens of telescoping stabilizer legs, two hundred meters long even fully retracted. The stern of the ship was obscured by the glow of an efflux trail so enormous and bright that Jaina felt like she was flying into a comet's tail.

Finally, the canopy's blast-tinting darkened. Jaina dropped the nose of the StealthX and shot away from the *Rockhound,* counting on the brilliance of the vessel's huge efflux spray to blind distant eyes to the silhouette of a departing starfighter.

"Okay, Rowdy," Jaina said, addressing her astromech droid by the new nickname she had given him. "Bring up the passive scanners and prep the shadow bombs."

A long whistle of inquiry filled the cockpit, and Jaina looked down to see a question scrolling across the primary display. SHADOW BOMBS? WHAT DID CAPTAIN CALRISSIAN *SAY* TO YOU?

"This is no time for jokes, Rowdy," Jaina said. "Besides, your humor protocol is lame. Who installed it, anyway?"

Rowdy replied with a mocking tweedle. I WILL NEVER TELL.

Jaina chuckled. It was already an old joke between them, since she herself was the one who had designed and installed the protocol. During a recent bout of melancholy over ending her engagement to Jagged Fel, she had decided to spend a little downtime pursuing what had been one of her favorite teenage passions: tinkering with stuff. The result had been a new humor routine for her astromech droid—and one that had the unexpected benefit of reversing the R9 series' tendency to self-enhance their preservation routines. The bolder version was a definite improvement, at least to Jaina's way of thinking. But she still had not decided whether the lame jokes were a reflection of her rusty programming skills, or a subconscious effort to echo the bad jokes her brother Jacen used to tell back on Yavin 4—before *he* became Darth Caedus and *she* became his executioner.

An alert chime sounded from the cockpit speakers, and another message rolled across the display screen. BOGEYS COMING FAST.

The screen switched to a tactical map showing three generic starcraft symbols speeding toward the *Rockhound*'s tail. A fourth symbol, hanging at the top of the display, was not approaching at all.

"*That* doesn't look like a turbolaser assault in the making," Jaina observed. "Rowdy, how sure are you of your sensors?"

ALL SENSORS ARE FUNCTIONAL AND CONCORDANT, the R9 reported. WE HAVE FOUR POTENTIAL TARGETS, AND WE HAVE ONLY FOUR REMAINING SHADOW BOMBS AND NO LASER CANNONS. IF THAT IS NOT CHALLENGE ENOUGH, I CAN ALWAYS SHUT DOWN ANOTHER ENGINE.

"Very funny." As Jaina spoke, she was watching data readouts appear beneath each of the symbols on the screen. "Didn't I just *say* this is no time for jokes?"

WHO IS JOKING?

Jaina was too busy studying tonnage estimates to respond. The three craft approaching the *Rockhound* were carrying far too much mass to be starfighters, while the vessel hanging back was only about half the mass of the ChaseMaster frigates the Sith were using. In fact, its thermal profile lacked the high-output signature of military-grade engines at all, and there were no energy concentrations large enough to suggest a turbolaser preparing to fire.

"Rowdy, give me more on those bogeys in the lead." As Jaina spoke, she began to ease back on the control stick, bringing the StealthX up and pointing its nose toward the trio of tiny blue flickers still closing on the *Rockhound*. "They can't be fighters, or they would have attacked by now."

A magnified enhancement of the lead bogey appeared on Jaina's display. The image suggested a blocky craft about twenty meters long, with a wedge-shaped bow and four undersized ion engines attached to the stern. Thermal imaging showed a main cabin packed with at least twenty beings, while a small energy concentration just beneath the roof seemed to suggest the presence of a cannon turret.

Jaina frowned. "Maybe Lando was right," she said. "That looks like an assault shuttle."

NEGATIVE. THE HULL ARMOR ON AN ASSAULT SHUTTLE WOULD DEFEAT OUR THERMAL IMAGING, Rowdy reported. IT IS SEVENTY-EIGHT PERCENT LIKELY THAT ALL THREE CRAFT ARE LIGHTLY MODIFIED BDY CREW SKIFFS.

"Okay . . . and I suppose the *lightly modified* means that cannon turret on the roof?" Jaina asked.

AFFIRMATIVE. BDY SKIFFS ARE NOT SOLD WITH ARMAMENT OPTIONS.

"And *that's* why pirates love them." As she spoke, Jaina was trying to recall the latest intelligence on the rash of pirate attacks that Jaden Korr was investigating. The last she'd heard, he was still focusing on the middle Hydian Way, which was a long way from the Maw. "Vessels without military-grade sensors usually can't see a small cannon turret, so they don't get too worried when they see a BDY skiff coming."

SO WE ARE NOT BEING ATTACKED BY SITH?

"Apparently not," Jaina said, feeling relieved. A Sith frigate would have been a problem. But three shuttle-loads of pirates? That, she could handle. "It looks like someone is trying to board us."

The display returned to tactical scale, and Rowdy added a designator label beneath the large vessel, still hanging back at the top of the screen. AND THIS DAMORIAN S18 LIGHT FREIGHTER IS THE MOTHER SHIP?

"That's right," Jaina said. "Classic pirate tactics—get close and send over some fast shuttles."

THEN THIS IS GOING TO BE MORE FUN THAN WE THOUGHT, Rowdy reported. A DAMORIAN S18 IS LARGE ENOUGH TO CARRY *SIX* BDY SKIFFS.

"*Now* you tell me."

Just because an S18 *could* carry six skiffs didn't mean it *was,* but Jaina had to assume the worst. She continued toward the approaching vessels, trying to think of a way to take out six shuttles and a mother ship with only four shadow bombs, and quickly realized there wasn't one. Those pirates were no idiots. The three shuttles were staying at least a kilometer apart—well beyond the blast radius of a shadow bomb—and they were approaching in a staggered line.

"Rowdy, arm bomb three," she said, designating number three because bomb racks one and two were empty. She continued to close on the lead shuttle until the tiny flicker of its efflux tail had stretched into a blue dagger as long as her arm, then ordered, "Activate our transceiver and open a hailing channel."

A bleep of protest sounded over the cockpit speaker, and Jaina glanced down to find a message on the display. A STEALTHX EMITTING COMM WAVES IS NO LONGER A STEALTHX. IT IS JUST A POORLY ARMED, LIGHTLY ARMORED X-WING SAYING *COME GET ME.*

"We're required to issue a warning before opening fire," Jaina said. Her target was just visible to the naked eye, a tiny durasteel box with a wedge-shaped head, being pushed along by an efflux tail as long as a cannon barrel. "And you know how I feel about breaking the law."

THERE IS AN EXCEPTION FOR CLEAR INTENT, Rowdy pointed out.

"Better safe than sorry," Jaina said. "Besides, I want them thinking about *us,* not the *Rockhound.* Do I have that channel yet?"

An affirming *twoweet* filled the cockpit and the transceiver touch pad on Jaina's control stick turned green.

I UNDERSTAND, Rowdy scrolled. YOU ARE JUST TRYING TO MAKE THIS MISSION INTERESTING. COUNT ME IN.

"Glad you approve," Jaina said, wondering if the droid might be getting a little *too* brave. "Launch bomb three."

She felt a soft bump beneath her seat as a charge of compressed air pushed the shadow bomb out of the torpedo tube. Reaching out in the Force, she began to guide the bomb toward its target, then placed her thumb over the transceiver touch pad.

"Attention, BDY crew skiffs: Turn away *now,*" she transmitted. "This will be your only warning."

During the two full seconds of silence that followed, the lead skiff swelled to the size of a bantha outside Jaina's cockpit. She could see the flexible ring of a telescoping air lock affixed to the hull at the front of the passenger cabin, the band of the transparent viewport stretched across its wedge-shaped bow . . . and the flattened dome of a weapons turret, swinging its laser cannons in her direction.

A gravelly female voice came over the cockpit speaker. "Turn away or *what,* Jedi Solo? We know—"

The transmission dissolved into a stream of static as the shadow bomb detonated. Lacking any real shielding or armor, the shuttle's crew cabin simply vanished into the silver flash of the initial explosion. The stern and bow spun away trailing bright beads of superheated metal; then the StealthX's blast-tinting darkened, and all Jaina could see was a ball of white fire dead ahead. She pulled the stick back and rolled away, pointing her nose toward the hidden bulk of the mother ship.

A soft chill of danger sense tickled her between the shoulder blades. She slipped her thumb off the transceiver pad and went into an evasive climb, juking and jinking so hard she felt the craft vibrate as Rowdy slammed into the walls of his droid socket. The crimson streaks of cannon bolts began to brighten the void all around, flashing past a lot closer than she would have liked. Even without a comm signal for their targeting systems to lock onto, the pirate gunners were doing a good job of keeping her in their crossfire.

The gravelly voice came over the cockpit speaker again. "That wasn't much warning, Jedi Solo."

Instead of replying, Jaina ordered Rowdy, "Get me a location on that transmission. Is it coming from one of the skiffs or the mother ship?"

Before Rowdy could answer, the voice spoke again, "You didn't even give me time to issue a recall order."

Space outside turned crimson as a cannon bolt glanced off the StealthX's weak shields. Knowing the enemy would see the bolt's change of vector and realize exactly where she was, Jaina instantly rolled into a spiraling dive . . . and cringed as space again turned red. Half a heartbeat later another bolt struck, then blossomed into a golden spray of dissipation static.

An alert buzzer sounded inside the cockpit, and Jaina glanced down to see a message flashing on her display: SHIELD OVERLOAD.

"No kidding." She pulled her nose up and corkscrewed back toward the two shuttles, and the stream of fire quickly drifted away from her StealthX. "What about that transmission source?"

THE SIGNAL ORIGINATED FROM THE MOTHER SHIP.

"Thought so." Jaina swung onto an interception course with the nearest shuttle, then said, "Arm bomb four."

She had barely spoken before cannon fire began to flash past again, turning the void as bright as a bonfire. She spun into an evasive helix and continued toward her target. The enemy continued to close in on her, the bolts streaking past so close that the canopy's blast-tinting went dark and stayed that way.

"Rowdy, are we still transmitting?" she asked.

A negative chirp came over the speaker.

"What about leaks?" Unable to see her target through the darkened canopy, Jaina dropped her gaze to her display and began to fly by instruments. "EM radiation? Fuel? Atmosphere?"

Again, a negative chirp.

"Keep checking," Jaina ordered. "They're tracking us *somehow.*"

A message scrolled across her primary display. BY SILHOUETTE? ASHTERI'S CLOUD IS STILL BEHIND US.

"I don't think so," she said, fully aware of the difficulty of tracking a distant speck of darkness by sight alone—especially one that was spiraling toward its target at thousands of kilometers an hour, with the gunners blinded by the flashing of their own laser cannons. "Not without the Force."

A soft ding announced that they had closed to launching range of their second target. With the canopy still darkened by the constant barrage of cannon bolts, guiding the bomb to its destination by sight was out of the question. So Jaina expanded her Force awareness in the direction of the shuttle until she felt the living presences inside. She was not surprised to sense a heavy taint of darkness in them, but she *was* shocked by how calm they seemed, by how focused and disciplined they appeared to be.

Of course, that was about to change. "Launch bomb four."

Jaina felt the gentle bump of the shadow bomb being forced from the torpedo tube. She reached out for it in the Force—then grew distracted by the all-too-familiar *bang-screech* of a cannon hit. Alerts and alarms immediately filled her ears, and the StealthX went into an uncontrolled . . . *twirl*? It felt like she was in one of those thrill rides that spun around the central axis of the car, plastering their passengers against their seats. Jaina eased the stick in the opposite direction and slowly brought the starfighter back in line . . . then realized she had lost control of the shadow bomb, and her heart rose into her throat.

"Uh, Rowdy?"

YES?

"Any idea where number four went?"

IT DID NOT STRIKE THE TARGET, Rowdy reported. OR US . . . YET.

"Not funny," Jaina said. The extra velocity of the launch had probably carried the shadow bomb far enough away from the StealthX to avoid triggering the proximity fuse—but when it came to baradium warheads, *probably* wasn't much of a safety margin. "No joking when there's baradium involved."

YOU DID NOT WRITE THAT INTO THE APPROPRIATENESS ROUTINE, Rowdy complained.

"Consider it an addendum."

Noticing that the canopy's blast-tinting remained dark, Jaina checked her tactical display and saw that she had overshot her target by only a couple of kilometers. Despite her erratic course, both shuttles still seemed to know where she was, more or less, and they continued to pour fire in her direction. She banked into a turn, starting back toward the nearest craft, and found her stick heavy and slow.

"Rowdy, what's our damage?" she asked. "I've got a sluggish stick."

THAT IS HARDLY SURPRISING, Rowdy replied. THE VECTOR-PLATE POWER ASSIST IS OUT, AND WE HAVE LOST THE END OF OUR UPPER RIGHT S-FOIL.

The attitude thrusters, of course, were located on the foil ends.

"Great," Jaina said. She checked the tactical display and saw that the remaining skiffs had closed to within a dozen kilometers of the *Rockhound.* That left time for only one more pass before the pirates reached the tug and began boarding operations. "Adjust the power levels to compensate, and arm bomb five."

OUR MANEUVERABILITY IS LIMITED, Rowdy warned. AND THE SHIELDS HAVE NOT YET REGENERATED.

"No problem." Jaina assumed a course parallel to her targets and began to overtake them, trying to align her interception vector so the nearest skiff would be directly between her and the farthest. "I don't need shields to take down a bunch of pirates."

EXPERIENCE WOULD SUGGEST OTHERWISE.

"That was just a lucky hit," Jaina said. "Never happen twice."

Despite her words, the cannon bolts continued to come fast and close. Her blast-tinting was so constantly dark that the interior of the cockpit felt like a closet during a lightning storm, and she could not shake the feeling that those gunners were too *good* to be ordinary pirates. Maybe they were ex-military—something like retired Space Rangers or Balmorran void-jumpers, perhaps even a band of outlaw Noghri.

The interception vector on her display finally lined up with both shuttles, and the blast tinting grew semi-clear as the farthest stopped firing to avoid hitting the nearest. Jaina quickly swung in for a flank attack and accelerated, easing the stick this way and that, fighting to keep her interception vector aligned with both targets. As she drew near the first skiff, its cannon bolts grew brighter, longer, and closer, and again the canopy turned as dark as space itself.

Jaina reached out in the Force, focusing on the dark-tainted presences ahead, and said, "Launch bomb five."

Again came the gentle bump of a shadow bomb being forced from its tube. She caught hold of it in the Force—and felt the StealthX jump as cannon bolts started burning through its light armor.

"*Stang!*" she cursed. "Who *are* those guys?"

A cacophony of alerts and alarms filled the cockpit. Jaina shoved the stick forward, diving for safety beneath the shuttle's belly where, at such close range, the cannon barrel would not be able to depress far enough to target her.

And this time, she did not release the shadow bomb. She kept her attention focused on the sinister presences inside the shuttle, pushing the bomb toward them even as her StealthX spiraled out of control. Rowdy tweeted and whistled, trying to draw her attention to the urgent messages scrolling across the display, and the second shuttle resumed fire, stitching a line of holes down the fuselage.

Then a white brilliance filled the void, so bright and hot that it warmed Jaina even inside her vac suit, and she felt the searing rip of two dozen lives being torn from the Force.

Afterward, everything remained quiet and dark inside the cockpit, and Jaina thought for an instant the detonation had taken *her.* Then her stomach grew queasy. The blazing blue of the *Rockhound*'s efflux tail flashed past above her, and she realized her shoulder was straining against her crash harness. Her ears were ringing with damage alerts and malfunction buzzers, and her throat was burning with the acrid fumes of system burnouts. She hit a chin toggle inside her helmet, then coughed into her faceplate as it slid down to seal her inside her vac suit.

"Activate suit support." She grabbed her stick and began to right her tumble, bringing the starfighter under control *gently,* in case the superstructure had suffered any damage. "Give me a damage assessment."

NOT AS BAD AS IT COULD BE, Rowdy reported. WE STILL HAVE TIME TO STOP THOSE LAST PIRATES—AS LONG AS WE SUFFER NO MORE LUCKY HITS.

Jaina surprised herself with a grin. "I like your style, Rowdy." She glanced down and found the last shuttle highlighted on her tactical display, less than a kilometer behind the *Rockhound* and already starting to climb toward its belly. "But I was wrong. Those *weren't* lucky hits."

An inquiring beep sounded inside Jaina's helmet.

"Their gunners have been using the Force." Jaina swung around and accelerated so hard that her battered StealthX began to wobble and pitch. "That's why they hit us every time I launch a shadow bomb—they can find me in the Force."

PIRATES HAVE THE FORCE?

"*These* pirates do," Jaina said. The last skiff came into view and began to swell, four tiny circles of blue arranged around a boxy gray stern. "Arm bomb six."

Rowdy emitted a confirming tweedle, then scrolled a message across the cockpit display. IT HAS BEEN NICE FLYING WITH YOU, JEDI SOLO. THANK YOU FOR GIVING ME A SENSE OF HUMOR SO I WILL FIND THIS AMUSING.

"Relax, will you?" The hair on Jaina's neck stood up, and a stream of cannon bolts began to fly back over the skiff's stern. "They have a blind spot."

Jaina pushed their nose down, and the stream began to fly past dozens of meters overhead. A moment later the skiff passed beneath the stern of the *Rockhound* and, dwarfed by the tug's two-kilometer immensity, continued forward between the massive stabilizer legs.

Knowing what would happen the instant the gunners felt her reach for their craft in the Force, Jaina hung back half a kilometer, then said, "Launch bomb six."

When she felt the charge of compressed air shove the shadow bomb free of its launch tube, she grasped it in the Force and pulled up hard. As she had expected, the skiff rolled on its back, trying to bring its weapons to bear before the bomb struck home. Jaina was already rising into its ion stream, nearly scraping her canopy on the *Rockhound*'s belly as she guided the bomb toward the four blue circles of the BDY's thrust nozzles.

Rowdy issued a shrill alarm tweedle, no doubt warning her about the dangers of remaining inside the skiff's ion tail. The friction alone would be pushing the StealthX's skin toward the combustion point, and Jaina could feel for herself how the turbulence was straining the starfighter's battered frame. Still, she remained inside the efflux, her attention fixed on the bright blue circles until they finally swelled into the silver flash of a detonating shadow bomb.

Half a second later the StealthX hit the bomb's shock wave and Jaina slammed against her crash harness. The temperature inside her vac suit shot up so quickly, she thought her hair would burst into flames. The spatter of ricocheting debris rattled through the starfighter, and then there was nothing ahead but the dark-pocked sky of the *Rockhound*'s vast white belly.

Jaina brought the StealthX under control. The starfighter's superstructure was showing through the nose in a couple of places, and its fuselage was vibrating so badly that she feared it was coming apart around her.

She began to ease away from the *Rockhound*'s underside.

"Rowdy, how are you doing back there?" she asked. "Still with me?"

There followed a short silence, then a single fuzzy beep finally came over Jaina's helmet speakers.

"Glad you made it," she said. "What's that mother ship doing?"

A blurred message scrolled across the cockpit's main display. TO DETERMINE THAT, WE WOULD NEED A FUNCTIONING SENSOR ARRAY.

"Good point." Jaina could see that the forward array had been melted completely off, so it made sense that the aft equipment had suffered heat damage, as well. "Can you open a channel to Captain Calrissian for me?"

A scratchy beep sounded inside her helmet, and a moment later Lando's static-distorted voice asked, *"Jaina?"*

Jaina pressed a thumb to the transceiver pad on her stick. "In the flesh," she said. "Do you have that mouse problem under control yet?"

"Just blasted it myself," Lando replied proudly. "Ornate will plot new jump coordinates as soon as you're aboard."

"Tell her to start plotting *now,*" Jaina replied. She could see the hangar mouth's dark rectangle only a few hundred meters ahead, and she wasn't planning on making a gentle approach. "Jump the second she has them."

"Jump?" Lando echoed. "No way, not until ByTwoBee tells me you're aboard and—"

"*Lando*! Just make sure the barrier field is off." The hangar mouth was starting to swell rapidly as Jaina approached, and Rowdy was filling her helmet with wave-off alarms and speed alerts. "If you wait for me to buckle down, the *Rockhound* will be taking cannon bolts up her thrust nozzle. The situation is worse than we thought. A *lot* worse."

"That's hard to believe, considering how bad it was to start with." Lando's voice faded as he issued orders to RN8, then asked, "Okay, Jaina, worse than we thought *how*?"

"Well, you were right—and so was I." As Jaina spoke, floodlights began to shine down from inside the hangar. Ignoring a cacophony of alerts from Rowdy, she brought up the nose of the StealthX and streaked toward its gaping mouth. "They *were* pirates. *Sith* pirates."

Chapter Two

THE SWEEP BAR ON THE *JADE SHADOW*'S SENSOR DISPLAY arced across the screen, slowly shading the region above the planetary horizon a deep blue. Once the entire area had changed hue, Ben authorized the reconnaissance drone to alter its course and start the next pass. To his surprise—and relief—the entire screen remained blue, and a message scrolled across the bottom: FINAL PASS. ALL CLEAR.

"That's it," he said, swiveling around to face Vestara Khai. Ben was sitting on the main flight deck in the copilot's chair, and Vestara was seated across from him in the navigator's chair. The *Shadow* remained on the river beach, below the volcano where Abeloth had kept her lair. "There's nothing in orbit big enough to be a spacecraft. Agreed?"

Vestara continued to study her display, slumped down in her seat with one arm in a sling, looking pained and exhausted after more than two days of sensor monitoring.

Finally, she nodded. "No *Rockhound,* no ChaseMaster frigates . . ." She turned to face Ben, her brown eyes steady and appraising despite her wound and her fatigue. "But what about your cousin's StealthX? That wouldn't show up in a standard sensor sweep, would it?"

Ben forced a smirk, trying to hide the little ache he felt

inside. With Vestara, no question was ever innocent, no suggestion free of a hidden agenda.

"You heard what it went through," he said. "Do you really think even Jaina Solo could keep it in one piece for two days?"

A slow smile came to Vestara's lips, looking a bit like a sneer because of the scar at the corner of her mouth. "I guess I'll take your word for it," she said. "So, yes, I agree."

"That both sides have honored their agreement?" Ben clarified. "That all vessels, except our *Shadow* and Lord Taalon's *Emiax*, have withdrawn from the vicinity?"

Vestara let her breath out. "Look, you don't have to get snarky. I *said* I agree."

"I just want to be sure," Ben replied. "You Sith can be pretty slippery about your agreements."

"And that's *news* to you?" Vestara retorted. "Your reactor is just running hot because we took you by surprise. Your father *knew* Taalon would try to take him out. He just didn't expect it to happen *before* we finished Abeloth."

"Taalon was trying to *capture* Abeloth." Ben took a deep breath, forcing himself to remain calm. "Who'd expect a Sith High Lord to try something so . . . so *stupid*?"

To Ben's surprise, Vestara laughed out loud. "Good point," she said. "That *was* a nork-headed move. But Taalon learned his lesson. And he knows he isn't going to learn much about Abeloth's true nature without your father's help. So we're all back to working together."

"For *now*."

Vestara shrugged and admitted, "For now. But until that changes, what's the harm in being nice to each other?"

Ben sighed, knowing exactly where the *harm* lay. After all, this was the girl who had exaggerated her injury to keep him distracted while her father tried to murder his father—and he was wise enough to know she would try it again. Sith girls played rough, and they *always* cheated.

But her game was the kind two could play, and Ben was just as capable of exploiting an edge as Vestara was. "No harm, I guess. Just don't expect me to let my guard down."

Vestara smiled and considered him for a moment, then said, "You haven't yet." She glanced aft toward the *Shadow*'s medbay, where Dyon Stadd had lain in a healing trance for the last two days. "Speaking of being nice, I wonder how our patient is doing. Maybe we should . . ."

Vestara trailed off and glanced out the forward viewport, frowning and tilting her head. Ben thought for an instant she was just trying to distract him again, but he could feel her surprise fluttering in the Force, and he didn't think she could fake *that*. He looked in the same direction she had glanced and saw only Taalon's shuttle squatting on its S-shaped landing struts, its drooping wings frowning down so far the tips nearly touched the bone-colored beach. A dozen meters beyond the shuttle, a sandy bank rose from the river's floodplain to become the floor of a jungle valley, and beyond the jungle canopy loomed the volcanic ridge where Abeloth's cave was located.

When Ben did not see anything unexpected, he asked, "What's wrong?"

Vestara continued to look out the viewport. "Nothing *wrong*," she said. "I just felt someone touch me in the Force."

Ben cocked his brow and waited for her to elaborate.

"My father, I think," Vestara said, looking back to Ben. "It's been a while since he did that when he wasn't angry, so it took me a bit by surprise."

"Sure," Ben replied, not buying her story at all. She was volunteering information he hadn't asked for, and *that* wasn't like Vestara. He expanded his Force awareness toward the ruins where Abeloth had died—and where his father was working with Gavar Khai and High Lord Taalon to learn more about Abeloth—and was relieved to feel only the tense wariness to be expected of a Jedi Grand Master in the company of two powerful Sith. "So much for working together."

"Ben, please. Your father is a Jedi. He doesn't get angry the way mine does." Vestara paused to study Ben's face—no doubt to see if she was having any effect—then seemed to reconsider and looked away, shaking her head and speaking in a soft voice. "You need to understand, if High Lord Taalon found out I had told you something like this—"

"*I* can keep a secret," Ben interrupted. "Even for you."

"Ouch," Vestara said, recoiling visibly. "Not nice."

"But deserved." Ben put a deliberate chill in his voice. "Don't play on my emotions, Vestara. It reminds me of why I don't like you."

A look of hurt came to Vestara's face, but she raised her chin and met his eyes. "Do I deserve that, Ben?" she asked. "We're on opposite sides of this thing, and maybe that makes us enemies. But we don't have to hate each other—that's a choice we make ourselves."

To Ben's surprise, there was a quaver in Vestara's voice, and everything he had been trained to watch for as a Galactic Alliance Guard officer told him she wasn't faking it. Her tone and volume were even, she held his gaze without forcing herself, and her posture remained confident yet comfortable. Most of all, he could feel in the Force that Vestara did not want him to despise her—and that it wounded her to think he did.

Ben felt the anger and bitterness of her earlier betrayal drain away, and he started to feel guilty about using them to hide from his true emotions. The fact was, he wasn't as angry with Vestara as he was with himself. He had let his feelings for her—feelings that he barely understood—blind him to her basic nature. She had been born a *Sith,* and that meant treachery came to her as naturally as breathing did to him. If he had forgotten that in the heat of a chaotic battle, wasn't it more his fault than hers?

Ben rose and placed a hand on his lightsaber, then said, "Vestara, I don't *hate* my enemies—but you're not going to play me twice. What did you sense?"

Vestara studied him for a moment, no doubt weighing how serious he was, then finally said, "Relax. I was going to tell you. I just need a promise—"

"No promises. I don't keep secrets from my father." Ben spoke with more heat than necessary, for the one time he had made the mistake of doing exactly *that,* his mother had died—and her killer had become Darth Caedus. "Especially not Sith secrets."

"I'm not asking you to. But you can't let High Lord Taalon—or my father—know that *I* told you. Either one would kill me for letting slip my own middle name. For this . . ." Vestara let the sentence trail off, then shrugged. "Well, you know what would happen. My people don't take betrayal lightly."

Ben knew that much was true. But Vestara's eyes remained hard and dark, and he *also* knew that she was still trying to manipulate him—trying to play on his sympathy and his sense of responsibility. Perhaps that was the only way of relating to her peers that she understood, to lie to them and exploit them. He started to wonder just how much of what she had become was a product of her environment . . . and whether she might be open to a different kind of life.

Ben nodded. "Don't worry. Taalon won't hear a thing."

"From you *or* your father?"

"*Jedi* honor their promises," Ben confirmed, "in word and spirit."

"You'd better." Vestara turned back toward the viewport and fell silent for moment, then finally said, "Okay. Ship is returning."

Ben let his hand slip away from his lightsaber and remained standing. It was the last thing he had expected Vestara to say, but it made sense . . . and it was also just alarming enough to make a good lie. He studied her a moment, looking for signs that she was trying to play him again, and didn't find any.

In a neutral voice, he said, "You told me that Ship isn't under Sith control."

Vestara looked back to him, her lips pursed in admonishment. "When I told you that, Abeloth was still alive," she said. "And I don't know that Ship is under our control *now*—only that he's coming."

"To do what?" Ben pressed. He could think of two possibilities, and neither was good for the Skywalkers. "To avenge Abeloth?"

"Or to share what he knows about her with Lord Taalon," Vestara replied. "Ship didn't tell me—but either way, you and your father are in trouble. Maybe you should think about coming over to the dark side. I'm sure the Circle of Lords would be happy to find a place for someone like you."

"Thanks, but . . . I'd rather die."

Vestara shrugged. "Have it your way." She tilted her head up at him, and her brown eyes suddenly looked both huge and deep. "But I'll miss you . . . a little bit, at least."

"Nice to know," Ben said, half grinning. "But you're getting ahead of yourself, don't you think?"

Vestara shook her head. "Afraid not," she said. "Ship *is* coming, and he's very angry."

Ben met her gaze. Beginning to think he and his father

really *might* be in trouble, he asked, "He didn't tell you anything else?"

Vestara looked him straight in the eye. "Nothing."

"I can check that, you know."

Vestara flourished her hand at him. "Be my guest."

Half convinced she was just using Ship to distract him from some other development, Ben reached out in the Force again. To his dismay, he felt an ancient presence approaching the planet.

Ben? The voice came to Ben inside his head, as full of portent and menace as he remembered. *Why are you not dead?*

Ben suppressed a shudder. *Just good, I guess.*

You have grown arrogant. Ship seemed more amused than irritated. *That is a valuable quality in a ruler.*

I'm no ruler, just a Jedi Knight, Ben replied. *And I'll be your destroyer, if you come near this planet.*

If you could destroy me, you wouldn't be warning me away, Ship noted. *But your audacity shows promise. It is not too late to join us, Ben.*

Ben was too insulted to reply. Ship wasn't a true sentient being, so perhaps it could not understand why the idea of following in his cousin's footsteps would fill him with revulsion.

Darth Caedus was a mere shadow of what shall come, Ship warned. *The Jedi are weak and doomed, and the Lost Tribe is destined to restore the Sith Empire to the galaxy.*

The Lost Tribe couldn't overthrow a Hutt crime lord, much less take over the galaxy, Ben replied. He could sense a new pride in Ship's presence, an optimism bordering on self-deception . . . and, in sentient beings at least, unchecked pride was the easiest of all weaknesses to exploit. *It'll take more than a few thousand Sabers and a flotilla of outdated patrol frigates to take down the Galactic Alliance.*

In time, young Jedi, in . . . Ship fell silent in midthought, and a cold wave of anger rippled through the Force. *You have grown clever, Ben. I won't underestimate you again.*

Ben felt a sudden chill in the Force as Ship withdrew from his touch. He would have liked to take a moment to gather his thoughts and consider what he had tricked Ship into revealing. But he could feel the weight of Vestara's gaze upon him, and by remaining silent too long, he would be sacrificing an opportunity to build on what he had learned.

As soon as Ben's gaze dropped back toward her, Vestara asked, "Believe me now?"

Ben snorted. "Not at all." He fixed her with an accusing glare, then asked, "Didn't you tell me you don't know much about Ship?"

"I *don't,*" Vestara insisted. She was working hard to make eye contact, which Ben recognized as a sure sign of a practiced liar. "But I didn't tell you all of the little bits that I *do* know."

"No kidding," Ben said. "Starting with the fact that Ship has been working with the Lost Tribe all along."

Vestara let out her breath and looked away, then admitted, "Okay, starting with that. He was kind of our savior. Had he not come looking for us, we'd still be stuck on . . . our home planet."

Ben smiled. "Kesh." He extended a hand to her. "I *have* heard the name before, you know."

Vestara nodded. "I know. But old habits die hard."

She allowed Ben to pull her to her feet, then stepped so close he found himself tensing to block an attack. She smiled, the scarred side of her mouth giving the expression a slightly sinister appearance, and looked deep into his eyes.

"You *do* know why I told you what Ship was to my people, don't you?" she asked.

"Sure." Ben continued to hold her gaze—*and* her

knife hand. "To build trust and make me feel indebted to you."

A flicker of disappointment shot through Vestara's eyes, but the smile remained on her lips.

"That, too." She touched her palm to Ben's chest, then asked, "Are you going somewhere?"

"Back to the ruins," Ben said. "I think Dad should know Ship is coming, don't you?"

"And you've never heard of a comlink?"

"It might be better if Lord Taalon didn't overhear," Ben said. "At least until I'm there with him."

Vestara considered this for a moment, then nodded. "You might have a point there." She glanced aft, toward the medbay, then said, "You go ahead. I'll look after Dyon."

Ben smiled. "Nice try." Still holding her by the hand, he stepped toward the rear hatch. "You're coming with me."

Vestara resisted for only a moment, then sighed and allowed him to pull her along. "Fine, but he's *your* friend. Don't blame me if his bandages are all pus-soaked when you get back."

Ben stopped. "I changed them less than two hours ago."

"And *I* changed them an hour after *that,*" Vestara replied. "From what I saw, his wounds are infected."

Given the amount of bacta salve that had been slathered over Dyon's wounds, infection seemed unlikely. More probably, Vestara was simply trying to keep Ben from warning his father about the coming change to the balance of power—and *that* told him all he needed to know about what Ship had actually said to her.

Ben nodded as though convinced by her argument. "Okay, it'll only take a second to check on him," he said. "And there are a couple of collection bags you probably need to change, anyway."

"*Me?*" Vestara objected.

"If the bacta salve isn't working, we're going to have to break out the strong stuff." Still holding Vestara's hand, he led the way aft through the main salon and past the galley. "And *your* thumbprint won't open the security cabinet where it's stowed."

Vestara's only response was a resigned grunt. At the entrance to the port access corridor, Ben used the pretext of courtesy to pause and wave her down the passage ahead of him. She, of course, paused and motioned *him* ahead.

Ben shook his head in mock disbelief. "Always so suspicious."

"Always so tricky," Vestara countered. "I've seen how dirty you Jedi fight."

Ben cocked his head and studied her, then asked, "Are we *going* to have another fight?"

A pained look came to Vestara's eyes. "Not soon, I hope."

She slipped past and led the way down the corridor . . . then drew up short at the medbay's open door. Assuming the worst, Ben stopped three steps behind her and reached for his lightsaber.

"You're . . . you're *awake*?" Vestara gasped. "How?"

Any suspicion that her astonishment was part of an act was quickly alleviated by the sound of Dyon Stadd's groggy voice.

"Just . . . tough." A bunk rail clanked as Dyon pulled against a safety restraint. "Hey, can you help me get this off? I've got to use the refresher something awful."

"Actually, you *don't*," Ben said, stepping past Vestara into the medbay. "That's probably just the catheter you're feeling."

"*Catheter?*" Dyon croaked. He was lying beneath a thin medbay blanket, with sweaty hair and sunken eyes. Both wrists were in safety restraints, a precaution to prevent him from thrashing about in his sleep and ripping out the IV drips in his arms. "How long have I been out?"

"Not as long as you should have been," Ben said, going to his side. Dyon's Force aura still felt tenuous and feeble, as though he were only about half alive, but his breathing did not seem labored, and he appeared reasonably alert. "How are you feeling?"

"I was mauled by a rancor once," Dyon said. He turned to meet Ben's eyes, but his gaze remained oddly vacant. "This is worse."

"I'll bet." As Ben stepped closer, he shot a hand out and grabbed the top edge of the blanket. A clank sounded as Dyon's hand jerked instinctively against his wrist restraints, but his eyes remained dead and expressionless. Ben frowned and asked, "How's your sight?"

"Ah." Dyon's head sank back in his pillow. "That's what you were testing."

"And you didn't answer my question." Ben pulled the blanket down and saw that the bandages wrapped around Dyon's torso remained clean. At least *that* was as he had expected. "Did you *see* my hand move, or just sense it through the Force?"

Dyon's eyes remained fixed on the ceiling. "I hear prosthetic eyes are even better than real ones."

Ben sighed and started to assure Dyon that he was right about prosthetic eyes—then heard the soft hiss behind him and turned to find the medbay door sliding shut. He raised a hand toward the control panel, but before he could use the Force to depress the slap-pad, a muffled sizzle sounded inside the circuitry box. Half a heartbeat later the tip of a crimson lightsaber burned through the cover plate and destroyed the retraction mechanism with a quick circle.

"Vestara!" Ben crossed to the door, his own lightsaber already in hand. "You *don't* want to do this."

"Not really." Her muffled voice was already fading as she raced toward the exit ramp. "But I have my orders."

Ben reached the door. Too wise to actually *look* through the hole Vestara had cut through the control panel, he expanded his Force awareness to the rest of the *Shadow.* He found her presence well forward and already descending the boarding ramp.

"She did it *again*?" Dyon asked.

Ben glanced back to find Dyon's head turned toward the door, his vacant eyes fixed on the hole that used to be a control panel.

"I thought you couldn't see?" Ben replied.

"I can't." Dyon's gaze drifted toward Ben's face. "But I can smell burned circuits and feel how angry you are. Even an academy flunk-out can figure that out."

"Actually, I'm not all that angry." Ben turned back to the door, then ignited his lightsaber and began to cut his way out. "She didn't even try to kill me."

Chapter Three

THE PYRE SMOKE HUNG LOW AND BLACK OVER THE COURTyard, making it difficult for Luke Skywalker to concentrate on the figures carved into the stone arcade . . . and perhaps that was the point. His Sith companions did not like him wandering the ruins alone, trying to understand Abeloth and the Font of Power without them, and they were certainly capable of using smoke to express their feelings. Unfortunately, he had discovered nothing to warrant their displeasure—only more of the eerie reliefs they had uncovered everywhere as they stripped away the temple's veil of carnivorous plants.

Dominated by sinuous shapes that seemed to change from vines to serpents to tentacles with each blink of the eye, the reliefs resembled a style called "ophidian grotesques" back on Coruscant. But Luke recognized these as something far more ancient and sinister. He had seen similar sculptures in half a dozen places around the galaxy, on worlds like Shatuun and Caulus Tertius—worlds that had died in cataclysms as old and mysterious as the Maw itself. Nobody seemed to know who had created the sculptures, and they were only found on planets that had been rendered uninhabitable eons before the dawn of recorded time.

A faint shiver of danger sense alerted Luke, and he turned to see Sarasu Taalon approaching through the greasy pall of smoke. Like all native Keshiri whom Luke had met, Taalon was slender and good looking, with lavender skin and violet eyes. His long face had been etched by age lines, though just deep enough to give him a dignified appearance grimly at odds with the hostility and narcissism that permeated his Force aura.

The smoke began to billow away as Taalon drew near, and Luke realized that the Sith was using the Force to clear the air around him. This simple task would have taxed his own abilities no more than it did those of the High Lord, but the Force was a sacred thing to Luke, not some tool to be utilized for one's personal comfort and convenience. That was the fundamental difference between Sith and Jedi, he thought: Sith believed the Force existed to serve *them,* and Jedi regarded themselves as servants of the Force.

Taalon stopped at Luke's side, his nose wrinkling at the smell of charred flesh that still lingered in the air. "You have a fondness for the odor of burning Sith, Master Skywalker?"

"If you mean, do I like it better than the smell of Sith left rotting in the jungle, then yes," Luke answered, not turning away from the column he had been studying. "Especially when they have been left in the heat for two days already."

Taalon waved a slender hand in indifference. "Time matters little to the dead, Master Skywalker, and we had work to do," he said. "But I apologize if the odor offended you. Given that it was only Sith you were smelling, I had thought you would find it satisfying."

"I don't relish *anyone's* death," Luke replied. "And I was sorry for your loss."

This last part drew a snort of disbelief. "You can't lie to a Sith, Master Skywalker."

Luke turned to Taalon with a smile as confident as it was serene. "If that were true, you'd know that I'm *not* lying. I took no joy in the deaths of Lady Rhea and her team aboard Sinkhole Station. And I'll take no joy in killing you and Gavar Khai—after you've forced me to it, of course."

Taalon's smirk narrowed to a thin-lipped frown. "You see, that's where we are different, Master Skywalker. When our work together is done, I'm very much looking forward to killing *you.*"

Luke shrugged. "We all need a dream, Lord Taalon." He returned his attention to the battle-scorched arcade and traced a finger down a ropy carving. It might have been a serpent climbing the column, or a vine twined around it; like all of the carvings in the temple, it was abstract and mysterious. "Until then . . . these reliefs obviously had some deep significance to whoever built this place. Do they mean anything to you?"

The frown departed Taalon's face, taking with it the glimpse it had offered of the ugliness hidden beneath his flawless features. He and Luke were working together only because they both knew that nobody would learn anything if they had to spend their time fighting. So far, during the two days it had taken to clear the jungle from the ruin and reclaim the dead from the planet's carnivorous plant life, the High Lord had been surprisingly cooperative—a sure sign that he intended to kill Luke the instant he decided his Jedi counterpart had lost his usefulness.

After a moment, Taalon said, "It could mean many different things to my people, depending on what it is. If it is a serpent, then it's associated with cunning and sudden death. A vine would be associated with patience and slow death, a tentacle with destiny and inescapable death, a rope with bondage and disgraceful death, a root with rejuvenation and feeding off death, an entrail with instinct and death by torture—"

"Thanks, I've got the idea," Luke interrupted. It had not occurred to him that the carving might represent an entrail, but he had to admit that some sections did seem to have a certain smooth, slightly flattened shape. "Do your people have any symbols *not* associated with death?"

"Death is what awaits us all when the Destructors return." Taalon turned to Luke. "Do you know of the Destructors, Master Skywalker?"

"Why don't you enlighten me?" Luke's reply was designed to avoid a direct answer. He knew enough about Lost Tribe politics to know that Vestara would pay in blood for anything she had let slip—at least *accidentally.* "The name certainly sounds ominous."

"With good reason, Master Skywalker—with very good reason."

Taalon went on to explain what Luke already knew: that according to Keshiri legend, a species of mysterious Destructors came back every few eons to wipe out civilization and return the galaxy to its natural, primitive state. When the original Sith had crash-landed on their world more than five millennia in the past, the native Keshiri had greeted them as the legendary Protectors, who were destined to save the world when the Destructors came again—a prophecy now embraced by the Sith themselves.

Taalon pointed at the sinuous carvings on the column, then continued, "These *symbols,* as you call them, have always been associated with the Destructors."

"You think Abeloth was a Destructor?" Luke asked, astounded. "And you still tried to make a *prisoner* of her?"

"There was no time to examine the artwork, if you'll recall." Taalon pointed toward the interior wall of the arcade, where a long row of three-meter doorways led into a series of cavernous habitation cells. Inside, Luke knew from their earlier explorations, were Wookiee-sized benches and stone bunks large enough to sleep rancors. "But just because Abeloth tried to hide in a ruin adorned with such artwork doesn't mean she *is* a Destructor. She seems rather too small to belong in this place, would you not agree?"

Luke faced the far side of the courtyard, where Gavar Khai was simultaneously tending the funeral pyre and keeping a watchful eye over Abeloth's corpse. Hidden beneath a blood-soaked robe being used as a death shroud, her body was about the size of a normal human woman—a bit on the tall side, perhaps, but too small to justify the huge furniture in the habitation cells.

Finally, Luke said, "At least in that form, she is."

He turned back toward Taalon and found him facing the center of the courtyard, where the Font of Power was gurgling inside its pall of yellow steam. Luke could feel that it was imbued with the same dark Force energy he had sensed the first time he had come here, in the company of his Mind Walking guides from Sinkhole Station. Whatever the fountain's connection to Abeloth might be, he knew that its dark power would be an irresistible temptation to Taalon.

"You may be right, Lord Taalon. This ruin wasn't where Abeloth lived." Luke glanced toward the top of the ridge, where her lair was located. "We might learn more by returning to her cave."

A predatory smile twisted across Taalon's lips. "Come now, Master Skywalker," he said. "I can feel the fountain's power as clearly as you can."

"The *fountain* didn't make my Jedi Knights lose touch with reality, and it's not what we're here to investigate." Luke turned toward the far side of the courtyard, where Gavar Khai was struggling to keep the pyre aflame on a diet of tree ferns and club mosses. "That would be Abeloth."

"Whose source of power was *here,* perhaps?" Taalon retorted. "In this fountain?"

As the High Lord spoke, Gavar Khai stepped away

from the pyre, positioning himself between Luke and Abeloth to preclude any attempt to retrieve the body. A robust man with long black hair, he had a hard face with clean lines and even features, and eyes so deeply brown they seemed the color of night. Judging by his interactions with Vestara, Khai was a good enough father—a little too stern, perhaps, but also loving and proud. Luke admired him for that much, at least. He realized he and the Sith would never part ways without doing combat, but fighting Khai would be a sad duty, and Luke would regret killing him.

From behind Luke, Taalon continued, "If you are going to reveal only what is convenient, Master Skywalker, our bargain is not worth the keeping."

Luke stopped and allowed his shoulders to slump. He had no idea what would happen if Taalon drank from the Font of Power—whether it would kill him or bestow on him the unlimited power promised by Luke's guides on his first trip to the ruin—and he truly did not want to find out. Unfortunately, any attempt he made to discourage the High Lord was doomed to backfire, and so he would have to pursue another strategy.

Besides, there was clearly *some* connection between Abeloth and the fountain, and Luke needed to learn about it as badly as his counterparts did. He turned, but remained where he was.

"I don't know a lot," Luke said, "and I won't be responsible for what you do with the information I *do* have."

Taalon's voice assumed a superior tone. "Then you *have* been here before."

"In a manner of speaking, yes." Luke crossed to the edge of the sulfurous plume, then stopped and looked back over his shoulder. "Do you agree to my terms or not?"

Taalon's eyes grew narrow and pensive. "Interesting," he said. "Are you trying to frighten me . . . or *tempt* me?"

"Just trying to honor our bargain," Luke said. "And *you're* the one who's insisting."

Taalon thought for a moment, then finally turned to Khai. "Do nothing unless the Jedi attacks."

Khai inclined his head. "As you command, High One."

Luke stepped into the steam. His sinuses and throat went raw after his first scorching breath, but he continued forward, using the Force to clear the fumes away from his face. As he drew nearer to the sculpted-tentacle basin, the power of the fountain itself began to pour through him, making him feel cold and queasy and vile inside. It looked much the same as it had during his first visit, a jet of dark water about as thick as his leg, rising from some well of dark side energy so deep and ancient that it felt as old as the galaxy itself.

Taalon stopped next to Luke and let out a soft breath that might have been a gasp of awe—or a hiss of fear. He stared into the column of brown water for a long time, allowing its power to wash over him, then finally stepped away from Luke and let his hand drop toward his lightsaber.

"I've kept my side of the bargain," Taalon demanded. "What do you know of this place?"

Luke continued to look into the column of brown water. "Well, it's a very powerful nexus of the dark side."

"*That* much I can sense for myself." Taalon's voice grew menacing. "I trust you have more to offer?"

Luke nodded. "Someone tried to trick me into drinking from it." As he spoke, a small pair of vortices appeared in the yellow steam, spinning at about head height above the basin. "They told me that if I had the courage to drink from the fountain, I would have the power to achieve anything."

"Who is *they*?" Taalon demanded.

Luke could feel the cold brush of Taalon monitoring his Force aura, trying to determine whether he was lying. He ignored the sensation and continued to watch as more vortices appeared in the sulfurous steam. The first set began to slow and grow more substantial, taking on the ovoid shape of eyes.

"My patience grows short," Taalon warned. "If you believe you can deceive me, you are mistaken."

"It was my guides from Sinkhole Station," Luke explained. The first set of eyes began to glow with the same golden anger he had seen on his previous visit, and he glanced away, making the movement quick and obvious. "They weren't very trustworthy."

"Or so you would have me believe." As Taalon spoke, his gaze shifted toward the fountain, and he let out an audible gasp as more sets of eyes began manifest around the first. "Who are *they*?"

Luke could only shake his head. "Your guess is as good as mine," he said. "Destructors? Manifestations of the dark side? More beings like Abeloth?"

"*Prisoners . . .*" Taalon said, leaping to his own conclusion. He shot Luke an angry glance. "Just as you hoped *I* would become."

Luke put on an innocent face, then protested, "*I* wanted to go back to Abeloth's cave."

"A ploy," Taalon said. "Had you shown your eagerness, I would have sensed your trap."

"You're too clever for me again, Lord Taalon." As Luke spoke, he experienced the familiar jab of his son's Force touch. Ben felt worried and seemed to be trying to warn him about something, urging him to stay alert and keep his guard up. Obviously, something must have gone wrong back aboard the *Shadow*—but there was no use letting Taalon know. Luke turned back to the fountain and, maintaining a deliberate air of calm, pointed at one of the more alien-looking sets of eyes. "Any idea what species those might belong to?"

"None at all." Taalon stood gazing from one set of golden eyes to another for several moments, then gave a sudden shiver and looked away. "But their promises are not to be trusted."

"*Promises?*" Luke's surprise was as real as his alarm. The darkness in the fountain had clearly reached out to Taalon in a way that it had not to him, and whether it was promising to reveal Abeloth's true identity or the secret of drawing on the fountain's power, that could only mean trouble. "They're actually *speaking* to you?"

Taalon turned to Luke with a sneer. "Your act grows annoying, Master Skywalker." He spun on his heel and started away from the basin. "It was a cunning trap, but nothing in this galaxy is harder to trick than a Sith High Lord."

Chapter Four

WHEN VESTARA LOOKED OVER HER SHOULDER, SHE SAW only the fern-and-fungus jungle swallowing her path. When she paused to listen, she heard only the hammering of her own heart. When she pulled the hot, humid air through her nostrils and down into her heaving lungs, she smelled only the sour taint of her own fear. But she knew Ben Skywalker was behind her, just twenty or thirty meters down the slope. She could *feel* him, a fierce, fiery presence in the Force, clambering up the ridge behind her, tireless and determined and unforgiving.

It was her own fault, of course. Vestara could have tossed a thermal detonator into the medbay as she locked Ben inside, or she could have taken a minute to sabotage the *Shadow*'s fusion core before rushing away. But she had told herself that Ben was too quick and cunning to eliminate so easily, that trying to kill him would only decrease her chances of reaching Lord Taalon with the news of Ship's return. The truth was, she simply had not *wanted* to kill Ben. She had allowed her fondness to become weakness, and Vestara detested weakness . . . especially in herself.

Continuing to bound up the ridge, and drawing on the Force to combat her growing exhaustion, Vestara dared to glance back. She saw no sign of Ben, only a handful of fronds still fluttering in her wake. They would be still by the time he passed, and the thick undergrowth was perfect for an ambush. All she had to do was think of a way to negate his danger sense . . . or to overwhelm it. If she could find a circle of paroxispore or a brake of acid-feather, Ben would not know where the true threat lay. She would be able to camouflage herself nearby and—even with one shoulder only half usable—remedy her mistake. Her father would never need to hear of her weakness . . . and neither would High Lord Taalon.

Resolved to find a good place for an ambush, Vestara turned her gaze up the slope again and found a large, gray-green blossom hanging in front of her. It had no stamen or pistil, just a long tubular anther filled with a fine, rust-colored pollen.

"Ah, *shrak*!"

Vestara planted her heels and tried to whirl away, squeezing her eyes shut, but she was too late. There was already a spasm rolling up the anther, and a cloud of crimson pollen exploded into her face, filling her eyes with bright stinging pain. Her vision blossomed into flame-colored blindness. Knowing that to remain motionless was to die—no doubt slowly and painfully—she continued her spin and Force-leapt blindly away.

Whether she had turned across the slope or down it, Vestara had no idea—and she was never going to find out. She was still in the air when she slammed into a snarl of vines and simply hung there, bouncing. Thinking she had just gotten tangled, she reached for her lightsaber—then felt a vine tighten around her wrist and pull it away from her body. She tried to jerk free, but the vine was secured to her sleeve by a potent, sweet-smelling resin. When she grabbed it with the Force, its grasp grew tighter, stretching her arm out straight, pulling so hard that she feared her shoulder would pop out of its joint.

Vestara tried to blink her vision clear and succeeded only in coating her eyes with resin and making them sting even worse. She pulled her other arm from its sling and began to inch her hand toward her parang, trying to move slowly enough to avoid triggering another attack.

Something woody and sinuous slid up the inside of her arm and began to apply pressure in the opposite direction. Vestara's heart began to hammer inside her chest, her breath coming in short gasps of panic. Another vine slithered up her leg, then twined itself around her torso and began to squeeze. Her thoughts began to whirl through her mind in a wild cyclone of anger and terror. After surviving so much on this world—attacks by carnivorous plants, Abeloth's manipulations, being marooned with no hope of rescue—the thought of returning to it had filled Vestara's heart with dread. But she *had* returned, because Lord Taalon had commanded it, and here she was again, blind and bound and about to become dinner for a tree.

"I . . . really . . . *hate* . . . this planet."

Vestara grabbed her lightsaber in the Force and slipped it off its belt hook. The last thing she needed was for Ben to find her like this, and not only because she would be at his mercy. He had a bad habit of thinking he was saving her life, which usually manifested itself in a cocky grin that suggested he expected something in return—like maybe being honest or *not* betraying him when the chance came. She floated her lightsaber off to the side until it was several meters away, then depressed the activation switch.

The weapon came to life, emitting the familiar drone-and-crackle of a power supply focused through one of the Lost Tribe's efficient Lignan crystals. Directing the blade by its sound, she slashed through the vines above her head and adjacent to her. Instead of dropping to the ground, Vestara tumbled away head-over-heels and found herself hanging upside down, caught now by her ankles and one arm. She used the Force to bring the lightsaber around above her feet.

Her legs quickly fell free and swung down until they were even with her head. Now she was hanging parallel to the ground, caught only by her waist and one arm. Believing she just might spare herself the embarrassment of being rescued by her Jedi rival, she floated the lightsaber into her free hand so she could cut more accurately, then twisted her body around, reaching up above her waist.

"Stop!"

Ben, of course. Vestara dropped her chin in frustration, then slashed through a vine. Her feet swung down just as she had expected, but they did not touch ground, and she found herself hanging by her wrist.

"Vestara, no!" Ben blurted. His voice was coming from four or five meters away, a little below her and well off to one side. "What's wrong with you? You'll kill yourself!"

"*Sure* I will," Vestara said, raising her blade above her head. "That's just like you Jedi, trying to take advantage of a blind girl."

"Blind?" Ben sounded genuinely surprised. "Vestara, I'm serious—you're hanging over a cliff."

"A cliff?"

Vestara deactivated her lightsaber and returned it to its hook. Then she pulled a spare energy bar from a thigh pocket and let it drop. She did not hear it hit the ground.

"Okay, so I'm hanging over a cliff." Vestara could not keep the quaver out of her voice—and she did not bother trying. She was usually very good at concealing her emotions, but Ben had been using the Force to track her when she ran into the blossom, and he would have sensed her terror in her aura. "What are you going to do about it?"

She did not sense Ben moving any closer. "Why should I do *anything*?"

"Ben, you're wasting time." Vestara's eyes burned as if someone were spraying hot ashes into them, and she could feel the lids beginning to swell. If she didn't get the pollen flushed out soon, she would be blind for days—and on this planet, being blind was a death sentence. "If you were going to kill me, you wouldn't have told me about the cliff."

"Maybe I like you where you are."

Vestara exhaled in exasperation. "I should have killed you when I had the chance."

"You didn't," Ben replied. "Have a chance, I mean."

Vestara turned her head in his direction, then used the Force to draw her parang from its scabbard and send it flying toward his voice. A strangled cry of surprise escaped Ben's lips, and she heard the undergrowth rustle as he dived out of the weapon's path.

"There's *always* a chance, Ben," Vestara reminded him. As she spoke, the vine tightened around her wrist, and she had an uneasy feeling that she was being drawn into the crown of whatever tree had captured her. "Now stop wasting time and tell me what you want."

"Not much." Ben sounded closer now, as though he had come over to the edge of the cliff. "I'd just like to know where you're going in such a hurry."

Vestara furrowed her brow, trying to puzzle out what Ben hoped to learn by asking such an obvious question. "Where do you think I'm going?" she asked. "The same place you are."

"To the ruins," Ben confirmed, "to tell Taalon that Ship is on its way back?"

Vestara whistled as though she were impressed. "You Jedi are *smart*. I didn't expect you to figure *that* one out."

"That part was easy." Ben's voice was even, betraying no hint that her sarcasm was bothering him. "What I want to know is, why you didn't take the *Emiax*?"

It was a revealing question, and one so unexpected that Vestara had to consciously still her Force aura to keep from betraying her surprise.

"Why do you *think* I didn't take it?" she asked, buying time to think. Whatever Ben threatened, no matter how angry he was about her latest betrayal, he wasn't going to leave her hanging there blind and doomed—he couldn't afford to, because he needed her to find his way through the jungle. "The *Emiax* is Lord Taalon's shuttle."

"And you were afraid I'd shoot it down," Ben finished, supplying a better answer to his own question than Vestara ever could have. "Smart girl."

"I have my moments," Vestara said. Again, she had to work to conceal her surprise. It hadn't occurred to her that Ben would actually *fire* on her after she had gone to such pains to spare his life . . . but these Jedi were full of surprises, which was what made them so dangerous. "Here's what *I'd* like to know. After you broke out of the medbay, why didn't you just take the *Shadow* and fly back to the ruins? You would have beat me by an hour."

"That's easy," Ben said, leaving a long pause that suggested he was developing an explanation. "I was, uh, worried about you."

"*Worried?*" Vestara echoed. "About a *Sith*? One who has betrayed you *how* many times?"

"You're just an apprentice," Ben replied easily. It did not sound like he was moving any closer, and the feeling in Vestara's stomach definitely indicated that she was being pulled up into a tree. "There's still time to redeem you."

"Cute," Vestara said. Her eyelids felt as big as her thumbs now, and she could feel pus starting to ooze out of her tear ducts. "But I wouldn't hold my breath, Ben—and I wouldn't leave me hanging here any longer, either. Two more minutes, and I won't be able to see for weeks."

"And that would matter to me *why*?"

Vestara smirked in the direction of his voice. "Because if you knew where the ruins were, you'd know you can't get to them in a spaceship," she said. "They're in the jungle, in a ravine at the foot of the volcano. Where did you think you were going to land?"

Ben let out an angry huff, then retorted, "So you lied to me about the reason you didn't take the *Emiax*?"

"So you expect me to believe you really would've have shot me down?" Vestara flashed him a sultry smile—at least she *thought* she was flashing it in his direction. "Come on, Ben. Help me down. I really *do* need to get this pollen out of my eyes."

"Why should I?" Ben demanded.

"Uh, because you'd like to find your father before Ship finds Taalon?" Vestara replied. "Once the High Lord realizes that Ship is coming back—"

"I *know* what will happen when Taalon thinks he doesn't need my father anymore," Ben interrupted. "What I *don't* know is why I should trust you."

Vestara frowned and fell silent. That *was* a hard question—and one for which she had no good answer. "Look, Ben, you *need* me."

"And you need me," Ben replied. "So give me a reason to help you down."

"A *reason*?" Vestara asked, growing more confused by the moment. "I've already given you one. Without me, you won't find your father in time."

"That's an argument, maybe even a fact," Ben insisted. "But it's *not* a reason. If I'm going to help you down and find something to help your eyes in this medkit—"

"You brought a medkit?" Vestara interrupted.

"I'm a Jedi Knight," Ben replied. "I *always* bring a medkit."

Vestara had to smile—then the vine tightened around her wrist again, and she felt herself start to rise faster.

"Okay, what do you want Ben?" she asked. "We're running out of time here."

"You know what I want," Ben said. "Your word."

"My *word*?" Vestara echoed. "You mean, just a promise?"

"Not just a promise. *Your* promise."

"*My* promise?" Vestara felt sure Ben had to be pulling a trick—maybe some kind of Force binding or Jedi mind-lock—but she couldn't sense anything unusual happening. "That's all?"

"You'd have to mean it," Ben replied. "If you want my help, you have to promise: no more betrayals."

Vestara felt herself biting her lips, and that was when she realized what Ben was doing to her: he was playing on her emotions, trying to beat her at her own game.

She suppressed a smile. "For how long?" she asked. It wouldn't do to seem too eager; he wouldn't believe her if she surrendered too easily. "I'm not promising *anything* forever."

Ben paused before answering, and Vestara knew she had him.

Finally, he nodded. "Fair enough—until Ship arrives. That's when reactor cores are going to start going critical anyway."

Vestara pretended to consider this for a moment, then shook her head. "Until you have a chance to tell your father about Ship. If I don't tell Lord Taalon that he's returning, I'll be running for my life with you and your father . . . *again*."

"Would that be so bad?"

Vestara nodded. "I'm no Jedi, Ben—and I don't want to become one."

"Okay, if you're sure," Ben said. Vestara felt him grab her in the Force. "So, I have your word?"

"Yes, Ben." Vestara grabbed her lightsaber again and

ignited the blade. She cut herself free of the last vine and felt Ben floating her toward him. "You have my word."

For what it's worth, she added silently.

Once they crested the ridge, Ben abandoned all pretense of needing advice to locate the ruins. The pyre smoke was wafting up through the jungle so thick and acrid that he had to use the Force to avoid the embarrassment of gagging in front of Vestara, and then it was a simple matter to descend into the stench. With her vision still blurry and her eyes continuing to drain, Vestara stayed close on his heels, holding on to his equipment belt and using the Force to steady herself on the steep slope. Walking that close behind him was the last place he would have preferred to have an armed Sith, but Vestara's promise to him was stronger than she knew—and any trust he placed in her would only increase its power.

After a few minutes, wisps of dark fume began to drift through the fronds and moss, and Ben felt Vestara's hand tense on the back of his belt. He pretended not to notice, but kept his lightsaber ready and his thumb near the activation switch. He could feel their fathers and Taalon a few hundred meters down the slope, wary and alert, more suspicious of his unexpected return than alarmed by it—and *that* meant Ben still had time to warn his father about Ship.

They continued to descend, and the jungle began to grow less dense. The ruins slowly came into view below, set in a small gorge at the foot of the volcano. The ancient complex had a simple plan, with a gray stone courtyard ringed on three sides by an arcade built into the face of a ten-meter cliff. The open end of the court overlooked a steaming swamp draped in moss and vines, but the centerpiece was a gurgling fountain swaddled in acrid yellow vapor.

Thirty meters from the fountain stood Gavar Khai, a

dark-hooded figure feeding chopped fronds and chunks of fungus to a large, smoldering pyre. Ben's father and Lord Taalon were nowhere to be seen, but their Force presences could be felt under the opposite slope, presumably exploring a warren of subterranean rooms beyond the arcade.

Ben stopped and spoke over his shoulder in a near whisper. "Remember your promise?"

"How could I forget?" Vestara replied, also whispering. "I don't make that many of them."

"I'm flattered—I guess." Ben stepped to the edge of the cliff, which was actually the roof of the arcade on their side of the ruin, then said, "How's your vision?"

"Good enough to imagine my father's face," she said. "I won't be able to stall long, so I hope you've thought of a good reason for abandoning our post."

"Not really," Ben said. "But by the time that matters, it won't matter anymore."

Vestara's Force aura rippled with confusion. "What does *that* mean?"

"Just trust me . . . and be ready." Ben turned sideways. "The next step is a long one."

He stepped off the roof, trailing one hand along the stone wall and using the Force to slow his descent. Behind him, Vestara released his belt and simply dropped. At the last instant, she extended a hand over her head and broke her fall by pulling against the top of the arcade, landing well ahead of Ben—and as gently as a feather. It was a sobering reminder of just how naturally the Sith of the Lost Tribe used the Force, and of how little the Jedi really knew about them.

By the time Ben was on the ground, Vestara was already crossing the courtyard toward her glowering father, her stride purposeful and confident despite her injured shoulder and the trouble her oozing eyes were causing her. Ben paused to brush off his robes, allowing Vestara ample time to betray him . . . because he knew she *would not.* She would realize the opportunity was intentional and suspect a trap, and Vestara feared mistakes more than she feared death. Rather than risk looking foolish in front of her father and Lord Taalon, she would honor her word and discover how good it felt to keep a promise . . . and once she had taken that first step toward redemption, Ben would *have* her. He would keep drawing her into the light a little at a time, just as his father had done with his mother, and eventually Vestara would grow accustomed to its warmth and move out of the shadows forever.

But Gavar Khai barely glanced in Vestara's direction as she stopped before him. Instead he kept his gaze fixed on Ben, one hand ready to launch a bolt of Force lightning and the other resting on the pommel of his lightsaber. Ben allowed father and daughter a few seconds alone, then smiled like a nervous suitor and started across the courtyard to join them. He could feel his own father's curiosity through the Force, a dull pang of uneasiness in the pit of his stomach, and he responded by concentrating on his feelings of urgency and alarm, a silent warning that their strained alliance was about to snap entirely.

Once Ben had joined the Khais in the smoke-clouded air next to the pyre, Gavar Khai finally turned to his daughter. "High Lord Taalon told you to stay with the Jedi, did he not?"

Vestara dropped her gaze and nodded. "He did."

"Then what are you doing *here*?" Khai demanded. "He was relying on you to prevent them from betraying us."

"Yes, I know." Vestara shot a demanding glance in Ben's direction, silently threatening to break her promise unless he came to her rescue. "But there were . . . *circumstances.*"

Khai narrowed his eyes and glanced in Ben's direction, then looked back to Vestara. "Let us hope High Lord

Taalon finds your *circumstances* acceptable," he said. "He is not one to easily forgive disobedience."

Vestara swallowed hard and dropped her gaze. "I await his judgment." She gave Ben a sidelong glare, clearly warning him not to push her. He smiled and remained silent; a promise meant nothing if it was easy to keep. She fought off a sneer and looked back to her father. "Once the High Lord hears the facts, I'm confident he'll understand."

Khai studied her for a moment; then his expression grew worried. "You should not be confident, daughter . . . not at all." His gaze lingered as the color drained from her face. Then he turned to Ben and stepped forward until they stood chin-to-nose. "Now, young Skywalker, tell me what you did to my daughter?"

Ben rolled his eyes and, without tipping his chin back, met Khai's gaze. "I saved her life."

Khai's expression grew even stonier. "And you had to blacken both eyes to do it?"

Ben glanced over at Vestara's purple, swollen eyes and realized that it did look as though she had been hit. Vestara smirked and looked away, letting him know that he was on his own. He returned the smirk with a one-sided grin, then looked back to her father.

"You'd rather I leave her hanging in a bloodvine?"

A hint of fear flashed across Khai's face, then vanished as quickly as it had appeared. He made no move to step away or seem any less threatening, but Ben knew that he had made his point—and that the time had come to prove to Vestara that he could be trusted not to betray her, either.

"That's what I thought," Ben said. "And she didn't disobey anyone's orders. She was chasing *me.*"

Khai scowled. "She was behind you?" he asked. "And you are still alive?"

Ben rolled his eyes. "Skywalkers aren't easy to kill," he said. "You should know that by now."

A cold presence entered the courtyard about five meters behind Ben, then a silken Keshiri voice said, "Oh, we *do* know, Jedi Skywalker—you may be certain of that."

Vestara and her father pressed their sword hands to their chests and bowed, and Ben turned to see High Lord Taalon crossing the courtyard toward him. Next to the Sith walked Ben's own father, his expression as curious as his Force aura was energized and wary.

Taalon stopped two paces short of Ben, at optimum striking distance for his lightsaber, then demanded, "So the question becomes: why were *you* disobeying orders?" He pivoted so that he was standing at an angle to Ben and Luke, smoothly placing himself in better position to address them—or to defend himself against them. "I'm aware that you Jedi don't place the same value on discipline as we Sith do, but surely when a father gives a command, he expects his son to obey."

Luke faced Taalon directly and frowned. "That works for you? With teenagers?" He put on an expression that managed to look both surprised and doubtful. "I hope you don't expect me to believe that."

Taalon's eyes went cold. "I assure you, Master Skywalker, I won't be distracted by your mockery." He turned back to Ben. "Now, will you instruct your son to answer me? Or shall I have to ask Vestara?"

Taking his father's cue to act the part of an unruly teenager, Ben spoke without permission. "It was the smoke." He waved an arm toward the funeral pyre, gesturing so energetically that Taalon flinched and half reached for his lightsaber. "I picked it up on the *Shadow*'s sensors and thought there might be a . . . a problem."

"A fight, you mean," Taalon surmised. "And so you

crossed the ridge on foot, because you thought we would still be in combat . . . *an hour later*?"

"Well, yeah." Ben glanced in Gavar Khai's direction, then scowled as though Taalon's explanation made perfect sense. "There are two of you, so I thought it would take Dad a while to finish you off."

"Your lack of faith hurts me." Luke's stern tone was belied by the amusement in his Force aura. "Clearly, we need to elevate your training sessions."

Taalon's expression turned sour. "I hadn't realized you Jedi were such comedians. When I return home, perhaps I will bring a few of you along to amuse our young ones." His eyes turned colder and angrier than ever. "Until then, I see that if I want a *truthful* answer, I must get it out of Vestara."

"I'm certain my daughter will tell you everything you wish to know," Khai said, a little *too* quick to promise his daughter's cooperation. He turned to Ben. "But what of your wounded friend? Has he died, or did you simply abandon his care?"

Khai was stalling, trying to force Ben to reveal the reason he and Vestara had abandoned their post. Maybe he had been eavesdropping when the pair stopped at the clifftop to discuss their agreement, or maybe he simply sensed the same thing Ben did—that Vestara liked Ben enough to lie for him. In either case, Khai was only trying to protect his daughter, and it was hard to blame a father for that.

"Dyon is on the mend," Ben said. "He was alert enough to take care of himself, or I wouldn't have locked Vestara in the medbay with him."

Taalon's brow rose, and he turned to Vestara. "Young Skywalker *tricked* you?"

Vestara let her chin drop. "I'm afraid so, High Lord." The flush that came to her cheeks was deep enough to look like true embarrassment, and Ben could detect no hint of deception in her Force aura. "He asked me to help him change a bandage, then stepped outside and sealed the hatch."

"I see." Taalon clasped her shoulder and turned her toward the arcade on the far side of the ruin. "You can explain over here . . . in private."

"Yes." Vestara glanced back, shooting Ben an angry scowl that suggested she now considered her promise completely fulfilled. "That might be best."

Gavar Khai remained behind with Ben and Luke, his expression stoic and unreadable as his daughter vanished into the shadows with Taalon. Ben fidgeted beneath his gaze, wishing that the Sith would step away to feed the pyre fire, or do anything that would give Ben a chance to have a few quiet words with his father. Finally realizing he would need to make his own opportunity, Ben turned toward the arcade.

"I didn't mean to shove Vestara into the fusion chamber," he said. "Lord Taalon's not going to *hurt* her, is he?"

"She'll be punished." Khai's tone was sharp and blaming, and he could not stop himself from staring into the arcade after his daughter. "How severely depends on how badly she failed her assignment."

"It wasn't *that* bad." Ben allowed his very real concern to creep into his voice. "It's not like she actually lost me."

Khai continued to stare into the arcade. "But you are the one who saved *her* life, and that will trouble Lord Taalon."

"Oh—well, I won't make the same mistake with *him*."

As Ben spoke, he nudged his father with an elbow, then made a walking motion with his fingers and pointed into the jungle. He felt bad about the trouble Vestara was in, but he needed to get his father away from there before Ship arrived—and he had no idea how soon that might happen.

Unfortunately, his father seemed to have other ideas. Luke simply shook his head at Ben's fingers, then nodded across the courtyard toward Abeloth's shrouded corpse. He wasn't leaving without a body to take back for analysis.

Ben scowled and mouthed the word, *Ship*!

Luke's brow shot up, but he made no motion toward the jungle.

Soon! Ben mouthed.

"What are you two whispering about?" demanded Gavar Khai's angry voice. "We have had enough Jedi tricks for one day."

"This is no trick," Luke said, turning toward the arcade where Taalon had taken Vestara. "But Sith or not, I won't stand by and allow a sixteen-year-old girl to be beaten."

Without awaiting a reply—and ignoring for the moment the fact that there was no indication that *anyone* was being beaten—Luke started across the courtyard. Taken even more by surprise than Ben was, Khai stood with his jaw hanging for a couple of heartbeats, then finally seemed to realize that he needed to do something.

By then, Luke was only a couple of steps from the arcade.

"Wait!" Khai extended his hand, using the Force to jerk Luke to a stop. "You can't interaaaggggghh!"

The objection came to a shrieking end as Luke whirled around, using his own Force strength to supplement Khai's. The Sith left the ground and flew across five paces of courtyard into the iron-tight grasp of Luke's artificial hand.

"Someone needs to intervene," Luke said calmly. "And since her *father* won't, *I* will."

Ben knew what his father was doing, of course, and he was already stepping toward Abeloth's shrouded body, reaching out to grasp it in the Force and float it around the far side of the funeral pyre. As gruesome as it seemed to sneak off with a stinking, three-day-old corpse, he understood why his father insisted on retrieving it. Assuming they were actually able to reach the *Jade Shadow* with Abeloth's body and return it to the Jedi Temple, it was impossible to say how much Cilghal might learn by studying the thing. She might be able to identify a species, or at least hazard a guess as to what kind of being Abeloth had been. And if they could not return to Coruscant with the cadaver itself, at least they might be able to take tissue samples and make a couple of vids.

But most important, by taking the corpse themselves the Skywalkers would prevent Taalon from keeping it. Given what the Lost Tribe's intentions had been—to subjugate Abeloth and turn her into their own living Force weapon—it was a risk well worth taking. Ben just wished he had thought to bring a thermal detonator along—except, of course, that it would have been a violation of their truce with the Sith.

Ben had just made it past the funeral pyre and was only three steps from the jungle when he felt Abeloth's corpse being drawn back into the courtyard. Cursing under his breath, he snatched the lightsaber from his belt and began to pull harder, then heard a familiar female voice behind him.

"Oh no you don't, Ben! *That* wasn't part of the deal."

Ben exhaled in frustration and, pulling harder than ever, spun around to find Vestara pursuing him around the pyre. Coming around the other side was Taalon himself, his lightsaber in hand and his eyes burning orange with rage. Luke and Khai remained out of sight beyond the pyre, still arguing and—judging by their Force auras—unaware of what was happening on the other side of the flames.

"Well done, Vestara." Taalon ignited his crimson

blade and started to circle toward Ben's flank. "See to Abeloth. I'll handle the boy."

A pang of sadness and loss shot through Vestara's Force aura, but she merely inclined her head. "As you wish, Lord Taalon. I'm just glad I was right."

She began to exert herself more fully in the Force, pulling hard enough that Ben knew it would prove impossible to hold the body *and* defend himself from Taalon. He reached for his father in the Force . . . and cursed, "Aw, *bloah*!"

Taalon sprang, coming in fast and hard with a vertical slash that felt almost contemptuous in its power and bluntness. Ben easily pivoted aside, simultaneously releasing Abeloth's body and sending it toward the pyre with a powerful Force shove. Then he continued his pivot and landed a spinning back kick square in the small of Taalon's back and began to think he just might win this fight.

And *that,* of course, was a very bad mistake.

Instead of flying splay-limbed into the jungle as Ben had expected, Taalon used the Force to plant himself like a tree and did not budge a centimeter. Ben's knee buckled, slipping, popping, and erupting in dull, aching pain. In the next instant Taalon's elbow was slamming into his temple, landing with such bone-crunching power that, had Ben not used the Force to send himself cartwheeling away sideways, the fight would have ended right there.

Ben was still tumbling when he saw Taalon's crimson blade slashing for his midsection. He brought his own lightsaber around to block—and felt the invisible hand of the Force pushing his arm aside, leaving a clear path for the High Lord's strike.

"Wait!" Vestara's voice boomed across the courtyard like a thermite detonation. *"It's a trick!"*

"A trick?" Taalon echoed.

Ben suddenly found himself hanging upside down, his

ankle locked in the High Lord's crushing grasp and his eyes fixed on the crimson blade that was no more than a centimeter from pushing into his chest. In the next instant Luke and Gavar Khai came rushing around the pyre together, their lightsabers ignited but not yet crossing. When they saw the situation—and how close Ben was to death—both men stopped in their tracks.

Taalon glanced at them only briefly, then looked back toward Vestara. "Explain."

"They switched bodies," Vestara said. "I don't understand how, but they did."

Ben turned his head toward her voice and found her standing next to the pyre, using the Force to levitate the corpse over which they had been fighting. The bloody shroud had been torn away during the tug-of-war, and now he could see that the corpse was not Abeloth's at all.

In fact, it wasn't even female.

"This *isn't* Abeloth," Vestara continued. She floated the corpse toward Taalon, and Ben found himself looking at a much-battered, but still recognizable male face. "It's Dyon Stadd!"

Chapter Five

OUTSIDE THE TEMPLE, A THOUSAND MANDALORIAN thugs stood clustered around their QuickStryke assault sleds, dressed in full battle armor and looking generally hot, bored, and eager to start something. Behind them sat a pair of *Canderous*-class heavy hovertanks and a squadron of ungainly vyrhawk fighter-bombers, and in the Walking Garden across the plaza more than two dozen sniperscopes were flashing in the foliage. Han Solo was starting to think Daala just might be serious about taking over the Jedi Order—that she might actually believe that mere military force was enough to bend the Jedi to her will.

As he watched, the QuickStrykes fired their repulsorlift engines, retracted their struts, and began to hover. The Mandalorians came more or less to attention, balancing their weight over both feet and swinging their weapons toward the Temple. Even the vyrhawks ascended to strafing altitude, their stubby wings and barrel-bristled noses winking with the rosy tips of energizing weapons. The sudden change of posture put the media on high alert, sending news presenters scrambling for their makeshift broadcast stages and cambots swarming into the unoccupied land between the Mandalorian lines and the Jedi Temple.

A couple of seconds later, the dark ribbon of a Gallactic Alliance Security hovercade streamed into view. Coming from the direction of the Government Center, it consisted mostly of speeder bikes, armored aircars, and cannon sleds. In the center of the procession were two large medical vans and a floating limousine that bore the emblem of the Galactic Alliance's Chief of State.

"Okay, that has to be Daala." Han turned away from the viewport and faced the small band of Jedi standing in the Temple's majestic mirrsteel foyer. "Looks like we're on."

"Yes, *finally*," Saba Sebatyne said. The Barabel stepped to the viewport, her thin tongue shooting between her pebbled lips as she glowered out at the hovercade. "How did you know Chief Daala would come in person?"

"Easy." Han started to slap the Master on her shoulder—then recalled how Barabels reacted when touched and quickly lowered his hand. "Daala is a power-hungry—"

"Han," Leia interrupted. She nodded at Allana, who was standing close beside her. "Admiral Daala is the Chief of State. She deserves to be referred to with a certain . . . decorum."

"—politician." Han glanced down at Allana and winked, then continued, "And power-hungry politicians love to gloat. No way is she going to miss *this*."

"An astute observation, Captain Solo," Kenth Hamner said, also stepping forward. He stopped just at the edge of Han's personal space, looking as dignified and grave as he usually did these days. His always resonant voice grew deeper and more demanding. "But I worry about your tone. If your idea works—"

"It *is* working," Allana interrupted. Her thin eyebrows were lowered in determination, and her bright gray eyes burned with the same frustration she no doubt sensed in the Force auras around her. "Otherwise Daala wouldn't even be here, and *you* know that as well as anyone!"

Hamner's lips tightened, and he addressed his reply to

Han. "I'm not disagreeing with you, Captain Solo. I'm just urging you not to be quite so . . . *smug.*"

Behind Hamner's back, Allana scowled and would have interrupted again, had Leia not laid a restraining hand on her shoulder. Han bit his lip and did his best not to aggravate the situation by smiling. He had insisted on bringing his granddaughter along because he wanted her to learn how to play a good hole card when someone else had most of the chips. But it was beginning to look like the lesson of the day would have more to do with internal politics—namely, that even Jedi Grand Masters could be nerf-brains.

Hamner seemed to sense Han's drifting thoughts and shifted, placing himself between Han and his granddaughter. "Remember, our goal here *isn't* to embarrass Chief Daala," he continued. "It's to convince her to lift the siege—"

"To *force* her," Octa Ramis corrected. A slender Jedi Master about ten years older than Jaina Solo, Ramis was almost as tall as Han—and, on occasion, was known to exhibit a temper just as volatile. "Let's be very clear on that, Grand Master. If this doesn't work, the Council *will* be discussing other means."

Hamner nodded. "Of course." The Force was hardly necessary to sense the bitterness in his voice; even the Masters were no longer bothering to hide their frustration with his cautious leadership. "I'd just like to remind Captain Solo that the goal is to *end* the crisis, not exacerbate it."

"No worries." Han unbuckled his holster-belt and rolled it around his old DL-44, then handed it to Leia. "I don't usually laugh in a chump's face until *after* I close the deal."

Hamner closed his eyes and exhaled hard, then turned to Kyle Katarn. "Maybe we should send someone else."

Katarn stroked the short-cropped beard that covered his blocky jaw, then asked, "Because?"

"Because Captain Solo *isn't* a Jedi," Hamner replied evenly. "And because he doesn't have the . . . *patience* to deal with Daala."

"We've shown Daala too much patience already," Kyp Durron said.

Cleanly shaven for a change—and reeking of algora-spice cologne—Kyp was standing with the two Jedi Knights who were key to Han's plan. The first was a tall Chev male named Sothais Saar, the second a small human woman named Turi Altamik. Cilghal had assured everyone that the pair's recovery from the Force psychosis was as complete as it was mysterious, and Han had known the healer far too long to doubt her judgment. Still, he would have felt a lot more confident if she had been there to keep a bulbous Mon Calamari eye on things. Instead she was down in the Asylum Block, running confirmation tests on the half dozen patients the GA did not know about.

"And Han has done too much for the Order—given too much of his own family's blood—to be dismissed like that," Kyp continued. "How many times does he need to prove himself?"

Kyp turned toward Corran and Mirax Horn, who were waiting a little apart from everyone else at the base of a soaring milkstone pillar. Corran's long face was as haggard as Han had ever seen it, with a tangled, untrimmed beard and a brow so furrowed it looked like a Gamorrean's. Though Mirax had at least brushed her hair and pulled it away from her face, her appearance was even worse, with hollow cheeks and sunken eyes.

Corran gave a single, quick nod of agreement. "Han has earned the Order's trust a hundred times over." He shot a scowl in Hamner's direction, then added, "I don't see how *anyone* could suggest otherwise."

Mirax joined her husband in glowering at the acting Grand Master. "Honestly, after what they've been through, it's an insult."

Hamner's eyes flashed at the cynicism in the voices of both Horns, and Han realized that if he didn't set his plan in motion *now,* the Masters were going to be too busy arguing to back him up. He kissed Leia on the cheek, then dropped to his haunches and looked Allana in the eye.

"Keep a watch on these guys," he said. "We don't want them missing my signal because they're, uh, discussing something."

"You mean *arguing.*" Allana shot a scowl in the Masters' direction, then said, "But don't worry. *I'll* be watching."

Han chuckled. "Looks like I'm in good hands, then." He rose and glanced over Allana's head toward Saar and Altamik. "You two clear on your part?"

Saar replied with a nervous nod. "Of course." Like all Chevs, he had pale skin and a heavy brow that made him look like a human thug—an impression that was only reinforced by the tailored cut of his shimmersilk robe. "We wait for your signal."

"Then just behave normally," Turi added. As petite and athletic as Saar was tall and husky, she had green, mischief-filled eyes and a smile diabolic enough to suggest she'd be a lot of fun in a firefight. "And let Daala do the rest."

Han flashed her a lopsided grin. "You got it, kid. I'll handle everything else."

He winked at Leia and turned toward the massive Temple doors. A pair of Jedi Knight guards peered through a security port, then wished him well and opened a small hatch in the base of one of the huge doors. He stepped out into the portico and stood looking down on the Mandalorian siege camp that lay spread across Fellowship

Plaza. How this was not being blasted as illegal by every media outlet on the planet, he could not understand. If Daala had called in the GA's *own* military, she could have at least claimed that she was merely taking action to protect the citizenry from a mysterious threat to public health. But the Jedi had a lot of friends in the GA military, and so she had turned to her Mandalorian allies instead.

Han had only a moment before a flock of hovercams came streaming toward him, weaving and bobbing as they jockeyed for a clear line of sight—and reminding him far too much of a swarm of bloodsucking skeetos. Knowing that Leia and the Masters would be eavesdropping on every sound he made, he took a deep breath and started down the stairs, singing one of his favorite Sy Snootles tunes, "Crazy Wicked Witch."

The hovercade streamed over the Mandalorian line at a velocity approaching breakneck, then whipped around in front of the Temple and came to a nose-dropping halt at the base of the stairs. A dozen aircar hatches flew open, disgorging fifty blue-armored Galactic Alliance Security troops who quickly shouldered their weapons and began to peer through heat-sensing scopes in search of snipers.

Han stopped on a landing, about a dozen paces up the stairs from Daala's limousine and the medwagons, and held his vest open to prove he was unarmed. That didn't keep the officer in charge, a lanky human captain whose face remained hidden behind a reflective helmet visor, from giving him a thorough frisking that was documented in close detail by the swarm of hovercams whirring about their heads.

After the captain finished and stepped away, Han put on a hurt expression and stared after the man in feigned shock. "I feel so . . . dirty," he said. "Maybe next time you could buy me dinner or something."

"I don't believe you're Captain Harfard's type . . .

Captain Solo," Daala said, emerging from her limousine. Dressed in a white tunic and slacks that looked an awful lot like the uniform of a Grand Admiral, she ascended the stairs and stopped a pace away from Han, then lifted her chin and glared at him in obvious disappointment. "I was expecting to see Grand Master Hamner, or at least one of the Council Masters."

"Yeah, sorry about that." Recognizing the captain's name from a few earlier GAS run-ins, Han allowed his gaze to linger on Harfard for a moment, then cast a pointed glance at the massive security detail the man was overseeing. "We didn't want to scare you—any more than we already have."

Daala's eyes narrowed. "Adequate security is a sign of prudence, Captain Solo, not fear." She looked past him toward the Temple. "But I really don't care who the Jedi send out to surrender."

Han's mouth started to water, the way it always did when he managed to put a player on tilt. "Surrender?" he demanded. "Who said anything about surrendering?"

Daala's gaze snapped back. "Master Hamner did," she said. "He commed me himself to say the Jedi are ready to turn over the maniacs they have been harboring."

"Maniacs?" Han pretended to be confused for a moment, then nodded as though he suddenly understood. "Oh, you mean the *patients.*"

"Yes, the patients," Daala confirmed. "Call them what you will. I want them. Now."

"But just the psychotic ones, right?" Han clarified. "You don't want the ones who just have sinus infections or stomach flu or stuff like that, right?"

Daala's glare turned suspicious. "I want the *barvy* ones, Captain Solo: Sothais Saar, Turi Altamik, and all of the other unstable Jedi who pose a danger to the citizens of this planet." She raised her chin and spoke directly to the holocams hovering overhead. "And to this galaxy."

"And then you'll lift the siege." Han phrased this not as a question, but as a condition . . . and he made sure he was also speaking into a holocam mike. "That's the agreement."

"I'll lift the siege *after* I'm satisfied that the Jedi are no longer sheltering psychotic Jedi Knights," Daala said carefully. "And I *am* going to search the Temple. Let's be very clear about that."

Han rubbed his neck, pretending to hesitate, then finally nodded. "Okay, fair enough." He looked toward the medwagons resting on their struts behind Daala's limousine. "You brought the brain-breaker?"

"If by brain-breaker you mean xenopsychiatrist, then yes. I brought the best." Daala turned toward the limousine and flicked her fingers in a summoning motion. Out stepped a tall, middle-aged Bith with a dignified bearing and a huge cranium so deeply green it was almost emerald. "Allow me to present Dr. Thalleus Tharn, chair of xenopsychiatric medicine at the Greater Coruscant University. His honors and titles are too numerous to recount, but I have every confidence that Master Cilghal will know his reputation."

Han whistled, truly impressed, then extended a hand as Tharn stepped onto the landing. The xenopsychiatrist made no attempt to reciprocate, instead dropping his ebony eyes to study the appendage as though it were being offered as an object of contemplation rather than greeting. Never one to accept a slight gracefully, Han continued to hold his hand out until Tharn was finally forced to sidestep in order to avoid it.

"I never shake hands," Tharn said, clasping his hands behind his back. "I'm also a surgeon."

Han's brow shot up. "You mean you cut people open by hand, yourself?" he asked. "No droids?"

"Brain surgery is more art than medicine, Captain Solo, and droids are not capable of art." Tharn's voice was deep and refined, the kind that Han sometimes heard narrating advertisements for luxury airspeeders and men's personal grooming products. "I'm sure you wouldn't want someone with sore fingers excising a suspicious node from *your* prefrontal cortex."

"I wouldn't want *anyone* digging around in there. No telling what they might find." Han hitched a thumb toward Daala. "The Chief tell you why you're here?"

"She did," Tharn assured him. "To oversee the sedation and transfer of the Jedi patients to a facility where they can be safely secured."

"In carbonite," Han added, more for holocam's benefit than Tharn's. "She told you that part, too, right?"

Tharn nodded. "Of course."

"And you think that's okay?" Han allowed some of his very real outrage to show in his wide eyes and sharp expression. He needed to get Tharn on live HoloNet saying that carbonite was the last resort—and the easiest way to get a brain-breaker to do anything was to make him think he needed to calm someone down. "To freeze a being solid, then hang him on a wall like some trophy?"

Daala quickly stepped forward. "Dr. Tharn isn't here to debate—"

"Unfortunately, Captain Solo, I *do,*" Tharn said, motioning Daala to stand aside. "Until we find a way to cure these patients, freezing them in carbonite is the *only* responsible thing to do. Jedi Knights are just too powerful to have wandering about in a psychotic state." Tharn's tone grew rhythmic and soothing. "Surely you agree with that."

Han rolled his lips over his teeth, trying to pretend that this *wasn't* going even better than he had hoped, then finally sighed and dropped his head. "So you think they *can* be cured?"

The Bith gave him a reassuring nod. "I'm looking forward to the challenge."

"That's not a yes," Han noted.

"It's not a no, either. I give you my word, Captain Solo, I won't rest until we can thaw them out. No one here enjoys freezing Jedi Knights in carbonite." Tharn turned to Daala. "Isn't that true, Chief Daala?"

"Of course, Doctor." The coldness in Daala's eyes betrayed her lie, but she managed to put enough sincerity in her voice to avoid sounding vindictive. "Once we can be certain the sick Jedi are no longer a threat, they'll be released immediately."

Han resisted the urge to smile. "Then I guess we should get on with this." He let his shoulders slump like a man defeated, then turned to Captain Harfard and spoke the words that Saar and Turi were waiting to hear. "Tell your bucketheads to hold their fire, will you? They're coming out."

"*Who's* coming out?" Harfard demanded.

"Sothais Saar and Turi Altamik, for starters," Han said. "Assuming you don't blast them, there'll be a few others."

Daala sensed the trap and quickly looked to Tharn. "Do you think that's wise, Doctor?" Her demanding tone suggested her own opinion. "Wouldn't it be better to take custody of the pris—um, *patients*—under more controlled circumstances?"

Tharn paused a moment, as though considering the merits of her suggestion, then nodded sagely. "Indeed it would." He turned to Captain Solo. "If you could just have someone open an entry bay, my orderlies will be happy to go in and remove the patients."

Han ignored him and continued to look at Daala. "Our mistake," he said. "When you told Kenth you wanted a public surrender, we thought you meant out here in front of the news, where everyone could see how well you're going to treat the patients."

"I meant that I wanted the situation resolved publicly," Daala replied. "I didn't mean we should endanger scores of beings by making the actual exchange out here in Fellowship Plaza."

"Well, *stang.*" Han turned toward the Temple entrance, where Saar and Turi were already stepping out of the portico with their hands raised high in the air. "I wish you'd told me that earlier."

A low growl sounded inside Harfard's helmet as he barked an order, and a knot of blue-armored guards closed ranks around Daala. There were already hundreds of Mandalorian weapons pointed at the two Jedi, but a couple of dozen GAS commandos went rushing up the stairs to intercept the pair.

Han turned toward the wall of guards surrounding Daala. "There's nothing to be afraid of, Chief Daala," he said. "But if you're scared, we could let—"

"I am *not* scared, Captain Solo." Daala pushed through the knot of guards and turned to Harfard. "I think it's safe to have the troops stand down, Captain."

Harfard made no move to obey. "With all due respect, Chief, this could be a Jedi trap."

Daala looked up the stairs toward Saar and Turi, who were standing, calm and unarmed, with their hands raised, while dozens of blue-armored GAS commandos thrust blaster nozzles in their faces.

"They've already sprung their trap, you idiot," Daala whispered. "Stand down . . . *now!*"

Harfard's helmet remained turned in her direction for a moment, then he finally muttered something into his commset and turned away. The guards surrounding Daala quickly retreated to a less intrusive distance, and the ones surrounding Saar and Turi assumed a less aggressive stance, pointing their weapons at the two Jedis' chests instead of their heads.

"Very clever," Daala said to Han. "Who are they?"

Han scowled, genuinely confused. "Who are *who*?"

Daala pointed up the stairs. "Those two impostors," she said. "Obviously, they *aren't* Sothais Saar and Turi Altamik."

"Nice try," Han said, sneering. Whether Daala really believed they were impostors or just wanted to plant that doubt in the public mind, he should have realized she wouldn't give up easily. "But that's them."

"And you expect the Galactic Alliance to take your word for this?" Daala asked.

"'Course not," Han said. "You can have them prove it."

"How?"

"Just have them do something only Jedi can do." Han motioned for Daala to follow him and started up the stairs. "They're either Jedi, or they're impostors. But they can't be both, because the Order doesn't have enough Jedi Knights in it to have doubles."

Daala remained on the landing behind him. "There's no telling what kind of illusions a Jedi Knight can create with the Force."

Han turned back to Daala, his lips drawn tight in disgust. "Come on, you *know* those tricks only work on the weak-minded." A hovercam floated down for a close-up, and he made a point of squinting at Daala as though he were trying to understand exactly what she was implying. "Say, you're not trying to tell me that the Galactic Alliance has a weak-minded Chief, are you?"

Daala's face flushed with anger. "You know better than that, Captain Solo." She remained on the landing. "But there's also plastic surgery."

"And *there's* a surgeon." Han leveled a finger at Tharn. "He ought to be able to tell if they've had any work done in the last few days."

Daala remained where she was, silent and no doubt trying to think of a way to turn the situation around.

"Fine," Han said. "I'll have them come down."

As Han turned to wave the pair down, Harfard rushed up and pressed a blaster nozzle into his ribs. "Hold it there, Solo. We won't let you endanger the Chief of State."

Han sneered down at the blaster, then said, "Assassination isn't really Jedi style, you moron." He shifted his glance to Daala. "Will you call this narglatch off? If you haven't guessed it by now, we've found a cure."

"Why don't we let Tharn be the judge of that?" Daala waved Harfard aside and motioned for the two Jedi to come down. "That *is* why you asked me to bring him along, is it not?"

The tightness of Daala's smile suggested she still felt sure of what Tharn would say—and that was probably her worst mistake of the day.

Han nodded. "Sure thing. I'm looking forward to seeing the master at work." He caught Tharn's eye and looked up at the swarm of hovercams, then added, "I'll bet your *colleagues* are too, Doc—especially the ones who'll be giving HoloNet commentary on your technique."

Tharn's eyes bulged as he realized what Han was implying, and he turned immediately to Daala. "This is hardly the proper venue for an evaluation," he said. "I'll need to take them back to my hospital for proper observation."

"You sure you want them in your lab, with no one but a few Mando goons guarding them?" Han rubbed his neck, feigning concern for the Bith's welfare, then lowered his voice and spoke in a menacing tone. "They might still be dangerous, and you said *yourself* that the only safe way to keep a crazy Jedi was on ice."

The epidermal folds in Tharn's cheeks drew down tight, and he appeared to contemplate Han's words with an air of disdain. Then his green cheeks paled to chartreuse as he realized what Han was threatening—that taking the Jedi back to his own laboratory would result in its destruction—and he quickly shifted his gaze back to Daala.

"Perhaps I *can* make a preliminary field assessment," he said. "I trust that will prove satisfactory."

Without awaiting permission, he ascended the stairs toward Saar and Turi, a whirling mass of hovercams circling his head. Daala scowled at Han, who merely shrugged and silently mouthed, *Your expert.*

Tharn stopped in front of the two Jedi and stood in silence, looking first deep into Saar's eyes, then into Turi's. After a moment, he peered up at the Chev's raised hands.

"Jedi Saar," he said, "please tell me why your hands are raised."

Saar furrowed his heavy brow, then shrugged and pointed his chin toward the line of Mandalorians spread across Fellowship Plaza. "Because I don't want to get blasted?"

Tharn nodded. "That seems reasonable." He turned to Turi. "Jedi Altamik, can you explain why those Mandalorians might want to blast you and Jedi Saar?"

Turi's upper lip curled into an edgy half smile. "Sure—Sothais and I have been a bit barvy lately." She shifted her gaze away, looking past Tharn down toward Daala, then added, "But we're better now, Chief Daala . . . *honest we are.*"

The faint rustle of laughter from beyond the Mandalorian lines told Han all he needed to know about who was winning the public relations battle in Fellowship Plaza. The Jedi had Daala on the defensive—and she knew it. To Han's surprise, she acknowledged Turi's jibe with a sour smile and a dip of the head.

"I'm glad you think so, Jedi Altamik," she said. "But

if it's all the same to you, I'd prefer to hear that from Dr. Tharn."

"I understand," Turi replied. She looked back to the Bith. "To tell the truth, I'd kind of like to hear him say it, too."

Another murmur of laughter broke out from the media encampment, this one louder than the first. Tharn waited for it to pass, then nodded.

"Just a few more questions, Jedi Altamik." He turned back to Saar. "Jedi Saar, do you trust me?"

Saar thought for a moment, then shook his head. "To tell the truth, Doctor, not all that much."

This reply drew no laughter, but Tharn took it in stride. "In your position, I don't think I would trust someone hired by Chief Daala, either," he said. "But please rest assured that whatever I do here, it's for your own benefit."

Saar regarded him warily. "If you say so."

"I *do.* And please lower your hands. Nobody here is going to blast you without a direct order from Chief Daala." Tharn continued to look at Saar, but addressed himself to Daala. "That's correct, is it not, Chief Daala?"

"If that's what you want, yes," Daala replied.

"It is." Tharn waited until Saar had lowered his hands, then turned back to Turi. "You, too, Jedi Altamik."

Turi lowered her hands. "Thanks, Doc."

"Your gratitude is not really necessary, Jedi Altamik," he said. "But your trust is. Will you trust me?"

Turi's green eyes grew thoughtful, her gaze turning inward as she reached out to examine his Force aura. After a moment, she nodded. "Okay."

"Excellent."

Tharn turned back to Saar, bringing a knee up between the Jedi's legs so swiftly that the Chev was doubled over and groaning before Han quite realized what he was seeing. A hush of astonishment spread across the plaza, followed an instant later by the clatter of hundreds of blaster rifles being raised to armored shoulders. Tharn's hand shot up, signaling for the troops to hold their fire, then he drew his knee back to strike Saar again.

In the next second, Tharn was high in the air, hanging aloft two meters beyond Turi's outstretched hand. "*Doc!*" she cried. "Why in the *blazes* did you do that?"

"I was conducting a field test," Tharn explained. He seemed surprisingly at ease for someone who had just assaulted a Jedi. He craned his neck around to look back down at Daala. "And since I still seem to be alive, Captain Solo is clearly correct. These Jedi have obviously been cured."

Daala was too astonished to be angry. "You *must* be joking."

"I assure you, I am not." Tharn turned back to Turi, then said, "Would you please put me down, young lady? You've already proven that you are in control of yourself."

A stunned Turi slowly lowered Tharn back to the landing. "You're as barvy as we were, Doc," she said. "You could have gotten us *all* killed."

"Only if one of you had lost control, and I could see from the moment you left the Temple that wasn't going to happen." Tharn gestured toward Saar's still-groaning figure. "*That* was just to prove it to Chief Daala."

And, Han realized, to make himself look good in the public eye—nothing like kneeing a Jedi in the groin on live HoloNet to make sure everyone remembered your name. But Han wasn't going to begrudge the Bith his fifteen moments of fame; even if it *had* taken a none-too-subtle threat, Tharn had defied Daala and done the right thing. For that, he was going to need whatever benefit his newfound celebrity brought.

Han turned to Daala and motioned up the stairs, to where Turi was holding Saar by the arm and trying to help him stand up straight. "If you're satisfied," he said.

"I think Jedi Saar could use someplace private to recover."

Daala nodded. "Of course." She flashed a vengeful glare in Tharn's direction, then added, "I'll have that plaza cleared as soon as Dr. Tharn certifies that *all* of the patients still in Jedi custody have recovered."

"Sounds good." An immense wave of relief rolled through Han, but he forced himself to keep a neutral face. He had seen defeat snatched from the jaws of victory often enough to know that *now* was no time for one of his trademark smug grins. Han turned to Tharn. "I'm pretty sure Master Cilghal will be happy to show you anything you need to see."

Actually, Han wasn't completely sure of that, since Cilghal wasn't all that sure of what had happened to cure the barvy Jedi Knights. But that was *her* problem, and now that Han had forced Tharn to throw in with the Jedi, the good doctor wasn't going to be looking too hard for reasons to make a negative report.

Han waited while Tharn made a show of ascending the stairs and taking Saar's free arm, then turned back to Daala.

"I guess that just leaves us with one last thing to discuss."

A vengeful light came to Daala's eyes, and Han's heart began to sink even before she spoke. "What thing would that be, Captain Solo?"

"Valin and Jysella Horn," Han said, deciding to go for broke. "We'll be coming to pick them up, just as soon as your bucketheads drag their barricades out of our hangar exits."

Daala's smile turned cold. "Then you'll be making the trip for nothing," she said.

Determined *not* to take the Galactic Alliance Chief of State by her lapels on live HoloNet, Han grabbed the sides of his trouser legs, *then* demanded, "You're going to keep them in carbonite? When you *know* Cilghal can cure them?"

"I don't know that she *can*. In fact, I don't know anything about this cure at all." Daala paused and ordered Harfard to lift the siege, then turned back to Han. "And until I *do* know everything, Captain Solo—until I'm one hundred percent satisfied that the Jedi are holding *nothing* back from me—the Horns will be remaining in GAS custody."

Chapter Six

KENTH HAMNER SHOULD NEVER HAVE TAKEN LUKE SKYwalker's chair at the Council meetings, not because he was unworthy of it, but because Jedi were not soldiers. They honored beings rather than rank, and if a leader expected to command their obedience, he first had to win their respect. Kenth saw that now, and he knew it had been a terrible mistake to claim the trappings of Grand Master before proving that he deserved them. At the time, he had believed that assuming the title would cement the support of the Order behind him. Instead, it had done just the opposite, reminding the Jedi that he was *not* Luke Skywalker—that he was, in fact, a replacement foisted on them by an ex-Imperial Chief of State who had once stood for everything the Jedi opposed.

And the problem with Daala herself was much the same. She was old-school military, very much the ex-admiral who believed she deserved not only deference, but immediate and unquestioning obedience. Sadly for all, the Jedi saw her in a much different light—as little more than a former enemy who had not yet earned their trust *or* their respect. The combination was a recipe for the disaster it had become, and Kenth could see in the hard faces around him that Han Solo's inability to win a graceful victory had only pushed matters to the brink of cataclysm.

With the exception of Luke himself, all the current members of the Jedi Council were there, either in the chamber or—in the case of Kam and Tionne Solusar—attending via HoloNet. Corran Horn was staring into the speaking circle with one of those saucer-eyed gazing-into-the-Core expressions that never seemed to leave his face these days. Flanking him were Kyle Katarn and Kyp Durron, their lips tight with the anger they were biting back. To Kenth's right sat Saba Sebatyne, her scaly tail extended through the chair's comfort-slot, the tip twitching and rasping on the larmalstone floor. Opposite the Barabel, Cilghal sat upright and motionless, her hands grasping the armrests of her chair and her bulbous eyes all but hidden by their membranous covers.

Next to the Mon Calamari sat the Council's newest member, a golden mountain of fur and fangs whom Kenth himself had nominated. Standing a full head taller than most Wookiees, with a boxy snout and a thin line of white fur covering a scar across her throat, Barratk'l was of a species that had been enslaved by the Empire because of its great strength and endurance, the Yuzzem. In contrast with her fierce appearance and powerful build, she had an abundance of patience and good-natured common sense that were all too rare on the Council these days.

Octa Ramis, of course, was on her feet, her brow lowered in anger, her fist banging like a slammed door as she struck it against her palm. ". . . holding them hostage!" she was saying. "This, we can no longer permit. We have shown the entire galaxy that Valin and Jysella no longer pose a danger to anyone, and the time has come to demand their return—or to recover them ourselves."

Kenth closed his eyes, retreating into his thoughts and silently urging Nek Bwua'tu to awaken from his coma. Together he and Bwua'tu could force Daala and the Council to come to terms and end this thing. But Kenth was himself in no position to extract the necessary concessions from Daala, and that left him with only two options—accede to his Masters' demands for action, or continue stalling and hope Bwua'tu awoke soon. Since only one of those choices did not lead to more violence between the Jedi and the government they were sworn to serve, his choice was clear.

Without opening his eyes, Kenth asked, "Master Ramis, the Mandalorian legion has barely cleared the plaza. Do you really think *now* is the best time to test our détente with Chief Daala?"

"I do."

Kenth's eyes popped open. "You can't be serious."

"As an asteroid headed dirtside," Ramis replied. "It's the last thing Daala will expect."

Saba's tail stopped twitching. "This one agrees," she said. "GAS will still be on alert. But even so, they will not be much trouble."

"And Daala won't have a response prepared, so we'll have the publicity initiative," Kyp agreed. He stood and began to pace in front of his chair. "If we move quickly, we might be able to keep this entirely out of the press—maybe even force her into claiming the release was on her authority."

Kenth began to feel light-headed. "You're talking about a raid against an *Alliance* facility, a raid that may end up killing *Alliance* soldiers. Have you lost your minds?"

The Masters paused to look his way for only a moment, then turned back to their discussion.

"Forcing Daala to claim *she* released the Hornz is good," Saba said. "This one would like to hear more."

"Well, *this* one wouldn't." Kenth drew himself upright in his chair; he had to cut this discussion off before the idea gathered any more momentum. "Mandos are one thing, but we are *not* going to take arms against Galactic Alliance personnel. Is that clear?"

Only the Solusars, Barratk'l, and Cilghal nodded. The rest of the Masters turned toward him with blank or slightly puzzled expressions, as though they were wondering why he thought his pronouncement should matter to them. Clearly, his leadership of the Council was hanging by a thread—a very frayed thread.

It was Corran Horn who broke the silence, finally seeming to return from his trance to stare across the circle at Kenth.

"And what are *you* going to do?"

Kenth scowled. Had Corran *really* just dared him to try to stop them from taking action? He rose to his feet, then said, "I don't think I like your tone, Master Horn."

Corran remained seated and spoke in a deliberately soft tone. "At the moment, *Grand* Master Hamner, I couldn't care less what you like." Bracing his palms on his knees, he leaned forward and studied Kenth with eyes so cold they seemed dead. "What I *do* care about is this: my children have been frozen in carbonite for months, and Daala no longer has any reasonable excuse to hold them. Both Valin and Jysella are Jedi Knights, and if you're unwilling to stage a raid to extract them, I'd like to know how you intend to get them back."

"Ah." Kenth sank back into his seat, feeling as uncertain of himself as he did embarrassed. It was a bad sign when a leader's stress began to make him defensive and paranoid, and he knew he should be relying on someone else to help him keep his perspective. But with Bwua'tu in a coma, where could he turn? It looked as though only Barratk'l supported him, and considering the situation, it would be unfair to undermine her standing on the Council by using her as his confidante. "My apologies, Master Horn. I thought you were asking something else."

"Clearly," Cilghal replied in her gurgling voice. "But the question Master Horn *did* ask is a good one. If you are reluctant to stage a raid, how do you propose to recover our Jedi Knights?"

"And don't even think about saying we're going to leave them there until we sort this out," Kyp added. "The Order can't allow *anyone* to hold our people hostage to our cooperation. We'd have every two-chit crime lord in the galaxy trying to hang his own personal Jedi in carbonite."

Seeing by the faces of the other Masters that his only choice was to agree or watch his fellows plan a disastrous raid, he steepled his fingers and nodded.

"We're *going* to recover Valin and Jysella very soon, I promise you," he said. "But I'd like to do it without starting an all-out war with Chief Daala."

"I don't see how that will be possible." It was Kyle Katarn who said this, and—coming as it did from one of the Council's most careful and deliberate thinkers—it was a statement that hit like a punch to the gut. "Natasi Daala is a woman of her convictions, and it's her conviction that the Jedi must be reined in. Unless you intend to allow that . . ."

Katarn paused and tilted his head in inquiry.

When Kenth responded with only a quick headshake, Katarn continued, ". . . then it *will* be necessary to confront her." He turned and ran his gaze around the circle of Masters. "The only thing we don't know is how soon."

Kenth could have kicked Katarn. Instead he turned to the other Masters and spoke in a deliberately calm voice.

"What Master Katarn says *may* be true. But don't we owe it to the Order, the Alliance, and the citizens of Coruscant to at least *try* to avoid war?" He looked to the two Masters likely to be most concerned about an outbreak of violence, Kam and Tionne Solusar. "We have only *just* forced Daala to lift the siege. Remember, she may believe that we were the ones behind the assassination attempt on

Admiral Bwua'tu. Let's give her a little time to discover the truth and realize she's *still* standing on the brink of a very nasty fight. Let's see if we can't make her blink, shall we?"

When the entreaty was met with silence rather than objections, Kenth realized he had a bought a few precious days for Bwua'tu to recover. He breathed a silent sigh of relief and steeled himself to take up the next item on the agenda—the StealthX strike force they had been trying to launch to reinforce Luke.

And *that,* of course, was the moment when the door opened and Han and Leia Solo marched into the Chamber.

"No wonder she wants hostages!" Han said, already striding toward the HoloNet control console. "You're not gonna believe this!"

Kenth scowled at Leia. "Jedi Solo, haven't I asked you and your husband not to barge into Council meetings? *Repeatedly?*"

"The Masters need to see this," Leia replied, not even bothering to pretend she was apologetic. "There's a freedom march on Blaudu Sextus."

"*Where?*" Kenth had never even heard of the planet, and he could not imagine why a protest there would be important enough to interrupt a meeting of the Jedi Council. "Jedi Solo, if this is just an excuse to—"

"In the Regulan system," Han interrupted, "out near Dubrava."

"Dubrava?" Kyp asked, turning in his chair. "I didn't know there *was* anything near Dubrava."

"*Barab One* is near Dubrava." Saba's dark eyes fell on Kyp and remained there, as though she considered anyone who did not know the galactography of her home sector a potential meal. "It is in the Albanin sector, along with Hidden Tegoor, Blaudu Octus, and, of course, Blaudu Sextus."

"Oh, *that* Blaudu Sextus," Kyp said, nodding as though he had merely needed reminding. "Of course."

Saba sissed at him, then directed her attention to the circle in general. "Blaudu Sextus invites slave labor from Blaudu Octus." She turned back toward the Solos. "Is it the Octusi on the march?"

"You guessed it," Han said.

Han pressed a sensor on the console, and a hologram appeared over the projection pad in the center of the speaking circle. The image depicted a line of centauriform aliens, with an Ithorian-like torso and head rising from the forequarters of a shaggy, barrel-chested nerf. They were marching single-file through a warren of cut-stone buildings, carrying sloppily rendered placards that depicted broken shackles and manacles. Although they were moving at a fast trot and filling the air with a high-pitched keening that would have been painful to hear in person, the marchers appeared eager to avoid causing property damage, remaining in a narrow line to avoid trampling the airspeeders parked in front of the buildings. In the foreground of the hologram appeared the impish figure of Madhi Vaandt, a doll-faced Devaronian female with pointed ears, narrow bright eyes, and white hair almost as wildly kept as Octusi fur.

". . . can see, the Octusi are a gentle species. Even when they choose to throw off the shackles of slavery, they show the utmost concern for the safety and property of others," Vaandt was saying. The scene shifted to a poorly lit spaceport in the dead of night, where a trio of huge MandalMotors troop transports sat almost invisible in a darkened corner of the landing field. "So why, then, was *this* the scene last night, at an industrial spaceport just twenty kilometers away?"

The scene assumed the greenish blue tint generated by a light-gathering lens. Several hundred Mandalorian commandos appeared, debarking the transports in assault sleds, in hovertanks, and on foot. Kenth's stomach immediately grew hollow and queasy, and even before he could grudgingly ask Leia for a report, Saba was on her feet, her scales bristling and her fangs bared.

"Chief Daala goes too far!" A loud crash sounded behind her as her heavy tail slammed into her chair and sent it toppling to the floor. Betraying no sign she had even noticed, Saba continued, "The Octusi are no threat to the Blaudunz. Octusi never fight . . . not even to save their own lives!"

"Perhaps you should give us a background report on these cultures, Master Sebatyne," Kenth suggested. Glad for an excuse to close the holofeed before the other Masters grew outraged as well, he signaled Han to kill it. "Maybe it will help us understand Chief Daala's thinking."

"What's to understand?" Han asked. "Daala sees defiance, Daala crushes defiance. It's the same strategy she learned sitting on Tarkin's lap."

Despite the sarcasm, Han deactivated the hologram, and Saba became the sole focus in the circle. The Barabel took a moment to collect her thoughts, flicking her tongue between her pebbly lips, then raised her gaze to address her fellow Masters.

"The Octusi are the natives of the Blaudu system," she began. "They are a simple-minded species, and most Blaudunz—the colonizers of Blaudu Sextus—do not accept that they are truly sentient."

"*Are* they?" asked Ramis.

Saba spread her hands. "That is for Master Cilghal to say, not this one," she replied. "The Octusi speak and understand nearly a hundred wordz, but they do not read or write, and they have no concept of time beyond *now, later,* and *before*. They use simple hand toolz to dig and to shape stone, but they do not understand leverz or pulleyz."

"Then it would depend on whose definition of *sentience* we apply," Cilghal said. "By the standards of the Old Republic, they would be classified as a primitive species and protected by the same laws that protect children and the mentally disabled. By Imperial standards, they would be classified as advanced livestock and treated as chattel."

"And under Alliance law?" Kenth asked.

"From Master Sebatyne's description," Cilghal replied, "I would consider them quasi-sentient. It wouldn't be legal to enslave them, and any legal dealings would need approval by a government-appointed advocate."

"What about their relationship with the Blauduns?" Kam asked from his hologram. "From Master Sebatyne's reaction and Madhi Vaandt's report, the two species hardly seem antagonistic."

"They are not," Saba said. "The Blaudunz own their Octusi, this is true. But they regard them as working petz and treat them well."

"Are they imprisoned?" asked Kyle.

Saba shook her head. "They are escorted *to* their work every day, but that is only because they would spend the day wandering otherwise. When they are done working, they are free to do as they wish."

"And they don't try to escape?" Tionne asked, her voice projecting from her hologram.

"There is nowhere to escape *to*," Saba explained. "Blaudu Sextus is a mining world, and its native plant life is either poison or not worth the eating. When the Octusi grow hungry, they must return to their masterz for food harvested from Blaudu Octus."

"And they always return to the correct master?" Tionne clarified.

"Not alwayz," Saba replied. "Sometimes, they go to someone else when they are hungry. It is not legal for a Blaudun to feed someone else's property, so they are returned to their rightful ownerz. But if it happenz several times, it is assumed the Octusi wishes to change ownerz, and the Blaudunz come to an arrangement."

"Well, that *sounds* like slavery," Kyp said. "Kind of."

"But they're allowed freedoms most slaves are not," Kenth pointed out. He directed his gaze back to Saba. "Tell us how the Octusi are taken from their home to Sextus. Perhaps that will clarify the situation."

"It won't," Saba replied. "The Octusi ask to be taken."

"Ask?" echoed Kyp. "As in, *Would you please move me a couple of worlds down-system and let me be your slave?*"

"Yesss," Saba hissed. "Blaudu Octus has a steep axial tilt, so the Octusi must spend their lives migrating, following the seasonz in search of good grazing. It is a hard life of moving fast, and they rarely live more than twenty standard yearz—barely long enough to rear their offspring."

"But they have a longer life span on Blaudu Sextus?" Kyle asked. "That's why they want to serve the Blauduns?"

"In a way, yes," Saba said. "When an Octusi becomes too slow to keep up, the band will often seek out a harvesting ship from Sextus and ask the Blaudunz to take their beloved one. It is better than dying alone in hard weather, and Octusi have been known to live eighty yearz in the care of the Blaudunz."

"And the Octusi know this *how*?" Kyle asked. "Because the Blauduns tell them?"

Saba shook her head. "Because *other* Octusi tell them," she said. "The Blaudunz bring slaves to help with the harvesting, and they are free to tell younger Octusi about life on Blaudu Sextus."

"Nothing is ever simple," Kyp observed. "It sounds like slavery, and it *doesn't.*"

"Yes, there is a lot to consider." Kyle spoke in a slow, thoughtful tone that suggested he had grown more interested in the abstract question than the real problem—and that was a big relief to Kenth. At the moment, he could not afford to get into a heated argument with his Masters about whether the Jedi Order should be doing more to support Freedom Flight's drive to eliminate slavery from the galaxy. "What about discipline and neglect? Do the Blauduns abuse their slaves?"

"There are bad beingz in every species," Saba replied. "But the Blaudunz have lawz against mistreating any creature, and those lawz are enforced."

"Which is rather beside the point, if I may say so." Leia spoke without permission, not even bothering to glance Kenth's way to seek it. "It's the Mandalorians that are the problem, *not* the revolt."

"Yes, exactly," Saba said. "The Octusi will not fight, but they will not yield. Now that they have risen in protest, they will continue to protest until they have won."

"Won *what,* precisely?" Kyle asked. "Emancipation? Wages?"

"It is strange that they would demand either," Saba said. "They are free to return to Blaudu Octus on a harvesting ship anytime they wish, and they have alwayz been confused by the idea of money." She looked toward Leia. "What does the report say?"

Leia thought for a moment, then shook her head. "The only thing Madhi has mentioned so far is freedom," she said. "Nothing specific."

"Which strikes me as suspicious," Kenth said. "If the Octusi are free to live where they choose, free to return to their homeworld to die, and free to spend their leisure time as they wish, it's hard to believe such simple beings even *understand* the ways in which they *aren't* free."

"What are you saying, Grand Master?" Barratk'l asked. Her voice was a bit less deep and gravelly than that of most Yuzzem. She had once suffered a grievous throat wound, and when it was repaired, she had asked to have her vocal cords thinned so that her speech would be more understandable to other species. "That it is permitted to keep slaves, as long as they lack the intelligence to realize what they are?"

"You *know* better, Master Barratk'l." Kenth fixed the Yuzzem with an icy glare and held it until she finally averted her gaze, then turned to Han. "Would you replay the feed you just showed?"

"Sure." Han touched some controls, and a moment later a holographic line of Octusi slaves was trotting through the speaking circle. "From here?"

"That's fine, thank you," Kenth replied. "Now would you freeze the scene and magnify one of those Octusi—one carrying a sign?"

Han scowled in puzzlement, but did as he was asked, and a moment later the hologram depicted a single life-sized Octusi. With shaggy white fur and a long, barrel-shaped abdomen connecting his hind- and fore-quarters, he resembled the beast of burden that his Blaudun masters claimed he was. But in the broad, flat trunk rising up from his forequarters, there was a gracefulness hinting at the tranquil nature Saba had described, and in his broad shoulders and hammer-shaped head there was a gentle beauty born of the uncomplicated integrity of a simple soul.

When Kenth activated his laser pointer, though, it was the broken shackles depicted on the sign that he illuminated.

"Master Sebatyne, have these beings *ever* been shackled?"

"No. Why would they be shackled when they have nowhere . . ." The Barabel let her question trail off, her eyes bulging as she seemed to comprehend the reason for Kenth's question. "Shackles would be rare, Grand Master Hamner. *Too* rare."

"So where did they learn the symbolism?" Kyle asked.

He turned to the other Masters and added, "Grand Master Hamner is right. Someone put them up to this."

The other Masters glanced around at one another, searching for a face that seemed to have some idea as to who might benefit from such a thing. Kenth allowed them ample opportunity to find someone, then finally cleared his throat.

When all eyes turned in his direction, he said, "I believe I have a theory. You've all heard of Freedom Flight, of course?"

The Masters nodded, and Han Solo chimed in, "For a secret organization, they've taken on a pretty high profile."

"The saviors of slaves usually do, Captain Solo," Barratk'l said. There was a defensiveness in her voice that Kenth found surprising, and he found himself wondering whether there might be a reason for that—a reason that might explain why Freedom Flight seemed to simply *assume* it should be able to count on Jedi help. "It is a hazard of protecting the wretched and crushing the mighty. They remember who you are."

Han gave her an approving grin. "Hard to argue with that," he said. "But how does it make sense for them to stir things up on Blaudu Sextus? There are countless stinkholes in the galaxy where things are a lot worse. Why start a revolt on a world where it's hard to be sure they *are* slaves?"

It was Leia who replied. "Because of Madhi Vaandt."

She stepped over to the control console and reached over the top to touch a control. The HoloNet returned to a live feed, where the hologenic reporter was interviewing a hairless green biped who stood only about chin height to her. He had sunken eyes, a long dagger-thin nose, and a broad smiling mouth that made him look rather perverse and wicked. As Vaandt peppered the unfortunate Blaudun with barbed questions about owning another being, Leia spoke over the tinny voices coming from the audio feed.

"What's changed lately?" Leia pointed at Vaandt's image. "*Her.* It's no coincidence she happened to be on Blaudu Sextus when the slaves went into revolt. Someone tipped her off—the same people who convinced the Octusi they were repressed in the first place: Freedom Flight."

Kyp shook his head. "I don't see it," he said. "The whole Blaudun–Octusi thing isn't ugly enough. If you're trying to draw attention to the plight of slaves in the galaxy, there are so many other places you can make a bigger impact."

"Yeah, but no other place where you *know* Daala is going to *have* to send in the troops," Han said. He looked to Saba. "I'm betting the Blauduns don't have much in the way of riot police."

"This one doubtz the need ever occurred to them."

"And since the Octusi are too stubborn to stop on their own, you know there's going to be a confrontation," Kyle said. He glanced in Barratk'l's direction, his brow furrowed in thought—no doubt because he was wondering the same thing Kenth was: whether a new Council member from a once enslaved species would involve herself in such a thing—whether she would risk the lives of thousands to liberate hundreds of millions. "And you know it's going to happen on live HoloNet."

"No, it will not be a confrontation." Saba fixed a bulbous eye on Barratk'l, then added, "Freedom Flight has made a mistake in their calculationz. This will be a slaughter."

Barratk'l's eyes widened noticeably, and she growled, "I hope you aren't saying *I* helped them plan."

Saba studied her for a moment, then replied, "No. This one is saying that Freedom Flight has made a mistake, and it would be good to let them know before it bringz blood."

"Which is exactly what Freedom Flight *wants,*" Kyle said. His voice had assumed the deep, confident tone it usually did when all the pieces of a puzzle had come together for him. "There's nothing like public outrage to force quick change, and if Daala blasts thousands of pacifist slaves on live HoloNet, it's *going* to create public outrage."

"But how does Daala fall for it?" Corran asked, raising his gaze for the first time since the subject had shifted away from Valin and Jysella. "If she's smart enough to keep the Jedi bottled up inside our Temple, she's smart enough not to fall for a trap like that."

"Only if she knows everything," Han said. "Whoever's behind this is picking out-of-the-way worlds for a reason. Even Ken—er, *Grand* Master Hamner—didn't know anything about the Blaudu system before this."

"But I *would* have before I sent in troops," Kenth replied. He was so accustomed to subtle digs that he allowed Han's to pass unanswered. "No, my guess is that there are things *we're* not seeing here. For instance, why did Daala use Mandalorians?"

"Because she wants to make a point," Han replied. "Nothing says *don't stir the soup* quite like a brigade of Mando bucketheads showing up on your doorstep."

Kenth shook his head. "No, she used Mandos because she was hoping to handle this swiftly and quietly," he said. "What if she had the extra Mandos on alert in case things heated up here on Coruscant?"

"You mean in case the Alliance military started to show signs of siding with *us*?" Kyle asked.

"That would be one reason, yes," Kenth said. He did not reveal that he *knew* this to be the case, as he had promised to hold in confidence all of the information Bwua'tu had shared with him. "She would have more faith in the Mandos to put down the revolt quickly—and to have no scruples about how they did it."

"And she *would* think that just because Octusi are pacifists, they're pushovers," Kyp said, nodding enthusiastically. "She's still that much of an Imperial."

"That would mean Freedom Flight *knew* about the Mandalorian reserve," Leia observed. Her expression was thoughtful but certain. "Otherwise, they wouldn't expect Daala to respond so quickly—and they wouldn't have had Madhi Vaandt waiting to expose her."

"You are saying Freedom Flight must have a spy inside Daala's office," Saba surmised. She cocked her scaly head in contemplation, then dipped her chin. "This one agrees. It explainz much."

"Yeah, it's beginning to look like these Freedom Flight guys have spies *everywhere*," Han said. "Kind of makes you want to know who *they* are."

Whether Han meant the comment to be a jab at Barratk'l was difficult to say, but the anger that flashed through her dark eyes suggested how she had taken it. Not wanting Barratk'l's relationship with the rest of the Council to turn sour so quickly, Kenth scowled in Han's direction.

"If Master Barratk'l had anything to do with Freedom Flight, I'm sure she would have told us by now." He waited until Han finally rolled his eyes and looked away, then gave Barratk'l a warm smile. "It's not as though there would be any reason to hide such a laudable endeavor from the Council."

The Yuzzem's eyes softened, and Kenth knew he had earned her gratitude. Only eight more Council members to go, and he *might* be able to consider himself worthy of the chair he was occupying. He looked away from Barratk'l and ran his gaze around the rest of the Masters.

"So," he said, "now that we understand the situation, what are we going to *do* about it?"

The blank looks that greeted the question suggested

two things to Kenth. First, the Masters' opinions of him had fallen so low that this was the last thing they had expected him to ask. And, second, he still had a chance to win them back.

"I think it goes without saying that we can't permit a slaughter of this magnitude," Kenth began, "no matter what kind of impact it might ultimately have on the condition of other slaves in the galaxy."

Support came from an unexpected corner—Corran Horn. "Agreed. There is no tomorrow, only what we do, or fail to do, today." He was quoting a new precept the Council was currently thinking of adding to the Jedi Code as a reminder to young Jedi Knights that the pursuit of noble ends never justifies base means. "We need to end this revolt before it turns into a bloodbath."

Kenth paused and ran his gaze around the circle, giving each Master an opportunity to object. When none did, he said, "Ending this revolt will put the Jedi Order temporarily on the side of the slavers and the Mandalorians. Can we accept that?"

"This one cannot," Saba objected. "We can also end the revolt by chasing the Mandalorianz away."

"I don't see how," Tionne said. "If the Octusi will keep marching until they win, we've only delayed the confrontation."

"Sometimes delay *is* prevention," Saba replied. "The Blaudunz and the Octusi are not enemies. Without interference, they will come to their own arrangement—without blood."

Kenth remained silent, waiting for someone else to point out the flaw in Saba's plan. When no one did, he realized he would have to do that himself.

"Are you suggesting the Jedi take military action, Master Sebatyne?" he asked. "Because, at the moment, that is just not possible."

"Of course it is not possible." Saba's tail thumped the

floor so hard that Kenth felt the impact through the seat of his chair. "We have the Sith to fight."

"So you're suggesting . . . what, exactly?" Kyp asked. "Because chasing off an entire brigade of Mandalorians is a pretty tall order, even for a Jedi Knight."

"You are right, Master Durron," Saba said. "We may have to send two."

The silence that followed suggested that the rest of the Masters were as stunned by the suggestion as Kenth was.

After a moment, Kyle asked, "Are you suggesting that we send Tesar and Wilyem?"

"No." Saba's head snapped around so quickly that Kenth wondered for an instant whether someone had reached for a lightsaber. "Why would you think *that*?"

"My apologies," Kyle said, frowning in puzzlement. "I thought you *meant* to suggest them."

"Tesar and Wilyem are busy." Saba glared at Kyle a moment, then looked back to the circle. "We must send someone else."

Kenth did not recall hearing of any mission involving the two Barabels. And these days, not hearing about *anything* involving a Jedi worried him. He thought for a moment, trying to recall the two Barabel females who had helped the Solos sneak a load of psychotic Jedi off the planet a couple of months ago. They had been the youngest members of the Wild Knights when Saba appeared with the band during the war with the Yuuzhan Vong, and they had flown with honor and ferocity in a half dozen space battles.

"What about Zal and Dordi?" he asked, finally recalling their names.

"This one said *no!*"

Saba stood and whirled so fast that Kenth had to exert an act of will to keep from leaping to his feet. Several other Masters did not bother, rising to stand in front of their chairs with their hands hovering over their lightsabers.

Saba glanced at their hands, then snorted in derision. "Dordi and Zal are not available, either. Barabel Jedi Knightz are *not* available."

Kenth remained in his chair, more puzzled by Saba's anger than he was frightened by it. In a calm voice, he asked, "And why not?"

Saba's scales bristled, and her tail lashed around so fast that Kenth and Cilghal both had to jump to avoid being swept off their feet. "It'z private."

"Private?"

Kenth glanced over at the Solos for some explanation—and found them looking just as puzzled as he was. Whatever the Barabels were up to, they were keeping it completely to themselves—and a secret mission cooked up by Barabels could not be a good thing.

"Master Sebatyne," Kenth said evenly, "like it or not, I'm the acting Grand Master of the Jedi Order. When four Jedi Knights disappear from the Temple without authorization, it's my duty to find out why."

The Barabel continued to regard him with a fang-filled snarl. "No, it is *not*. What Tesar and the otherz are doing is no one's concern but their own."

Kenth dropped his head in frustration. "Master Sebatyne, what I'm asking . . ." He caught himself and looked back up. "No. What I'm *demanding*—"

"Master Sebatyne," Leia interrupted, "I think Grand Master Hamner may be concerned that Tesar and the others are acting against Chief Daala without his knowledge. After the actions of, um, certain Jedi Knights recently, it's a reasonable concern."

Saba looked from Kenth to Leia for a moment, her reptilian head rocking in thought. Finally, she looked back to Kenth.

"You think Tesar and Wilyem have gone *out*? To hunt . . . *Daala*?" Her fang-filled snarl changed to an equally fang-filled grin, and she began to siss so hard her shoulders shook. "No. This one . . . promises they remain in the Temple. They are not going anywhere . . ." More sissing. ". . . for *monthz.*"

A brief glance away from the Barabel revealed that the other Masters—and even the Solos, who knew Saba better than anyone—remained as puzzled as Kenth was. He shrugged and sank back in his chair, very tired and very ready for the Council meeting to be over.

"Very well, Master Sebatyne, I'll take you at your word." Without waiting for her to return to her seat, he looked past her toward Barratk'l. "I propose that we send Sothais Saar and Avinoam Arelis to Blaudu Sextus to convince the Octusi to delay their protest. Saar is a Chev, and he's been working on the slavery problem for some time now."

Barratk'l nodded. "I agree about Saar. But why Arelis? If you're worried about a relapse, it's better to send a Master. And I have a certain understanding of the issue myself."

Kenth nodded. "That's true," he said, "but we also have the Lost Tribe to consider, and we're going to need every Master available when we go to face them."

"Then you do plan to launch the StealthXz?" Saba asked, half rising out of the chair to which she had just returned. "When?"

"When we can do so without fighting our way off Coruscant," Kenth replied. "We won't help *anyone* by arriving all shot up."

"Then you may as well send Master Barratk'l to Blaudu Sextus." Kyp's tone was derisive, and he was shaking his head and staring at the floor. "Because we're *not* getting our StealthXs off this planet without a fight—not as long as Daala is in charge."

Kenth could see by the disgust in the faces of the other Masters that they shared Kyp's opinion, and he knew as well as they did that *this* was the true test of his leadership. If he could not convince the Masters to be patient, to trust him just a little while longer, they would simply launch without him.

Deciding the time had come to confront the problem head-on, Kenth took a deep breath. "Master Durron, the situation with Daala may not be as intractable as you believe."

No one in the Chamber could have missed his implication; they were Jedi Masters, a former Chief of State, and, well . . . *Han Solo.* And they were all regarding him with varying degrees of surprise, doubt, and outright disbelief.

Finally, Kyp cocked a brow in what was either incredulity or awe. "You're saying you have something in the works?"

Kenth put a little durasteel in his voice. "I'm not just *saying* it, Master Durron. I *do.*"

Several Masters asked the obvious question at the same time, but it was Saba's raspy voice that Kenth heard most clearly.

"*What?*" she asked. "You have planz you have been hiding?"

Kenth pulled himself up in his chair, trying to summon a commanding presence. "I'm sorry. I'm not at liberty to discuss it."

Again the Masters spoke at once, but this time the result was an insulted—and in some cases, outraged—cacophony, "*Sure,*" "*Very convenient,*" and from Han, "*You've got to be* kidding *me!*"

Kenth raised his hand for quiet. "Please. I'm serious about this, but I can't discuss it right now."

He might as well have been speaking Ssi-ruuvi. The Masters merely stared as though the Emperor himself had suddenly appeared in Luke Skywalker's chair—and it was no wonder. For the leader of the Jedi Council to say he could not trust his Masters with such important information was unthinkable, a preposterous affront to their integrity and their judgment. And Kenth had to make them accept it. He had given Bwua'tu his word that he would keep their arrangement secret, and he owed it to the admiral to honor his promise—at least as long as the old Bothan was still alive.

"Look, I apologize," he continued. "But you'll understand when the time comes."

"I think we understand now," Kyp said. He turned to the Solos. "Maybe you two had better go."

Kenth shook his head. "It's not because Han and Leia are here," he said. "And it's *not* a matter of trust."

"And that's *not* why I asked them to leave." Kyp stood and nodded the Solos toward the exit, then waited in silence until they were gone. Once the door had hissed closed behind them, he turned back to Kenth. "I want an explanation now, Grand Master. You do *not* keep secrets from the Jedi Council—not about this kind of thing."

Kenth remained in his seat. "Normally, I would agree. But just as Master Sebatyne is asking us to take her word about the absence of Tesar and the other Barabel Jedi Knights, I'm asking you to trust me on this. It really *is* to the Order's benefit."

"This one's secret is different," Saba retorted. "It involves only four Jedi Knightz. Your secret is about the whole Order. It concernz Master Skywalker and the Sith."

Kenth could only nod. "I know it does."

Octa Ramis sighed and ran a hand over her brow, then said, "It might help if you could at least explain *why* you can't tell us."

"Of course," Kenth said. "Quite simply, it's because I gave my word."

"You gave your word," Kyp repeated. "And you expect us to trust that?"

Inwardly, Kenth was cursing Bwua'tu's coma and the

assassin's bad timing, but outwardly he shrugged and gave Kyp a half smile. "*Hoped* might be a better word."

This actually drew a smile from Kyp. "I guess I can believe *that.*"

"Well, *I* can't," Corran said. He rose and straightened his robes. "I'm sorry, Grand Master Hamner, but I think you're just stalling."

Saba rose as well. "This one, too," she said. "The time has come to launch. There are Sith out there, and Master Skywalker needz our help."

"And what do you think is going to happen when you go?" Kenth demanded. "The entire Sixth Fleet is waiting in orbit, and they *will* fire on you, I promise."

"We will elude them," Saba said simply.

"And when the Mandalorians return to storm the Temple?"

"We will kill them, as we did before," Saba replied. "The time for restraint has passed. There are beingz out there more fearsome than Mandalorianz, and if we do not act soon, *they* will be the ones ruling Coruscant."

Saba turned away, signaling that the debate was over, and started for the door. When the other Masters followed, Kenth knew his gamble had backfired. They were tired of waiting, of sitting on their hands while Luke and Ben and Jaina confronted a whole tribe of Sith, and no amount of reason was going to stop them—even if he broke his word to Bwua'tu and revealed what the GA military had in store for them.

So Kenth placed his hand on his lightsaber and stood. "No!"

Saba stopped at his sharp tone and turned to face him. "Please, Master Hamner, do not make this harder than it needz to be."

"And don't think you can do it any other way." Kenth started toward her, still gripping his lightsaber, and continued, "I was placed in this office by Grand Master Skywalker, and if you want to remove me, you won't do it by ignoring me. You'll have to do it the old-fashioned way."

Saba's gaze dropped to his weapon hand. Her tongue flicked between her lips, and Kenth knew then that he had found her limit. She wasn't prepared to fight another Jedi for control of the Order—not when there were so many other things for the Jedi to fight.

Trying to press his advantage and settle the issue once and for all, Kenth stepped closer, looking from Saba to the others. "Is there *anyone* here willing to take it that far?"

That was when the Masters surprised him again. Instead of averting their eyes or attempting to stare him down, they turned almost as one toward Corran Horn, and it grew obvious to Kenth that *he* was the one who had pushed matters too far, that his life and the future of the entire Jedi Order depended on what kind of man Corran Horn really *was*.

Corran stood lost in thought, his gaze so distant and sad and vacant that Kenth was not sure he even understood what was being asked of him. The other Masters remained silent, and it took all of Kenth's willpower to do the same. He wanted to grab Corran by the shoulders and shake him, *hard*, and demand that he stand for the Alliance and restraint and political process. Instead he stood silent with the other Masters, awaiting the verdict of a man whose children Kenth had allowed to remain frozen in carbonite for months.

After a time, Corran's eyes seemed to focus again, and he looked up and met Kenth's gaze. "No, we're not ready for that." He shook his head and started for the door again. "Not yet."

Chapter Seven

ERAMUTH HAD FALLEN ASLEEP.

Or so it appeared to Leia. She couldn't check his aura to be certain because Force-use was forbidden inside the Ninth Hall of Justice, and she did not want to prejudice the jury by getting caught violating the rule. But a day after the siege of the Temple had ended, she and Han had a made a point of arriving early to snag seats behind the defense table, and now they were seated in the first row, a little to one side where they could see Eramuth in profile.

The dapper Bothan was slumped down in his chair, with his hands folded across his vest-covered belly and his chin resting on his chest. His breathing was deep and steady, his eyes were closed, and his long ears were twitching in response to a breeze blowing only through his dreams. If the old fellow *hadn't* fallen asleep, he had been bored into a coma by Sul Dekkon's slow and methodical examination of the prosecution's latest surprise witness, an Imperial Intelligence officer who had been aboard the *Bloodfin* when Tahiri killed Gilad Pellaeon.

". . . please tell us what your duties as a ComInt officer included, Lieutenant Pagorski?" Dekkon was asking in his raspy Chagrian voice. His skin was a richer hue than that of most of his species, so deeply blue it was better described as sapphire, and today the long lethorns dangling down the sides of his head were capped by dark spheres of polished ebonium. "Without violating any military secrets, of course. We just need a general idea."

"Very well, sir," Pagorski replied. She was wearing the full Imperial dress uniform, white jacket with epaulets over gray shirt buttoned high and tight. "Basically, we eavesdrop on enemy communications. That's why it's called ComInt. Communications Intelligence."

Pagorski's narrow eyes were fixed on Tahiri instead of Dekkon, and it was obvious from the hardness and anger in them that she had taken Pellaeon's assassination personally. That was fine; it would make her testimony easier to discredit—provided, of course, that Eramuth was alert enough to observe her obvious motivation for coming forward.

Dekkon continued his line of questioning. "During the Battle of Fondor in the most recent civil war, were you aboard the Imperial Star Destroyer *Bloodfin* in your capacity as a ComInt officer?"

"That's correct."

"So you were the officer in charge of intercepting enemy communications for the entire Imperial fleet?"

"No, sir," Pagorski replied. "That would have been Captain Ellis."

Dekkon looked up from the datapad in his hands. "That's right—forgive me." He adjusted his heavy features into an expression of apologetic chagrin—a sign that the Chagrian was trying to keep Eramuth's attention focused on the mistake rather than the next question. "And what has become of Captain Ellis?"

"Captain Ellis was killed in action, sir." Pagorski's eyes blazed with anger. "During the mutiny."

"The mutiny that occurred after the Moffs' order to aid Colonel Jacen Solo . . . whom we now know as Darth Caedus?"

"That is correct, sir." Pagorski continued to glare at Tahiri. "Lieutenant Veila murdered Admiral Pellaeon because she knew that without him in command, the Moffs would take Colonel Solo's side against Admiral Niathal."

Dekkon hesitated almost imperceptibly, no doubt anticipating the objections to hearsay and prejudicial phrasing that should have been rising from the defense table. But Eramuth's chin remained on his chest, leaving Tahiri to sit beside him, no doubt wondering whether it would be more harmful to let the jury see her nudging her counsel, or to let the characterization pass unchallenged.

Always eager to press an advantage, Dekkon paused only half a second before continuing. "And before the murder, had Admiral Pellaeon already given orders to aid Colonel Solo's rival, Admiral Niathal?"

"Yes, sir."

"And, in your capacity as a ComInt officer, did you have occasion to intercept a communication between the defendant and Colonel Solo of the Galactic Alliance, in which the defendant informed him of Admiral Pellaeon's decision to support Admiral Niathal?"

"I did."

"Was the communication encrypted?"

"Of course," Pagorski answered. "During a military operation, *everything* is encrypted."

"But you were able to decipher the signal and eavesdrop on the conversation between the defendant and Colonel Solo?"

"I was."

"And how did you accomplish that?"

A superior smirk came to Pagorski's lips, and Leia knew that much of what followed would be a lie. The lieutenant had come forward at the last minute not—as she had claimed—because it had taken that long for the Imperial

Navy to grant her request to testify. Rather, she had waited because doing so made it impossible for the defense to challenge the claim she was about to make.

"I'm sorry, Counsel, but that's classified Most Secret," Pagorski said. "I warned you that I wouldn't be able to discuss the technical details of the interception when I came forward."

"Yes, so you did." This time, Dekkon pushed on without pause to what was surely very questionable testimony. "But you *are* free to tell us when this occurred in the chain of events."

"I am," Pagorski confirmed. "It occurred shortly after the command rift developed between Admiral Niathal and Colonel Solo. Admiral Pellaeon announced that he was going to throw the Empire's support behind Admiral Niathal, and Lieutenant Veila initiated an encrypted comm transmission to her superior."

Leia frowned, and Han fidgeted in the seat beside her. From everything she had heard about the battle, no such communication had taken place. Apparently, Tahiri did not recall making the call, either, for she started to lean over to whisper a denial into Eramuth's ear—but found him still napping. Clearly uncertain of what to do, she stopped and turned her attention forward again.

Dekkon continued to press his case. "Can you tell us what was discussed during that transmission?"

"I can. Lieutenant Veila reported Admiral Pellaeon's decision and requested orders. Colonel Solo instructed her to change the admiral's mind."

Tahiri was leaning forward now, her green eyes narrowed and her scarred brow lowered. Leia knew the expression meant that Tahiri was simply trying to figure out why Pagorski was lying, but she wasn't sure the jury would see it that way. To a jury, Tahiri's posture might very well look like a fallen Jedi Knight—or former Sith apprentice—attempting to intimidate a witness.

"Did he instruct her to kill him?" Dekkon asked.

"No, quite the opposite," she said. "Lieutenant Veila asked how far she should take matters, and Colonel Solo replied, 'Don't kill him. He's too popular with the Imperial Navy.'"

A shocked murmur rolled through the courtroom, and the judge—a stately Falleen female with a finely scaled face and long hair worn in a topknot—hit a button on her bench. A sharp, piercing tone filled the chamber, immediately bringing the court to order, and the judge scowled out at the spectators for a moment before nodding to Dekkon to continue.

Dekkon spun toward Tahiri, his long shimmersilk robes swirling about his legs. "You're saying Colonel Solo specifically ordered the defendant *not* to kill Admiral Pellaeon?"

Pagorski nodded. "I am."

"And you're certain it was Colonel Solo and the defendant you were hearing?" A puzzled frown flashed across Dekkon's blocky blue face as his gaze fell on Eramuth's dozing figure, but he quickly recovered and returned his stare to Tahiri. "It could not have been some other colonel and lieutenant discussing whether Admiral Pellaeon should be assassinated?"

"No, it was Colonel Solo and Lieutenant Veila," Pagorski confirmed. "We were very certain of that."

"How?"

Again, Pagorski smirked. "I'm sorry, Counselor, but you know I can't reveal that."

A fatherly smile came to Dekkon's face. "Of course you can't." He turned to face Pagorski again and paused for a moment, no doubt considering how far he could test the limits of proper testimony while his foe was napping. After a moment, he seemed to decide that he needed to seize every advantage he could, and he asked, "So, why *do* you think Lieutenant Veila killed him?"

Pagorski turned her icy gaze on Tahiri. "Because she was ambitious."

"Ambitious?"

"Admiral Pellaeon was a man with a durasteel will," Pagorski explained. "And Lieutenant Veila was serving as an aide to one of the most ruthless leaders the galaxy has ever known. When the admiral refused to change his mind, I imagine she grew angry and frustrated with having to report her failure. She vented that anger by murdering a legend of the Imperial Navy."

The courtroom broke into murmurs again. Han pressed against Leia's shoulder, and the warm rasp of his whisper filled her ear.

"Where are the objections?" he demanded. "Even *I* know that last answer was conjecture!"

Leia laid a calming hand on her husband's knee, then—knowing she would be ejected from the courtroom if she were caught—gave Eramuth a gentle Force nudge. The Bothan's head rolled to one side, his muzzle opening just long enough to emit a loud, throaty snort.

A stunned silence descended over the courtroom for perhaps half a second, then the spectators' gallery broke into a chorus of ill-concealed chuckles. Judge Zudan stabbed the ORDER button atop her bench and called for silence, the scales of her stately Falleen face turning crimson with irritation. Several of the jurors eyed Eramuth in shock and shook their heads in open disbelief. Tahiri turned around in her seat, her brows arched in a silent appeal for help.

Han leaned forward, reaching across the bar to pat her shoulder. "Don't worry, kid," he said. "He's got everything under control."

Tahiri glanced over at Eramuth, who was still asleep, then shook her head and whispered, "You're a worse liar than Dekkon's witness up there."

Han scowled, but before he could make a retort, Dekkon was nodding. "A legend indeed." The Chagrian faced the defense table. "Your witness, Counselor."

Tahiri turned forward again, glancing over at Eramuth with an expression as confused as it was alarmed. She had told the Solos more than once how impressed she was with her Bothan attorney, how sharp and cunning and—surprisingly—*ethical* he seemed to be. So it seemed likely that the concern in her eyes was as much for him as it was for herself, that she worried—as Leia did—that the strain of a high-profile trial might be proving more than an elderly Bothan could handle.

"Counselor Bwua'tu?" the judge inquired from her bench.

Eramuth let out a long, sleepy snort.

"Counselor *Bwua'tu*?" Zudan repeated. When Eramuth's only response was to allow his head to roll to one side, the judge directed her attention to Tahiri. "Would the defendant be kind enough to awaken her counsel?"

"Of course, Your Honor." Tahiri gently shook the Bothan by his shoulder, at the same time whispering, "Eramuth . . . *Eramuth . . . !*"

Eramuth's eyes opened the third time his name was called. He glanced around the chamber briefly and seemed to realize what had happened, then quickly pulled himself upright, far too alert—in Leia's opinion, at least—for someone who had been in such a deep slumber only instants before.

"My apologies," Eramuth said, straightening his vest. "I was concentrating."

This brought a wave of chuckles from the spectators, and even a couple of smiles from the jurors' box. But the judge's expression remained sober. She returned silence to her courtroom with a stern glower, then turned her attention back to Eramuth.

"Your witness, Counselor. Perhaps you'd like the sten-bot to repeat the last ten minutes or so of testimony?"

Eramuth shook his furry head. "That won't be necessary, Your Honor. I was resting my eyes, not my ears." He waggled his ears back and forth to illustrate the point, then rose to his feet. "I'm ready to proceed."

Zudan eyed him warily, but said, "If you're sure."

"Of course, Your Honor." Eramuth stepped around the defense table with such conviction that Leia began to believe he really might have been resting his eyes. The Bothan paused for moment, visibly stretching his back, then marched up to the lectern, propped his elbows on the surface, and leaned toward the witness box. "So, Lieutenant Pagorski, can you sense the Force?"

Pagorski's expression went from smug to confused. "The Force, sir?"

"You know." Eramuth executed an expansive wave over his head. "The energy field that surrounds us and permeates us, that binds the galaxy together with all living things and gives the Jedi their power. The Force."

Pagorski gave a curt nod. "I know what the Force is, Counselor."

"Then my question should be a simple one," Eramuth said. "Can you sense it?"

"No." Pagorski frowned and shook her head. "I can't."

"Oh." Eramuth seemed almost disappointed. "You're quite sure?"

Pagorski frowned and glanced toward the prosecution's table as though seeking guidance. When the expressions of Sul Dekkon and his three assistants remained completely inscrutable, she looked back to Eramuth and nodded.

"Yes, sir. I'm very sure."

Eramuth gave a dramatic sigh, then let his shoulders slump and returned to the defense table. He had barely taken his chair before Tahiri was pressed to his shoulder, whispering into his ear so harshly that Leia did not need to strain to overhear.

"That's *it*? She gets up there and lies—"

"My *dear.*" Eramuth's hand shot over and squeezed Tahiri's leg so hard Leia could see the muscle flexing in the old Bothan's shoulders. "I have just established that Lieutenant Pagorski could not have heard *everything* that passed between you and Captain Solo. Isn't that enough for one day?"

Leia saw Tahiri's shoulders sag at the same time she heard Han groan.

"Colonel," Tahiri whispered.

Eramuth frowned. "What?"

"Jacen was *Colonel* Solo," Tahiri explained. "Not Captain."

Eramuth's ears dropped. "Didn't I say Colonel?"

Before Tahiri could respond, Judge Zudan's sharp voice demanded, "Are you done with the witness, Counselor?"

Eramuth motioned for Tahiri to be silent, then rose. "I'm sorry, Your Honor, I was consulting with my client."

"I *asked* if you were finished with the witness, Counselor," Zudan repeated. "You didn't dismiss her."

"I'm done with her for now, Your Honor," Eramuth said. "But I'd like to reserve the right to recall her at a later time."

Zudan nodded as though that was a wise idea. "I'm sure you would. The witness is excused with instructions to remain available in the waiting room." The Falleen turned just long enough to see Pagorski acknowledge the order with a nod, then looked back toward the defense table and motioned Eramuth and Dekkon forward. "I'd like counsel to approach the bench, please."

Tahiri took one glance at the frowning jury and let her head drop, but Eramuth simply patted her on the shoulder, grabbed his cane, and strolled toward the bench. He was barely gone before his client turned and motioned to Leia and Han. As they huddled together, Leia thought the young woman looked confused and worried, and more frightened than anytime since the war against the Yuuzhan Vong.

"What do you think?" Tahiri whispered. "Is he too old to take this?"

"Hey, don't underestimate the *old guy,*" Han said. "We've got tricks you've never even heard about."

Tahiri gave him a disapproving scowl. "Do you *really* think this is a trick?"

Leia frowned, thinking, then finally shrugged. "I don't know," she said. "There were a lot of opportunities to discredit Pagorski's testimony—maybe even have it completely stricken—and Eramuth didn't take them."

"Yeah, but Dekkon's a smart guy," Han pointed out. "If Eramuth wants to trap him, it's got to look convincing."

"*Convincing,* not foolish," Tahiri said. "Unless his strategy is to make the jury feel sorry for me, I have *no* idea what he's doing."

"And you don't want to just trust him?" Han asked. It was an honest question, not an argument, and *that* suggested to Leia that even Han was having doubts. "You've been pretty happy with him until now."

Tahiri thought for a moment, then nodded. "I know," she said. "But this is my *life* . . . and Eramuth's, too, if the strain is more than he can handle."

Leia fell silent for a moment, trying to think but really just worrying . . . imagining how it would feel to lose this last link to her two sons, to the shining star that had been Anakin *and* to the all-destroying vortex that Jacen had become. Tahiri had loved her youngest son and gone to war with him, had watched him die and lent him her strength so that he would know he was not dying alone in a distant place. Then Jacen had taken that love and twisted it to serve his own dark needs, and somehow she had survived and returned to them again, not quite whole, yet stronger than ever and ready to answer for her misjudgment. If Leia lost her, she would be losing so much more than the woman who had been a close friend to *both* her sons in their last hours—she feared she would lose what remained of her sons themselves.

Still pretending to think, Leia took a couple of moments to compose herself, then turned to Han. "Eramuth *is* taking on a lot by himself," she said. "Dekkon has a whole team of assistants sitting at his table. It might not hurt to get Eramuth some help."

"Yeah." Han turned to Tahiri. "We could talk to Tendra Calrissian and see if she knows someone who can take that second chair—maybe the third and fourth ones, too."

Tahiri's gaze dropped. "Eramuth doesn't want anyone sitting at the table with us," she said. "He says it will make me look guilty."

"So who says they have to sit at the table?" Han replied. "It's *your* throat that killtab will be going down. The decision is yours."

"I know." Tahiri licked her lips, looking guilty and reluctant. Then Eramuth's gravelly voice barked something harsh at the judge, and she looked back toward the bench.

"Okay," Tahiri said, nodding. "Go ahead and ask. What can it hurt?"

"Nothing," Leia assured her. She watched Eramuth spin away from the judge's bench, his ears flattened and his fur bristling. "He might even appreciate the help."

"Yeah, stranger things have happened." Han winked at Tahiri, then added, "Don't worry, kid, he's Bothan. He'll do *whatever* it takes to win—even if it means taking help."

Tahiri's face brightened, but before she could reply, Eramuth slipped behind the defense table and dropped into his ancient wooden chair with a heavy thump. Tahiri mouthed a silent *Thanks* to the Solos, then leaned toward her attorney.

"What's wrong?" she asked.

"Judge Zudan has ordered me to get a medical evaluation, that's what!" Eramuth flashed his fangs toward the bench, then added, "She *claims* she wants to make sure I'm still competent!"

Chapter Eight

THE TRAIL WAS A HUMAN-SIZED TUNNEL THROUGH THE undergrowth, and it ended about a kilometer into the jungle, where a large bipedal lizard had fallen prey to the poisonous barbs of a drop-bramble. The reptile had a broad, flat back still green with chlorophyll and a thick tail that was still drumming the ground to warn its herd-mates away. It was watching Luke with a single blue eye that seemed more trusting than frightened, but it was already oozing yellow froth from both nostrils and suffering violent muscle spasms, and it was obvious that nothing could be done for the creature but help it to a peaceful end. He touched it in the Force, urging it to sleep, and once the nictitating membrane drew across the eye, he drew the blaster he had found it necessary to carry on this strange world and ended its misery.

The whine of the bolt had barely died away before Luke sensed his companions rushing up behind him, their alarm hot and electric in the Force. He turned to meet them, holstering his blaster and shaking his head.

"Sorry, it's not her." He pivoted aside, allowing Sarasu Taalon and Gavar Khai a clear view of the lizard lying dead at the end of the trail they had been following. Behind the two Sith came Ben and Vestara, their lightsabers drawn but not ignited. "Just an unlucky wyvarl who didn't watch where she was going."

Taalon tightened his lips and stepped to Luke's side,

then flicked a finger in the wyvarl's direction. The lizard rose into the air and floated toward them, dragging with it a tangled nest of poisonous drop-brambles. Once the reptile had drawn close enough, the High Lord drew his lightsaber, then ignited it and cleaved the wyvarl down the length of the body. He continued to levitate the two halves while he inspected the interior organs to be certain it really was a lizard, then sent them tumbling into the jungle with a wave of his hand.

"This isn't working," he said. "We're tracking nothing but wyvarls and drendeks."

"We could always split up," Luke suggested. "The more ground we cover, the better our chances of catching her before she recovers."

Taalon tipped his head forward, peering at Luke out the tops of his eyes. "Yes, I am sure you would like to be rid of us."

"Not really," Luke replied. Searching alone or in two small groups, they would *all* be more vulnerable to the planet's voracious plant life—and to the treachery of their supposed allies. But after two days of following false trails, it was beginning to look like they needed to take the risk. "We need to change tactics, though. We're not going to find Abeloth this way."

"No doubt because you have hidden her true body so well," Gavar Khai said, coming up behind Luke and Taalon. "You are fooling no one, Master Skywalker—only wasting our time."

Luke sighed. After discovering that the body they had been holding at the Font of Power did not belong to Abeloth, it had taken a three-hour standoff merely to convince the Sith that it would be a good idea to return to the *Jade Shadow* and check the identity of *whoever* it was that Ben and Vestara had been caring for in the medbay. Unfortunately, by the time they arrived, the patient had already fled, leaving the reluctant allies with nothing to show for their earlier battle against Abeloth except frustration, uncertainty, and mutual distrust.

When Khai was not contradicted by his superior, Luke turned to face the wide-shouldered Sith. "I wish I *were* wasting your time, Gavar. I truly do." He motioned back down the trail. "But since I'm not, let's go back to the ships and see if we can think of another way to approach this."

Khai remained in the middle of the trail, but he flicked his grim eyes past Luke's shoulder, seeking instructions from Taalon.

"Let's do as he suggests, Saber Khai," Taalon said. "It will be more . . . *comfortable* to discuss the matter back at the ships."

The hint of a smile tightened Khai's thin lips, suggesting that he understood Taalon's words to mean the same thing Luke did: there was going to be an argument, and if that argument erupted into violence, the Sith's superior numbers would be more advantageous on the open terrain of the river beach.

"As is your will, High Lord."

Khai inclined his head to Taalon and shot Luke one last glower, then turned and slipped past Ben and his daughter to the front of the line. Luke had already surrendered all hope of keeping his back clear of Sith, so he exhaled slowly and consciously, silently attuning himself to his danger sense, and started down the path after his son and Vestara.

After the Sith girl's duplicity during the fight against Abeloth, Ben seemed to be a lot more wary around her, and that was a big relief. But Luke would have been fooling himself to think the attraction had ended there. She was a smart, beautiful young woman with an engaging personality, and Ben was an adolescent male still coming to terms with his hormones. It was going to take more than a few lies and a deadly betrayal to dampen his feelings. That was plain to see in the glances he kept stealing at her, now that he was walking behind Vestara instead of ahead of her, and in the way he stumbled whenever the terrain grew uneven.

Luke extended an arm and held his hand behind Ben's ear. When Ben did not sense its presence even after half a dozen steps, Luke shook his head in exasperation and swatted his son above the ear.

"Hey!" Ben looked over his shoulder and frowned. "What was *that* for?"

"Pay attention," Luke ordered. He shifted his eyes toward his own shoulder, sliding them in Taalon's direction. "We're on a death planet here."

Ben's eyes lit with understanding, and his scowl grew guilty. "Yeah, okay," he said, looking forward again. "But you could have just said something."

"And you're sure I *didn't*?" Luke said.

He could tell by the way Vestara's head cocked that *she* was sure, but Ben merely dropped his gaze and began to watch his footing more carefully. Luke knew that he had embarrassed his son by pointing out that he was distracted, and that was fine with him. Embarrassed was better than dead, which was exactly what Ben would be if his mind was still on girls when the fighting started.

After a few minutes of walking, they reached the crimson river that ringed this side of Abeloth's volcano. On the opposite beach sat their three starships, the Skywalkers' *Shadow* and the Sith's *Emiax* flanking the veiny red sphere of the recently arrived Ship. With an outer hull pocked by scorch blossoms and blast craters, the ancient meditation sphere continued to show the aftereffects of tangling with an ace Jedi pilot in a StealthX. But the worst damage wasn't apparent from the exterior. Jaina had put a couple of cannon bolts up the exhaust nozzle, damaging the power plant so badly that Ship had taken days to limp back to the planet.

Khai led the group along the top of the riverbank until they were above their raft, then descended the sandy slope to prepare for the crossing. Vestara followed close behind her father, but Luke used a Force tug to keep Ben atop the bank with him. Taalon stopped two paces away, presenting his flank to Luke so that he would be able to defend himself if the need arose suddenly.

"Is there a *reason* you wish to retain the high ground, Master Skywalker?" Taalon rested his hand on his lightsaber. "Or do you think the time has come to part ways?"

"Before we know what's become of Abeloth?" Luke shook his head. "I'd rather take my chances with Sith—but that *doesn't* mean I'm going to be careless."

"A clever answer," Taalon replied. "It suggests much and promises nothing."

"You already have my promise, and it hasn't been broken." As Luke spoke, he continued to look across the river toward the starships. "Didn't Vestara report that Ship was under Abeloth's control?"

"*Was* being the crucial point," Taalon replied. "The Sith control it now."

Luke turned to face the Keshiri. "How sure are you of that?"

"Very sure." Taalon narrowed his eyes. "If you're planning to use Ship as an excuse—"

"Not an excuse," Luke said. "But has Ship explained why it returned here after the fight? It must have seen the rest of your fleet leaving the Maw."

"Yeah," Ben said. "It was kind of surprised to find out *I* was still here—and I got the impression Vestara felt the same way."

"You believe Abeloth summoned Ship?" Taalon asked. "To help her escape?"

Luke nodded. "I believe that's one possibility—especially if that was Abeloth instead of Dyon that Ben and Vestara were looking after in the medbay."

Taalon considered this, then looked down the bank to where Vestara and her father were preparing to launch the raft. Khai was using the Force to levitate the raft back toward the river's edge, while his daughter was holding the line that would keep it from floating away.

"Vestara, you have been listening?" Taalon asked.

Vestara turned and nodded. "Of course, High Lord."

"Is young Skywalker right?" he demanded. "Did Ship seem surprised to find you here?"

Vestara did not even need to think before nodding. "Ben is half right." She glanced toward Ben and flashed him a quick smile. "Ship was already on his way when I felt him coming. I didn't need to call him."

"That is no proof that Skywalker is telling the truth, Lord Taalon," Khai said. He lowered the raft to the sand. "If Ship came for Abeloth, why is it still *here*?"

"Probably because Ship is so damaged," Ben replied. He turned his gaze back to Vestara. "How long did it take Ship to arrive after we felt it coming? Three hours?"

"Easily," Vestara confirmed. "We crossed the ridge to the fountain ruins, realized that we had the wrong body, then crossed the ridge again and found an empty medbay in the *Shadow.* That was at *least* three hours, and Ship didn't arrive until later, after we had already started to search for Abeloth."

"Right," Ben said. "So if Abeloth was counting on Ship to rescue her, she was disappointed. In its condition right now, the *Shadow* or *Emiax* would have caught up in about two heartbeats and blown them *both* back to atoms."

"Which begs the question of why Abeloth would call Ship in the first place," Taalon pointed out. "If she couldn't use it to escape, what good is it to her?"

"Would she have *known* Ship was damaged?" Luke asked. "When *I* reach for someone in the Force, I don't have a feel for their condition until *after* I make contact."

Taalon's expression turned thoughtful. "Perhaps."

"And perhaps *not,* High Lord," Khai said. "A plausible story is not always a true one. By all accounts, Abeloth has lived on this planet for dozens of millennia. Why would she pick *now* to leave?"

"First, because she's wounded and being hunted," Ben said. "Second, because she *can.*"

All three Sith frowned, and Ben glanced over at Luke, clearly wondering how much he should reveal about what they had surmised about Abeloth's past. Deciding that the more they revealed right now, the more likely the Sith were to believe, Luke nodded.

"Go ahead," he said. "Maybe it will convince them of the truth."

"We will not be *convinced* until we have Abeloth's body in our hands again," Taalon said, turning to Ben. "But go ahead. I'm sure it will make an interesting story."

Ben's eyes flashed, but he nodded. "You know what happened at Sinkhole Station, right?"

"You mean the explosion that destroyed my frigate?" Taalon demanded.

"Yeah, *that,*" Ben replied, completely unintimidated by Taalon's sour tone. "Well, we think that Sinkhole Station may have been built to keep this planet locked inside a shell of black holes."

"To what end?" Khai demanded. "Are you saying this planet was Abeloth's *prison*?"

"We're saying it might have been," Luke clarified. "There's a lot we don't know, but our trouble didn't start until after, well, a *crack* developed in the shell."

"A crack?" Taalon asked. "What kind of crack?"

"The kind that we all came through," Luke replied. "When Ben and I discovered Sinkhole Station, it was already malfunctioning, and a gap had opened in the shell. We don't understand the technology any better than you do, but it was clear enough that something was going wrong."

"And given that it was floating around in a million pieces the last time we passed by, it sounds like maybe Abeloth has been trying to shake her way free," Ben said. He waved his arm around at the planet in general. "So we're thinking this place was probably a prison, *not* a fortress."

Taalon considered this for a moment, then said, "A very plausible story."

"It's more than a story," Luke said, growing frustrated. "It's a theory that fits the facts—which is about all we have to go on right now."

"Not entirely." Taalon's voice grew cold. "Because we Sith also have a theory to fit the facts—which is that you are hiding Abeloth's body from us because you wish to keep to yourselves all knowledge of her nature."

Luke rolled his eyes in exasperation. The trouble with Taalon's theory was that it was *half* accurate. He had no more intention of sharing with the Sith any true knowledge about Abeloth's nature than *they* did of allowing him and Ben to leave the planet alive. But first things first—they had to find their quarry and finish the job.

"Look, we've been over this. Abeloth *is* alive, and I have no idea where she's hiding." Luke started down the bank toward the raft. If Abeloth remained alive, then Callista—or whatever Callista had *become*—probably remained with her. Given a chance to concentrate in peace, he might be able to focus on her Force presence and locate their quarry that way. "Unless you have a better idea, I'm going back to the *Shadow* to meditate on it."

"To *meditate*?" Taalon said, remaining on the bank behind Luke. "I have a better idea than that, I think."

Luke half expected his spine to start bristling with danger sense. Instead he saw Ship wobble aloft and wheel around toward them. He glanced back and saw Taalon looking in the vessel's direction, his eyes half closed in concentration.

"You think *Ship* is going to help us?" Luke asked.

"You're the one who noted that it had been under Abeloth's control," Khai reminded him. "Perhaps the High Lord can learn something useful from it."

"I wouldn't hold my breath," Ben grumbled. "Ship has probably been spying for her since it got back."

Taalon shot Ben a smirk. "I can handle Ship, young Skywalker. You're talking to a Sith High Lord now, not an adolescent apprentice girl."

Angry disbelief flared in Vestara's eyes, suggesting that she believed the same thing Luke did—that Taalon was badly overestimating his control of the vessel. Ship passed overhead and dropped onto its struts atop the bank, its eye-like viewport facing the High Lord. From Luke's position a little behind and below the vessel, it was possible to see that the long, triangular hull breach caused by the power-plant explosion was already half mended, with edges that were now smooth and puckered inward instead of jagged and flared outward. Even the craters left by Jaina's cannon hits were starting to close, and the scorch blossoms had faded from a deep, sooty black to more of a charcoal gray. How Ship was repairing itself, Luke had no idea—but the way it had been sitting quiet and shut down, trusting the Sith to keep watch over it, reminded him a lot of a healing trance.

Taalon turned to Ship. "Is Abeloth still alive?" he asked. "Share your answer with the others, so the Jedi will know I am being honest."

Luke's spine bristled with the chill of a dark side touch, and then Ship spoke.

The dead do not move themselves. Its voice was wispy and low, audible only within the mind. *If the Skywalkers did not hide her, then she must be alive.*

Taalon frowned. "That's no answer."

It is the only answer I have, Ship responded. *She re-*

leased me when I was wounded. What became of her later, you know better than I.

Luke stepped to Taalon's side. "Let's assume that she *is* still alive."

"Yes, let's," Taalon agreed. He kept his gaze focused on Ship. "Where would we look for her?"

A glimmer appeared in the viewport—not inside Ship, but in the viewport material itself—and Luke had the feeling that Ship's attention had shifted to him.

You know where to find the answer.

Luke felt a dark tentacle of longing taking form inside him, slithering higher and starting to grow, and he *knew* that Ben had been right. Abeloth had survived—and Ship remained under her sway.

You have been there before.

Unsure whether Ship was speaking to him alone, or to Taalon and everyone else, Luke did not reply. Instead he pointed his son around behind Ship. Khai motioned Vestara up the bank to join him, then came to stand next to Luke, leaving him flanked on both sides by Sith.

After a moment's silence, Taalon finally looked over at Luke. "What did it say?"

Knowing Taalon would sense a lie, Luke merely shrugged and shook his head. "Nothing we can trust," he said. "Ben's right. Ship is spying for Abeloth."

Jedi liar! The gleam faded from Ship's viewport as it shifted its attention away from Luke. *He is only trying to hide it from you.*

Taalon shot Luke a sidelong glance, then asked, "Hide *what*?"

Luke sighed and, knowing that Ship would say the name if he did not, answered, "The Pool of Knowledge."

The planet's greatest treasure. A slit opened in Ship's flank, and it extruded a long boarding ramp. *Come aboard, all of you. I'll take you there.*

Chapter Nine

TOO LARGE TO DESCEND INTO THE JUNGLE GORGE, SHIP was hovering just above the narrow cleft, the far end of its boarding ramp resting on a patch of rocky rim. Beyond this outcropping, a vine-tangled slope climbed steeply to the right, ascending through several kilometers of tree ferns and club mosses to the fume-belching crater atop the volcano's summit. To the left, the slope fell away just as sharply, descending a thousand meters to the base of the mountain, where a vast swamp lay quivering with the volcano's pent fury.

In the bottom of the gorge lay the only hint of the pool they had come to find, a tiny yellow-brown rivulet so filled with mud and sulfur that Ben could not imagine it coming from anything called the Pool of Knowledge.

Vestara stepped into the hatchway next to Ben. "So where's this Pool of Knowledge?" she asked. "Where are *we*?"

"I don't know about the pool, but we're on the same side of the ridge as the fountain ruins." Ben stepped out onto the ramp and pointed toward the jagged summit. "The notches in the crater look like they're in pretty much the same place." He turned and waved a hand toward the swamp at the foot of the mountain. "And the only swamp I've seen is near the fountain, too."

Vestara followed him onto the ramp and examined

the terrain, then glanced over with a half smile. "Show-off."

"It would be more impressive if young Skywalker could tell us where to find this Pool of Knowledge," Taalon said. He stepped into the hatchway behind them and peered in both directions. "I'm beginning to fear the Jedi are right about Ship being a spy. This is terrain for waterfalls, not pools."

The pool is here, Ship insisted. *The elder Skywalker has seen it.*

Taalon's suspicion filled the Force, and he turned to look back into Ship's interior. "You have been here before?"

"I've been to the *pool,*" Luke corrected. "But that was while I was Mind Walking. It doesn't mean I can find it in the physical world."

Taalon's Force aura grew acrid. "If you hope to take me Mind Walking again—"

Skywalker can find it here, Ship insisted. *He knows what to look for.*

Taalon narrowed his eyes, then cocked a lavender brow in the direction of Luke's voice. "Is that so?"

Luke did not answer quickly, and Ben knew his father was weighing options. Ryontarr, the Jedi deserter who had served as Luke's Mind Walking guide during the visit to Sinkhole Station, had claimed that anyone bathing in the Pool of Knowledge would see *all that has passed and all that will come.* And that kind of knowledge was simply not something that Taalon—or any Sith—could be allowed to acquire.

After a moment, Taalon let his hand to drop toward his lightsaber. "*Well?*"

Luke sighed, then stepped into the light just inside the hatchway. "Look for a grotto," he said, peering down into the chasm. The crowns of the tree ferns lay thirty meters below, and the ground was probably another twenty meters beneath that. "Somewhere in the bottom of the gorge. That's all I can tell you."

Taalon smirked. "Are you *sure*?"

"Well, I could warn you not to go inside alone, but I doubt you'd trust me on that."

"What makes you think you won't be along to join us?" This from Khai, who was standing on the ramp between Ben and his father. "No one here is foolish enough to trust a Jedi he cannot see."

"We need to split up," Luke said. "It's a long gorge, filled with jungle so dense we'll have to cut it away just to see the canyon walls. Every day we spend doing *that* is another day Abeloth spends recovering."

"Which is probably why she had Ship bring us on this galoomp chase in the first place," Ben added.

"*Assuming* she's still alive," Taalon said.

"You don't believe she's dead any more than I do," Luke replied. "If you did, you wouldn't be here looking for a way to find her."

"Perhaps I enjoy your company, Master Skywalker," Taalon retorted. "The opportunity to learn so much about your Order is not likely to come my way again soon."

"On that much, I think we agree." Luke pointed up the gorge. "How about if Ben and Vestara head upstream, while the rest of us go downstream?"

Taalon's gaze shifted toward the ramp. He studied Vestara for a few moments, no doubt using the Force to impress on her the importance of not letting Ben out of her sight, then turned back to Luke.

"Very well, two groups." Taalon nodded to Vestara. "You have your orders."

"And be wary of ambushes," Khai added. "Master Skywalker may be right about Ship's loyalties."

Vestara inclined her head, acknowledging her father's concern, then glanced over at Ben. "Ready?"

Ben felt an affirming Force nudge from his own father. "Sure." He started down the ramp toward the gorge rim. "Don't wait on me."

"I'm going to *have* to," Vestara said from behind, "if you insist on taking the long way around."

As she spoke the last few words, her voice seemed to be growing more distant and to be coming from beneath Ship. Ben turned to see her already several meters below the ramp and floating down into the gorge under clear control. He glanced toward her father and found Khai gesturing in her direction, obviously using the Force to lower her. Ben was more surprised than he should have been; he had been around these Sith long enough to know they employed the Force as casually as most beings used comlinks or holoprojectors.

Ben glanced over at his own father and cocked a brow. Luke rolled his eyes at such casual overuse of the Force, but nodded and tipped his head toward the gorge. Vestara was as much a Sith as her father and Taalon, and it wouldn't do to have her down there searching for the Pool of Knowledge alone—not even for a few moments. Ben took two quick steps toward Ship, then jumped off the ramp and felt his stomach rise as he plummeted into the chasm.

Vestara had already disappeared into the jungle below, and Ben dropped so fast and so long he began to worry he would crash down on top of her. Then his stomach sank with sudden deceleration as his father's Force grasp tightened, and he saw a nest of cobervine coming up below him. He snatched his lightsaber off his belt and used the Force to push himself in the opposite direction. Several of the vines struck at him anyway, but it was a simple matter to render the plants harmless by slicing the fangpods away before they reached him.

Once Ben had passed beneath the jungle canopy, he felt a warning prickle from his father and responded by flooding his aura with confidence and reassurance. An instant later he slipped free and dropped the last twenty meters to the ground, using the Force to break his fall.

He landed in a tangle of shoulder-high ferns whose barbed fronds were coated with a sticky digestive acid. He quickly used telekinesis to push them aside, then joined Vestara over on the bank of the stream.

It was larger than it had looked from above, easily four meters across and close to half that in depth. The water was more amber than brown, and clearer than Ben had thought, allowing him to see a meter or so below the surface. Vestara was staring into the stream, her light-saber in hand and her knees ready to spring. But he could tell by her tense shoulders that she hated being in this place as much as he did, that her memories of Abeloth frightened her even more than the half-recalled terrors he had felt during his time at Shelter.

Ben stopped beside her and peered down into the water. He could see a handful of ribbon-like weeds bending against the current, stretching in their direction.

"I really hate this planet," he said. "How you survived all those weeks marooned here, I can't imagine."

"It wasn't all that difficult, as long as you were with Abeloth." Vestara did not remove her eyes from the water while she spoke. "The hard part was knowing what she was—as much as that's possible—and convincing yourself to stay close to her anyway."

Ben thought back to his own early brushes with Abeloth and shuddered. It had always been her *need* that had frightened him before, the impulse to draw other beings closer and smother them in the all-consuming furnace of her own dark energy. But now that she had been killed—or wounded, or driven back into her true form of existence, or whatever had happened to her—he had a bad feeling she just wanted them dead.

A deep rumble sounded someplace far back inside the mountain, then Ben saw a ripple running upstream and felt the soft jungle soil beginning to settle beneath his feet.

"Yeah, well, I don't think Abeloth is going to give us much choice in the matter this time," Ben said. He jerked a thumb over his shoulder, toward a gorge wall hidden somewhere in the jungle behind him. "What do you say we start looking over back there?"

Vestara shook her head, then finally lifted her chin and peered across the stream. "We'll have better luck over there." She pointed to the other side. "Can't you smell it?"

Ben took a deep whiff of jungle air and smelled nothing but decaying vegetation. "Smell *what*?"

"The breeze." Vestara Force-jumped across the stream and began to sniff. "It's cool, and it smells like a cave."

"It can't be that easy."

Vestara glanced over her shoulder. "That mean you aren't coming, Jedi?"

Ben flushed. "I'm coming." He gathered the Force and sprang across the stream, alighting on the bank next to her. "Someone needs to keep you out of trouble."

Instead of making a comeback, Vestara surprised Ben by turning to contemplate him. She lowered her brow and gazed into his eyes for a moment, almost challenging him to challenge *her,* then finally shrugged and shook her head in disappointment.

"That's why you Jedi are going to lose this galaxy to us," she informed him. "You're *afraid* of trouble."

With that, she spun away and began to march through the jungle, using the Force and her lightsaber to clear a path. Ben fell in behind her—though not *too* close behind her, lest she not be paying attention on a backswing. He wanted to make some retort, of course, but he understood the ways of the Sith too well to fall into that trap. Emotions were dangerous, unpredictable things, and Vestara probably believed that if she could goad him into losing control, she just might have a chance of pulling him over to the dark side. And Ben knew that if she failed, that if he could show her how strong *his* side of the Force truly was, that someday she would step into the light beside him.

All he had to do was be patient.

As they drew nearer to the gorge wall, Ben began to feel the breeze Vestara had mentioned. The air was damp and cool, and she was right. He could smell a definite hint of rock and mildew, and something more caustic, too—perhaps sulfur. Within a few steps, the ground started to rise sharply, and they began to catch glimpses of a tangled curtain of moss fluttering in the jungle ahead.

Ben risked moving close enough to grab Vestara's shoulder. "Okay, so it *was* that easy. But hold up here for a second."

"What for?" Vestara continued to clear vegetation, increasing her pace and drawing half a dozen steps closer to the mossy curtain. "Come on, Jedi. Show some initiative."

"It's called the *Pool of Knowledge,* Vestara." Whatever happened, Ben knew that he could not allow her to enter the pool before his father arrived—that even if she survived, the experience would change her into something he had no chance of pulling back into the light. "Does that really sound like something we should mess with?"

"Sure."

Vestara used the Force to hurl the last meter of vegetation aside, then drew up short. The grotto could be seen less than two paces ahead, a fluttering rectangle of shadow only half visible through the yellow moss hanging down the gorge wall. About the height of a Wookiee and wide enough to admit a speeder, the portal looked more like an underground hangar entrance than a cave—especially when Vestara slashed the moss curtain away, revealing a lintel and support columns carved with the same ophidian grotesques they had found at the Font of Power.

Vestara smiled. "Knowledge is good for you, right?"

"Not *always*." Still holding his own lightsaber, Ben stepped toward her—and the grotto entrance. "Some knowledge destroys."

"Don't be silly. Knowledge is just . . . memory and thought." Despite Vestara's bravado, she paused at the entrance to glance back at Ben—and at the unlit lightsaber in his hand. "How can it destroy *anything*?"

Ben remained where he was. "Has your mother always been faithful to your father?"

Vestara scowled at him. "What business is that of yours?"

"It isn't," Ben admitted. "But what if you knew she hadn't been? Would you be obligated to tell your father?"

"Of course," she said. "He's a Sith Saber, and she is . . . well, she *isn't*."

"And what would happen then?"

Vestara's eyes went hard, revealing more about Keshiri society than she probably realized. "I see no point to your questions," she said. "My mother would never be unfaithful to my father."

"Of course not. But if you knew that she *had* been, you'd be obligated to tell your father." Ben paused, then added, "And *that* is knowledge that destroys. Just one example. Are you sure you want more? Are you sure you're *ready*?"

Vestara glanced toward the grotto entrance, and her expression turned more thoughtful than troubled. "The Pool of Knowledge can do that? How?"

Ben saw his mistake at once, of course. To the Sith, no

knowledge was forbidden, no mystery better left unsolved. To them, it was all just information, to be gathered and utilized in their pursuit of galactic domination—which meant they could never be permitted to enter the Pool of Knowledge. Ben and Luke would *have* to stop them.

And Ship had known that when it brought the Skywalkers and the Sith here together. Ship *wanted* them to fight.

"Vestara," Ben said, "you're going to have to trust me on this, but we need to back out of here and think about what we're doing."

Vestara barely glanced back. "Nice try, but the only place I'm going is in there." She swung her lightsaber toward the grotto entrance. "With you or without you."

"Hold on." Ben extended a hand. "*Think.* Why did Ship bring my father and me along?"

"To help us find the Pool of Knowledge, of course."

Ben waved at the cave entrance. "Does it *look* like you needed our help?"

"So I got lucky," Vestara said. "It happens."

Ben shook his head. "You know better than that. Ship put us down right on *top* of the Pool of Knowledge. It wanted to make sure we found the grotto quickly, so we'd all still be relatively close together."

A light came to Vestara's eyes. "The ambush my father warned against?"

"In a way," Ben said. "Ship is trying to start a fight between us again—between your side and ours, I mean."

When Ben said no more, Vestara cocked her head slightly and demanded, "What are you keeping from us, Ben?"

"Plenty," Ben replied. "And that's not going to change. But trust me, it would be better for everyone if you just forgot we ever found this place."

The reply came from behind Ben, halfway back to the

stream and in a deep, silky voice that was chilling in its calm menace. "It's too late for that, Ben."

Ben's heart jumped for his throat. His thumb dropped toward his lightsaber's activation switch, and he pivoted sideways, so he could see the stream *and* the grotto. Taalon was leading Luke and Khai up the path toward them, his lavender eyes fixed not on Ben but on the dark portal that Vestara had cleared just a couple of minutes earlier. The crooked ribbons of pollen and spores that streaked the robes of all three men suggested they had come in a hurry—as did the beads of perspiration clinging to their brows in the humid jungle air.

Ben glanced back toward Vestara. "You summoned them?"

Vestara shrugged. "As soon as I realized we had found it," she confirmed. "That's the difference between young Sith and young Jedi, Ben. We are taught to follow orders."

Ben nodded. "Yeah, I see that." He stood aside and let Taalon pass. "But when are you taught to *think*?"

Taalon answered for her. "After we teach them to *obey,* young Skywalker. A sharp arrow is worthless if it doesn't fly true." He stepped to the grotto mouth and peered inside. "Let's go inside and see what you hoped to hide."

"You go ahead," Ben said. "I've got a problem with dark side nexuses."

Taalon turned back to Ben. "Was there something in what I said that made you think I was *asking*?"

"It's okay, Ben," Luke said. He caught Ben's eye, then slid his gaze toward the grotto and gave a little nod. "I think we'll *all* want to see what the pool reveals."

Ben paused a moment for show, trying to uphold the impression he had been cultivating among the Sith of being an unruly teenager. Clearly, his father had a plan, and it involved being outnumbered in a tight, dark space.

Hoping it didn't involve a thermal detonator as well, he sighed loudly and stepped up behind the others.

"Oh, no—after you." Taalon pivoted aside and waved Ben toward the grotto entrance. "I insist."

Ben scowled and, receiving a nod of permission from his father, said, "Thanks for nothing. If I sense any traps, I'll be sure to leave them for you."

"That will be fine, young Skywalker," Taalon replied. "It's the traps you can't sense that I wish to avoid."

The admission sent a shiver down Ben's back, but he stepped into the grotto entrance and felt no danger in the damp gloom. From ahead came the sound of dripping water, a single *blep* every two seconds or so. There did not seem to be any living presences within the chamber, only a miasma of sulfurous fumes so thick and rank that even a whiff made Ben feel physically ill.

After a moment, Luke said, "Go ahead, son. The only traps in there will be of our own making."

"Which are always the worst kind," said Taalon. "Is that not true, Master Skywalker?"

"Certainly for the weak," Luke said. "But Ben will be safe enough."

Recognizing a cue when he heard one, Ben stepped forward and discovered that the grotto was not as dark as it had appeared from outside. A cold, diaphanous light rose from a small pool in the center, filling the chamber with a silvery glow and revealing that the cavern walls were covered in a meshwork of tiny crevices. Seeping from most of those crevices were tiny wisps of yellow, acrid fume—the source of the sulfur smell that Ben had noticed earlier.

He stepped to the edge of the pool and saw that it lay not in a shallow natural bowl as he had expected, but in an artificial basin with deep, sheer sides. The edges had been decorated with the same grotesque patterns that had been carved into the pillars and lintel at the grotto's entrance.

Reflected on the surface of the pool was someone that he barely recognized, a man who had Ben's own strong chin and wavy reddish-brown hair. But he looked twenty years older, with wise blue eyes and a smiling face deeply etched by laugh lines. The figure was dressed in a brown homespun Jedi robe over dark combat armor, and he was holding a lightsaber with a hilt somewhat longer and thinner than normal, similar to those the Sith carried.

Guessing that he was looking at an image of himself in a couple of decades, Ben gasped and started to back away—then sensed Vestara coming to stand beside him.

"It seems you'll age well."

As she spoke, Vestara's image appeared in the pool, not next to Ben where she was actually standing, but facing him from a short distance away. Like Ben, she appeared to be older and more attractive, with high cheeks and oval eyes that seemed even larger than they did now. But there was also a loneliness in her expression that made her appear more hardened and sad, especially when she smiled and extended a hand in his direction.

Vestara stepped closer, pressing her shoulder to Ben's, then continued, "And it seems we won't be strangers to each other." She turned to face him directly. "I wonder how we find out whether that's going to be a good thing . . . or a bad thing?"

"You *don't,*" Luke said, stepping into the grotto behind them. "We're here to find out where Abeloth went. Nothing else."

Taalon entered on Luke's heels and said something about utilizing every resource to its fullest, but Ben did not catch the exact words. His attention was locked on the pool, where Vestara's reflection was changing before his eyes, twisting into something grotesque and alien—something that was vaguely human and just barely female, with a long cascade of yellow hair that reached nearly to her feet. Her eyes were sunken and dark, like a pair of deep wells, and she had a broad, full-lipped mouth so wide that it reached from ear to ear. She seemed be running—or, rather, *rippling*—along a sandy beach somewhere adjacent to a crimson river—

"Our *ships*!" Ben whirled toward the grotto exit and found himself facing a wall of robed chests. "*That's* why Ship brought us here—so she would have time to steal one of our craft and escape!"

Ben started to step around the others, but Gavar Khai quickly moved to block his path. "Explain yourself."

"Abeloth!" Ben said, thrusting an arm back toward the pool. "I saw her. She was on the beach where we left the *Shadow* and the *Emiax*—and she was running."

"Toward the vessels?" Taalon demanded. "You saw that?"

Ben nodded. "Not the ships, but it was the same beach." He started toward the exit again. "It's going to take half a day to get back. We've got to hurry."

"Not until we are sure." Khai used the Force to push Ben back toward the pool, then looked to his daughter. "Vestara?"

"I wasn't, uh, *looking* at the time." The pitch of her voice suggested surprise. "But I think he's right. We should go back *now*."

Puzzled by the urgency in her tone, Ben spun around and found her whirling away from the pool. Her eyes met his and flashed in alarm, then quickly slid away. Reflected on the water behind her was a walled city filled with lacy glass spires and living trees twisted into sculptures of remarkable complexity. Surrounding the city on three sides were high, steep mountains blanketed in a jade-green forest. On the fourth side, a plain of verdant farmland swept down to a turquoise sea, where the sands of a lavender beach lay shuddering beneath an unending assault of whitecaps.

Kesh.

Even had Ben not guessed by Vestara's reaction what the pool was showing him, he would have known by the angry outburst that erupted from her father that he was looking at the mysterious homeworld of the Sith.

"Jedi treachery!" Khai extended a hand and used a blast of Force energy to splash the image away, then turned to glare at Ben. "I should have killed you days aaah—"

Khai's threat came to a startled end as he went sailing across the Pool. He slammed into the far wall of the grotto and remained there, pinned in place by the invisible hand of the Force.

"*Days* ago, Gavar, you might have had a chance to succeed," Luke said, stepping to the pool. "Now that the odds are more even, you'd do well to avoid threatening my son." He glanced over at Ben and flashed a quick smile, then added, "The next time, he just might take you seriously."

Wondering if this was his father's way of starting the fight that *had* to be coming, Ben pivoted around to guard their flank. But the other two Sith appeared less concerned with the developing situation than with the undulating surface of the pool. Taalon was kneeling at the edge of the water, scowling down at the broken reflection of what might have been a large white throne. Vestara was standing at the High Lord's shoulder, apparently unaware of—or unconcerned by—her father's predicament.

Taalon waved a hand over the pool, using the Force to still the shimmering waters, and Ben's heart climbed into his throat. Sitting on the throne, wearing a simple aurodium crown, was a slender red-headed woman. She looked a lot like Tenel Ka, except that she had two arms and a small, button-ended nose that clearly came from the Solo line. Hanging from the belt of her gown was a long, curved lightsaber with a rancor claw in the hilt, and standing guard around her, with their weapons drawn and ignited, were a dozen Jedi Knights representing a dozen different species. One of those Jedi, the human, had the same square chin and wavy red hair that Ben had seen in his own reflection just a few minutes earlier.

Taalon turned to glare at Ben. "Who is she?"

Ben shrugged, trying to calm himself and still his Force aura before he answered. A dark fury came instantly to Taalon's eyes, and Ben realized that the High Lord already knew that he intended to lie.

"Uh, Dad?"

A lightsaber snapped to life behind him, and Ben realized no further explanation was required. Knowing he would have only one chance to stop Taalon before Taalon stopped *him,* he jerked his own weapon off his belt. He stepped forward, rolling the hilt around for an overhand strike and angling left to force Vestara to pivot out of his attack path.

But Vestara did not react as expected to the sound of the igniting lightsaber. Her mouth simply gaped open, and her green eyes locked on the sizzling blade in disbelief and confusion. Ben brought his free hand around to trap her weapon arm against her flank and push her aside when she tried to counterattack.

No counterattack came. Vestara's expression merely melted into disappointment, and her gaze slid away, filled with sorrow and surrender. A cold, sick weight filled Ben inside as he realized what she was thinking, that their flirtations had meant nothing to him and he had planned to kill her all along. Ben drew up short and, unable to reach past her to strike at Taalon, whirled around behind her.

A loud splash echoed through the cavern, and Ben knew he was too late. He came around with his lightsaber in both hands, at middle guard between him and Vestara. She had finally taken her own weapon in hand and stood prepared to defend herself, but she still appeared more puzzled than ready. A couple of meters to their side, Ben was vaguely aware of his own father diving toward the far side of the cavern, and the delicate *clinkle* of Gavar Khai's shikkar shattering on the stone floor behind him.

Vestara tensed to spring, confused no longer. Ben sprang forward, swinging his lightsaber at her forward knee. She ignited her own blade and flipped it down to block; then a hardness came to her eyes and her parang began to rise from its sheath.

Ben was already snapping his hips around, launching a vicious roundhouse kick at her sore shoulder. "Out of my way!"

The blow caught her high on the arm, driving her injured shoulder up toward her head. There was a loud *pop,* and Vestara staggered away, one arm hanging limp. Ben stepped to the edge of the pool and, below its surface, saw Taalon's dark-robed figure swimming underwater toward the far end. Ben stepped after him, gathering himself to dive.

"Ben, no!" His father Force-shoved him back. "Take—"

The order vanished beneath a deafening crackle, and suddenly the blinding blue flicker of Force lightning filled the grotto. Ben pulled his blaster with his free hand and traced the dancing forks to their source on the far side of the pool, where Gavar Khai crouched on the stone floor spraying bolts at Luke.

Ben squeezed his blaster trigger half a dozen times and saw Khai slam into the cavern wall with smoke rising from his robes and armor. He sensed danger, turned to his side and saw Vestara flying at him, her blade weaving baskets of crimson light as she whirled it through an attack pattern.

Ben turned the blaster on her, then had to ignite his own blade to deflect the bolts she sent flying back toward his head. They met half a heartbeat later, the power of Vestara's attack driving his guard down despite her injury and smaller size.

He dropped flat on his back, then aimed his blaster up behind her guard and squeezed off three quick bolts. She threw her chin back, and that was all the opening Ben needed to spring up and land a Force-enhanced elbow strike to her solar plexus.

Vestara went flying back . . . and slammed Taalon in the flank as he came leaping out of the water. The pair cartwheeled sideways, the High Lord filling the air with curses until they slammed into a wall. Taalon rose to his knees, then Ben saw a fist rise and fall, and Vestara groaned in pain.

Luke was on the pair instantly, his lightsaber droning and sparking as he pounded at Taalon's defenses. Determined to finish the High Lord while they had the advantage, Ben rushed to join his father.

On the other side of the pool, Gavar Khai's dark figure struggled up and limped toward the fight. For an instant, Ben wondered whether he had seen Taalon strike Vestara—and whether a father's anger might be enough to turn a Sith against his Lord.

Then Khai's parang floated from its sheath and came spinning across the pool toward Ben. He brought his lightsaber around to block . . . and only managed to slice the glass weapon in two. The hilt went tumbling away and shattered against a wall. But Khai still held the blade in his Force control, and it came swinging back toward Ben. He tried to twist away and felt the broken shard push between his ribs. His flank erupted in fiery pain, and his breath left him in an anguished gasp.

Knowing what was coming next, Ben whirled to face Khai—and found his lightsaber slicing through empty air as Khai leapt toward his father and Taalon. Ben dropped his blaster and extended his hand, intending to Force-slam Khai into the grotto wall. The Sith countered with a Force shove of his own, hurling Ben back toward the grotto entrance.

"*Dad!*" Ben's voice was a raspy croak. "Behind . . . you!"

He should have known better than to worry. As Khai ignited his lightsaber, Luke was already ducking and reaching up to grab a passing ankle. With a quick, circular jerk, he brought Khai smashing down on Taalon and Vestara. Then he rolled his blade around, brought it down, and sent a Sith forearm sliding across the grotto floor. Whom it had belonged to, Ben could not tell.

In the next instant his father was riding a bolt of Force lightning into the grotto wall beside him. Ben ignited his lightsaber and shoved the blade into the crackling energy, disrupting the current and freeing his father.

"Dad, arrraagh—" The question came to an anguished end as the glass lodged in Ben's side grated against his ribs. Being careful to grab it by the dull side, he reached over and jerked out the shard. "Dad, are you—"

"Go." Ben felt his father's hand on his shoulder, shoving him toward the exit. "*Fast.*"

Ben obeyed instantly, his chest filling with fire as he dashed for the exit. His father was only two steps behind him, but once they had cleared the mouth of the grotto, Luke stopped and reignited his lightsaber. Thinking the Sith were in hot pursuit, Ben turned to fight—and found his father hacking at one of the pillars beneath the entrance's massive lintel.

"Dad, wait—"

"Go!" Luke hacked another chunk from the column. "Hurry."

Ben made no move to obey. "But . . . Vestara's in there." The act of speaking filled his chest with fire, and he couldn't get air, but he forced himself to continue. "Taalon was beating—"

"She'll survive." The column snapped with a bang like a sonic boom, and one end of the lintel dropped, filling the entrance with rubble and dust. Luke whirled, cleaving through the opposite column with a single stroke, then continued around and started toward Ben. "*You,* I'm not so sure about."

Chapter Ten

JAINA WOULD HAVE LIKED TO THINK THE BRITTLE CALM of the Council Chamber had come in anticipation of the briefing she and Lando were about to give, but everything she saw told her otherwise. Eight of the ten current members were there in person, all watching the entrance so they would not be forced to look at one another. Kenth Hamner's face was stony and indifferent, Kyle's inscrutable, Kyp's openly resentful. Corran Horn avoided a clenched jaw only through an obvious act of will, and Saba's cheek scales were bristling. Cilghal's eye pods were bulging, Barratk'l's nostrils were flaring, and Octa Ramis's hands had turned white from clutching her chair arms. Even the Solusars, participating via hologram from the Jedi academy on Ossus, looked ready to rap a few knuckles.

Clearly, Jaina's TOP URGENT request to brief the Council had interrupted a heated exchange, and she had no doubt her report was only going to aggravate the Masters' mood. On the bright side, it would at least remind them that there were dangers in the galaxy greater than Natasi Daala—dangers that the Jedi could meet only with a bold and united leadership. Once she and Lando finished their presentation, even Kenth Hamner would recognize that.

With Lando at her side, Jaina entered the Council circle and bowed. "Thank you for seeing us so quickly."

"Given the rumors of where you've been, I saw no reason to doubt the urgency of your request." Hamner's eyes and voice grew icy. "We'll discuss your unauthorized actions after your briefing—*immediately* after."

The lump that formed in Jaina's throat was born of anger more than fear, but she swallowed her ire and inclined her head in what she hoped was a look of contrition. The important thing here was to get the Masters moving in the same direction, and she would not do that by antagonizing the temporary Grand Master of the Jedi Order.

That could come later.

"I look forward to the discussion, Grand Master," Jaina said. "Regarding the briefing, however—before we start, it would be helpful to know what you've heard about my trip."

It was Kyp who summarized the Council's knowledge for her. "We've heard that you went to . . . *evaluate* Luke's situation." His gaze shifted toward Lando, who was standing at Jaina's side looking dapper, worried, and exhausted. "Apparently, you ran into Lando and joined him aboard the *Rockhound.* After some excitement on Klatooine, the pair of you followed Luke, Ben, and a flotilla of pretty nasty allies into the Maw. We're thinking you were trying to find out what's been turning Shelter Jedi barvy and eliminate it. Is that about it?"

Jaina nodded. "It is."

"We asssume you were successful," Saba said. She flashed a broad, fang-filled grin. "Because the mad ones have recovered."

Jaina's heart did not soar—the news she was bringing was too grim for that—but it definitely *rose.* "I can't tell you how glad I am to hear that."

"And I am, too," Lando said, sounding far from relieved. He reached into his pocket and extracted the datachip they had prepared on their journey back from the Maw. "Because you're going to need every Jedi Knight you can find."

"There was trouble with your allies?" Kyle asked.

"They double-crossed us, but we expected that," Lando confirmed. "What we didn't expect was *this*."

Lando casually flipped the datachip in the general direction of the Council circle. Kyle Katarn raised a hand, summoning the chip to his grasp, then slipped it into the reader-slot in the arm of his chair. A moment later the holograph of a Rebaxan MSE-6 droid appeared above the projection pad hidden in the center of the circle.

Jaina explained what they were seeing. "This is an impostor droid a pirate group used to impersonate Lando's voice aboard the *Rockhound*. Its commands redirected us to an ambush point, disabled our comm and sensor systems, and crippled my StealthX."

"We've already delivered it to Lowbacca for analysis," Lando added. "He's taking it apart now."

"Thank you," Hamner replied drily. "I'm sure those are the orders we would have given anyway."

"We're hoping Lowbacca can tell the Council something about the programming style." Lando's explanation was directed primarily to Kenth, and his tone was pointed. "It might help you locate the pirates' home base."

The image changed to a recording of the cockpit tactical feeds as Jaina went out to challenge the ambushers.

"As you can see," Jaina continued. "They came at us in three BDY crew skiffs, launched from a Damorian S-eighteen light freighter."

"I *do* see," Hamner said. His voice assumed a disapproving tone. "You filed a TOP URGENT request in order to inform the Council that you were assaulted by . . . *pirates*?"

"That's right." Lando did not bother to hide his irritation. "Except *these* pirates also redirected us to Ashteri's

Cloud. And there's only one way they could have known to choose those coordinates for an ambush."

"You're saying they *knew* you would be coming out of the Maw." Kyp shifted forward in his seat, then clarified, "You're saying they had to be Sith."

"Yes," Jaina said. "After the mouse droid sabotaged my StealthX, the only weapons I had left were shadow bombs. Every time I launched one, their gunners found me. They felt me using the Force."

"So . . . *Sith,*" Barratk'l growled. "A double cross. Then Master Skywalker and Ben must be—"

"No," Lando interrupted quickly. "They're fine—at least they were when we left orbit."

"We're not sure of the details, because we never made planetfall," Jaina added. "But after Abeloth's death, Luke came to some kind of arrangement with the Sith to investigate her nature. Only three people from each side stayed behind, and everyone else was ordered to leave."

"And you're sure the Sith obeyed?" asked Octa Ramis.

"We're sure they left when we did," Jaina replied. "And it wouldn't be easy to return. The planet was tough to reach."

"The Sith lost a frigate going in," Lando added. His voice assumed a note of pride. "And they would have lost another if the *Rockhound* hadn't been there to pull it to safety. They could *probably* make it back on their own, but they wouldn't be eager."

"And I think I would have felt it if something *had* happened to Uncle Luke or Ben," Jaina added. Noticing Hamner's mouth starting to sag at the corners again, she turned to Kyle Katarn. "Will you advance to the next image, please?"

Kyle pressed a control on his chair arm, and a holographic map of the known galaxy appeared over the projection pad. Scattered along the hyperspace lanes were nearly four hundred bright red squares. Near one edge, in the Corporate Sector, was a large cluster of twenty-seven red triangles.

"This map is derived from the one Jaden Korr has been assembling during his piracy investigations," Jaina explained. "We spent most of the trip back filtering out attacks that don't fit the same profile as the one against the *Rockhound.*"

"Basically, we were looking for two things," Lando explained. "A recent port call, followed by the total disappearance of the vessel—no survivors, no wreckage, no flotsam or bodies."

Jaina stepped forward and pointed to the twenty-seven red triangles in the Corporate Sector. "These triangles represent a fleet of old ChaseMaster frigates that disappeared on their way to a decommissioning yard," she explained. "We *know* that they were taken by the Lost Tribe, because High Lord Taalon had a squadron of twelve with him."

The Force shuddered with the alarm of every Master in the Chamber.

"And the circles?" Cilghal asked. "They represent assaults you merely *believe* to be Sith in origin?"

Jaina nodded. "That's correct," she said. "There's no way to be certain, at least until we locate the Lost Tribe's home base, but they fit the same profile."

The chamber fell silent as the Masters contemplated what they were seeing. After a moment, Corran Horn rose and stepped over to the holograph, running his gaze along each of the major hyperspace lanes. All eyes were on him, watching in silence as he paused at each of the circle symbols, studying the description of the missing ship and the cargo it had been carrying. Finally, a look of horror came over him, and he turned to face his fellow Masters.

"There are Sith *everywhere,*" Corran announced. "And they're building a war fleet!"

Chapter Eleven

AT ONE END OF THE MEETING ROOM STOOD A WELL-stocked bar and snack center, and at the other a round borlestone conference table surrounded by a variety of chairs and stools chosen to accommodate the galaxy's most common body types. The lighting was indirect and soft enough to encourage relaxed conversation; even the transparisteel viewing wall, looking across Fellowship Plaza toward the pyramidal grandeur of the Jedi Temple, was tinted amber to create an atmosphere of warmth and well-being. The style was not what Leia would consider typically "Sullustan"—but, according to Lando, Luewet Wuul was no typical Sullustan.

Leia took a seat at the table and motioned for Lando and her other two companions to do the same. "We may as well make ourselves comfortable," she said. "For a Senator, 'just a few minutes late' usually means an hour."

"You'll find Luew an exception to that rule," Lando said, heading for the bar. "He prides himself on courtesy—and on his Maldovean Burtalle. Anyone else?"

Jaina stopped just inside the entrance. "Uh, Lando, we can't afford to offend this guy." She began to walk along the wall, pretending to examine the artwork and craftsmanship while she searched for hidden eavesdropping devices. "And I don't recall the receptionist inviting us to help ourselves."

"I'll take that as a yes." Lando placed five glasses on

the bar counter. "And don't worry about Luew. He's *already* on our side."

"You'd better be right about that," Han said, going toward the bar. "Because if this gets out, Daala will hang us with it."

"No, she won't," Leia said. "Because we're not going to mention *that* part to Luew."

Han frowned. "Which part?"

"The part about Jedi *working* with the Sith," Lando said. He produced an ice bucket and used a pair of tongs to drop a sapphire cube into each glass. "And Leia's right. Luew doesn't need to know about that part—and he wouldn't want to."

Leia grimaced, then cast a meaningful glance toward Jaina, who was just finishing her sweep. "I hope he still *doesn't.*"

Lando flashed a confident smile. "No worries. The way Luew talks, he's the last one who'd allow eavesdroppers." He selected an amber jug off the bar shelf, then shot Jaina a wink. "Besides, why do you think he's leaving us alone in here? He expects you to sweep for listening devices. He wants you to know you can talk freely."

"Considerate guy," Jaina said, turning back toward the table. "Or one with really good techs. I can't find anything."

Leia extended her own Force awareness throughout the room and, experiencing no hint of uneasiness, nodded. "Okay," she said. "So why don't you have a seat and tell us how it went with Grand Master Hamner?"

Jaina rolled her eyes, then plucked at her flight suit. "He dismissed the Masters three hours ago, and I'm still in the same thing I was wearing when we left the *Rockhound.*" She shook her head in dismay, then looked up with an expression of equal parts dismay and frustration. "He spent the entire time accusing me of sabotaging his attempts to reconcile with Daala."

"Reconcile?" Han echoed, returning to the table with a handful of coasters. "With *Daala*? How'd you keep from laughing in his face?"

"It's too scary to laugh, Dad," Jaina said. "Honestly, I think the pressure is getting to him. Master, er, *Grand* Master Hamner really seems to believe he can cut a deal with her."

"He has to *try,*" Leia said. "We can't fight Sith if we're busy fighting Daala."

"Yeah, well, trying to cut a deal with Daala is a waste of time," Han said. He began to fling coasters like sabacc chips, tossing one in front of each seating area. "The only way to deal with Daala is to deal her out."

Leia frowned. "Han, what do you mean by that?"

"You know what I mean," Han said, taking a chair. "And don't give me any poodoo about it being premature. Daala tried to take us out, and *Amelia* was there. She's lucky I haven't gone after her already."

"*Someone* tried to take us out," Leia corrected. Han was referring to a dinner a few weeks earlier, when their visit to the Pangalactus Restaurant had been interrupted by an assassination attempt. Leia found the incident more sad than angering, as the dinner had been their last with Jagged Fel before Jaina broke off the couple's engagement. "We don't *know* that Daala sent them. We can't even be sure *we* were the targets."

"You want to give me odds she *didn't,* and we *weren't*?" Han countered. "She set us up with that whole *we can negotiate* act."

"Okay, so let's say Daala *did* set us up," Leia said. Han had never had much patience for verifying the obvious, so unless she wanted the meeting to start with a rant about Daala's Imperial treachery, she needed to nudge him into a more constructive area of thinking. "What are you going to do about it? Launch another coup?"

Han winced at this reminder of their son Jacen's disastrous takeover of the Galactic Alliance government, and he answered in a calmer voice. "I wasn't thinking of *us,* exactly."

"I hope you're not thinking of the Jedi, either," Leia said. "Because the Senate—and the public—would only take that as proof that Daala is right to fear us."

"Let's hope it doesn't come to that," Lando said, joining them with a tray of drinks. "Kenth is right about one thing—the Jedi have as many friends in the Senate as Daala does, and you can put a lot of pressure on her by letting them know what's going on."

"I'd say that has about a ten percent chance of working," Jaina said. "What do we do when it backfires and she starts arresting Senators?"

Lando flashed one of his brilliant smiles. "That, my dear, is when the Jedi step in to *save* the Alliance." He placed a tumbler full of burtalle in front of Jaina. "You just need to be patient—and find a way to bring Kenth around before the Sith make their move."

"You think we have that much time?" Leia asked.

Lando set a tumbler in front of her, then nodded. "With Abeloth dead, yes, I think so," he said. "If she were still alive, the Jedi wouldn't have a chance. But as matters stand, her attack on the Shelter students may have been a lucky break for the Jedi."

"How do you figure that?" Han scoffed. "By giving Daala a bunch of barvy Jedi Knights she could use as an excuse to go after Luke and the Order?"

It was Jaina who replied. "By forcing the Sith to reveal themselves before they were ready. If Ben and Luke hadn't been exiled, they would never have gone to Sinkhole Station—and we wouldn't have known about the Lost Tribe."

"Exactly," Lando said. "But now we have a chance to mobilize."

"We?" Leia arched a brow, then asked, "Are you sure you want to involve yourself in this, Lando?"

Lando looked at the floor for a moment, then said, "To tell the truth, it's the last thing I want." He grabbed a tumbler off the tray and emptied it in a long gulp, then placed the glass back on the tray. "But with a whole planetful of Sith on the way, I doubt there's going to be a choice for *anyone*."

He placed the last two tumblers on the table, one in front of Han and one in front of a Sullustan-sized stool with a well-worn nerf-hide seat, then returned to the bar to refill his glass. With a contemplative silence hanging over the room, Leia took a sip of the burtalle. It was as special as Lando had claimed, with a deep, malty flavor tinged by musky notes from the moagwood aging casks. It was also extremely potent, leaving her tongue and the roof of her mouth feeling dry and smoky.

Han took a sip from his own tumbler, then raised his brow in approval. "I'll say this for the Senator—he serves some of the best jet juice I've ever had."

A bright Sullustan voice rang out from the back entrance. "I'm glad you approve, Captain Solo. Coming from you, I take that as quite a compliment."

Leia turned to see a distinguished-looking Sullustan in a gold-trimmed vest entering the room. With heavily wrinkled dewflaps and long bags hanging beneath his eyes, he was clearly an elder of his species. Yet he bore himself like a young man, carrying his shoulders thrown back and walking with a confident gait. When Leia and the others started to rise to greet him, he was quick to wave them back into their seats.

"We don't have time for that nonsense," he said, going straight to the table. "I've got a subcommittee hearing to chair in . . ." He checked his chrono. ". . . fifteen minutes, and Lando said this was urgent. So let's get straight to it."

"Very well, Senator Wuul," Leia said. "The reason we asked—"

"Not *that,*" Wuul said, raising a hand to silence her. He slipped onto his stool and snatched the drink Lando had left for him, then drained it in a single gulp. "The burtalle. And call me Luew. Only the opposition calls me *Senator.*"

He raised the empty tumbler above his head, signaling Lando for a refill, which, Leia noticed, was already on its way. Once Lando had traded the empty glass for a full one, Wuul's head suddenly snapped around, and he peered at her out of a single dark eye.

"You're not the opposition, are you, Jedi Solo?"

Leia flashed a reassuring smile. "Of course not, Luew." She grabbed her own drink and clinked glasses with Wuul, then said, "Any friend of Lando's is a friend of ours. And please . . . call me Leia."

Luew responded with a crafty smile, then took a small sip of his fresh burtalle and placed the glass on the table. "Glad to hear it, Leia." He turned his gaze first to Han, then to Jaina, and said, "Okay, now that we understand each other, why don't you tell me what's so urgent that you had to come over here in a dirty flight suit, young lady?"

Jaina's cheeks reddened, but she sat up straight and replied with a single word. "Sith."

Instead of reaching for his drink as Leia had expected, Wuul slumped and shook his head in dismay.

"*Another* one? I thought we were finally finished with those azkancs." The vile term had barely left Wuul's mouth before he winced and glanced over at Han. "No offense intended, Captain."

"None taken," Han assured him. "But if it was just one azkanc, we wouldn't be here. Luke and Ben have run into a whole planetful."

Wuul cocked his head in confusion. "A planetful? Of Sith?"

"We don't actually know that it's a whole planetful," Jaina clarified. "But there are a lot. They call themselves the Lost Tribe, and we think they've spent the last two years putting together a battle fleet."

"A *fleet*? Of *Sith*?" Wuul seemed too shocked to comprehend what he was hearing. "But I thought they only came—"

"Yeah, in twos," Han finished. "So did I. But that's kind of a recent development. Near as we can tell, these guys have been marooned on some world called Kesh for the last five thousand years."

"I see." Wuul's dewflaps went from pink to pale green, but he seemed to gather his wits and sit upright. "And *they* have been responsible for the madness afflicting the young Jedi Knights?"

"Uh, no." Han looked to Leia for guidance as to how much he should reveal. "Not really."

"Their illness was caused by an ancient being named Abeloth," Leia explained. "She made contact with the Jedi Knights while they were still children, when we were hiding our young ones in the Maw during the war against the Yuuzhan Vong."

"But that's not really important now," Jaina added. "Abeloth has been destroyed. What we need to worry about is the Sith."

Wuul's gaze shifted to his burtalle, and Leia thought he would take another drink in an attempt to calm himself. When he surprised her by merely gazing into the glass while he contemplated what he had just been told, she realized that his hard-drinking act was just a ruse designed to put other people at ease—and, perhaps, to cause them to underestimate him.

After a moment, Wuul nodded and returned his gaze to Leia. "The Jedi can't handle the Sith with Daala breathing down their collars. Is that correct?"

Leia nodded. "Exactly."

Wuul contemplated this for a moment, then asked, "And what do you expect *me* to do about that? I'm the chair of the subcommittee on mineral taxation. I don't have that kind of leverage over Daala."

Lando stood up and slapped a hand on Wuul's shoulder. "Luew, old buddy, we're not looking for leverage. And you know it."

Wuul's brow rose. "I do?" He looked up, feigning an innocence his Force aura did not exude, then he saw the expression on Lando's face and exhaled loudly. "Okay. But after this, we start from even again."

Lando's chuckle verged on a true belly laugh. "Fair enough," he said. "What's a little sabacc debt compared with the possibility of a Sith empire?"

"I'm glad you see it that way." Wuul motioned to the tumbler in front of Lando's chair. "Now sit down and drink some of that burtalle while I prepare a little gift for my new friends."

"Thanks," Lando said, smiling and returning to his chair. "Don't mind if I do."

Wuul pulled a small datapad from inside his tunic and thumbed some keys, then slid the pad across the table toward Leia. "That's a list of everyone in the government and the military who owes me a favor—and who can be counted on to keep it." He continued to hold the datapad beneath his fingers. "But I trust you're not talking about another coup."

Leia hesitated, glancing across the table at Jaina. So far, they had not revealed anything the entire galaxy was not going to learn within the next couple of weeks anyway—there were already rumors coming out of Hutt space that there had been some Sith involvment in the slave revolt on Klatooine. But the Council's plan for dealing with Daala had to remain a closely held secret until the trap was sprung—and Senators with gambling debts did not usually make the most trustworthy of partners.

When Leia did not reply quickly enough, Wuul's face sagged. "I see." He pulled the datapad back and turned toward Lando. "I don't know how you could think I'd involve—"

"It's not a coup," Leia interrupted. She also turned to Lando. "How much does he owe you?"

Lando's eyes lit in comprehension. "Not much." He flashed an artificial grin. "Just twenty-five."

"Twenty-five hundred?" Jaina asked.

Lando shook his head, and Leia's heart fell.

"Twenty-five *thousand*?" she clarified. That wasn't a lot next to a Senator's salary, but politicians had been known to sell out for less. "Lando, I wish you'd mentioned this earlier. I'm not sure the Masters would have approved coming to Luew if they had known he had gambling debts."

Lando continued to smile. "Why?" he asked. "It's a private matter between Luew and me."

"And it isn't twenty-five *thousand,*" Wuul added gruffly. "What do you take me for? A chump?"

"Twenty-five *million*?" Han asked, whistling. He turned to Leia. "Look, I don't think you need to worry about Luew. With that kind of money on the table, *nobody* is going to sell us out."

"Relax, will you?" Lando said. "Luew wouldn't sell you out at *any* price."

"Thank you, Lando," Wuul said. "Also, just for the record, it isn't twenty-five million."

A stunned silence fell over the room, and Jaina asked, "Blazes, Luew. How much *are* you into him for?"

"Twenty five *credits,*" Wuul said, clearly irritated. "Just twenty-five, no zeros. I'm sure that seems like Jawa change to you Jedi, but it's the same sabacc no matter what the stakes."

"We haven't played high stakes since before Luew took office," Lando explained.

"It just wouldn't be right," Wuul added, "the chairman of the committee on mineral taxation taking all that money from the owner of a mining world."

"Oh dear, Luew," Leia said. She felt a little guilty and foolish for leaping to such a wrong conclusion, but the possibility of corruption was not something she could ignore—not when Kenth's plan depended so heavily on *honest* politicians. "I think we owe you an apology."

"Nonsense—you'd have been wrong *not* to investigate." Wuul waved a dismissing hand, but without meeting Leia's gaze. "Now let's talk about this bill you want me to write. I assume that, basically, you want the Jedi's current status written into law, with guarantees of financial support and military cooperation."

Leia raised her brow. "Are we that obvious?"

"Only to me, my dear," Wuul said. "You need this bill to come from someone you can trust, but someone not normally aligned with the Jedi, because Daala will be on the lookout for *that.* You also need someone who can bring a lot of votes your way, because you'll have to override the Chief of State's veto—and that makes it fairly obvious what you want from me."

Jaina nodded, but looked nervous. "I really hope Daala isn't this smart," she said. "Because if it's that easy for her to figure this out, the galaxy is in big trouble."

"Unfortunately, she *is* that smart," Luew said. "And that's the weak spot in your plan. We can't make this happen without talking to each other. Sooner or later, Daala is *going* to catch a whiff of our communications and realize what we're doing. Once she does, we need to bring the bill to the floor before she can gather enough support to block a vote."

"Why don't we just attach it to something she *can't* have blocked?" Leia asked.

Wuul shook his head. "They outlawed that little maneuver when they chartered the Galactic Alliance," he said.

"To tell the truth, I'm surprised the Jedi decided to take the political route after the attempt on Bwua'tu's life. With the support you have in Hapes and the Empire, I'm surprised you're not threatening to just leave Coruscant."

"Probably because we're not the ones in charge," Jaina said, allowing her frustration to show. "And Grand Master Hamner is afraid to call Daala's bluff."

"Actually, he thinks a political solution would be better for everyone, if we can work it out." Leia shot her daughter a disapproving scowl, then turned back to the Senator. "But what does the attack on Bwua'tu have to do with anything? Even Chief Daala doesn't seem to think the Jedi were involved with that."

"That's not quite right," Wuul corrected. "The rumors I hear actually have her saying, 'If the Jedi were that incompetent, I wouldn't be worried about them.'"

Lando cocked his brow. "Meaning?"

"Meaning she can't imagine the Jedi failing," Wuul explained. "So she's wondering whether it was someone trying to make the attack *look* like Jedi, or a Jedi plan she just doesn't understand yet. By all accounts, she was really thrown for a loop when Asokaji accused her of ordering the admiral's assassination in retaliation for the arrangement with Grand Master Hamner."

There was a moment of stunned silence as Leia and her companions contemplated the arrangement to which Wuul might be referring. As Bwua'tu's aide-de-camp, Rynog Asokaji would be privy to the admiral's most closely guarded secrets—including any clandestine bargains he had struck with Kenth Hamner.

Finally, Han blurted out, *"Arrangement?"*

This was quickly followed by a demand from Jaina, "What arrangement?"

Wuul's wrinkled brow rose. "You don't know?" He raised a hand and rubbed a finger across his lips as he considered their ignorance, then shrugged and said, "Apparently, Admiral Bwua'tu was worried that the Order intended to launch its StealthX wing to break Chief Daala's siege. So he cut a deal with Grand Master Hamner. Hamner agreed to keep the StealthXs in their hangars, and Bwua'tu promised to block any attempt to use the military against the Temple."

Leia went cold inside, and she could tell by the fury in Han's and Jaina's faces that they felt just as betrayed as she did. She wasn't angry about the agreement itself. Tensions *had* been high during the siege, and taking steps to defuse them had probably saved a lot of lives. What angered Leia was that Hamner had done it without consulting the Council. He had taken it upon himself to leave Luke and Ben unsupported against an entire *tribe* of Sith—to hold the security of the Jedi Temple above the security of the entire galaxy—and he had not even bothered to inform the Masters of his decision. And why? Obviously, because he knew they would have disagreed with him. Those were not the actions of a good leader—they were the compromises of a man out of his depth.

When the silence in the chamber grew uncomfortable, Wuul said, "Look, my friends, my information is coming to me secondhand, through General Jaxton of Starfighter Command, so it's quite possible I have some of the details wrong."

"Maybe," Han growled. "But the ones you have right explain a lot."

Wuul dropped his gaze. "I see." He reached out and absently began to spin his burtalle glass, then asked, "It seems the bill is just a stalling tactic—one aimed at you. Shall I still pursue it?"

"Yes, absolutely," Leia answered. "The whole Council agreed to it. I doubt they'll have a change of heart just because he's been keeping things from them."

"Besides, it *would* be the best solution to the problem—

for everyone," Lando pointed out. "Just because it's a long shot doesn't mean we shouldn't take it."

Wuul cocked his head to look up at Lando. "Yes, you *do* have a love for long shots, don't you?" He thought for a moment, then said, "Very well. I'm going need some things from you."

"Of course," Leia said. "Whatever we can do to help."

Wuul raised a hand and extended his thumb. "First, I need to know I won't be endangering Alliance citizens. You're *sure* the creature that has been spreading this illness is no longer a threat?"

Lando nodded. "We didn't see the corpse ourselves, but Luke said over the comm she was dead."

"They're going to try to bring the body back for analysis," Jaina added. "Plus, well, everybody's sane again."

"True." Wuul smirked, no doubt recalling the image of Han forcing Daala's own expert to certify that Sothais Saar and Turi Altamik were completely sane. "It certainly looked that way on the news."

Even Jaina smiled at this. "Yeah, I wish I could have seen that."

"No problem," Han said proudly. "I've got the whole thing on vid."

"Mine's in full holo." Wuul paused a moment, then turned to Jaina. "Second, we're going to need a distraction to keep Daala's mind on something aside from what we're doing in the Senate."

"Okay," Jaina said. "What do you have in mind?"

"The integration of the Empire," Wuul said.

Jaina's expression grew confused, and she looked to Leia for clarification.

"The assassination attempts have had an upside for Jagged," Leia explained. "He's finally backed the Moffs into a corner. It looks like he'll be able to bring the Empire into the Alliance after all."

"Which will only strengthen Daala's hand when it

comes to the Jedi," Wuul observed, continuing to watch Jaina. "So we need those negotiations to start unraveling, and *keep* unraveling until after the Senate passes my bill. The more time Daala has to spend tossing those beetles back into the pot, the longer it will take her to catch on to what I'm doing."

"That makes sense," Jaina said cautiously. "And you want me to . . . what? Steal their charter agreement?"

Wuul's dewflaps sagged in disappointment. "I was thinking of something a little more difficult to repair," he said. "New conditions, greedy holdouts, language quibbles . . . whatever hurdles you can convince Head of State Fel to throw Daala's way."

Jaina's mouth tightened, and her Force aura began to draw in on itself. "I doubt I can convince him to do anything like that."

A devious grin came to Wuul's small mouth. "Don't sell yourself short, Jedi Solo." He extended his hand and laid it over hers. "You're quite an attractive mating prospect, by human standards. I'm sure it will be easier than you think to convince Head of State Fel to help us."

Jaina bit her lips, then dropped her gaze and did not reply.

Leia reached over and gently pulled Wuul's hand away from her daughter's. "It's not public knowledge yet, Luew, but Jaina and Jag broke off their engagement a few weeks ago."

"Yeah," Han said. "Over the same kind of thing."

Wuul looked from Leia back to Jaina. "I'm very sorry to hear that, my dear." He reached out and patted her hand again. "But I'm sure you can convince him to take you back. You're a Jedi."

Chapter Twelve

THE AMPUTATION WAS THE LEAST OF NEK BWUA'TU'S wounds, but it was the most visible, with the stump of the arm resting atop a pillow next to the old Bothan's chest. His thick fur had been shaved away to just above the elbow, where the end of the limb was wrapped in a white, seepage-stained bandage. His midsection had been cut and burned so badly that even a 2-1BXS combat-trauma surgical droid had required thirty hours to repair and replace the damaged organs, and now his torso lay completely hidden beneath a hard-shelled bactabath body cast. It reminded Daala of the ribbed blast armor that her turbolaser crews had worn, back when she had actually commanded Star Destroyers.

"The trouble with lightsaber amputations is they cauterize," Dr. Ysa'i was saying. A golden-furred Bothan of about Bwua'tu's age, Ysa'i was a highly acclaimed orthopedist specializing in his own species. "You see, Bothan nerves can't be stimulated to reattach after they've been burned apart."

Daala raised her hand in a wave of indifference. "Nek is an old soldier. He's lost more important things than an arm." She motioned toward the holographic brain-activity image floating above the head of his bed. At the moment, it looked like a heavy sea, with high swells rolling from one end to another. "*That's* what we can't afford to lose. How long before he awakens?"

Ysa'i's ears flattened. "Comas are hardly my area of expertise, Chief Daala," he said. "I'm just here to take—"

"*Now* would be a very bad time to put a plate of poodoo in front of me," Daala interrupted. She continued to look at Bwua'tu as she spoke, wishing they could tape his eyes shut. An FX medical assistant droid had told her that exposing "the patient" to visual stimuli, such as the vidscreen hanging above his bed, increased the likelihood he would eventually awaken. But it also made him look dead, especially with the moisture preservative making his eyes glisten, and she did *not* like seeing Bwua'tu that way. "You've had training. How long before I have my Chief of the Navy back?"

Ysa'i allowed a low snort of discomfort to escape his snout. "I'm not a neurologist," he said. "But I doubt anyone can give you the answer you're looking for."

Daala sighed. "That bad?" She let her chin drop, then said, "Okay, tell me what you do know."

Ysa'i's voice developed a note of arrogance. "That's what I'm *trying* to do, Chief Daala." He stepped closer to the head of the bed and slipped a leathery finger into the holograph. "Brain images are fairly easy to read, at least on a superficial level. These rolling waves indicate there *is* activity, but it's very deep and nonreactive. Something is definitely happening in there, but I doubt it's a reaction to *us*—or anything in his external environment."

"I believe that's because the waves are rounded and regular, correct?"

This question came from the other side of the bed, where Bwua'tu's chief aide-de-camp, Rynog Asokaji, was standing. A Bith male with an old burn scar across the cheek folds on one side of his face, Asokaji had angrily accused Daala of ordering the assassination attempt in retaliation for Bwua'tu's secret effort to work out a compromise with Hamner. To his surprise—and Daala's, too—she hadn't grown angry at him in return. Instead she had praised his courage in defending his superior, then advised him to ask permission the next time he felt the need to speak frankly. The pair had been on good terms since.

Asokaji continued, "I was told that when the waves grow sharper and the pattern more irregular, it will indicate that he's listening to our voices."

"Or responding to something else in the environment, yes," Ysa'i clarified, still addressing himself to Daala. "A neurologist can tease more information from the patterns than I can, Chief Daala. But the sharper, higher, and more irregular the waves, the greater the likelihood that he's going to awaken."

"Then it appears there's no reason to hope the admiral will awaken anytime soon," Wynn Dorvan said. He returned to the bedside next to Asokaji, still holding the comlink he had stepped away to use. A human of unremarkable looks and brown hair neatly trimmed in a conservative cut, he had the appearance of a conscientious lifetime bureaucrat—which he was. "So why would Admiral Bwua'tu need to be fitted for a prosthetic hand *now*? Isn't that a bit premature?"

Ysa'i's muzzle curled at the implied challenge to his medical authority, but Daala recognized the deeper significance of her assistant's question. Wynn had noticed an inconsistency in the situation. To his meticulous way of thinking, inconsistencies often concealed deceptions, and—given that it had been an assassination attempt that had put Bwua'tu into the medcenter in the first place—any deception concerning the admiral's care was not to be tolerated.

When Wynn met Ysa'i's half snarl with a determined glare, Daala sighed. "The hand fitting is my doing, Wynn." The confession did not embarrass her so much as make her feel vulnerable, for she had learned during her long military career that every sentimental indulgence revealed a weakness that could be exploited. "I don't want Nek waking up to a stump."

"Very wise," Ysa'i agreed, a little too quickly. "Having the prosthetic will make the transition easier."

"Let's hope so," Daala said. Choosing to forgive the doctor's somewhat obvious attempt to curry favor—he *was* Bothan, after all—she reached over the rail and squeezed Bwua'tu's knee. "The Alliance needs you back, old friend."

She started to withdraw her hand, but Ysa'i reached out to stop her. "Wait." He pointed toward brain-activity holograph. "He's responding."

Daala looked up and saw that a long chain of sharp peaks had appeared amid the rolling hills. Realizing that it had been *her* touch that had drawn the reaction, she experienced a flutter of schoolgirl joy—and immediately felt a bit silly. She and Bwua'tu were too old and too jaded for such romantic nonsense . . . and yet, she couldn't help being more protective of him than ever.

"What should I do?" she asked Ysa'i.

"First, have someone call Dr. Javir," Ysa'i said, naming the medcenter's chief neurologist. He thought for a moment, then added, "Second, keep touching the patient. Perhaps speak to him, see if it increases the activity."

"Very well." Daala nodded, and Asokaji immediately turned toward the exit. Daala turned her attention back to Bwua'tu, looking into his glistening, vacant eyes, and began to speak. "Admiral Bwua'tu, wake up. I need your report on the assassination attempt *yesterday*, and you've been lying around here for over a week."

She glanced up at the activity monitor and found the peaks unchanged, no higher or sharper.

"Keep going," Ysa'i urged.

Daala squeezed Bwua'tu's knee again. "You're being

remiss, Admiral. I'm giving you a direct order to wake up and report."

She paused and glanced over at Ysa'i.

"No change," the doctor said.

"Nek, are you *listening* to me?" Through the sheet, Daala began to run her fingers against the grain of Bwua'tu's leg fur—that always got him going. "I need to know who attacked you."

"There!" Ysa'i said. "Follow that. His attention spiked."

"Nek, we think the lightsaber wounds were a misdirection," Daala continued, "because, well, you survived."

Bwua'tu's eyes moved, not much, but it seemed to Daala that the pupils had definitely dipped toward his lower eyelids.

"Nek, we need to know who did this to you," Daala said. "And we have no leads."

She paused again, waiting for Bwua'tu's eyes to move, or for Ysa'i to say something encouraging about the monitor.

When neither happened, Daala pressed on, "Nek, if they're willing to attack *you*, they're a threat to the entire Alliance. You've got to help us figure out who did this to you."

His pupils moved again, this time rising slightly to the right—away from her. She paused, hoping Ysa'i would report another spike on the monitor.

It took more than a second. "There—in a different area. He's definitely interested."

"In *something*," Daala said. She removed her hand from his knee. "Any change?"

"Not that I have the training to see," Ysa'i replied. "But the monitor is capturing this on a chip. I'm sure Dr. Javir can interpret the data more accurately than I can."

Instead of replying, Daala continued to watch Bwua'tu's eyes. It took only a couple of seconds for his pupils to shift again. She turned to look in the same direction—and felt the excitement of a few moments earlier draining away.

Bwua'tu's gaze was fixed on the vidscreen above his bed, where the impish figure of Madhi Vaandt was broadcasting from a plaza surrounded by the looming, cut-stone buildings of Blaudu Sextus's capital city, Arari. Behind the newscaster, thousands of shaggy-furred Octusi were racing past, squealing and shrieking as they fled a line of Mandalorian QuickStryke assault sleds.

"*Madhi Vaandt,*" Daala growled. She glanced over at Wynn, who was watching the vidscreen with an expression that seemed a lot less surprised than it should have. "I thought we were going to suppress her reports."

Wynn shrugged. "Needmo said he'd pull her off the assignment voluntarily," he explained. "Apparently, he was lying."

"And you took a *newscaster* at his word?" Daala asked. "It's not like you to be so careless."

"I *wasn't.*" Wynn shot a meaningful glance at Ysa'i, then added, "Needmo would have challenged a formal suppression order as a matter of principle, and we would have had to demonstrate material relevance in open court. I thought an informal request was the better option."

What Wynn was being careful *not* to say in front of the doctor was that the informal request had been their *only* option. To avoid a direct link between her government and the effort to suppress the slave revolt, Daala had arranged for a local mining company to hire the Mandalorian mercenaries with laundered funds. Defending a formal security order in court would have meant running the risk not only that the order would be overturned, but that the entire arrangement would be revealed to Needmo—and therefore the general public—in the process.

Daala exhaled in frustration, then nodded. "You're

right, of course," she said. "But no more playing nice with Perre Needmo. If one of his reporters airs so much as a *stang,* I want him off the air."

Wynn nodded. "I'll alert the Galactic HoloNet Commission."

"You might want to hold off on that until *after* Admiral Bwua'tu awakens," Ysa'i said. He pointed at the brain-activity image. "The situation on Blaudu Sextus seems to be catching his interest."

The holograph had blossomed into a virtual mountain range, with spires and peaks shooting up in all quarters. Daala checked Bwua'tu's pupils and found them locked on Madhi Vaandt, tracking her image as it shifted to different parts of the display.

"Nek?" Daala asked. "Is it *her*?"

The image on the vidscreen shifted to a close-up of one of the Octusi, and the peaks on his activity graph began to subside.

"That's strange," Daala said. "There must be some connection."

"A connection?" Asokaji asked, stepping back into the room. "Is he coming awake?"

"It's too early to tell," Ysa'i replied. "At least for me."

"But there's *something* happening," Daala said. "He seems interested in Madhi Vaandt." She looked up. "Can you think of a reason?"

Asokaji's face grew a deeper shade of blue, and he could not help shooting a quick glance in Wynn's direction—a glance that was returned just as quickly, then broken off. Daala found herself confused for a moment, until the image of Vaandt's face appeared on the vidscreen again. With sharply pointed ears, shaggy white head fur, and long narrow eyes, she was, Daala had to admit, quite bewitching.

"A reason aside from the fur, I mean." Daala's tone was crisp without being sharp. "She's beautiful, but I don't think that's what is catching Nek's interest. There's some connection to the attempt on his life." She looked back to the brain-activity image, which had once again blossomed into peaks and points. "There has to be."

Asokaji glanced at Ysa'i and reported that Dr. Javir was on her way, then fixed his attention on the vidscreen and furrowed his brow in thought. Daala pointed to the remote control on the far side of Bwua'tu's bed and made an *up* motion with her thumb, and Wynn turned on the sound. The image switched to a close-up of a Mandalorian assault sled herding a crowd of terrified Octusi out of the plaza, while Vaandt's report continued in a voice-over.

". . . claim they were contracted to protect the interests of the Sextuna Mining Corporation, but that seems unlikely." The image switched to a giant strip mine carved into the flank of a desolate mountainside somewhere on Blaudu Sextus. "*This* is Sextuna's nearest interest, located over eighty kilometers from the protest march in central Arari."

The image switched back to Vaandt's impish face. "Until the Mandalorian assault sleds arrived and began to run down protesters too determined to flee, the march was entirely peaceful. Even now, after a provocation that was clearly one-sided, the only reported casualties are Octusi." The vidscreen displayed a large, shaggy-furred body that had been crushed beyond all recognition. "Given recent events at the Jedi Temple, this reporter is left wondering just *what* these Mandalorians are trying to protect—and *who* they're really working for."

A deep rage began to burn inside Daala's chest, and she looked across Bwua'tu's bed. "She's going too far with this, Wynn. We need to do something about it."

"I understand," he replied evenly. "I'm just not sure

what we *can* do—unless you're willing to risk the uncertainties of open court."

Translation: *Unless we want the whole galaxy to know that Vaandt's right, we have to take our lumps.* Daala clenched her teeth and looked away—and that was when she saw Bwua'tu's eyelid twitch.

"Did you see that?" she asked, turning to Ysa'i. "He blinked."

"I didn't, but you mustn't allow it to raise your hopes," Ysa'i said. "It's an automatic reflex."

Daala looked back to Bwua'tu, waiting for him to blink again. He didn't, but she could see for herself that his activity image was peaking and spiking every time Vaandt's image appeared on screen.

"No, Doctor, it means something." She glanced back up at the vidscreen, where Vaandt was just doing her sign-off with an image of Arari's smoking skyline in the background. "I think there's some connection between Madhi Vaandt and the attack."

Asokaji's scarred cheek folds widened in shock, and he glanced over at Wynn with an expression that suggested he thought Daala was losing her mind.

"Something troubling you, Rynog?" Daala asked. "Speak freely."

"Thank you, Chief," he replied. "But it doesn't make sense. Why would a reporter involve herself in an attack on Admiral Bwua'tu?"

"I didn't say she was *involved*," Daala corrected. "I said there was a connection—and, at the moment, that's all we have."

"Is it?" Asokaji asked. "I know you're convinced that this couldn't have been a Jedi attack because it was botched, but maybe it *wasn't* botched. What if the goal wasn't to assassinate, but to incapacitate?" He pointed at the body cast covering Bwua'tu's midsection. "Only a Jedi could do *that* and be sure not to kill."

Daala raised her brow. She had to admit the possibility had not occurred to her, but it didn't feel right, either. She looked to Wynn and cocked a brow.

Wynn thought for a moment, then said, "Sometimes a lightsaber attack is just a lightsaber attack. But I don't see the *why.*" He turned to Asokaji. "If Bwua'tu was trying to help Hamner work out a compromise with Chief Daala, why would the Jedi want to kill him?"

"Because not all Jedi *want* a compromise," Asokaji said. "Hamner told the admiral that he was having difficulty convincing the other Masters to be patient. Perhaps a splinter group decided to take matters into their own hands and put a stop to the negotiations."

"It's not out of the question," Daala admitted, recalling the assassination attempt on the Solos—an attempt that had spoiled her own efforts to negotiate a compromise. "There's no question that *someone* wants to keep us at each other's throats."

Asokaji nodded. "Exactly." His gaze was fixed on Bwua'tu's form, and Daala did not need to be a master of Bith facial expressions to see that he was thirsty for revenge. "We need to bring the Jedi into line, Chief, before it's too late. If they'll go after Admiral Bwua'tu, they'll go after you."

Wynn's face grew pale. "Rynog, we don't know that they *did* go after the admiral," he said. "In fact, what little evidence we have suggests it *wasn't* them."

"You underestimate the Jedi." Asokaji circled the bed and pushed between Daala and Ysa'i. "Give the order, and I'll have five thousand space marines storming the Temple tomorrow."

Daala was tempted . . . *sorely* tempted. But as much as she wanted to bring the Jedi to heel, she didn't want to destroy them unless it was absolutely necessary. And even if she'd thought it *was* necessary, she would not have entrusted the job to someone whose judgment was so obviously clouded.

She turned to Asokaji. "Thank you for the offer, Commander, but I don't see the Jedi faking a Jedi attack in an effort to throw us off their trail. Too many things can go wrong."

Asokaji's shoulders fell. "You're letting them get away with it."

Daala shook her head, then laid a hand on Asokaji's arm. "No. I assure you, whoever did this to Admiral Bwua'tu is *going* to pay. But I want it to be the true attackers, not their patsies."

An audible sigh of relief sounded from Wynn's side of the bed. "Very smart, Chief. We don't want to play into the assassin's hands."

"No, we don't," Daala agreed. "What we want is to find out who they are. We also want them to know we're looking for them—and we want them scared. We want them *very* scared."

Wynn's expression grew worried. "Am I to assume you have some idea of how to accomplish that?"

"Yes, you are." Daala's gaze returned to the vidscreen, where Madhi Vaandt was delivering a final recap of the day's events on Blaudu Sextus. "Dr. Ysa'i, would you please excuse us? We're about to have a very secret conversation."

Chapter Thirteen

THE FIST DESCENDED AND SENT VESTARA FLYING, COMpletely out of the grotto and onto the rubble pile that High Lord Taalon had Force-blasted from the entrance earlier. She tumbled across the stones backward, tucking her chin to prevent her skull from cracking against the stones but otherwise leaving herself unprotected. Three somersaults later, she slammed into a chunk of broken pillar and finally came to a rest, her head spinning and her body aching. Her barely healed shoulder had begun to throb again, and a line of stinging dampness confirmed that her old abdomen wound had reopened.

Two pairs of boots began to crunch toward her from the grotto mouth. Vestara struggled to her feet and stood at attention. This was the third time she had been punched, and she knew High Lord Taalon would not want to kneel down when he inspected his work. Her tunic and trousers were torn in a dozen places, exhibiting an impressive array of cuts and already darkening bruises. She had a split lip, a bloody nose, and two black eyes, but so far nothing that seemed likely to cause permanent disfigurement.

Despite her fear that High Lord Taalon would find it necessary to change that, Vestara would not have dreamed of begging for mercy. The fight against Luke Skywalker had left her father in far worse condition than she was, with a pair of blaster burns and an amputated forearm. Even Taalon was having trouble breathing because of some cracked ribs, and his cheek was as swollen and black as a guama fruit. Most alarming, his fall into the Pool of Knowledge had done something to his eyes. The pupils had grown so large that meeting his gaze was like staring down a pair of wells, and if Vestara looked long enough, it seemed to her that she saw two dim stars twinkling in the bottom.

The two men circled Vestara twice, appraising every detail of her injuries, and finally stopped in front of her. Taalon sent a chill down her spine by looking her up and down for several more moments, then turned to her father.

"What do you think, Saber Khai? Have we done enough?"

Khai's expression grew hard and thoughtful, but there was an almost imperceptible arch to his brows that suggested how painful the question was for him to answer. The last thing he would want was to see Vestara seriously injured, and yet he had to know, as *she* did, that asking for too little might easily get her killed.

After a moment, Khai shook his head. "It's certainly clear she's been beaten, but will that fool the Jedi? We need something disfiguring—a broken nose, perhaps, or a burst eyeball."

Vestara tried not to show her fear as Taalon studied her face and contemplated her father's suggestion. The nose could be repaired by any competent surgeon, but the eye would be a handicap forever. To the discerning taste of the Keshiri, even the best prosthetic would be evident and considered a blemish worse than the scar at the corner of her mouth.

Instead of raising his hand to strike, though, Taalon shook his head. "Skywalker is clever. A serious injury, he would view as an effort to win sympathy and reinforce Vestara's story."

Khai nodded. "Yet this will be enough to play the *boy's* sympathy," he observed. "He's still very naïve."

"Indeed. We also avoid the question of how a mere apprentice managed to escape from us without injury." Taalon grabbed Vestara beneath the jaw and turned her head to inspect his handiwork more closely. "Has the Skywalker boy fallen in love with you?"

Vestara felt the heat rising to her cheeks, but she answered honestly. "I'm not sure it's love yet," she replied. "But I *do* know he entertains fantasies of turning me to the light side."

Taalon's brow cocked. "*Does* he?" He glanced over at Khai. "How would you feel about a Jedi daughter, Saber Khai?"

Khai's smile was quick and cynical. "Nothing would make me prouder, High Lord . . . as long as she remains Sith on the inside."

"Yes, that *would* be necessary," Taalon confirmed. He continued to hold Vestara by the jaw. "And you, child? What are your feelings about the Skywalker boy?"

Vestara let her eyes drop, then admitted, "I'm not sure, my lord." She did not even consider trying to lie; any attempt was doomed to fail, and it would only make Taalon suspicious of her motives. "I think I may be falling in love with him, but . . ."

She let the sentence trail off, not sure what else she had intended to add.

"*But?*" Her father's voice was stern. "You're not sure?"

Knowing better than to take the opening her father was trying to make for her, Vestara glanced up and shook her head. "No. I just don't want to."

To her surprise, this drew a sympathetic smile from Taalon. "But you *must*, my dear," he said. "If young Skywalker senses that you are falling in love with him, then he will fall in love with you."

Vestara's eyes grew wide. "You wouldn't forbid it?"

"*Forbid* young love?" A snort of amusement escaped Taalon's broken nose, sending a spray of blood down Vestara's ripped tunic. "My dear, there are some things even a High Lord cannot forbid. All I demand is that you *use* what you feel—just as you would use your anger or your pain. Can you do that?"

Vestara nodded, eager and relieved. "Of course."

"Good." Taalon continued to hold her by the jaw, bending down and moving in close. "You understand what we require?"

Vestara nodded. "I'm to learn the identity of the Jedi queen," she said. "The one you saw in the Pool of Knowledge."

"No!" Taalon squeezed her chin so hard that Vestara feared he intended to break her jaw after all. "You are to learn *everything* about her—not just her identity."

"Yyy-ee-sss." Vestara could barely squeeze out her reply. "I understand."

"I doubt that." Taalon continued to squeeze, the black emptiness of his gaze drawing Vestara in, making her feel dizzy and hollow inside, as though she were falling, tumbling down into the dark wells of his eyes. "This is an important assignment, Vestara—more important than slaying the Skywalkers, or discovering the truth of what became of Abeloth. It may be the most important assignment I have ever given *any* Sith."

"My lord, I'm honored," Vestara said, feeling truly flattered. "May I know *why*?"

Taalon glanced back toward the grotto. "Because I have *seen* it, my child." He finally released Vestara's chin, but she continued to feel trapped, lost in the abyssal darkness of his gaze. "Destiny has but one throne, and if a Jedi queen claims it, the Sith cannot."

A heaviness came to the jungle air, and the flattery of a moment earlier became a burden Vestara felt ill prepared to carry. She knew she was strong in the Force, but the

Skywalkers were mighty, and even Ben was a battle-tempered warrior whose experience went far beyond hers. The only advantages she could claim were her charm and her treachery, and she was not fool enough to believe they would make her the equal of Luke Skywalker *or* his son.

When Vestara's astonishment kept her silent longer than was proper, her father stepped in to cover. "So our goal must be to discover this queen's identity?" he asked. "And kill her before she can assume the throne?"

"Let us not limit ourselves, Saber Khai," Taalon said. "It may be that even the Jedi do not know their queen's identity yet. Perhaps she has not even been born."

"My lord Taalon," said Khai, "if the queen has not yet been born, how do we know there is anything for Vestara to learn? Or that the Jedi know any more than we do?"

"Because of *when* they attacked," Vestara said, recalling how quickly the fight had erupted after High Lord Taalon saw the image of the Jedi on the throne. "Ben tried to get me to pretend we hadn't found the grotto. Then, once we were inside, his father attacked the instant High Lord Taalon saw their queen."

"Precisely." Taalon stepped away and turned to peer into the fungus jungle. "The Jedi know something about this queen . . . and I know Vestara. She *will* discover what that is."

Chapter Fourteen

WHIRLING THROUGH THE JUNGLE WAS A BLIZZARD OF bird-moths. They were as bright as jewels, saballine blue and rardo red and coratyl yellow, and they were squeaking and chirping like a thousand tiny astromechs during an ion barrage. Some were as small as a human fingernail, but a few were the size of a Bith's head, and nothing was trying to eat any of them. The stalks of the club mosses had grown knobby with tree turtles, and the ferns sagged with the weight of dangling wing-snakes. Most disconcerting of all, the ground tremors had stopped and the volcano had ceased rumbling.

It was, as the saying went, all too calm. And as Luke reached the jungle's edge, where a sandy bank descended to the beach, he saw why.

Dozens of huge drendek lizards were wheeling over the river, their great wings blotting out the blue sun. Closer to shore, a colony of long-legged reptiles that looked like a cross between eopies and emaciated nerfs stood ankle-deep in the crimson water, drinking in peace while a carpet of golden smotherpads floated nearby. Thirty meters from the shore, the Sith's *Emiax* sat squatting on its S-shaped landing struts, its drooping wingtips hanging down so far they almost touched the azure sand.

"Hey!" Ben said, stopping at the jungle's edge beside Luke. "The *Shadow*'s gone!"

"Very observant, Jedi Skywalker," Luke said. "But if you expect to impress me, tell me who took her."

"Too easy, old man." Ben looked high into the sky, suggesting that he had come to the same conclusion Luke had—that Abeloth had stolen the ship and escaped the planet. "I suppose this makes me a Master?"

"Not quite." Luke glanced over, quietly checking to make sure Ben's wound had not come unglued—and that he was holding up okay after their long run from the Pool of Knowledge. "To make Master, you'd have to bring her back."

"The ship? Or just Ab—?"

Ben's question was cut short by a muffled crackle of Force-lightning coming from deep in the jungle behind them. They dropped over the sandy bank and whirled around to peer back through the foliage. Even drawing on the Force to sharpen his vision, Luke could see only twenty meters or so through the bird-moth blizzard and tangled curtain of fronds. He extended his Force awareness in the direction from which the sound had come and sensed only the planet's primordial miasma of life, voracious and alien and tinged with darkness. Fortunately, both Skywalkers were already hiding in the Force, so it seemed unlikely the Sith could sense their location any better than he could theirs. But with Ben injured, the *Shadow* gone, and Abeloth on the loose, that was not much comfort.

"Sith," Ben whispered. "Probably chasing Vestara."

"Or wanting us to *think* they are," Luke replied. He pulled a thermal detonator off his equipment harness and started back up the bank. "Go prep the *Emiax.*"

Ben grabbed his elbow. "Dad . . . no."

Luke looked back, saw the concern in his son's eyes, and sighed. "You're worried about the girl?"

"I *saw* Taalon hit her during the fight," Ben said. "They might believe her interference was on purpose."

"If they believed that, she'd be dead already," Luke replied. "Ben, I know you like bringing pretty girls to the light side, but Vestara isn't like Tahiri. She was *raised* Sith."

"Dad, that Force lightning was meant for someone, and it wasn't us," Ben replied. "It *has* to be Vestara."

"No argument there. They're trying to set her up to infiltrate."

"They already *did* that," Ben replied. "How many times do you think they're going to use the same old trick?"

"Until we quit falling for it."

Ben winced, but seemed to recognize the truth of what Luke was saying and nodded. "Okay, maybe it *is* the same trick," he admitted. "But it doesn't matter. Vestara is still a Sith, she still knows where Kesh is, and *that* makes her the best intelligence we have on the enemy. Can we really afford to give that up?"

Luke dropped his chin in surrender. "I suppose not," he admitted. "But I'm *not* taking a chance with that girl. Any false moves and—"

"I know: blast her." Ben nodded. "I just think she deserves a chance."

"A *last* chance." Luke returned the detonator to his equipment harness, then pointed his son toward *Emiax* again. "You're going to have to bypass hatch security, so try to enter from the far side of the ship. It may buy you a couple of extra minutes if the Sith arrive before you're in."

"Will do," Ben said, smiling. "That's what I admire about you, Dad."

"Always thinking?"

Ben shook his head. "So much confidence in your son." He started down the bank in leaps in bounds. "How long do you think it'll take me to pop a hatch lock older than you are?"

Luke would have made a retort about older locks being better engineered, but his audience was already at the bottom of the bank. He returned the detonator to his equipment harness, watching as his son rushed across the beach toward the *Emiax*. The young Jedi's robes were ripped open, revealing an entire flank and hip stained brown with dried blood, and a puckered line showed where the wound had been closed with first-aid glue. The reminder of how close Ben had come to being killed made Luke ache with fear, but it also filled him with tremendous pride to see his son handling the injury with such humor and grace. And—though he remained convinced that forbearance was wasted on Vestara or *any* of the Lost Tribe Sith—Luke could not help admiring the young man's compassion and determination to give others a second chance, or even a third.

Luke pulled his blaster, then crawled up over the bank and took a hiding place in the undergrowth. The jungle remained still, and for several minutes he lay smelling the musty soil, half expecting his ankle to cramp beneath the crushing pain of a constrictor vine, or his throat to fill with the venomous blossom of a fangthorn. But nothing attacked, and he was smart enough to understand just how frightening that was. Abeloth had *played* them, Jedi and Sith alike.

How far back her plan extended, Luke could not say. Perhaps escape had been her intention even during the war against the Yuuzhan Vong, when she had reached out to Ben and the other younglings at Shelter. Or perhaps she had fled her planet only in desperation, to escape those who had come to enslave or destroy her. The only thing Luke knew for certain was that her "death" had been a ruse—and that now she was aboard the *Jade Shadow,* flying out into the galaxy, alone and free.

Luke began to worry that the Sith might be approaching from a less obvious direction—then, finally, he saw a curtain of fronds shudder. Vestara appeared an instant later, running swiftly and in Force-enhanced silence. The arm beneath her injured shoulder was once again hanging limp, and her face was swollen, bloody, and mottled with bruises.

Luke felt a pang of pity for her. Whether inflicted in anger or as part of a stratagem, the beating she had taken had clearly been real. Of course, he found it suspicious that none of her traumas was disabling or disfiguring—but then again, he might have dismissed even severe injuries as little more than a ploy to win Ben's sympathy.

Vestara raced past his hiding place and stopped at the jungle's edge, her shoulders sagging as she peered down on the river beach. Luke could not test her Force aura without running the risk that she would sense his presence, but the way she braced her hands on her hips and kicked at the ground suggested she was more angry at the *Shadow*'s absence than frightened by it. Still, she was hardly the kind to panic, and her apparent calmness did not *necessarily* mean her flight had been a ruse.

But when Vestara uttered what he assumed was a Keshiri curse and remained on the edge of the bank, awaiting her pursuers, Luke knew her life had never been in danger. The beating had been a ploy designed to play on his son's affections, and it made Luke's stomach churn to know how hurt Ben would be when he learned how callously the girl was trying to manipulate him. Sadly, that was not a wound Luke dared help his son avoid. Ben would understand beguilement only after he had been exploited by it; he would accept the weakness of the human heart only after his own heart had betrayed him. Before he could be the truly great Jedi he was destined to become, Ben needed to learn these lessons in his gut as much as in his mind. It tore Luke up, but as a father all he could do was watch and be there to catch Ben when he fell.

Vestara had been standing at the jungle's edge for only a moment when the muffled thud of running boots sounded in the foliage behind her. She turned and, as High Lord Taalon emerged from the fronds, she began to speak in Keshiri. To Luke's astonishment, Taalon replied with a fork of Force-lightning that caught Vestara square in the chest and sent her tumbling over the sandy bank and out of sight.

Luke waited until Taalon had stepped more clearly into view, with the half-hidden form of Gavar Khai moving through the jungle behind him, then disengaged his blaster's safety. The two Sith must have sensed their danger, for by the time Luke had depressed the trigger and sent a flurry of bolts screaming toward them, both were already diving for cover. On the way down, Taalon took a bolt under the collarbone and a second along his neck, but Khai simply vanished into the undergrowth.

Continuing to lay suppression fire with one hand, Luke pulled the detonator off his equipment harness and set a three-second arming delay, then switched the fuse to MOTION and tossed it onto the ground about a meter in front of him. He backed away still firing, and by the time the two Sith began to return fire, he was already leaving the jungle. He reached out to Ben in the Force, felt only impatient alarm in response, and realized that his son was having trouble overriding the *Emiax*'s hatch security. Luke sprayed a dozen more bolts back into the jungle, then stopped firing and hazarded a glance down toward the shuttle.

Ben was standing on the near side of the craft, his lock slicer pressed to the hull just above the hatch controls. He was frantically punching keys and watching the slicer's screen, searching for some clue to the security scheme. Halfway down the embankment, Vestara was just beginning to recover from the effects of the Force lightning, her body still trembling and jerking as she struggled to her knees. A thin wisp of smoke was rising from her torso, where the heat of the attack had burned a hole in her robes.

Luke returned his attention to the jungle, and a few moments later a frond shuddered. He sent a flurry of bolts flying toward the movement, fell quiet for a few seconds, then opened fire at a shadow that might—or might not—

have been a figure lying in the undergrowth. He was rewarded with a loud Keshiri curse, and the shadow rolled out of view.

Deciding the Sith would now grow cautious and approach more slowly, Luke retreated a couple of meters down the bank, then bounded to Vestara's side. Her face was battered, a trio of lightning burns showed through a hole in her robes, and the odor of charred cloth filled the air around her. She certainly *appeared* to be someone in dire need of Jedi protection.

Luke wasn't fooled, of course . . . but he *did* feel sorry for her. He pulled her to her feet and started across the beach toward the *Emiax,* where Ben had grown so frustrated that he had stuffed the lock slicer back into his equipment belt and was now examining the hatch seam with his lightsaber in hand.

"Abeloth stole the *Shadow,*" Luke explained, dragging the still-shaky Vestara along by an elbow. "So you're going to help us borrow the *Emiax.*"

"I . . . I'm not sure I *can,*" Vestara said. "High Lord Taalon is the only one who knows—"

The thunderous crackle of a thermal detonator sounded from atop the sandy bank. They glanced back in time to see a ten-meter sphere of jungle vanishing in a crackling ball of white. Once the dazzle had faded from Luke's eyes—revealing only a glassy, rimless crater where an instant before there had been towering tree ferns and club mosses—he looked back to Vestara.

"What do you think?" he asked. "Did that trap get Taalon and your father?"

Vestara raised her chin. "Would it have gotten *you?*"

"Not even close." Luke smiled and started across the beach again, this time dragging her along at a run. "Which leaves you with a choice—help us with the *Emiax,* or stay behind and explain to High Lord Taalon why you failed at your assignment."

"*Assignment?*" Vestara echoed. Like any good spy, she was playing innocent until the last. "I don't know what you're talking about."

"I *saw* your reaction when you realized the *Shadow* was gone." Luke reached down and plucked the lightsaber off her belt. "And if it's going to come to another fight, I'd be a fool to let it start with uneven odds."

Always a quick thinker, Vestara needed only two steps to make up her mind. She turned toward the *Emiax,* where Ben had ignited his lightsaber and was just preparing to plunge the blade into the hatch seam.

"Put that lightsaber away, you nerf-brain!" She pulled free of Luke and sprang across the last ten paces to the shuttle. "All you need is the Force."

"It has an internal latch?" Ben asked, brow rising. "Like the *Shadow*?"

Vestara rolled her eyes. "Nothing that complicated, Ben." She shifted her gaze to the control panel, and the hatch seal broke with a soft hiss. "You just needed to disengage the cabin lockouts."

As the boarding ramp dropped into place, Ben's face reddened. "That was next on my list."

"Sure it was."

Vestara grabbed Ben's hand and started up the ramp with him. In the same instant a prickle of danger sense raced down Luke's spine, and he turned to see Taalon and Khai standing in the crater left by the thermal detonator. He opened fire immediately, forcing them to drop for cover, and retreated toward the boarding ramp.

Luke had not even reached the bottom when he felt himself being lifted with the Force and carried aboard the *Emiax*.

"You Jedi," Vestara said. Luke dropped to the deck at her feet, then watched as the ramp-toggle rocked into the RAISED position. "Don't you use the Force for *anything*?"

Chapter Fifteen

WITH THE SLAVE REVOLTS ON KLATOOINE AND BLAUDU Sextus now claiming as much attention as the Pellaeon murder trial, the crowd in the Ninth Hall of Justice spectator area had gone from standing-room-only to barely packed. Tahiri couldn't say whether that was a good development for her or bad, but she *did* know that it had brightened her counselor's mood. In contrast with his careworn appearance of the past few days, this morning his eyes were bright and his fur glistening. As he strode to the defense table, his posture was confident, his bearing energetic, his expression almost smug. Considering how Sul Dekkon had been dominating the courtroom so far, something had clearly changed. Tahiri just hoped it wasn't her counselor's grasp of reality.

As the Bothan placed his antique briefcase on the table, she reached up and fingered the lapel of his tailored suit jacket. The white fabric was an exorbitantly expensive wool made from tauntaun undercoat. The jacket completed a double-vested white suit that had been out of date a decade before Tahiri was born. Still, it worked for the old boy in a way that the formal robes and tabards he had been wearing until now had not.

"You're looking quite dapper today," Tahiri said. "You must have slept better."

Eramuth smirked down at her. "My dear, I haven't been sleeping *badly*." He looked over her head and smiled at

Sul Dekkon, his long upper lip rising just enough to give the gesture a predatory edge. "But opposing counsel is about to have some sleepless nights, I promise you."

"That's good to hear," Tahiri said, trying to put some hint of faith in her voice. "Because, to tell you the truth, I've been getting a little worried."

"No need, I assure you." Eramuth's gaze lingered on his opponent for a time, then finally shifted toward the aisle in the spectator section. "I'm doing fine."

"Actually, it's not *you* I've been worrying about."

"Is that so?" Eramuth's voice grew distracted as the Solos arrived with Lando Calrissian and an attractive Lorrdian woman who had long braids of amber hair falling over her shoulders, both front and back. "Look what we have here, my dear: the up-and-coming Sardonne Sardon." He sounded surprised.

Before Tahiri could object—or explain Sardonne's presence—Eramuth stepped away from the table and went to the bar, which separated the court proper from the spectator aisle. The identification surprised Tahiri. Not only was Sardonne two generations younger than Eramuth, she had never met him in court and was—as Lando had put it—"a well-kept secret" whose competence had not yet drawn the attention it deserved.

Eramuth surprised the younger counselor by reaching across the bar and offering his hand to her. "What a pleasure to meet you, my dear. I've reviewed several of your cases. The Travaless speeder-theft acquittal was particularly brilliant."

Sardonne's dark-lashed eyes widened in surprise. "You reviewed the *Travaless* case?" she asked. As Tahiri had requested, her formal robes remained concealed beneath a full-length overcoat. "Even *I* barely recall that."

"Never forget *that* one, my dear," Eramuth replied. "Arguing that the defendant's delusions justified bypassing the security system was inspired. But actually *proving* that she had, in her own mind, *purchased* the vehicle was pure genius."

Sardonne's smile stretched nearly from ear to ear. "Thank you, Counselor. Coming from you, that means a great deal to me."

"It's well deserved, my dear . . . *very* well deserved." Eramuth released her hand and glanced over at the crowded row of seats behind the defense table. "But I wish you had let me know you would be observing today. I'm afraid I reserved only three seats."

Sardonne's smile did not waver. "Thank you, but I'll be fine."

Her gaze flickered toward the defense table so briefly that even Tahiri almost missed it—but Eramuth did not. His ears pricked forward, and he slowly turned to face Tahiri.

"We discussed this," he said. "I don't want a second chair."

"That may be so," Leia said, stepping to the bar. "But isn't what *Tahiri* wants the determining factor here?"

Eramuth's eyes narrowed, but the expression on his face was more disappointed than angry. He continued to stare at Leia for a moment, then finally whirled on his heel and faced Tahiri.

"Well?" he demanded. "*Is* this what you want?"

The general din was fading as spectators began to notice the tensions at the defense table. A pair of camdroids appeared from the crowd and began to float forward. Tahiri caught Leia's eye and shot a glance toward the camdroids, then turned to Eramuth.

"I've told you several times that we need help."

Tahiri spoke quietly, forcing Eramuth to come closer, but did not say more until she saw Leia flick a finger and send both camdroids tumbling toward the rear wall. Strictly speaking, it was illegal to use the Force inside the Hall of Justice—but it was just as illegal to bring a cam-droid inside a courtroom, so it seemed doubtful that Leia would be ejected.

Once the camdroids had been smashed against the wall, and Eramuth had taken a seat beside her, Tahiri continued in a whisper, "You've been dozing off in court, Eramuth, and every time I try to talk about bringing in help, you insist you don't need it and have me taken back to my cell."

"Because I don't *need* a second chair." Eramuth shot a disapproving glance in Sardonne's direction. "Especially someone who looks like *her.*"

"You just said she was brilliant!"

"She is," Eramuth admitted. "But you don't need brilliant. You need me."

"I need *both,*" Tahiri insisted. "And since *I'm* the one on trial for her life, I'm going to insist."

Eramuth snorted and stared at the table. "My dear, I *do* have a plan."

"Falling asleep is part of your plan?" Tahiri countered. "In *court*?"

"I know it's hard to believe—"

"*Eramuth,*" she interrupted. "I was a *Jedi.* How gullible do you think I am?"

"Not very, apparently." Without looking up, Eramuth asked, "You're certain of your decision?"

Tahiri glanced back at the Solos and Lando, who were just shuffling into their reserved seats, past a dozen reporters who had spent half the night waiting in line to be certain they would have front-row seats. When all three gave her encouraging nods, she let out her breath and nodded.

"I'm sorry to have to do it this way, Eramuth," she said. "But you didn't leave me any choice."

"Well, it *was* a conversation I was trying to avoid," Eramuth admitted. Unexpectedly, he laid a furry hand across hers, and Tahiri was surprised by the deep pain she saw in his eyes. "But no need to worry. I've had my feelings hurt by attractive young women before."

"Eramuth, I just think this trial has been wearing you out," she said. "And I need you at your best."

"I understand, my dear," Eramuth said, rising. "As you say, it *is* your life on the line."

He stepped over to a bailiff and asked for another chair, then went to the bar and personally opened the gate to admit Sardonne. She quickly entered, removed her overcoat, and passed it to the Solos—then spent the next couple of minutes awkwardly waiting for her chair. Despite the fact that all eyes were on her, she managed to look confident and unconcerned with the attention. But Tahiri knew better, for Sardonne's Force aura was ablaze with her excitement—and why not? Win or lose, the trial of Gilad Pellaeon's murderer would make her a household name.

The extra chair had barely arrived before Judge Zudan entered and activated a high, piercing bell tone to call the session to order. With her topknot pulled even higher than usual, her reptilian features looked even harsher, and her gaze immediately turned to Sardonne Sardon's seat at the end of the defense table.

"I see we have a new face at the defense table today," Zudan said. "Please declare yourself for the court."

"Of course, Your Honor." Sardonne rose. "Sardonne Sardon, with the defense."

"Thank you." Zudan turned to Eramuth. "I'm glad to see that you reconsidered my suggestion to take an assistant, Counselor."

Eramuth rose. "Actually, Your Honor, Counselor Sardon *isn't* my assistant," he said. "She'll be taking the defense as of today. I'll be withdrawing."

Tahiri probably shouldn't have been surprised—she had, after all, seen the hurt in Eramuth's eyes when she insisted that he take on a second chair—but she was.

Withdrawing on such short notice seemed unprofessional, to say the least, and she had expected better from Eramuth.

Apparently, so had everyone else in the courtroom. The chamber burst into an astonished din that did not fade until Judge Zudan stabbed her finger down on the bell button atop her bench and held it there. When the room finally fell silent again, she glared out into the spectator area and issued a stern warning about not interfering with the business of her court, then looked back to Eramuth.

"And what is your reason for *asking* to withdraw, Counsel?"

Eramuth struggled to his feet, looking even older and shakier than he had been over the past few days. "I'm sure the court is aware of the assassination attempt on my nephew, Admiral Nek Bwua'tu."

Zudan nodded. "Of course—as is the entire civilized galaxy."

"Thank you, Your Honor." Eramuth inclined his head as though accepting condolences she had not issued, then continued, "As long as he remains in a coma, I'm afraid my presence is required at his bedside to such a degree that—"

"Excuse me, Counselor," Zudan said, raising a hand to silence him. "But hasn't your nephew been in a coma for nearly three weeks now?"

"He has."

"And you have only now decided that it's interfering with your ability to provide an adequate defense?"

Eramuth shrugged. "It has only recently become apparent, Your Honor."

"I see." Zudan's narrowed eyes suggested that what she *saw* was the lie Eramuth was telling her. She turned to Sardonne. "And you, Counselor Sardon? Are you prepared to take the defense?"

Sardonne rose, her carefully controlled Lorrdian face betraying no sign of the surprise and anxiety that Tahiri knew she had to be feeling right now.

"Not at this time, Your Honor," she said. "But if I can ask for a recess of three or four days to prepare—"

"You can *ask,*" Zudan interrupted. Her gaze shifted to Eramuth. "Counselor Bwua'tu, your request to withdraw is denied."

Eramuth's ears flattened in anger. "But, Your Honor, my nephew—"

"I have made my ruling, Counselor." Zudan ordered the bailiff to bring in the jury, then leaned over her bench to glare down at the defense table. "I don't know what you people are trying to pull here, but rest assured that you *won't* be pulling it in my court. Is that clear?"

Sardonne was the first to answer. "Yes, Your Honor."

"Counselor Bwua'tu?" Zudan demanded.

"Your Honor, I assure you—"

"I'll take that as a yes, Counselor." Zudan turned her gaze on Tahiri. "And the defendant?"

"Yes, Your Honor." Tahiri sank down in her chair, contemplating what she already knew was going to be another bad day in court. "I understand completely."

Chapter Sixteen

TODAY THE BIG CIRCLE OF FUN LOOKED MORE LIKE A stockyard than a dirt field used to hold footraces and shoving contests. Several thousand shaggy Octusi were gathered in the primitive arena, singing and stomping and working themselves up for another parade through downtown Arari. Madhi Vaandt found it impossible to tell who was in charge, for there seemed to be dozens of elders making speeches, issuing instructions, and supervising the repair and replacement of the placards that the Mandalorians had shot up during the last march.

Nearly fifty Octusi, all proudly displaying the burn holes where they had been hit by blasterfire, were positioning themselves at the near end of the circle, almost directly in front of the droid-repair shop where Madhi and her crew were hiding. From her vantage point, in a darkened second-floor storeroom, it appeared the demonstration would be the largest yet, with the violence suffered during the last march only hardening the resolve of the slaves.

Madhi glanced toward the adjacent window, where her cam operator was crouching on the floor, attaching a small right-angle surveillance lens to his cam. A slender human male with graying blond hair and a weatherworn face, Tyl Krain had taken Madhi under his wing early in her still-blossoming career, teaching her not only the *hows* of getting the story but also the ethics of pursuing it, and her duty to present a fair and balanced report. In short, Tyl had helped shape a young, ambitious Devaronian female into a journalist whom even the legendary Perre Needmo felt comfortable airing—and Madhi loved him like a father for it.

Well, maybe not *exactly* like a father. He *was* a fairly handsome human, after all.

Tyl finished attaching the surveillance lens, then quickly adjusted the focal length and activated the display. Almost instantly his steely eyes grew wide, and he began to record.

"You spot the Jedi already?" Madhi asked.

Their mysterious contact in Freedom Flight had warned them that two young Jedi Knights, Sothais Saar and Avinoam Arelis, were on their way to Blaudu Sextus to prevent the Octusi from being slaughtered. It seemed doubtful that they could have made planetfall on Blaudu Sextus so quickly—the journey required a lot of staging stops and hyperspace jumps. But Jedi were capable of amazing feats, and the Freedom Flight contact *had* promised they were in for a surprise.

When her cam operator did not answer after a moment, Madhi asked, "Tyl?"

"*Not Jedi,*" Tyl whispered. With a wall of fifteen-centimeter stone separating them from a field full of bleating Octusi voices, there was little chance of being overheard, so it seemed obvious that something was very wrong. Without looking away from the hand-sized screen, he spoke to the Chev assistant standing at the back of the storeroom. "Shohta, get the power generator up and get us a HoloNet link. Perre will want this live."

Madhi immediately glanced back, looking down a narrow aisle flanked by shelves piled with droid parts, and nodded to the heavy-browed Chev waiting next to the door. A former slave whom Madhi had won in a drinking contest on Vinsoth, Shohta Laar had not yet adjusted to his freedom, and he still had a habit of awaiting Madhi's permission before he followed instructions from anyone else. Once the Chev had begun to assemble the equipment, Madhi returned to her window and peered out—then gasped aloud. Hovering in the alley mouths surrounding Big Circle were dozens of QuickStryke assault sleds, the barrels of their laser cannons depressed for close-in ground support. A partially exposed Mandalorian sat atop each vehicle, using a swivel-mounted auto blaster to cover a squad of debarking commandos.

The Octusi were casting a few wary glances toward the assault sleds, but continuing to organize and repair placards. Madhi knew from her time on the planet that the semi-sentient Octusi probably did not understand what the arrival of the Mandalorians meant. They were a gentle, rule-abiding species that could not conceive of others being otherwise. And since a peaceful assembly in their own Big Circle of Fun did not violate the rules established by their Blaudun masters, it simply had not occurred to them that the Mandalorians might intend them harm.

Madhi, on the other hand, had a very good idea of what was about to happen, and in her heart she ached to rush out and explain the danger to the Octusi. She wanted to urge them to flee, or at least to turn on their oppressors and go down fighting. And part of her wanted to take Tyl up on the roof, to reveal their presence so the Mandalorians would know the entire galaxy was watching as they did whatever they had come to do.

Instead Madhi called, "Shohta, how long? I want to be live on the 'Net when this thing blows."

"*Blows*, mistress?" Shohta asked. "You think there is going to be a riot?"

"A riot or a massacre," she said. "Maybe both."

The back of the room fell quiet as Shohta stopped work. When Madhi heard no indication of it resuming, she glanced back down the aisle. The Chev was standing idle and slump-shouldered, holding a power feed in one hand and a coupling socket in the other, his brutish Chev features sagging with dismay.

"Shohta!" she snapped. "We need to go live *now.*"

Shohta merely cocked his head. "So we can show a massacre live on the HoloNet?" he asked. "Shouldn't we do something instead?"

"We *are* doing something, Shohta," Madhi retorted. "Our *jobs.* And if you want to keep *yours,* get me that HoloNet link."

Shohta knelt down and connected the power feed to the generating unit, but his movements were slow and languid, a silent form of protest that Madhi had learned to recognize among slaves and the grievously oppressed. She let out a long breath and, starting to feel like a despot herself, spoke in a gentler tone.

"Look, Shohta," she said. "We're journalists, not Jedi. We don't involve ourselves in the story."

"Not even to save lives?" Shohta asked.

It was Tyl who answered, in a voice devoid of sympathy. "Not even to save lives." His gaze remained fixed on the cam display. "If we involve ourselves with the story, we *change* the story."

"And what is wrong with changing it?" Shohta demanded. "What is wrong with saving the lives of innocent beings?"

"What's wrong is that if we try to interfere, the most likely thing to happen is that we get killed *first.*" Tyl's voice had grown hard. "And then the galaxy will never know what happened here."

"We're not police and we're not medicos," Madhi added. "We're journalists, and our first duty is to report the facts."

"As you wish, mistress." Shohta depressed the power unit's activation safety and held it down, then slowly ran his gaze over the small control panel, searching for the priming switch that he had probably flicked a thousand times since joining Madhi's crew. "After the power unit is running, I'll have to find a good place for the antenna. We should have a link in ten minutes or so."

"Ten *minutes*?" Tyl tore his eyes away from his display and started to set his vidcam aside. "That's ridiculous, Shohta. If I have to do this myself—"

"*Tyl,*" Madhi interrupted. "Stay on the cam. Shohta will handle the HoloNet link."

Tyl's brow rose, but he nodded and looked back to his cam.

Madhi turned to Shohta. "Shohta, I understand how you feel. So does Tyl. But it's the truth that matters in this job, not our feelings about it." She paused, waiting for a nod that did not come, then continued, "If we go out there to interfere and somehow survive the experience, then *we* become the story—not the Mandalorians and what they've come to do."

"But a lot of lives might be saved," Shohta said.

Madhi shook her head. "*Those* lives might be saved," she said. "But more would be lost in the long run. We can't be there every time an army of thugs uses violence to put down a slave revolt."

"This way, the galaxy sees what's really happening," Tyl said, his gaze still fixed on the cam display. "Maybe the public won't care about a bunch of four-hooves on a world so far off the hyperspace lanes that the Empire never bothered to give it a survey number. But my guess is, when they see Mandalorians blasting Octusi in cold blood, they'll want it stopped."

"And not just on Blaudu Sextus," Madhi added. "On Tatooine, Karfeddion, Thalassia . . . and on Vinsoth, too.

If we keep doing our jobs and exposing the truth about slavery, maybe the public will demand that the Galactic Alliance stop turning a blind eye. Maybe it will start asking questions about who's been sending Mandalorians to put down the revolts." Madhi paused, allowing herself a smile of anticipation. "And when we tell them, they're going to want her head."

"Assuming we can *confirm* what we know," Tyl reminded her.

"We'll get there," Madhi assured him. "We'll connect her to the credit trail, or the Sextuna executives will get tired of taking the blame and admit she's the one who's really paying the Mandalorians. Something will turn up. It *has* to."

"By *her*, you mean Daala?" Shohta asked. "She has been helping the slavers?"

"We're pretty sure," Madhi said. "But we don't have the evidence to prove it yet."

Tyl looked from the cam display toward Shohta. "What you need to decide is whether you want to stop her," he said. "Whether you want to help *all* slaves, or just the ones you see out there."

Madhi saw the resentment in Shohta's eyes change to understanding, then to determination, and his fingers quickly found the priming switch he had seemed unable to locate just moments before. The generator gave a soft *clickclack*, then hummed to life. Shohta grabbed the antenna assembly and began to point it around the room, his eyes fixed on the interface screen as he tried to find the strongest signal.

"Link in two minutes," he reported. "I'm sorry for the delay."

"Don't waste time apologizing," Madhi ordered. She slipped her sound bud into her ear and activated the button mike on her tunic collar. "Just get me on the 'Net."

Madhi returned her attention to Big Circle and saw that the Mandalorians already had the field surrounded. Finally beginning to sense that something was wrong, the Octusi had stopped their preparations and were looking toward the main entry arch, located just a hundred meters or so from where the wounded veterans of the last demonstration were lining up. She stepped to one side of the window and leaned against the wall, straining to see what had caught the Octusi's attention.

Floating down the narrow lane directly in front of the repair shop she saw a QuickStryke urban assault car. Protruding from the commander's hatch were the head and shoulders of a helmetless Mandalorian male with blond, short-cropped hair and cold blue eyes. He had a long scar down one cheek and a flat, crooked nose that had obviously been broken several times—both signs, to Madhi's way of thinking, that he probably wasn't one of Mandalore's better hand-to-hand fighters. He held his chin a little too high, peering down on the Octusi as though he were a butcher selecting stock for his slaughterhouse.

"That commander looks familiar," Madhi said. As she spoke, an image came to her, a HoloNet report she had seen of the siege of the Jedi Temple. She pulled her datapad from her pocket and activated the search function. "Isn't he the one who blasted that apprentice on the steps of the Jedi Temple?"

"Sure looks like him," Tyl replied. "Rhal, I think. Something Rhal."

Madhi entered the name and moments later was rewarded with a news capsule of the incident. The apprentice, Kani Asari, had been Kenth Hamner's personal assistant, and the killer had been a Mandalorian commander placed in charge of the siege by Chief Daala herself. Madhi compared the killer's image with the commander outside, and her heart began to pound in excitement.

"Tyl, this is it," she said. "Belok Rhal was the Mandalorian *commander* at the siege of the Jedi Temple."

"So?" Tyl asked.

"So, Daala gave him complete authority at the Temple siege, and he killed an unarmed apprentice in full view of the media," Madhi said. "And now here he is, putting down a slave revolt on Blaudu Sextus."

"That's a coincidence, not proof," Tyl said. "It doesn't establish a connection to Daala."

"No," Madhi said. "But it *is* a fact—and we *do* report facts, don't we?"

Tyl thought for a moment, then reluctantly nodded. "Just be careful with your phrasing, okay?"

"No worries, I won't imply anything," Madhi said. Outside her window, the QuickStryke had come to a stop directly in front of the wounded Octusi, and Rhal gazed out over the Octusi, probably looking for a leader. "Shohta, how are we coming with the link?"

"We're connected to the relay satellite," he reported. "But I'm trying to buy more bandwidth. Their equipment is old out here, so we're only getting grade-three signal."

Madhi glanced over at Tyl. At grade three and standard bandwidth, her voice would be distorted and the vidimages grainy and jerky. But both would be recognizable—and the primitive quality of the broadcast might give the report an added note of urgency.

"Let's do it," she said.

Tyl nodded. "Keep the offer open," he said to Shohta. "And bring the parabolic mike to Madhi. We'll want an enhanced voice signal on Rhal."

As Tyl spoke, he raised one hand and began a silent five-finger countdown. Madhi made a quick mental list of the points she needed to cover in her introduction, keeping in mind that her feed was arriving at the Perre Needmo studio at the beginning of their workday, about six hours before they were scheduled to go on-air. By now, a vidimage of the situation in Big Circle was already streaming onto the control room, where a startled production assistant would be rushing to bring it up on a monitor and confirm that the automatic recording equipment was capturing the transmission. Next, he would feed the transmission into the studio's internal network and bring it to the attention of Perre Needmo and the senior production staff, who would decide whether to relay the report to the network immediately or save it for their own broadcast. Given the likelihood of the situation erupting into mass violence, Madhi was betting they would pass it into the network immediately—which meant her report would need to mention the *Perre Needmo Newshour* prominently and often, if she wanted to keep her employers happy.

Tyl's last finger folded down into his palm, and Madhi began to speak in a hushed, urgent voice. "This is Madhi Vaandt on assignment for the *Perre Needmo Newshour* on Blaudu Sextus in the Regulan system, an insignificant mining world on the galactic edge where the hands of power operate beyond the umbrella of Alliance law. The field below is Big Circle of Fun, an Octusi sporting arena in the capital city of Arari. As you can see, a mechanized company of Mandalorian infantry has surrounded a gathering of Octusi slaves preparing to begin a protest march through the downtown area. Although this will be the thirteenth such march in as many days, the Mandalorian company is a remarkable show of force. The Octusi are a pacifist species whose demonstrations have been marked by their gentleness and good order.

"It appears, however, that their Blaudun masters may

be growing weary of the inconveniences caused by the daily marches. Yesterday a group of Mandalorian mercenaries hired to put down the revolt opened fire on the front of the march, killing fifteen Octusi, wounding more than fifty, and causing a stampede that resulted in the first significant property damage of the revolt. Determined to avoid a repeat of the aggravation, today the Mandalorian mercenaries have trapped the Octusi in their staging area, surrounding them with light armor more suitable for urban combat than crowd control.

"Whatever the Mandalorian intentions, they seem determined to present an ominous front, as they have brought in a veteran commander with a reputation for ferocity."

Madhi glanced over at Tyl, waiting for the nod that would indicate the vidcam was now focused on Rhal, and saw Shohta approaching with a small parabolic mike that she could use to capture Rhal's words. Normally, journalistic ethics would prohibit eavesdropping on a subject without his knowledge, but since Rhal was in a public forum obviously preparing to make a public statement, an exception could be made. She nodded her thanks to Shohta and pointed it out the window at Rhal.

When Tyl nodded that he was ready, Madhi continued, "This is Commander Belok Rhal. No stranger to our news audience, he was in command of Mandalorian forces during the siege of the Jedi Temple on Coruscant. Chief of State Daala had personally charged him with persuading the Jedi to turn over Jedi Knights Sothais Saar and Turi Altamik, who were then suffering from the mysterious psychosis that had been plaguing Jedi Knights at that point. It remains unclear whether his authorization included a dispensation to commit murder, as only a handful of government officials know the full extent of his orders. But one thing is beyond debate: Belok Rhal is the man who killed a teenage girl named

Kani Asari on the steps of the Jedi Temple, in cold blood and in full view of the Coruscant media, just to make a point. And his presence here sends a chilling message."

Rhal's gaze finally settled on an Octusi Elder with a wrinkled face and gray fur, and he began to say something that Madhi could not quite make out from her hiding place.

"And I think we're about to hear exactly what that message is." She lowered her voice to a dramatic whisper. "Let's listen."

Madhi activated the parabolic mike, and a moment later Rhal's voice began to come through her earbud. It was just the way the feed would sound to listeners on Coruscant—a little fuzzy and distorted, but clear enough to convey the Mandalorian's words.

". . . been hired to put a stop to this illegal revolt, and we intend to do so." Rhal's voice grew menacing. "What is your name, slave?"

The Octusi stepped forward, until he was standing chest-to-armor with the QuickStryke. "I am Races-the-Water-Bringing-Wind of the Redolog family, Elder of the Quansasi Haulage Team. And what is your name, Mandalorian?"

"Not for you to know," Rhal replied. "You appear to be the leader of this mob. Is that so?"

Races-the-Water-Bringing-Wind inclined his head. "I am one of the Elders, yes." He laid a palm flat on the QuickStryke's nose armor. "And I am asking you to remove your carriages, Not-for-You-to-Know. They frighten our people."

"Then your people are wise." Rhal flicked something inside the command hatch, and his voice rang out across the circle. "Elders will come forward and present themselves."

A low murmur rolled through the crowd as dozens of elderly Octusi began to make their way forward. Races-the-Water-Bringing-Wind twisted his upper body around, turning his T-shaped head sideways so that he was looking up at Rhal with one eye and out over the crowd with the other.

"Why?" he asked.

"Because I ordered it," Rhal said. "As I told you, this revolt has come to—"

"No." Races-the-Water-Bringing-Wind boomed the word calmly, sharply, and loudly enough that it carried out over the circle and brought the migration of Elders to an instant stop. He turned back to Rhal and continued in his deep Octusi voice. "You are no one's master. You do not order us—"

The defiant words came to a shrieking halt as Rhal raised a blaster pistol from inside the commander's hatch and sent a single blue bolt burning through the Elder's head. Races-the-Water-Bringing-Wind's upper body folded back over his shaggy midsection, and then he collapsed onto his side, limp and dead before his body hit the dirt.

So shocked was Madhi that she forgot why they were here—until Tyl began to speak in a soft voice. "I'm going in for a close-up on the body." With a grade-three signal, his words would probably be audible only as background noise, but it hardly mattered. They had just captured a cold-blooded murder on vid, and their viewers would be too shocked to be wondering what the cam operator was saying. "You might want to do some personal reaction, then slip into conjecture about where this is all going to lead."

The suggestion brought Madhi back to her senses, and she slipped smoothly into a hushed narrative. "This is Madhi Vaandt for the *Perre Needmo Newshour*. What you have just seen is the cold-blooded murder of an Octusi Elder by the Mandalorian commander, Belok Rhal. The

Octusi crowd is obviously as shocked as we are, and there is no telling what will happen next."

Outside, Rhal leveled his blaster pistol at another Elder. Madhi deactivated her button mike long enough to whisper, "Tyl, get back on—"

"Got it," Tyl said, scraping his right-angle lens along the windowsill. "Stay live. The image might be fuzzy enough that you need to confirm what's happening."

Madhi clicked her button mike back on, but before she could resume, the parabolic mike began to pick up Rhal's voice again.

"You, slave, come forward."

The Octusi remained where he was and, in a loud booming voice, said, "No."

A blaster bolt screeched from Rhal's weapon, taking the Elder low in his forequarters. His huge mouth opened wide, and he let out a deep, thrumming howl of pain that was instantly echoed by all of the other Octusi in the circle.

"I don't know how well you can hear that over the HoloNet," Madhi narrated for her audience. "But the entire Octusi crowd has joined the wounded Elder in crying out. It's called the Song of Sorrow, and we witnessed the same thing yesterday . . ."

As Madhi spoke, a female voice began to sound in her earbud. "This is network control, letting you know that we're carrying this live on the news channel. We've just seen the murder, and we're estimating a five-second signal lag. Your vid is grainy, so keep telling us what we're seeing."

". . . when the Mandalorians opened fire in the streets of Arari," Madhi continued. Between the voice issuing instructions in her ear, the violence outside, and her own shock, her thoughts were racing and whirling through her mind like a beldon flying through a hurricane. But there was strange calm inside her, a recognition that this was what she had spent her life training to do . . . and that she was more than up to the task. "We are told that the Octusi use similar songs to communicate over great distances as they race over their native plains on Blaudu Octus."

Madhi fell silent as Rhal's speaker-enhanced voice cracked across the circle, splitting the Song of Sorrow like a thunderclap. "I won't ask you again, slave."

Rhal pointed his blaster at the injured Octusi.

The Elder folded his knees beneath him and dropped to the ground, then looked Rhal straight in the eye. "No."

"The courage of the Octusi is legendary in the Albanin sector," Madhi continued. "And yet, they are described as the gentlest of species. In their own culture, they engage in nothing more violent than the aptly named Shove-Dances, which young males perform during mating season."

Her last two words were drowned out by the shriek of a blaster bolt. A smoking hole appeared in the center of the second victim's chest, and the Elder collapsed forward onto the ground, his great, dark eyes still staring up at Rhal.

"We have just witnessed a second cold-blooded murder by the Mandalorian commander in charge of this company," Madhi reported. "It is difficult to understand the reasoning behind this excessive use of force. However, lawless actions are common out here on the galactic edge. Pirates plague the region, as do crime rings and bounty hunters. Perhaps Sextuna Mining Corporation feels justified in employing beings such as Belok Rhal to protect their fleets."

As Madhi spoke, a tremendous thrumming filled the circle, overwhelming the parabolic mike she was holding and filling her head with a painful boom that left her ears ringing. In the next instant the Octusi sprang into flight, rushing for the alleys and streets that the Mandalorians had blocked with their assault sleds. Rhal reached up to activate his throat mike, and Madhi barely managed to swing the dish back in time to capture what he was saying.

"Commence Operation—"

The last part of the command was lost to the ear-piercing wail of a blaster cannon barrage. The circle below erupted into a blinding meshwork of colored bolts and flashes, and the outer ring of Octusi fell almost as one.

"The Mandalorians have opened fire!" Madhi yelled, unconcerned about being heard above the roar and screech of so much blasterfire. "A massacre of unbelievable magnitude has begun before our very eyes here on Blaudu Sextus. And this reporter, on assignment for the *Perre Needmo Newshour,* must conclude that it was the Mandalorian commander's intention all along to provoke a stampede as justification for the cold-blooded atrocities that you are now witnessing. Hundreds of Octusi lie dead or dying already, and still the Mandalorians continue to fire . . ."

As Madhi spoke, the gunner's hatch on Rhal's QuickStryke flew open, and out popped the head of a female Mandalorian with short-cropped brown hair and a small, button-ended nose. She said something about being borked, then pointed up toward the window where Tyl's right-angle lens lay recording the massacre in the circle.

Rhal glanced up, and Madhi's parabolic mike captured his static-filled voice asking, *"Live?"*

The female nodded and said something that Madhi's parabolic mike *did* pick up: "You stupid idiot."

Rhal ignored her and grabbed the swivel-mounted heavy blaster in front of his hatch, then swung the barrel toward the droid-repair shop where Madhi and her crew were hiding.

Madhi dropped to take cover, but continued to report.

"It appears the Mandalorians have discovered our presence. They are not pleased to have their actions—"

A flurry of blaster bolts came shrieking through the window, filling the stockroom with the stone shards, smoke, and flying droid parts.

"—brought to light for you to see." The quaver that had come to Madhi's voice was unprofessional, she knew, but there was nothing she could do to disguise it. "We are under direct fire here, so please be patient while—"

The deafening crack of a cannon bolt shook the repair shop, spraying hand-sized stones across the room and filling the air with so much smoke that Madhi could no longer see Shohta waiting by the door. She glanced across at Tyl and found him holding a hand to his forehead. There was blood pouring down over his eye, and it was dripping onto the vidcam's display. But he was still squinting at the screen with his good eye, struggling to keep Rhal in the frame.

"—change locations," Madhi finished. She deactivated her collar mike, then tossed the parabolic mike out the window and scrambled across the floor to Tyl. "Will you forget about the shot for a minute? We've got to move! Now!"

Without waiting for a reply, she grabbed his arm and started to race toward the back of the room. Another cannon bolt struck the front of the storeroom, pelting them with fist-sized stones and dropping both of them to their knees. Tyl went limp. For a moment, Madhi thought he had been seriously injured.

Then she saw him toss the right-angle lens aside and reach for the wide-angle, and she knew he was fine.

Taking her lead from his example, Madhi activated her collar mike and began to narrate again. "My cam operator has quite a gash over one eye, so please forgive us if our images grow unclear. We remain under fire, and we are fleeing our observation post. Again, this is Madhi

Vaandt, bringing you events live from Blaudu Sextus for the *Perre Needmo Newshour*."

They reached the back of the room and found Shohta crouched over the uplink antenna and power generator.

"I don't know if you can see this, but my Chev assistant, the former slave Shohta, is attempting to shield our equipment with his own body." Madhi grabbed him by the arm and dragged him toward the door. "We'll keep transmitting until it's no longer possible, but I'm afraid we *will* be going off 'Net sometime soon."

The female voice began to sound in Madhi's earbud again. "This is great stuff—a Peamoney Award for sure," she said. "Keep it going as long as you can, and don't worry about medical expenses. The network has you covered."

"That's because there aren't going to *be* any medical expenses," Tyl grumbled. He braced the vidcam on one shoulder and grabbed the uplink antenna with his free hand, then nodded Shohta toward the generator unit and turned to Madhi. "Go!"

Madhi cracked the door open and peered into the hall, then sighed in relief. "No Mandos," she reported. "Let's go."

They stepped through the door and, still trailing a power feed and datalink to the abandoned equipment, scurried down the hallway to the stairwell.

"As you can see, we're attempting to relocate to a more secure position," Madhi reported. "We may have to abandon our generator and uplink antenna at any moment, so . . ."

Madhi reached the top of the stairwell and found herself staring down at Belok Rhal and a handful of armored Mandalorians. She stopped short.

"Tyl, you getting this?" she whispered.

"Wrong lens." He activated the vidcam floodlights,

filling the stairwell with illumination. "But we're sending pictures."

That was all Madhi needed to hear. She started down the stairwell toward the Mandalorians.

"Commander Rhal," she began, "the entire galaxy has just witnessed your company initiate an assault of incredible violence in the Big Circle of Fun. Would you care to explain these atrocities for the record?"

"No." Rhal pointed his blaster over Madhi's shoulder, no doubt in the direction of the vidcam. "Turn the cam off."

Madhi's knees began to shake, and she grew very afraid that she was going to lose control of her bladder on the intergalactic news.

"That's not going to happen, Commander Rhal," she said.

"No?" Rhal shifted the blaster barrel toward her chest, and Madhi knew she was about to die. "I beg to differ."

As Rhal spoke, two tiny circles of brightness appeared in the stone wall behind him. Madhi could not imagine what they were—but she felt sure it was nothing she wanted to point out to the Mandalorians. She began to descend the stairs, one hand turning the button mike on her lapel toward Rhal.

"The galaxy is watching, Commander. Would you care to comment on what you've done here today?" she asked. Behind Rhal, the bright circles turned into lightsaber tips, one green and one blue, and Madhi began to think she and her crew just might survive this assignment. "Are you truly in the employ of Sextuna Mining Corporation? Or do your orders come from somewhere else—somewhere closer to the Core?"

This last question, she knew, was pushing the boundaries of journalistic ethics. But considering that the man was pointing a blaster at her chest, she was going to allow herself some leeway.

"Is it possible, Commander Rhal, that your true employer is Chief of State Daala?"

Madhi saw Rhal's eyes narrow, and she knew that she had pushed things farther than was safe. The lightsaber tips at the bottom of the stairwell became lightsaber blades and began to cut through the thick stone as though it were flimsiplast, and Rhal's companions spun around, preparing to open fire on the two Jedi that the Freedom Flight agent had promised were on the way.

Rhal merely pulled the trigger of his blaster pistol . . . twice.

The bolts caught Madhi in the torso, knocking her back onto the stairs with a chestful of fire. She heard someone screaming and saw Shohta flying down the stairs toward her, his brutish Chev features twisted into a mask of grief, his big fists flailing in anger.

Meanwhile, Rhal's escorts began to pour fire toward the bottom of the stairs. Their efforts were, of course, useless. No sooner had they opened fire than the Jedi used the Force to send the lightsaber-weakened wall flying inward, knocking the Mandalorians over backward. In the next instant, a pair of young Jedi Knights, one a furious-looking Chev and the other a handsome young human, were standing at the bottom of the stairs, using the Force to slam the armored Mandalorians first against one wall, then against the another, denying them any chance to bring their weapons to bear . . . and making them suffer terribly for the attempt.

In the same instant, Shohta reached Madhi's side. Her vision was already starting to narrow and darken, but she saw her assistant tearing at her tunic, first exposing her wounds, then covering them with hands that her flesh was already too cold to feel.

Then Madhi saw Tyl descending the stairs, the vidcam

still on his shoulder and focused on the bottom of the stairwell. He stopped beside her and turned the lens on her face, tears pouring out down his cheeks. He knelt beside her but made no move to lower the vidcam and help her—and there wouldn't have been any sense in it. Madhi could feel what had happened to her, how much of her had been burned away by the Mandalorian's bolts, and she had been a journalist too long to deny the truth of her situation.

She looked up at Tyl and smiled. "Did you get the shot?" she asked. "Just tell me you got the shot."

Chapter Seventeen

WITH A LINE OF CORUSCANTI SKYTOWERS GLEAMING ON the horizon and the lush gardens of Fellowship Plaza spread out a thousand meters below, the view from Pinnacle Platform was breathtaking—even to a Barabel. The platform was the Jedi Temple's highest landing pad, an elegant blonstone deck large enough to receive diplomatic shuttles. On a clear day, a being with a predator's keen eyes could stand at its sanke-wood balustrade and watch bureaucrats taking lunch in Peace Park, or gaze down the Grand Promenade and ponder the security sleds swarming the silver cylinder of the Galactic Justice Center.

But the beings gathered on the platform that morning had no more interest in the spectacular view than the sleek Incom CrewComet descending to land. The shuttle was carrying Zekk, Tekli, and a handful of recovered Jedi Knights returning from temporary exile on Shedu Maad. Hoping to make the group feel comfortable and welcome after their recent bout of psychotic illness, the Masters had arranged an enthusiastic reception at the Temple's most prestigious entrance.

Unfortunately, a crisis on a faraway world had erupted just as the shuttle entered the atmosphere, and now all eyes were locked on the nearest datapad. It seemed to Saba that events on Blaudu Sextus were already shaping the future of the Jedi in ways she did not comprehend.

"Stun bolts, yes?" asked the Council's newest member, Barratk'l. "No officer would kill a reporter on live HoloNet."

"Belok Rhal would," Leia said. "Those were no stun bolts."

"This one agrees," Saba said, peering over the heads of both Solos at the datapad in Han's hands. He was holding it out for others to view, but being careful to keep the screen high enough to prevent Allana from seeing the violence. "If Rhal will kill on the stepz of the Jedi Temple, he will kill anywhere."

The grainy image zoomed in on a Devaronian journalist lying motionless in a narrow stone stairwell, then focused on a pair of smoking scorch holes that left no doubt about the nature of the bolts that had struck her chest. Saba noted the corpse's absolute stillness and the awkward angle of its limbs, and she knew that Madhi Vaandt had been dead before the holosignal reached Coruscant.

A tinny clatter sounded from the datapad's speaker—a section of stone wall collapsing off camera—and it was followed an instant later by the screech and drone of a blaster-on-lightsaber battle. The cam operator lingered on the smoke rising from Vaandt's body long enough to establish firmly that she had been killed, then zoomed out to show two Jedi Knights—a powerful-looking Chev named Sothais Saar and a slender, dark-haired human named Avinoam Arelis—fighting their way into the bottom of the stairwell.

For a moment the pair stood shoulder-to-shoulder, their bright blades weaving a basket of color as they batted blaster bolts back at their Mandalorian attackers. Then, moving so smoothly and swiftly that Saba almost missed it on the grainy transmission, they executed a perfect shield manuever, with Sothais stepping forward to protect both of them while Avinoam remained motionless, a little behind him and to one side. Dropping his lightsaber to his side, Avinoam raised his free hand and started to wag it gently. Armored Mandalorians suddenly began to fly back and forth, crashing into the stone walls and dropping to the stairs in flailing heaps of *beskar'gam* armor, spraying stray blasterfire everywhere.

The blurry image of Belok Rhal appeared at one edge of the tiny screen, pointing a blaster toward the cam and shouting orders that were not quite audible over the din of the battle behind him.

"*Stang!*" There was more alarm in Han's voice than anger, and Saba understood him well enough to realize that he was worried about the cam operator's safety. "I think we're about to lose our feed."

But even as Han spoke, another figure was moving into the frame, blocking Rhal's firing angle.

"This is Madhi Vaandt's production assistant, Shohta, reporting live from a droid-repair shop in Arari on the planet Blaudu Sextus." As Shohta spoke, he turned to present his profile to the cam, revealing the heavy-boned face of a middle-aged Chev. "As you know if you have been watching our live report . . ."

A flurry of wildly inaccurate blaster bolts came flying over Shohta and bounced out of sight. He cringed and ducked, but continued to speak.

"As you know," he repeated, "the mercenary commander Belok Rhal has killed Madhi in an attempt to prevent us from reporting the Mandalorian massacre of Octusi slaves taking place right now a few dozen meters beyond that wall. But Madhi Vaandt would not be silenced, and neither will we."

Shohta frowned in the direction of his cam operator, then nodded. He stepped out of the image to reveal Rhal, retreating up the stairs toward the cam and pouring fire down toward Sothais Saar. Saar was advancing calmly, his lightsaber blade barely moving as he deflected bolt after bolt into the stairwell walls. Behind the Chev Jedi Knight, Avinoam Arelis was disarming the half a dozen Mandalorian survivors he had already beaten into submission by Force-slamming them into the walls and one another.

"During our short time together," Shohta said from off cam, "one of the things that Madhi repeated to me many times is that it is a journalist's duty to report the story, not to interfere with it. I hope that, just this once, you will forgive me for disobeying her."

As Shohta spoke, a huge boot appeared in the image, then planted itself square in Rhal's back and sent him tumbling back down the stairs toward Sothais Saar. The Jedi used the Force to redirect the Mandalorian's fall, slamming him into the wall several times before bringing him to a stop within easy reach. It was impossible to hear what the young Jedi Knight said as he brought his lightsaber around toward Rhal, but the Mandalorian's face went pale, and he let the blaster tumble from his hand without attempting to fire.

Shohta's heavy-browed face appeared again, this time with tears streaming down his lumpy cheeks. "Madhi Vaandt died today so that the galaxy would know the truth about slavery: that it still flourishes on the edges of the Galactic Alliance, and that there are many powerful beings and corporations in the so-called civilized galaxy actively helping to preserve this immoral and illegal practice."

Shohta paused to look down and gather his thoughts, then addressed the cam again. "Fortunately, her death was not in vain." He stepped aside and waved his hand down the stairs, to where Sothais and Avinoam were securing their prisoners. "Thanks to Madhi Vaandt, the Jedi have heard the cries of the oppressed . . . and they have answered."

Atop Pinnacle Platform, the Force grew heavy and

still, for most of those present knew the truth—that the Jedi had *not* heard the call of the oppressed. The Jedi Council had sent Sothais and Avinoam to Blaudu Sextus not to *free* the Octusi, but to discover who was inciting the rebellion and put an end to it before it resulted in just this kind of massacre. But the mission had gone terribly awry. The two Jedi Knights had found themselves caught in circumstances that dictated they follow their hearts rather than their orders, and because of their decision, they had found themselves on live holo doing exactly what Jedi were *supposed* to do.

It had the will of the Force written all over it.

And Saba, at least, understood the message. The Jedi had lost their way, shying away from a fight with Daala when they should be taking bold action and moving against the galaxy's enemies—*all* of them. She stepped away from the Solos and turned toward Kenth Hamner, who had been watching the events unfold with Cilghal, Kyle, and a couple of other Masters. His face was white with shock and dismay, but at least she saw no anger in it. He understood as well as she did why the two Jedi Knights had involved themselves as they had, why they had not stood idly by while a journalist was slain and thousands of innocents slaughtered. Perhaps this was not going to be as difficult as she feared.

After what they had seen, perhaps even Kenth Hamner would agree that the time for action had come.

Saba took a moment to center herself, letting out a series of long, calming breaths and taking in the view. While they had been watching the events on Blaudu Sextus, the CrewComet had landed unnoticed and was now sitting on its struts, its cone-shaped nose still glowing white with entry heat, wisps of steam rising off its hull. But the ramps remained up and the air locks sealed—a sign, no doubt, that Zekk and the others had been watching the same report and were still sitting in the passenger cabin, as shocked as everyone outside.

Saba reached out to the shuttle in the Force, welcoming the passengers home, but also checking to make certain that she recognized their presences. The Jedi had just entered a new and dangerous era. With enemies moving against them—both here on Coruscant and in the galaxy at large—they could not afford to be complacent, not even in their own Temple . . . perhaps *especially* not in their own Temple.

When she was rewarded with the warm touch of half a dozen familiar Force presences, Saba nodded to herself, then let out a long breath and started toward Grand Master Hamner. He was already on his comlink, issuing orders through Temple communications. Whatever happened next, she could not grow angry. It was not impossible that he had reached the same conclusion she had—and even if he had not, she would need to remain calm to win the support of her fellow Masters.

Hamner must have sensed her approach and intention, for as Saba drew near, he signed off the comlink and turned to face her. His blue eyes had gone from steely to soft, his features from dignified to weary. Saba still found it a challenge to read human faces, but it seemed to her that Hamner's expression was one of sadness and defeat—that the grim set of his jaw remained only because he was too stubborn to surrender.

"Master Sebatyne," he said, acknowledging her with his usual military propriety. "An unfortunate turn of events on Blaudu Sextus."

"This one does not think so," Saba said. She had barely replied before she sensed herself and Hamner becoming the center of attention on the platform. The Masters had witnessed their confrontations many times, and even most Jedi Knights were aware of the tension between them, so it was only to be expected that when they came together, others would watch. "Sothais and Avinoam did well. They did what any Jedi should do."

Hamner nodded, but said, "They also disobeyed orders, and now we have a mess on our hands. This Chev reporter, Shohta, is drawing the wrong conclusion, and that is going to fan the flames of revolt along the entire galactic edge."

"And we are certain that is a bad thing?" Saba asked. "Perhapz the time has come for the Jedi to think of what is right, not what is convenient."

Hamner shook his head. "Saba, we've been through this a thousand times." He looked past her toward the CrewComet. "Our Knights are about to debark. What do you say we give them—"

"No." The word came from behind Saba, in a voice that was both gravelly and insistent, and Barratk'l continued, "You cannot put this off, Grand Master. What happened on Blaudu Sextus changes everything, yes?"

Hamner shook his head. "No," he said. "I've already sent orders instructing Sothais to turn Rhal and his men over to the Blauduns for prosecution."

"You *what*?" This came from Han Solo, who, along with most of the others on the landing deck, was crowding in to watch—or join—the confrontation between Saba and Hamner. "Rhal *murdered* your own assistant—"

"On the steps of the Jedi Temple," Corran Horn added.

"—doesn't that mean *anything*?" Han continued. "I can't believe you'd let him go like that."

Hamner's eyes began to harden again. "I grieve for Kani every day," he said. "And I'm as determined to see Rhal brought to justice as anyone here—but only *legally*."

"So you turn him over to the same mugwumps who hired him?" Han scoffed. "That's not justice, it's a joke."

"How can it be a joke if it's not funny?" asked a small voice down at waist height. Saba looked down and saw

Amelia Solo there, looking puzzled and earnest. "And besides, aren't Jedi supposed to obey planetary laws?"

Hamner smiled down at her. "Out of the mouths of babes," he said. "Amelia's right. If we bring Rhal back here to Coruscant, he's a problem for everyone."

"But if we leave him with the Blauduns, they *have* to punish him—and punish him *hard*—or it will look like they approve of the slaughter." Leia nodded, then looked over at Han and Corran. "It's a better solution than you think."

"It keeps *us* from looking like we sent two Jedi there seeking vengeance." Hamner shot Leia a look of gratitude, then turned toward the CrewComet. "Now that we've settled that—"

"We have settled nothing," Saba interrupted, purposely placing herself between Hamner and the shuttle. "As you say, Shohta's wordz will spark slave revoltz along the entire galactic edge. The Jedi must decide how we are going to respond, and we must decide *now.*"

Hamner closed his eyes in frustration. "*Now,* Master Sebatyne?" He shook his head. "I don't think so. It's going to take days for those fires to catch—"

"It is not the slaves this one thinkz of," Saba interrupted. "It is Daala."

"Master Sebatyne has a good point," Kyle Katarn said. "If Chief Daala didn't see the transmission live, you can bet she's watching a replay right now."

"And she'll think the same thing Shohta did," Kyp Durron said, nodding. "That the Jedi have decided to take a stand against slavery."

Hamner's eyes flashed with alarm, and Saba knew he finally understood the danger they were in. Daala would interpret the events on Blaudu Sextus in the worst possible light. She would conclude that the Jedi were trying to destabilize her government by forcing it to commit scarce resources to the farthest reaches of the galaxy.

Given her volatile nature and her military background, she might *also* conclude that she had no choice but to launch a preemptive strike—and launch it quickly.

"My apologies, Master Sebatyne. You're right, of course." He turned toward the Temple entrance. "Please convey my apologies to those aboard the shuttle. I'd better get on this right away."

"On *what,* Grand Master?" Saba called. "The Council has not come to a decision."

Hamner stopped and spun on his heel. "There's no decision to *come* to, Master Sebatyne. I need to make Chief Daala understand what really happened—and I need to do it before she convinces herself otherwise."

Saba shook her head. "This one does not believe so," she said. "This one feelz the hand of the Force in what happened today. This one believes the time has come for us to act with our heartz."

"With our *hearts,* Master Sebatyne?" Hamner echoed. "The Sixth Fleet is in orbit, with nothing to do but keep watch over us. A whole planetful of Sith is busy building war fleets to attack us. And you're telling me you *want* us to throw our support behind a galaxy-wide slave revolt? *Seriously?*"

"Yes," Saba replied. "Seriously. It is what the Force demandz of us."

Hamner shook his head. "I'm sorry, Master Sebatyne, but that's ridiculous."

"Maybe to *you,*" Barratk'l said. The Yuzzem stepped to Saba's side, a hulking wall of fur and fangs that stood a full head and a half taller than even a Barabel. "But maybe Master Sebatyne is not the only one who feels it, yes?"

Hamner turned toward Barratk'l wearily, his eyes filled with betrayal and disappointment. He was the one who had recommended that Master Barratk'l be recalled from her post on Nal Hutta and asked to join the Council. It was obvious from Hamner's expression that he had expected her to repay the honor by remaining loyal to him. But that wasn't how the Council worked. Masters were expected to speak their minds and vote their consciences, and it was clear, to Saba at least, that Barratk'l agreed with her.

Finally, Hamner said, "Barratk'l, the Yuzzem were enslaved under the Empire, so it's only natural that you would want to help others escape. But these are hardly the circumstances—"

"Then what are the circumstances?" Cilghal asked, surprising even Saba. "The Mon Calamari were also enslaved by the Empire, and I can no longer stand by in good conscience while other species suffer the same fate." She turned to Saba and nodded. "I feel it, too, Master Sebatyne. The Force is moving in this."

Once Cilghal had voiced her feelings, Hamner looked to the other Masters and, finding no support in any of their faces, he merely shook his head in determination.

"I appreciate your honesty," he said. "But when Grand Master Skywalker went into exile, he didn't ask *you* to stand in while he was gone. He asked *me*, and I must do what I think is best."

Hamner turned toward the door with an air of finality.

He had not even taken two steps before Han called out, "Tell them about the deal with Bwua'tu."

Hamner stopped in his tracks and spun around, his eyes wide with outrage and surprise. "*What?*"

"I said, 'Tell them about the deal with Bwua'tu.'"

Hamner clenched his jaw and balled his fists, obviously struggling to contain his anger.

Han looked him straight in the eye. "You can do it, or I can."

Saba could tell by the way that Han's pupils had opened that at least part of what he was saying was a bluff.

"Who knows?" Han continued. "They might even understand."

Kyp and Kyle looked at each other, then Kyle stepped toward Hamner. "Understand *what,* Grand Master?"

Hamner glared blaster bolts at Han, but said, "Admiral Bwua'tu commed me during the siege. He wanted to make a deal."

"And you didn't tell *us*?" Corran asked, clearly outraged.

"He asked me to hold it in confidence," Hamner replied. "He didn't want Daala to know."

"And this deal, what was it?" Corran demanded.

Hamner hesitated, obviously reluctant to break his promise to the admiral.

"It's the reason your *Grand Master* here doesn't want to do anything," Han prompted. "He's still hoping Bwua'tu will wake up and fix everything with a wave of his hand."

"Not exactly," Hamner said through clenched teeth. "But Admiral Bwua'tu *did* offer to use his influence to convince Daala to be reasonable."

"In return for what, exactly?" Kyle asked.

"Not launching the StealthX wing," Hamner said. "The Mandos saw us preparing when they stormed the Temple, and the last thing either of us wanted was starfighters battling over Coruscant."

Saba felt her blood turn cold. Hamner had been doing more than just keeping secrets from them. He had entrusted the Order's well-being to a *Bothan,* and he had been stalling his fellow Masters—*lying* to them—in the vain hope that his friend the Bothan would awaken and solve all his problems for him.

Clearly, Hamner had cracked under the pressure. Clearly, he was no longer fit to lead the Jedi Order.

Saba stepped forward. Speaking as gently as her Barabel voice would allow, she said, "This one thinkz it would be best if you resigned, Master Hamner."

Hamner's jaw fell. "*Resign,* Master Sebatyne? You must be joking."

Saba shook her head. "No joke, Master Hamner. This one has no confidence in you." She glanced around at her fellow Masters. Receiving one nod after another, she added, "We *all* have no confidence in you."

Strictly speaking, it was not a formal no-confidence vote. But there were enough Masters present to indicate what the result would be, and even Kenth Hamner was not stubborn enough to demand the formality when the outcome was a foregone conclusion. He glanced from one Master to another, his face growing a little paler each time a Master met his gaze and nodded agreement with Saba's pronouncement. When he had come to the last face, he turned to her with a trembling mouth.

"I do *not* resign, Master Sebatyne," he said. "And this is not over."

"It is for us," Saba replied. "Go inside, Master Hamner. Your presence is no longer required by the Council."

Chapter Eighteen

JAGGED FEL FOUND CHIEF OF STATE DAALA OUTSIDE her office, standing in the corner of a huge balcony that he had not known existed, looking past the shoulder of the Senate Building toward the gleaming silver pyramid that was the Jedi Temple. She was leaning out over the edge with both hands braced on the railing, her shoulders hunched in anger and her long coppery hair blowing in the humid breeze. Her posture reminded him of nothing quite so much as the linstone fiends hanging from the roof edges of some of Bastion's most ancient buildings, a guardian monster from a lost era, still standing watch and fuming at the vicissitudes of time and humanity.

Discerning no hint in her bearing of why she had asked to see him on such short notice—and seeing no advantage in startling her during a moment of private meditation—Jag cleared his throat and started across the balcony.

"If you're thinking of attempting a paraglider assault, I'd advise against it," he said, only half joking. "They'll see you coming from a kilometer away."

Daala snapped fully upright, clasping her hands behind her back, then spinning to face Jag. "I suppose they would," she said. "And there's that blasted Force to worry about."

"Yes, there's always the Force," Jag agreed. "It would be a mistake to underestimate its power."

The corner of Daala's mouth rose in a sardonic smile.

"I believe I have heard that before." As Jag drew near, she unclasped her hands and held one out. "Thank you for rearranging your schedule. I assume you're aware of events on Blaudu Sextus?"

"I've been watching the Public HoloNet reports." Jag forced himself to shake her hand—after all, a Head of State could not allow personal feelings to interfere with state business. "But if that's why you asked me here, I must admit that I fail to see how the outrages on Blaudu Sextus concern the Empire."

"No?" Daala turned back toward the Jedi Temple. "I should think that's obvious."

Of course—*Jaina.*

Jag stepped to the rail and, without answering, gazed across the vast plaza toward the silvery pinnacle of the Jedi Temple. He could not look on it without feeling a pang of longing and sorrow. After his exile from the Chiss Ascendancy, Jaina and the Solos had become the closest thing he had to a family, and he still found it difficult to accept that they were no longer a part of his life. How Jaina could break off their engagement over a matter of duty and conscience, he simply could not accept—and the effort of trying invariably left him feeling sad, lost, and alone.

After a moment, Jag said, "You should consider replacing your intelligence officer. Jedi Solo and I are no longer engaged." He turned and looked her straight in the eye. "She broke it off shortly after the assassination attempt at Pangalactus."

Daala made a point of holding his gaze. The attack at the famous theme restaurant had occurred weeks before, yet Imperial Intelligence remained unable to offer more than conjecture as to who was behind the assault. To Jag, that meant the party responsible had been a very competent plotter, and that placed Daala at the top of the suspect list.

When Jag did not look away, Daala finally dropped her eyes and said, "I hope you don't believe *I* was behind that."

"No, Jaina had her own reasons for ending things," Jag said, deliberately misconstruing her meaning. "Besides, when it comes to matters of the heart, she would hardly be inclined to take *your* advice."

Daala's mouth tightened almost unnoticeably. "I doubt it," she allowed. "But I'm sure you realize I was referring to the attempt on your life."

"What makes you sure the attempt was on *my* life?" Jag pressed. He knew better than to think Daala would ever let slip something incriminating, but he wanted her to know he remained suspicious. "Those YVHs were spraying more fire the Solos' way than mine."

"Who knows what they were firing at?" Daala offered a dismissive wave. "*I* certainly don't."

"Meaning you're not the one who sent them."

"Yes." Daala's voice grew hard and icy. "Meaning I had nothing to do with that attack—no matter *who* the target was."

"Then I'd be very interested to know who did," Jag pressed.

"So would *I*." Daala turned away from the railing and gestured toward a table, where her waiters had placed some pastries and a carafe of caf. "Wynn thinks it was part of a conspiracy to undermine my government by making me look like a monster."

"You're saying that the assassination attempt at Pangalactus was all about *you*?" Jag followed her to the table and pulled a chair out for Daala. "That's rather self-centered, even for you."

"I only wish you were right, Head of State Fel," Daala said, accepting the jab with a tight smile. "But I've been hearing some unpleasant rumors about a pro-Jedi bill being circulated by Senator Wuul. So I must admit that I'm starting to see a pattern."

"Then I suggest you stop engaging in that sort of behavior," Jag replied. He went to his own chair and sat. "You're making it rather easy for them to paint you in a bad light, don't you think?"

An angry glint finally came to Daala's eyes. "If you're referring to the situation on Blaudu Sextus—"

"And elsewhere," Jag interrupted.

"*And* elsewhere," Daala allowed, "I'm merely trying to keep order."

Jag took a napkin and placed it in his lap. "At least you've shown me the courtesy of not pretending that the Mandalorians were there under someone else's orders. Thank you."

"You're obviously someone who knows how to keep a secret," Daala replied. "And to be frank, I need your help."

"To put down the slaves?" Jag's thoughts started to race through his mind at lightspeed. Daala *had* to know he would never agree to such a thing, not unless she had something to offer him—or to threaten him with. "I'm sorry, but the Empire isn't in the habit of lending its military out for those sorts of things."

Daala allowed her face to harden with anger. "There is more happening here than a simple slave revolt. The entire galactic rim is about to erupt in violence and chaos," she hissed. "The Alliance can't prevent that alone."

"Then you might consider releasing the fleet you're holding in orbit."

"And play into Jedi hands?" Daala's hand came down on the table so hard that Jag's saucer and cup jumped. "That's what they want. That's why they've begun this ridiculous freedom campaign."

Jag's brow shot up. "You're saying the *Jedi* are behind Freedom Flight?"

"Isn't it obvious?" Daala retorted. "By igniting fires along the galactic rim, they compel me to divert my forces."

"And they give you an opportunity to make yourself look bad," Jag added, "by doing crazy things like sending Mandos to put down slave revolts."

"Exactly." Daala nodded and poured for them. "So you see why we need the Empire's help."

"I see why you *want* it," Jag said. "But you're overlooking something important."

"I doubt that." Daala returned the carafe to the table and offered the pastry plate to him. "You're about to tell me the Jedi would never do such a thing, aren't you?"

Jag tried to hide his surprise by reaching for a cream puff. "The thought had crossed my mind, yes."

"Of course it had," Daala said. "But if that's true, why have they been working with Sith?"

"Sith?" Jag repeated. He sank back in his chair, recalling his last conversation with Jaina, when she had begged him to lend her some Imperial ships. She had hinted that Luke had uncovered something huge on his journey, something that threatened the entire galaxy—and that certainly *sounded* like Sith. "Okay, maybe they've found another Sith. But if you think they're working *with* him, you've lost your mind."

Daala sat back, listening patiently, then smiled and said, "Not *another* Sith, Head of State Fel. A whole fleet of them. Perhaps a whole *civilization* of them." She withdrew a small datapad from her tunic pocket, then continued, "And I have *not* lost my mind. You've heard about the trouble on Klatooine, of course?"

Jag nodded. "The Fountain of the Hutt Ancients," he said. "Someone damaged it, and that's what touched off the whole slave revolt."

"Not *someone,*" Daala said. "*Sith.* Jaina Solo sat in judgment of them—and released half."

She slid the datapad across the table to Jag.

"Alliance Intelligence has compiled a report on the matter." She took a cream puff and cut it in half. "Enjoy."

Jag activated the datapad, then watched in a growing mixture of fascination and horror as a dour-faced Duros operative detailed what his team had discovered on Klatooine. The incident began when Luke and Ben Skywalker arrived with a fleet of frigates crewed by two separate species of Force-using beings. As the fleet departed, the crew of one of the frigates violated the Fountain of Hutt Ancients. A short time later, Jaina Solo and Lando Calrissian arrived and were asked to sit in judgment of the offenders. The most damning evidence was a brief vid of Jaina and Lando standing behind a Klatooinian elder as he read their verdict—a verdict that condemned the captain and crew of one Sith frigate, the *Starstalker,* to be executed by Klatooinians, yet left the captain and crew of a second frigate, the *Winged Dagger,* free to go.

The vid had barely ended before Daala asked, "So tell me, Head of State Fel: who do you think has lost their mind now?"

Jag looked up, his thoughts already leaping ahead to what Daala intended to do with the vid. "Why are you showing me this?"

"Why do you *think*? The galaxy is at peace . . . *at peace.*" Daala's face grew hard, and she leaned forward in her chair. "And *you* are going to help me keep it that way."

Chapter Nineteen

THE SHINING CRESCENTS OF ALMANIA AND ITS THREE moons were hanging bright against the dark velvet of space, a set of jewel-colored sickles gleaming with the diamond-colored light of the system's huge A4-class sun. Two of the crescents, the planet itself and the moon Pydyr, were mottled with patches of sapphire ocean and verdant land. Another crescent, the industrial moon of Drewwa, scintillated with the lights of a thousand factories, including those of Tendrando Arms and Amala Casketry. But it was the fourth crescent, the yellow dead moon of Auremesh, that drew Ben's attention.

The tracking signal they had been following since departing the Maw had vanished from the *Emiax*'s navigational display. Ben was fairly certain that his father would not have sent the deactivation signal without telling him, so the *Jade Shadow* must have taken a berthing inside a cave, a bunker, or some other structure with a roof thick enough to block the signal. Given that their quarry would be looking for a place to hide while she nursed her wounds and rebuilt her strength, an empty, deserted moon seemed like a good candidate.

Ben rubbed his thumb across the touchpad on the *Emiax*'s piloting yoke. A waypoint designator appeared on the navigation display, drifting toward Auremesh.

"No, we'll go to Pydyr," Luke said from the copilot's

seat, two meters across the spacious flight deck from Ben. "That's where she'll be hiding."

"Pydyr?"

This came from Vestara, sitting in one of the passenger's seats at the back of the flight deck. Even after she had helped them steal the *Emiax,* and fled from her father and Sarasu Taalon back in the Maw, Luke had insisted that she remain in either his presence or Ben's at all times. Given that she was more familiar with the shuttle's systems than the two Jedi were, it was a probably a wise precaution—even though Ben feared it would give her the impression that Jedi were just as paranoid and dangerous as the Sith.

"How do you know?" Vestara asked. "Do you Jedi have the ability to track *anyone* you've ever met?"

Out of the corner of his eye, Ben glimpsed the hint of a smile coming to Luke's face, and he knew what his father was thinking. After their first encounter on Sinkhole Station, Luke had used a Dathomiri blood trail to track Vestara halfway across the galaxy. Letting her believe that such feats were easy for Jedi would certainly give them an advantage in dealing with her. Ben glanced over as though seeking permission to answer and received a quick nod in reply. He glanced back at Vestara, whose many bruises had merely faded to pale purple even after a two-day healing trance, then raised his brow.

"You expect us to believe you *can't*?" Ben scoffed. His own wound was almost completely healed, thanks to a combination of trance, steristrips, and bacta salve. "Lies like that are what makes it so hard for Dad to trust you."

Vestara let her gaze drop, though not quickly enough to hide the surprise in her eyes. "Sorry," she said. "I guess I'm still Sith at heart."

"You see?" Luke asked, looking over to catch Ben's eye. "You can't change her, son."

Ben shrugged. "At least she's admitting it." He felt bad

for having spoken to her so harshly. But she was still probing for information on the Jedi, and he was not fool enough to assume that her questions were innocent. "That's a start."

The cabin remained silent for a moment, then Vestara asked, "Are you two enjoying this game?" There was just enough of a tremor in her voice to send a pang of guilt shooting through Ben. "Because if you are, we can continue all day. I was raised to be strong."

Luke studied her for a moment, then nodded. "And smart," he said. "I'll give your Master that much credit. She may not have shown you much about handling a lightsaber, but she *did* train you to wield that beauty of yours."

Vestara's Force aura grew cold and raw, but her voice remained calm. "Why, *thank* you, Master Skywalker. It's so good to hear that my training has been of *some* benefit." The buckle on her crash harness clicked open. "And now, if you don't mind, I need to make a trip to the refresher."

Luke waved her toward the back of the flight deck. "Go ahead," he said. "Ben and I need to prepare for our approach."

The surprise that rippled through the Force was as much Ben's as Vestara's. His father hadn't been insisting that they actually accompany her into the refresher when she needed to use it, but he had been adamant that one of them escort her to the compartment and wait outside.

Recovering from her own surprise, Vestara asked, "You're tired of watching?"

Luke's smile was bitter and tight. "We've got more important things to do," he said. "But if you misbehave, Ben will get the beating."

"*Me?*" Ben asked. His father would never actually beat him—but Vestara probably didn't know that, and it would be good to see whether it mattered to her. "Why *me*?"

Luke shrugged. "You're the one who keeps saying we can trust her."

"I keep saying we should give her a *chance*," Ben corrected. "There's a difference."

"So we're giving her a chance," Luke replied. "If you've got a problem with that, we can always flush her out an air lock."

Ben let his breath out, then glanced back at Vestara. "Can I trust you?"

Vestara gave him a crooked smile. "This time." She brought her knees together and began to dance on the deck. "And if you don't, we're *all* going to regret it."

"Okay, okay," Ben said. "But don't make me . . ."

Vestara was already out the hatch and racing into the day cabin behind them.

Ben waited until her footfalls grew inaudible, then looked back to his father. "Dad, if she really had to go that bad, why wait until she knew where we were headed? I think she was playing us."

"And you're surprised?"

Ben nodded. "Well, yeah," he admitted. "I can't figure out why you let her go."

"Because I need to send a coded message to Cilghal, and I can't do that and fly the ship." He reached into his tunic pocket and produced a pair of circuit boards. "And because . . . I also disabled the engineering hatch and the auxiliary comm station."

Ben smiled. The precautions would prevent Vestara from sabotaging the vessel or reporting its location. "I guess that's why you're the Grand Master," he said, shaking his head in admiration. "But I still can't figure out one thing. How do you know Abeloth is going to Pydyr instead of Drewwa or Auremesh?"

"Easy." Luke rose and stepped to the back of the flight

deck, then closed the access hatch and secured it from the inside. "I know what Abeloth is looking for."

Without offering any other explanation, he took a seat at the navigator's station, then activated the subspace transceiver and opened a channel to the Jedi Temple. When the communications officer at the other end acknowledged the signal, Luke merely began to tap the mike in an irregular pattern that Ben quickly recognized as the Jedi flash code. Without the encrypting equipment aboard the *Jade Shadow,* it was the only way to communicate with the Temple securely, especially since there was every possibility that the *Emiax* would automatically—and secretly—be copying every outgoing transmission and sending it straight to Kesh.

And as Ben listened, he began to realize just how important it was that no one but Jedi comprehend the message. His father was not only reporting the latest events in the Maw, but also asking the Jedi to send reinforcements to Pydyr as soon as possible. He was fairly certain that Abeloth had gone into hiding there, and when he and Ben flushed her into the open, they were going to need help destroying her—a *lot* of help.

The hatch handle jiggled just as Luke finished the message, and Vestara called, "Hey, who locked me out?"

"Uh, sorry, Ves." Ben glanced back at his father, who raised a finger and silently mouthed *one second.* "You must have tripped the security protocol when you rushed out of here. Just a minute."

Luke nodded and remained in his seat as a series of taps and scratches began to sound from the transceiver. Ben listened with growing alarm as they heard what had been happening back on Coruscant—the use of Mandalorians to first storm and then lay siege to the Temple, Daala's refusal to release Valin and Jysella Horn despite the evidence that all of the other psychotic Jedi had recovered from their illnesses, the vote of no confidence in Grand Master Hamner . . .

"*Ben?*" Vestara banged on the hatch. "What's going on in there?"

"Hold on," Ben called. "We're, uh, busy with our approach."

"*Approach?*" Vestara sounded doubtful. "Already?"

Ben did not reply. The interruption had caused him to miss a string of code, and he was still trying to figure out what the assassination attempt on Admiral Bwua'tu had to do with the trouble between Master Sebatyne and Grand Master Hamner. The message ended a moment later. Luke acknowledged it with a few quick taps, then urged the Council to send reinforcements quickly and shut down the unit.

As his father turned toward the hatch, Ben caught his eye and mouthed, *What's going on at home?* Luke only shrugged and shook his head.

Vestara banged on the hatch again. "Look, if you two don't want me hanging around—"

"Don't be silly." Luke released the lock and hit the control pad on the wall. "We want you right here where we can keep an eye on you."

The hatch hissed open. On the other side of the threshold stood a sour-faced Vestara, her eyes narrowed in suspicion and her Force aura droning with irritation.

Instead of stepping aside to allow her onto the deck, Luke asked, "Something wrong with the refresher?"

"No, it's fine." Vestara's brow furrowed. "Why?"

Luke's gaze dropped along her sleeves. "Your hands usually smell like sanitizer when you return," he said. "This time, they don't."

Vestara looked to the floor, attempting to feign embarrassment, but she was not quite quick enough to conceal the way her pupils widened in alarm. Wherever she had gone after leaving the flight deck, it hadn't been to the refresher.

"I must have forgotten," she said, spinning on her heel. "Thanks."

"Not at all," Luke said, starting after her. "I'll come along to make sure you remember this time. Ben can handle the approach until we return."

"Sure, no problem," Ben called back.

He didn't know whether to be amused, angered, or saddened by the situation. His father clearly had Vestara figured, which meant she was less likely to cause them problems. But what his father had figured out—that Vestara was still deceiving them—felt like a betrayal not only of Ben's trust, but of Ben himself. He was doing everything he could to show her that life didn't need to be so difficult—so filled with treachery and abuse. But Vestara seemed to be doing everything she could to make it clear that she just didn't care.

And maybe that was to be expected. Ben *was* trying to convince her to turn her back on not only her parents, but her entire culture, and even the world she grew up on. He could imagine how *he* would react were someone to try to convince him to turn his back on the Jedi.

Of course, Jedi didn't use beatings to discipline their students.

The shining crescents of Almania and its moons had grown so large in the forward viewport that they filled its entire expanse and were beginning to drift apart. Ben checked his navigation display and was not surprised to see approach-control channel designations for Almania and Drewwa flashing over their respective positions. But there was nothing for Pydyr. It was a fairly primitive world, still recovering from the destruction wreaked a few decades before by a Dark Jedi named Kueller, but it did have a spaceport. And that meant it should have had an approach-control system.

Had Ben been flying a StealthX instead of a VIP luxury shuttle, he might have attempted a covert landing. But instead of gravitic modulators and thermal dissipators, VIP luxury shuttles came outfitted with red nerf-leather seats and flight-deck beverage dispensers, and that meant that even if Pydyr didn't notice the *Emiax*'s approach, Almania and Drewwa would. There was nothing for him to do but a standard approach, so Ben set a course for the daylight side of the moon and activated the shuttle's comm unit.

"Pydyr Control," he commed, "this is the transport shuttle *Emiax* requesting an approach vector. Repeat: transport shuttle *Emiax* requesting approach vector."

Ben fell silent and awaited a reply, watching the moon swell from a crescent to a sea-mottled half sphere as the *Emiax* continued to draw closer. Half a dozen large landmasses were visible through a thin layer of clouds. Ben brought up a data file on the moon and discovered that the only significant population concentration was in the city of Corocus, located near the equator on the largest continent. He adjusted his course, swinging around the day side of the moon until he saw a geographic configuration that matched the image on his display—a horn of land pointing toward a large island.

"Pydyr Control," he commed again, "this is the transport shuttle *Emiax* on approach to Corocus. Please advise entry procedures."

After a moment, a raspy voice replied over the cockpit speaker. "Negative, *Emiax*." Even by the standards of an avian species, the Pydyrian's voice sounded thin and reedy. "Discontinue approach . . . divert to Almania. Pydyr is under . . . quarantine."

"*Quarantine?*" Ben pushed back into the pilot's seat, contemplating the instructions without obeying them. The Pydyrian certainly sounded sick, but that was easy enough to fake over a comm unit. Still, Ben found himself inclined to accept what he was hearing. Something just felt *right* about the stress in the Pydyrian's voice, and about the way he had paused to catch his breath. "Why?"

"Your own . . . protection," Control said. "This is a cross-species epidemic . . . very virulent. Divert at once."

As the Pydyrian spoke, Luke and Vestara returned to the flight deck. Instead of assuming her usual seat, Vestara came forward to take the navigator's seat, no doubt hoping for an opportunity to check the latest settings on the subspace transceiver. Ben saw the hint of a smile cross his father's lips and knew she would learn only what he intended her to learn.

"So, do we divert?" Ben asked. A sense of dread began to settle over him. He had read about some of the plagues that had ravaged the galaxy in the past, wiping out entire civilizations and leaving whole worlds devoid of sentient life. The last thing Ben wanted was to be responsible for spreading another one. "Maybe someone on Almania can tell us what happened."

Luke shook his head. "Stay on course."

"Uh, are you sure about that, Master Skywalker?" Vestara asked. Her Force aura was taut with the same fear that Ben felt, and there was an edge to her voice that suggested she would not allow herself to be taken to a plague world without a fight. "That guy sounds pretty sick."

Luke did not bother replying, and the Pydyrian's voice came over the cockpit speaker again. "Shuttle *Emiax,* be advised that our spaceport is closed to all traffic. You will not be allowed—"

"Pydyr Control," Luke interrupted. "*You* be advised that this is Grand Master Luke Skywalker of the Jedi Order, in pursuit of a stolen vessel of great personal significance, and we *are* going to land and recover it."

"Master *Skywalker*?" The Pydyrian sounded healthy for an instant, but quickly lapsed back into his reedy voice. "I assure you, no star yachts . . . have landed on

Pydyr in the last week. You would be condemning yourself and your companions to a long and . . ."

The words trailed off into a fit of coughing, and Ben felt more convinced than ever that the poor fellow was mere hours from death. But when he looked over at his father, he found no hint of concern or fear, only a knowing smirk and a jaw set in determination.

Ben realized then that nothing was going to dissuade his father from landing on the plague moon, not fear for their own safety or that of the galaxy, and his heart began to climb into his throat.

"We're not going to turn away, are we?" he asked.

Luke shook his head. "We'll be fine. Trust me."

"Why should we?" This question came from Vestara. "I can feel in the Force that something terrible is happening down there. How can you be so sure we won't be affected?"

To Ben's surprise, his father's smile grew wider, and it did not vanish as he turned to face Vestara directly.

"To begin with, I never mentioned what kind of vessel we were chasing." Luke looked back toward Pydyr. "And Control knew it was a star yacht."

Chapter Twenty

WITH A CLOUD OF DUST MOTES SWIRLING THROUGH ITS cavernous hangar and a long line of berthing bays sitting empty and dark along the back wall, the Corocus Spaceport looked more like a narglatch den than a planetary transit station. The giant maintenance cranes were bleeding orange corrosion from their rivets and weld-seams, and the faint wheeze of a leaky pressure coupling was whispering somewhere in the back of a darkened repair bay. Through the viewport window, Luke could see only one other vessel in the hangar, a classy BDY ZipDel light transport sitting across the way in the mouth of a transfer bay, its human crew peering out their own viewports toward the *Emiax*.

Their Force auras were trembling with fear, their faces mottled by blue blisters and weeping sores. Luke could see by the purple bags beneath their eyes that they were exhausted with worry, and it was clear by their unkempt hair and drooping shoulders that they were close to giving up hope. He held their gazes, then began a special breathing exercise designed to help him immerse himself in the White Current—two short inhalations followed by a single long exhalation.

Adepts of the White Current believed that the Current was separate from the Force, that followers of other Force-using traditions were drawing on some lesser form of mystic energy. Other traditions tended to view the White

Current as no more than a different manifestation of the Force. To Luke, they were *both* right. The White Current *was* different from the Force—but only in the sense that any current was a different thing from the ocean in which it flowed. In their essential wholeness, they were each other.

After a few breaths, Luke began to sense the White Current flowing past him, a feathery brush that made him feel refreshed and strong. He opened himself to it just as he would have to the Force, and it began to ripple through him, to fill him with a sensation of warmth and contentment. He surrendered himself to the current, let himself become a part of its flow and the flow to become a part of him.

Now that Luke had joined with the White Current, he began to see things through it—not as they *appeared*, but as they truly *were*. He turned his attention across the hangar again, pouring feelings of reassurance and calm into the White Current and using it to look at the two crew members of the ZipDel transport.

Their blisters and sores quickly faded from sight, and their flesh tone returned to a more healthy-looking pinkish beige. But their postures remained slumped and their eyes clouded with despair, suggesting that while their illness was merely an illusion, it was one they themselves accepted as real. Causing such suffering was an unthinkable cruelty to devotees of the White Current—and one that told Luke all he needed to know about where Abeloth was hiding.

"You two stay on the *Emiax*." Luke opened the hatch and started down the boarding ramp. "I'll go find out where they're hiding the *Shadow*."

"In just your robe, Master Skywalker?" The concern in Vestara's voice sounded genuine. "We have hazard suits aboard."

Luke glanced back. "A hazard suit?" Sensing another

chance to steer her toward a false conclusion regarding Jedi abilities, he flashed his most condescending smirk. "Why would anyone need a hazard suit when he has the Force?"

He descended the boarding ramp into the briny, fetid air of the hangar, then made his way through a cloud of still-swirling dust to the opposite side of the landing pad and ascended a brick staircase to the portmaster's office. Inside he found only two Pydyrians, both covered in the same bluish blisters and weeping sores as the humans he had glimpsed earlier. Small and slender, with long faces and delicate, vaguely avian features, the two Pydyrians were perched on roosting stools, their back-folding knees tucked beneath their seats and their toe-talons locked tight around wooden crossbars. Both were tilted precariously forward, the communications officer over his comm equipment and the portmaster over his slant-topped desk, and both appeared sick and on the verge of collapse.

Luke studied them through the White Current, as he had with the ZipDel crew, and saw that their illness was an illusion. As much as he wanted to believe it was Abeloth deluding the inhabitants of Pydyr, he had his doubts. Dozens of Sith—including a couple of Masters and a powerful Lord—had spent weeks in Abeloth's company without perceiving her true nature, and he himself had failed to see through her deceptions for days as she lay in the *Shadow*'s medbay disguised as Dyon Stadd. Given how easily he was penetrating *this* illusion, it seemed unlikely to be Abeloth's doing.

Luke crossed to the portmaster's desk and cleared his throat.

The Pydyrian barely raised his head. "You would be Luke Skywalker? *The* Luke Skywalker?"

"That's right," Luke said. Although his face might not be well known on Pydyr, his name most certainly was. Decades earlier, he and Leia had helped free the Almanian system from the tyrant warlord who had been on the verge of pushing the Pydyrian species into extinction. "I'm looking for my wife's star yacht, the *Jade Shadow.*"

The portmaster nodded. "So you have said. As I told you over the comm, nothing by that name has landed here." He used a slender hand with three long fingers to tap a command into a datapad on his desk, then turned the screen toward Luke. "Please look. You have just killed yourself for nothing."

"I doubt that." Luke peered down and found the spaceport traffic log on the screen. Though there were only fifty entries on the first screen, they went back nearly a month, and none of them was a *Horizon*-class space yacht. "The *Shadow* may not have landed in your spaceport, but I've already found all the evidence I need to prove the thief landed on Pydyr."

"As you walked across the landing pad?" the portmaster scoffed. He rocked back on his haunches and looked Luke directly in the eye. "You Jedi *are* good."

"Not that good," Luke said. He put a touch of Force behind his words, using it to plant the lie he intended to tell more deeply in the portmaster's mind. "You see, she's the carrier."

"The carrier?"

Luke pointed at the portmaster's sore-covered face. "Of the Weeping Pox," he said, making up his own name for the illusory disease. As much as he disliked lying, it was sometimes a necessity for any Jedi—and right now, his best option was to *use* the illusion, not fight it. "The thief is immune to this disease herself, but she's the one spreading it."

"*Spreading* it?" the comm officer echoed, coming alert. "Someone is causing this plague *intentionally*?"

"We don't know her motivations," Luke said, turning to the comm officer. "Perhaps she's just frightened. But we need to stop her."

The comm officer's eyes shrank to angry beads. "You should have stopped her before Pydyr."

"We haven't had much cooperation." Luke spread his hands. "I'm afraid she's proven very adept at persuading people to hide her."

The comm officer's gaze shifted toward the portmaster, either urging his superior to reveal what they knew—or seeking permission to do it himself.

"And that's a very unfortunate thing," Luke continued. "Because the longer it takes us to get her into a lab, the more beings will die."

"The *lab*?" the comm officer asked. "You think you can *cure* this?"

"That's what the scientists tell me," Luke replied. "If they can figure out why *she's* immune, they can replicate it."

The officer's eyes went back to the portmaster. "Najee, we must tell him."

"You already *have*, you fool," the portmaster answered.

"And he did the right thing." Luke fixed his gaze on the portmaster—Najee—and put an edge in his voice. "It's not just Pydyrian lives that are at stake. Where will I find her?"

Najee shrugged. "Who can know? We tracked her ship to the . . . to the seashore, well outside the city."

"Near a certain temple," Luke suggested. He watched the Pydyrian's expression sink and knew that he had guessed correctly—that he had been guessing correctly since the *Emiax* entered the Almanian system. Abeloth had come here to find the Fallanassi, a secretive order of women who were also known as Adepts of the White Current. "Najee, I know that the Fallanassi make their home here, and I have every reason to suspect the thief intends to hide among them. If I'm correct, their lives are in great danger."

"You *are* correct," the comm officer interrupted. "The

Jade Shadow approached under its own transponder code and—"

"*Sanar!*" Najee hissed. "The High Lady asked us not to speak of this."

"You remain silent if you wish." Sanar pulled his headset off and tossed it onto the comm console, then hopped down off his perch. "But if Luke Skywalker needs help saving the galaxy from this plague, the least I can do is show him where to start looking."

Chapter Twenty-one

FOLLOWING LUKE SKYWALKER AND HIS PYDYRIAN GUIDE without being seen was going to prove difficult—especially in the bright orange hazard suit Vestara was wearing to protect herself from the epidemic. If her quarry remained on foot, the huge columns and shadowy arcades of Corocus's blocky, mud-brick architecture would provide her with plenty of cover. But if they emerged from the spaceport in a speeder, she would need a speeder to follow, and in the deserted streets of Corocus that would quickly get her spotted.

Still, whether they emerged on foot or in a vehicle, Vestara had to keep them under surveillance. She had already used a public S-thread booth in the spaceport to send a dispatch to the Lost Tribe relay center on Boonta. Within the hour, the Circle of Lords on Kesh would know that the Skywalkers were hunting for Abeloth on Pydyr and that Vestara suspected they had already sent for Jedi reinforcements. It was difficult to guess how the Circle would respond, but respond they would . . . and it was her duty to be ready with as much intelligence on their enemies as she could gather.

Vestara studied the line of landspeeders resting on their struts along the side of the street, then selected one of the most common models and colors—a turquoise-blue Ubrikkian AirCushion—and stepped over to the driver's door. She used the Force to pop the locks from the inside, then lifted the door and slid into the driver's seat. The alarm system was flashing red and pinging softly, warning her that it needed to read a thumbprint. Vestara ducked down and looked behind the scanning pad. It was difficult to see clearly through the hazard suit's transparent faceplate, but after a moment she located the signal carriers and used the Force to jerk the two wires free of their contact points.

The alarm began to wail immediately. Vestara touched the ends of the wires together, silencing the siren in less than a second—then cried out in surprise as the vehicle's passenger-side door lifted open.

"Galactic Alliance Disease Control," she said, preparing to Force-hurl the intruder into the adjacent building. "I need transport to—"

"Don't," said Ben Skywalker's filter-muted voice. "Just . . . *don't.*"

Vestara looked up to find Ben, also wearing a hazard suit, standing outside the speeder. His lightsaber remained on his belt, but he was holding a blaster pistol—and pointing it at her.

"Ben." As she spoke, Vestara was wondering how long he had been watching her, and whether he had seen her enter the PanComm S-thread booth in the spaceport. "I'm glad you're here."

"Right," he said. "That's why you invited me."

Vestara cocked her head. "Would you have come any other way?"

"Of course not," Ben said. "We're supposed to be waiting aboard the *Emiax*. You are supposed to be taking a nice long sanisteam."

Vestara thought for an instant, then said, "That's right. How did you know I wasn't?" She shot him a playful smile and, wondering how effective her flirting could be from inside a hazard suit, cocked her brow. "Did you peek?"

"Didn't need to." Ben plucked at his orange hazard suit. "I checked the suit locker. Now let's go put these suits back where they belong."

Ben waved the blaster barrel for her to leave the speeder.

Instead, Vestara hit the repulsor activator. "I've got a better idea. Get in."

"I'm under orders." Ben leveled the blaster at her. "And for once, I should probably obey them."

Vestara rolled her eyes. "Ben, we both know you're not going to use that thing, and I'm *not* going to get out." She used the Force to depress her door toggle, and the driver's door dropped into place. "So you can either get in, or let me go alone."

Ben holstered his blaster. "You forgot the last option."

"What's that?"

"Pull you out of there by force."

Vestara raised her brow, surprised by his assertiveness. "As fun as wrestling you might be, Ben, aren't you forgetting something?"

Behind his faceplate, Ben's expression finally began to grow uncertain. "What?"

"I'm *Sith*." Vestara put some edge into her voice. "There's no telling how far I'll escalate things. It might even get deadly."

Ben's shoulders slumped, and he slipped into the passenger's seat. "Do I at least get to know where we're going?"

"Sure." As Vestara spoke, the nose of a SoroSuub landspeeder began to emerge from the spaceport parking garage behind them. She reached over and, sliding down in her seat, pushed Ben's head down. "We're following your father."

"*What?*" Ben tried to sit up again.

Vestara used the Force to push him back down. "I don't know about you Jedi, but we Sith are not in the habit of allowing our Masters to go hunting things like Abeloth alone—not without a backup plan."

Ben stopped struggling. "You think he's going after her *now*?"

"I don't know. But if they have traffic control on this moon, they have entry tracking." As Vestara spoke, a sleek-sounding landspeeder passed on the street. "So why didn't the portmaster just *tell* him where to find the *Shadow*? This has the feeling of a setup to me."

"Maybe." Ben grew more thoughtful. "Something might be up."

"I think something *is*," Vestara agreed. "So we follow at a discreet distance. If Master Skywalker doesn't need us, we go back to the *Emiax* with no harm done. But if there's trouble, we may be just the surprise that tips the balance in your father's favor."

"Okay, maybe you've got a point." Ben lifted his head enough to peer over the dashboard. "But I want you to know something."

"Yes?" Vestara sat up behind the pilot's wheel, fearing he knew about the message she had sent—and wondering why that felt like a betrayal to her. "What is it?"

Ben shot her a half smile. "You're a bad influence."

Chapter Twenty-two

THE DARK VEIL OF A STORM CLOUD WAS PUSHING IN from the sea, assailing the base of the cliff with an endless succession of rolling whitecaps. Between waves, hundreds of oval forms appeared from the water, many of them large enough to be starships but probably just boulders. Farther out stood the white spire of a distant island encircled by sea cliffs as high as the one upon which Luke was standing.

When Luke found no sign of the *Jade Shadow,* he turned to his Pydyrian guide. "I hope you're not trying to be clever, Sanar. If the *Shadow* went down at sea—"

"Not at all." Sanar pointed at the ankle-deep carpet of ground-vines in which they were standing. "Your ship is here, beneath us."

Luke dropped his gaze, immersing himself in the White Current in case he was seeing another Fallanassi illusion, and found only the same four-pointed ground-vine leaves that he had seen earlier. "Beneath us?"

"In a cave." Sanar stepped to the cliff's brink, then leaned out and pointed back under them. "Down there."

Using the Force to anchor himself in place, Luke stretched over the edge and looked down the sheer face. A hundred meters below, half hidden by a swarm of shrieking, sharp-winged seabirds, he glimpsed the dark shadow of a cavern's mouth.

"I see." Luke turned back to Sanar, then asked, "How do we get down there?"

The Pydyrian narrowed his small mouth in what was probably an expression of surprise. "You're a Jedi, aren't you?"

"I am," Luke agreed, "but Jedi don't fly."

"No?" Sanar looked more surprised than ever. "Then I have no idea. Perhaps we should go back and rent an airspeeder."

Luke shook his head. "No time for that. I'll just do it the hard way."

He withdrew a palm-sized cable launcher from his equipment belt and sent a stream of liquid wire shooting toward the rocks below. As soon as the line was long enough to reach the cave, he cut the flow and depressed the TEMPER button, sending a small electrical charge down its length. The wire solidified instantly, becoming a metal cable strong enough to carry several hundred kilograms. To secure the top end, he took a thumb-sized ground bolt from a belt pouch, threaded the cable through an eyeclamp, then affixed it to a blaster adaptor and fired the whole assembly into the ground.

A soft THWUNG let him know that the anchoring splines had deployed. Luke fed the line through a trio of braking hooks on his belt, then backed to the edge of the cliff and began to sit out over the empty air.

Sanar's thin brows arched in concern. "Master Skywalker, will you be needing me any longer?" He let out a wet-sounding cough—the first Luke had heard from him—then added, "I'm not feeling very well."

"You've done enough, Sanar. Thanks for your help."

"No—thank *you*, Master Skywalker." Even as he spoke, Sanar was already retreating toward his landspeeder. "If you have trouble recovering your wife's ship, call me for a ride. You have my comm codes."

The Pydyrian was inside the X-40 and closing the door before Luke could reply. The quick departure was not as alarming as it might have been. When they had first arrived and stood gazing out toward the distant island, an unexpected atmosphere of disquiet had fallen over the clifftop and slowly built into a tangible sense of peril. It was probably no more than a Fallanassi illusion designed to keep intruders away from their temple refuge. But Luke had felt Ben reaching out to him earlier with a sense of wariness and unease, and he was well aware that Sanar's eagerness to be gone might also be the first sign of a betrayal.

Luke took a moment to still himself in the Force and let it flow through him. He could feel a nebulous cloud of animal life in the windswept field atop the cliff, and in the sea behind him. He could even sense the waves of foreboding and mystery radiating from the distant island—no doubt the Fallanassi's refuge and home. But his danger sense remained quiet, and he did not sense anything at all in the cavern directly below.

Luke began to rappel down the chalky face of the cliff, taking his time and remaining alert to danger. He could think of a dozen reasons Abeloth might have come to Pydyr, and none was good. She might have come intending to recruit an army of protectors. Or she might have known of Luke's old romance with the Fallanassi leader Akanah, and come hoping to exploit the relationship—or take vengeance against Luke by killing an old suitor. Either way, the followers of the White Current were in terrible danger, and they needed to be warned.

As he drew near the cave, seabirds began to whirl about his head, diving and shrieking in an effort to drive him away from their nesting area. The cavern entrance was about twenty meters high and shaped like a lopsided O, with a slightly flattened bottom. He could just make out the *Shadow,* sitting on her struts about seventy meters in, a nebulous silver object only partially visible through a cloud of swirling, shrieking birds.

Before entering, Luke extended his Force awareness deep into the cavern—and felt nothing. Despite the thousands of birds, despite the cacophony and the air they stirred wheeling past to inspect him, he still felt no living presences anywhere ahead. He quickly pulled his blaster and lightsaber, then pushed off the cliff and descended in a free rappel, using the Force to pull himself deep inside the mouth.

After bumping aside half a dozen startled birds, Luke landed in a deep crouch about twenty meters in. He immediately dived for the cover of a nearby boulder and lay motionless, calling on his more mundane senses to locate the being responsible for deadening the Force inside the cavern. For a hundred heartbeats, he heard nothing but the birds and smelled nothing except their guano.

Then suddenly he could feel their presences, filling the cavern and spilling out over the sea. They were fierce little birds, frightened by his intrusion and on the verge of attacking. Luke poured thoughts of friendship and safety into his presence, and the birds began to quiet, both in the Force and in the cavern. He disentangled himself from the rappelling line and spun to his knees, taking care to keep his emotions calm as he peered around the boulder.

Walking toward him, Luke saw a tall, brown-eyed woman with tresses of curly brown hair hanging down her shoulders. Dressed in a simple white toga belted at the waist by a thin golden cord, she had high cheeks and a full-lipped mouth that seemed somehow sad despite its broad smile. She looked directly at Luke, and only then did he feel the waves of joy she was radiating into the Force.

"Luke Skywalker." She extended her arms toward him. "Welcome."

Luke rose and answered her smile with one of his own. Unlike everyone else he had seen on Pydyr, her appearance remained unblemished by the illusory pox, and there was no hint of fatigue or illness in her posture. He started across the cavern floor to greet her.

"Akanah. It's good to see you."

She scowled at his weapons. "You have a strange way of showing your pleasure."

Luke glanced down and flushed with embarrassment, but returned only the blaster to its holster. "I apologize." He gestured at the birds wheeling about their heads. "I've been pursuing a very dangerous . . . *being*, and when I couldn't sense these birds in the Force—"

"Naturally, you grew suspicious." There was a slight note of disapproval in Akanah's voice, and she cast a meaningful glance at the lightsaber still in his hand. "What must I do to persuade you that you have nothing to fear from *me*?"

"Only convince me that you *are* you," Luke replied. "Tell me the name of my mother."

Akanah arched a brow. "You hold a grudge a long time, Grand Master Jedi. I had *thought* you would be over that by now."

Luke knew by the sly smile that accompanied her words that he was not looking at an impostor. He and Akanah had met decades before, when she had tricked him into helping her find the Fallanassi by claiming that his mother belonged to their order. And while Abeloth might have known the facts of that meeting, she could not have known how Luke *felt* about the hoax—that he had come to understand Akanah's desperation and had forgiven her, and that they had even become romantically involved for a time.

Certain now that he was talking to the real Akanah—and *only* Akanah—Luke returned his lightsaber to his belt. "I *am* over it."

He stepped into her embrace and was surprised by the sudden sense of warmth and well-being he experienced. It felt good to know that Akanah still had fond feelings for him after all these years. But there was a pang of sadness, too, as he was reminded of the arms he would never again feel—and that he never again need fear making Mara jealous when an old girlfriend held him a bit longer than was appropriate.

Akanah seemed to sense the drift of his thoughts and stepped back, still holding his hands. "I heard about Mara. I am very sorry."

Knowing better than to force an insincere smile in Akanah's presence, Luke nodded and squeezed her hand.

"Thanks, that means a lot to me," he said. "We miss her, but Ben and I are doing fine now."

"I am glad to hear it." Akanah dropped her gaze to his weapons again. "Much more glad than I was to see you holding *those*. Surely you know better than to believe you have anything to fear from the Fallanassi?"

"Forgive my caution," Luke said. He felt as though he should have been relieved to see Akanah, but he was not. There was something reserved in her manner—something that suggested he should not take her help for granted. "My quarry has some frightening abilities. I couldn't take a chance."

Akanah shook her head sadly. "Why do we always fear what we do not understand?" She took him by the arm and started deeper into the musty cavern, their feet slipping on the uneven, guano-slickened floor. "That is why I wanted to see you before you departed. I hope you don't mind."

"Of course not. I'm glad you came." Now that they

had been together a few moments, Luke could feel a flatness in her Force aura—a hint that there was something she did not want him to sense. "But you must know I came for more than the *Shadow.* There's someone new among you—someone very dangerous."

Akanah nodded. "Yes, Najee said you were looking for the pox carrier," she replied. "There is no need to worry about her, Luke. We have the epidemic under control."

"There *is* no epidemic," Luke said, putting a bit of an edge into his voice. "And we both know it."

"Then why are you here?" Akanah asked. "Surely you are not arrogant enough to believe that the Fallanassi need Jedi protection—or that we *desire* it?"

Instead of answering, Luke stopped and turned to stare out the cavern toward the white island. "Then you *are* hiding Abeloth?"

"You knew that when you came to Pydyr," Akanah replied gently. "You also know that you are wrong to be here."

"Looking for Abeloth?" Luke shook his head. "You only believe that because you don't know what she is."

"I know that you are playing with the White Current," Akanah countered. "I know that your Jedi arrogance is what cost you your wife and your two nephews."

"My *Jedi arrogance*?" Luke fought to keep his emotions under control. The Akanah he remembered would never hurt him out of spite; if she was saying such things, it was either because she had changed, or because she believed them and thought he needed to hear the truth. "We've made some mistakes, yes—*I* have made mistakes. But the Jedi aren't like the Fallanassi. We don't hide from the galaxy, we embrace it and we live in it—and that means we must sometimes fight to defend it."

"To defend it, or control it?" Akanah asked, speaking softly. She took his arm and started toward the *Shadow* again. "The Jedi have lost their way—*you* have let them lose their way, Luke. First, they convince themselves that they are beyond light and dark—"

"That was never Jedi canon," Luke said. "A Sith infiltrator attempted to corrupt our beliefs."

"And she succeeded, did she not?" Akanah asked. "Consider the evidence. A Jedi Knight has assumed the throne of the Hapes Consortium. Jacen Solo took it upon himself to change the flow of the Current. And now, a Jedi Grand Master has joined forces with the Sith. If that is not corruption, I have no understanding of the term."

Luke fell silent, more surprised by the accusations than hurt by them. Akanah had no doubt learned about the Sith alliance from Abeloth herself. But how she had concluded that Jacen had wanted to change the future, he had no idea. Luke himself had come to that realization only gradually, after retracing his nephew's journey with the Mind Walkers and speaking with his spirit in the Lake of Apparitions. The only reasonable explanation was, again, Abeloth herself.

Half a dozen steps later, Luke finally asked, "Akanah, how can you know what Jacen was seeking? Is that something Abeloth told you?"

"*How* I know does not matter." Akanah's Force aura began to grow faded and hazy as she grew more guarded. "What matters is that you believe it, too."

They reached the *Shadow*'s stern and circled around to port. The boarding ramp had been left down, and Luke was dismayed to see a dozen of the sharp-winged birds flitting in and out through the open hatch.

"The failure is not yours alone," Akanah said, speaking in a gentler voice. "I sensed the shadow inside Jacen when he asked to study with us, but I allowed him to stay because he was your nephew . . . and because I believed I could help him find the light again."

"Thank you for trying," Luke said. "I know that you made an impression—Jacen spoke of you fondly, and with respect."

Akanah gave a dismissive wave. "It was a mistake," she insisted. "There was too much fire in him . . . too much will. I should have known he would leave before he was prepared."

"Prepared?" Luke asked, surprised. "You had plans for him?"

Akanah nodded. "To teach him to *accept*. He had so much Jedi in him, always believing that the galaxy was his to save." She stopped in front of the *Shadow*'s boarding ramp, and a cold fog began to obscure her Force presence. "That is why he became what he did, you know. It is why so many of your Jedi Knights become monsters. It begins innocently enough, with a vow to protect. But they have a habit of taking a burden greater than they can carry. Soon protection becomes control, and the Jedi protector becomes the Jedi ruler, just as Kueller did on Almania, just as Raynar Thul did in the Colony—just as Tenel Ka has in the Hapes Consortium. You assume too much, and the galaxy pays."

As Akanah spoke these last words, a ripple of excitement rolled through the Force from the cavern mouth, and Luke realized they were not alone. He extended his awareness in that direction and was not all that surprised to feel his son's presence just outside, hanging above the top edge—perhaps even on the same rappelling line he himself had used. And with Ben was Vestara's presence, damped down and—save for the burst of excitement that had given her away—almost undetectable.

If Akanah had felt the ripple, she showed no sign of it.

Deciding to follow her lead, Luke said, "There's great wisdom in what you say. But what of the evil in the galaxy? Should we allow the selfish to enslave the weak? The greedy to steal from the poor?"

"One cannot rid the galaxy of a killer without *becoming* a killer," Akanah countered. "One cannot fight evil without *doing* evil. Did the Jedi learn nothing when they decided to stand against the Yuuzhan Vong?"

"The Jedi stopped a brutal and savage species from conquering the galaxy," Luke replied, starting to grow irritated. "And later, we prevented a cruel retaliation against those same invaders."

Akanah shook her head. "You prevented a change from coming to the galaxy," she said. "That is *all* you did."

"So we should have allowed the Yuuzhan Vong to take everything?" Luke countered. "We should have gone into hiding and allowed them to sacrifice *trillions* of innocents to their imaginary gods? Is that what you're saying?"

"I am *saying* the Current is not ours to control," Akanah replied. "We cannot know where it will carry us, or what turns it may take getting us there. We can only trust to its purpose and not try to bend it to ours."

"And you believe that's what Jacen was doing," Luke said, once again probing for the source of her knowledge. "Trying to change something in the future?"

"No, I am convinced he *did* change something." Akanah waved Luke toward the *Shadow*'s open hatch. "And that is why I must ask you to go and leave the ancient one here with us. Perhaps, with our help, she will be able to undo the damage."

An icy lump formed in Luke's stomach. "Undo it?" He wanted to ask Akanah if she had lost her mind, but considering who she had just admitted the Fallanassi were sheltering, he was not sure he wanted to know the answer. "*How?*"

"Why do you ask questions when you already know the answer?"

Luke understood, of course. Abeloth had promised to return the Current to its original course. Perhaps such a thing was even possible—but that did not make it a good idea. Jacen had looked into the Pool of Knowledge and had a Force vision of a dark man in dark armor, sitting on a golden throne surrounded by acolytes in dark robes. But when Luke had looked, two years after Jacen had become Darth Caedus and been killed, his vision had been of Jacen's daughter, Allana, standing next to a white throne and surrounded by friends of all species. If *that* was the change Abeloth had promised to undo, Luke wanted no part of it.

Instead of ascending the *Shadow*'s ramp, Luke said, "Master Yoda once told me that the future is always in motion. We can never see it perfectly because it's always changing."

"Yes, you have told me about Yoda's teachings before, when we were . . . traveling." Akanah smiled at the memory, then continued, "We Fallanassi believe much the same thing—that it is impossible to know where the Current will take us, because the Current is ever-changing."

A flutter of exhilaration rose inside Luke, and he began to hope that he might yet persuade Akanah to cooperate. "Then why would you want Abeloth to change it *back*?" he asked. "If we don't know where it's going anyway, how can we know that the old course is any better than the new course? Or even that it's *different*?"

"Because now we *do* know," Akanah replied. "When Jacen changed its course, he changed it *to* something—to that vision you saw in the Pool of Knowledge, of the white throne—"

"How do you know about *that*?" Luke demanded, interrupting to prevent her from mentioning Allana while Vestara was outside eavesdropping. "Abeloth?"

"Then it *is* true." Akanah's voice grew more resolute. "Jacen has turned the current toward a destination of his choosing—and you have seen it."

"I've had a vision, yes," Luke said. "Whether that means he has actually turned the Current onto a new course, I have no idea."

Swells of alarm began to roll through the Force as Ben and Vestara suddenly grew very concerned about something happening outside the cavern mouth. Luke pivoted casually on one foot, turning to look out toward the sea and the white island, and saw that the birds had grown fiercely agitated.

"But if Jacen *did* turn the Current to a new destination," Luke continued, "and Abeloth changes it back, won't she *also* be fixing its destination? Won't she *also* be fixing a course that should be ever-changing?"

Akanah furrowed her brow, and Luke thought for a moment that he had shown her the lie in Abeloth's promise.

Then Akanah's eyes clouded with confusion, and her Force aura grew cold and shrouded. "That is a foolish question," she said. "Abeloth is beyond your understanding."

"Then explain her to me."

Instead of answering, Akanah looked toward the cave mouth. A pair of startled cries sounded from the cliff face outside, then Ben and Vestara plummeted into view, dropping headfirst toward the rocks below. Luke quickly reached out and grabbed them both in the Force, then pulled them both to safety.

They landed in a tumbling heap a few meters inside the cave and came to their feet standing shoulder-to-shoulder.

Reaching for his lightsaber, Luke turned to face Akanah—and found her already out of reach, backing away with a smile on her lips that was at once mad and gentle.

"Silly Jedi." She extended a hand toward the *Shadow*'s open hatch and motioned him toward the boarding ramp. "*No one* can explain Abeloth."

Chapter Twenty-three

ONLY THE NAMEPLATE HAD CHANGED. LOOMING UP among the elegant stone-and-mirrsteel spires of the corporate advocacy district, the hulking monolith of GAS Detention Center 81 remained the same permacrete misfit it had been when the sign read GALACTIC ALLIANCE STORAGE. With its purple cam bubbles, heavy blast doors, and fortified entry, the detention center looked like the urban bunker it was, and trying to bust *anyone* out of there was going to be about the craziest thing Han had ever done—on purpose, anyway.

But there wasn't much choice. Events on Coruscant were turning insane. With Kenth Hamner shoved to the sidelines, the Jedi Council had assigned the Solos to rescue Valin and Jysella Horn—or, more accurately, to steal the carbonite pods in which Galactic Alliance Security was storing the two frozen Jedi Knights. In the meantime, the Masters were developing a plan to reinforce the Skywalkers without having to engage GA forces first. If the Solos failed to complete their mission before the StealthXs launched, Daala's first move would almost certainly be to secure the pods somewhere so hidden even Jedi could not find them.

Three figures, one Mon Calamari and two human, emerged from the detention center and turned up the pedway toward Fellowship Plaza. From Han's vantage point, across the skylane and a hundred meters above the pedway, it was impossible to identify much more than their species and hair color—brown and black for the humans, not applicable for the Mon Calamari. The Mon Calamari and the large human were wearing brown Jedi robes, while the smaller, black-haired human—a woman—wore a loose-fitting pilot's jacket and trousers. As they walked, the woman leaned close to the brown-haired Jedi, and he wrapped a comforting arm around her shoulders.

"Corran is giving the signal, so it looks like Mirax got the tracking bugs attached to both pods." As Han spoke, a Rodian vagrant who had been sitting on the pedway before the Horns arrived suddenly snatched up his alms cup and started to meander after them. "And they've still got their tail."

"Only the usual?" Leia asked.

"All I see is a Rodian pretending to be a beggar," Han said. "There's probably a control officer and a couple of switch-offs working our side of the skylane, but no sign of a Doomsled or an arrest team moving in."

"Good." Leia's voice grew more muffled as she turned toward the center of the room. "How are we receiving?"

"Very well," reported the sultry voice of Natua Wan. Along with several other recently recovered Jedi Knights, the Falleen had *insisted* on being part of the rescue mission. Of course, Corran and Mirax Horn had also wanted to participate in the assault, but they were under constant observation and would only have drawn unwanted attention to the mission. "But something seems wrong with our overlay software. These path reports make no sense."

Natua's use of the plural gave Han a sinking feeling. "*Reports?*"

He turned toward the center of the chamber, where an oversized holopad was projecting a schematic of the interior of Detention Center 81. Near the heart of the holograph lay a web of green and yellow squiggles so filled with squares and rectangles that Han could not find the end or beginning of either line.

"Blasted circuit heads!" Han turned to R2-D2, who was plugged into the holopad, feeding it data transmitted by the tracking bugs. "You've got an interpretation problem. Did you check for a code algorithm?"

R2-D2 tweedled a sharp reply, which C-3PO promptly translated as, "Artoo-Detoo reports that he has already defeated the GAS code."

Another series of tweets followed. C-3PO ignored them and continued to look at Han.

"What else?" Han asked.

"My apologies, Captain Solo," C-3PO said. "But Artoo suggests that if you are unable to recognize a random progression, perhaps you shouldn't be leading this mission."

"A *what* progression?" Han left the viewport and went to stand at the holograph. "You mean this data is good?"

R2-D2 gave an affirmative whistle.

Han stared at the path reports, watching in growing concern as the colored lines changed directions at right angles, usually staying on the same plane, but occasionally descending or climbing as much as four levels. The pods did not seem to be moving toward any particular location, simply making random turns and floor changes that repeatedly crossed their own paths. Clearly, they were taking precautions to prevent the pods from being tracked back to their storage facilities.

"They're on to us," Zekk said.

Tall and square-shouldered, he was standing on the opposite side of the holograph with his fiancée, Taryn Zel. With Zekk's black hair and chiseled features and Taryn's fiery-eyed beauty, they were a handsome couple—and one that sent a sad pang through Han's heart every time he caught his daughter glancing in their direction. It was more envy than jealousy that made Jaina keep sneaking looks at how close they always seemed to be standing.

Han knew. Her thing with Zekk had always been more "fighting buddy" than "big love," and she had told him that she was glad he and Taryn seemed so happy together. But Han could also see that Zekk's happiness reminded Jaina of her breakup with Jag—of how the stars always seemed to be conspiring against them, pushing them into situations where they found themselves obliged to choose between duty and each other.

Han was no Jedi, of course. But it seemed to him they kept finding themselves in the same mess because the Force was trying to tell them that love didn't work that way. They couldn't keep putting everything else ahead of their relationship—not the Jedi Order, not the Empire, not even their family. It was all or nothing. When two people wanted to be together, they had to lock card values and push all-in together. In the game of love, that was the only way to win.

But Han knew better than to say any of that to Jaina. Even he knew it wouldn't be appreciated after she had already broken up with the guy. Besides, who wants to take romantic advice from her dad?

"Captain?" asked a flirty Hapan voice. "Oh, *Captain*?"

Han turned his gaze on the speaker and found himself looking through the holograph into Taryn Zel's gray-green eyes. "Yeah?"

Taryn shook her head in exasperation, then asked, "Are we still *doing* this?"

"Sure," Han said. "Why not?"

Taryn flashed a coy smile and said, "Good."

But Zekk was not so enthusiastic. "You're *both* crazy." He pointed at the still-growing path reports. "GAS knows we're coming."

"Not necessarily," Jaina pointed out. She was looking at the holograph from the side adjacent to Zekk and Taryn, standing between Leia and Natua Wan. "We've given them plenty of reason to be cautious. Running the pods around to confuse tracking devices could be standard procedure."

Taryn nodded agreement, then reached up and draped a hand over Zekk's shoulder. "When she's right, she's right," she said. "Jedi Solo has already embarrassed Colonel Retk once, and Yakas are beyond smart. *Of course* he would take precautions."

As Taryn spoke, C-3PO quietly dismissed himself and left the room, moving toward the front of the office suite. Han caught Seff Hellin's eye and nodded for the young Jedi to follow. C-3PO had orders not to allow anyone past the entrance, but given what they were about to do, there was no sense taking chances.

Once Han had returned his attention to the room, Zekk said, "What difference does it make if they *are* just taking precautions? We still don't know where they're keeping the pods, and that means we'll be inside too long. This will be a running battle, not a quick grab."

Taryn's eyes turned hard. "Are you suggesting we leave that poor Horn girl frozen in carbonite?" Like most Hapan women, she was not accustomed to being questioned by her mate, and there was an edge in her voice that suggested she was still having trouble adjusting to the idea that Zekk was most definitely *not* a Hapan man. "I'm afraid I just won't allow that."

Zekk's eyes twinkled with amusement. "The decision is Han and Leia's," he reminded her. "And Valin is frozen, too. Don't forget about him."

"What makes you think I *did*?" Taryn turned to Han and said, "If we're going to do this, I need to get moving. It won't be easy to make myself look like an uptight female boss, you know."

Han raised a hand. "We're gonna do it," he assured her. "But let's make sure we know what we're getting into, okay?"

As Han spoke, the green path report suddenly stopped advancing.

"Stang!" he cursed. "They just found one of the bugs."

Zekk turned to Taryn. "Didn't you say Hapan trackers are undetectable?"

"I did, but they can't overpower a signal neutralizer," Taryn said. "If that tracker doesn't come back online, it's probably because GAS has a neutralizer in the pod vault."

The yellow path report suddenly stopped advancing as well.

"And if *that* one doesn't come back?" Jaina asked, pointing at the end of the yellow line. It was three floors above the end of the green line, and about fifty meters toward the interior of the building. "Would that be because there are *two* signal neutralizers in *two* pod vaults?"

Taryn's eyes narrowed. "Probably," she said. "If GAS is worried about security, it *would* make sense to keep the prisoners in separate locations."

"That's certainly a possibility, Taryn," Leia said. "But raiding two locations is going to complicate things, even if we could be sure you're right. Is there a way to confirm that the trackers are still in operation?"

"They *are,*" Taryn insisted. "I can't prove it, but our devices use nanotech to fuse with anything they attach to. In less than a second, they become completely invisible. And they mask their transmissions as backgro—"

Taryn ended her explanation mid-syllable as C-3PO stepped into the room. He stopped just inside the door, but over one shoulder Han could see Seff Hellin looking frustrated and confused. Over the other was a tall, well-dressed man with a scar on his forehead. On the collar of his navy-style tunic, he wore the crest of the Imperial Head of State.

"Jagged?" Jaina gasped, starting toward the door. "What are you doing here?"

Before Jag could reply, C-3PO said, "Head of State Fel is requesting an audience with Captain Solo and Princess Leia." He turned his photoreceptors toward Han. "I asked him to wait in the foyer, but he was most insistent that he be seen at once."

"It's okay, Threepio."

Han nodded to Leia, and they followed Jaina through the door into the suite's empty, beige-carpeted outer office. Save for Seff, who silently mouthed the word *alone*, Jag was by himself—a fact that Han found telling. After the assassination attempt at the Pangalactus, Jag never went anywhere without his Chiss assistant, Ashik, and a sizable contingent of bodyguards.

"Thank you, Seff," Leia said, motioning the young Jedi Knight back toward the foyer. "You showed good judgment in not using force against the Head of State. But it might be wise to make sure there's nobody out there eavesdropping on us."

"Yeah," Han said, scowling at Jag. "And if there is, you don't have to be so nice."

"Certainly not on my account," Jag said. "If there's anyone out there, they aren't mine."

"Good," Jaina said.

She stepped forward, squaring her shoulders in a manner that Han recognized as just a little wary. Jag's unexpected arrival was clearly not a welcome surprise for Jaina; with a difficult raid coming up, the last thing she would want on her mind was Jagged Fel.

"Let's start with how you found us," Jaina demanded.

Jag smirked down at her. "I *do* have one of the best intelligence services in the galaxy."

Han's heart jumped into his throat, and he glanced over at Leia. "Great," he said. "If the *Imperials* know we're here—"

"There's no need for concern," Jag said, raising a

hand to stop him. "Ashik assures me that GAS is not aware of you."

Even Han could feel the relief flooding the room, but he didn't feel any better himself—especially since Jag had obviously just dodged Jaina's question.

"I need details, Jag," Han said. He hooked a thumb toward the next room. "We're putting a lot of lives on the line here, and Ashik's assurances don't cut it."

"I'm sorry, Captain Solo," Jag said. "As you yourself are fond of saying: trust me."

"That might be easier after we know what you're doing here," Leia said. She glanced toward the now closed door behind them. "And why you couldn't wait for us to come out."

"I couldn't wait because the Horns aren't the only ones with a team of GAS agents tailing them. Unless I'm back in the lobby soon, the ones tailing *me* are going to start wondering if I had some business in the Graser Building other than a meeting that ended . . ." Jag paused to check his chrono. ". . . twelve minutes ago."

"Fine," Jaina said. "So let's get to it. What do you need?"

Jag's eyes turned steely. "Very well, Jaina," he said. "The first thing I need to know is why you didn't tell me about the Sith—or the fact that the Jedi have actually been *working* with them."

Jaina's jaw dropped nearly as far as Han's heart. Leia merely bit her lips and glanced at the floor for a moment, then looked to Han.

"The leak couldn't have come from Wuul," she said. "He didn't know about the arrangement with the Sith."

"Then it's *true*?" Jag asked.

Jaina nodded, but it was Leia who answered. "I'm afraid so," she said. "Our StealthX wing has been trapped here on Coruscant—as I'm sure you're aware. And Luke and Ben needed some major support to destroy Abeloth."

Jag frowned. "Abeloth?"

"The huge threat I told you about," Jaina explained, "just before we broke up."

"*We* didn't break up," Jag reminded her. "*You* left because I wouldn't launch the Imperial fleet on just your say-so—"

"Hey, look," Han interrupted, "we'd love to leave you kids alone so you can work this out, but aren't we all on a schedule here?"

Jag flushed. "You're absolutely right, Captain Solo." He straightened his lapels and shot a glance Jaina's way. "And who broke up with whom is hardly relevant anymore. If you would be kind enough to explain this Abeloth problem, I'll fill you in on how I heard about the Sith."

"Fair enough," Leia said, stepping forward to take control of the conversation. "Abeloth is an ancient . . . well, *entity* that Luke and Ben found imprisoned in the Maw. When we hid our young ones at Shelter during the war against the Yuuzhan Vong, she made contact through the Force and planted the seeds of the madness that afflicted them recently."

"I see," Jag said. "But why would the Sith help Grand Master Skywalker destroy this Abeloth? I would think Sith would be happy to see Jedi Knights going insane."

"They *said* Abeloth was driving their apprentices mad, too," Jaina replied. "It turns out they were just trying to capture her. She's immensely powerful—and that makes her immensely useful."

Jag's face paled. "Please tell me they didn't succeed," he said. "Master Skywalker *did* destroy her . . . correct?"

"Well, we thought so," Han said. "But it turns out she escaped. We think she's on Pydyr right now, hiding out with the Fallanassi."

Jag began to look frightened. "I see," he said. "And the Sith? Do they know where she is, too?"

"Not yet," Han said.

"Not as far as we know," Jaina added. "But it's not going to stay that way. These are *Sith*, Jag—and there are thousands of them, maybe even millions. They're going to find her."

Jag shook his head grimly. "Unbelievable. Just when I thought things couldn't get any worse, you tell me they have." As he said this last part, he was looking at Jaina. "And this is why the Jedi remain determined to launch their StealthX wing?"

"Right," Jaina replied.

"Thinking like that, I see why Luke set you up to be Imperial Head of State," Han added.

"Yes, I *must* remember to thank him for that someday," Jag said, his dry voice suggesting that he was anything *but* grateful for the burden Luke had so unceremoniously dropped on his shoulders. "In the meantime, you need to contact the Temple. The Jedi should launch *now,* before the public learns about the arrangement with the Sith."

Han's stomach began to hurt. "And that's going to happen *how*?"

"The same way I learned of things. Daala has a vid of Jaina and Lando at the trial on Klatooine." Jag turned to Jaina. "It's bad, Jaina. Even I had trouble believing there was an acceptable explanation."

Han winced inside. If Jag was interested in working things out, he certainly wasn't earning any points that way.

Jaina's face remained stoic, her voice even as she asked, "If Daala has the vid, why hasn't she released it yet?"

"You Jedi really stirred things up when you sent Saar and Arelis to Blaudu Sextus. Daala wants *me* to send Imperial fleets to put down the revolts popping up along the rim." A tight smile crossed Jag's lips. "She seems to believe I would actually do that in exchange for not using that vid to embarrass the Jedi."

A broad smile came to Jaina's face. "And you're *letting* her?"

Jag dipped his head in acknowledgment. "For three days now."

"You'd *do* that for me?" Jaina asked, eyes wide with surprise . . . and joy. "After the way I broke things off?"

Jag's face remained stoic. "It's not entirely for you, Jaina," he said. "I'd like the Empire to develop a good relationship with the Jedi."

Jaina's smile did not vanish. "Close enough," she said, clearly reading something in his Force-aura that Han could not sense. "And, Jag, I'm sorry for the way I put you on the spot when—"

"Apology accepted," Jag interrupted, glancing from Jaina to her parents and clearly growing uncomfortable. "And thank you. It means a great deal to me, but the *Pellaeon* is preparing to break orbit, and Daala is going to know that I've been playing her soon enough." He shifted his gaze to Leia. "I wanted the Jedi to know before she did."

Leia cocked her brow. "Won't this kill the deal to bring the Empire completely into the Alliance?"

"It will," Jag replied. "But the more I come to know Daala, the more I realize that my Moffs are right this time. We wouldn't be joining an Alliance, we would be stepping into chains."

Leia clasped Jag's forearm. "Thank you for telling us first. That means the world to me—and I know it will mean the world to the Masters, as well." She rose on her toes to kiss his cheek, then turned to Han. "I think our decision has been made for us, dear. We have to go after Valin and Jysella *now,* even if our intelligence isn't quite complete."

Han nodded. "Isn't that what I've been telling you?" He clapped Jag on the shoulder. "We owe you one, son."

"Not at all, Captain Solo," Jag said. "I'm only doing what's right for the Empire."

"Yeah—and for everyone else, too," Han said. He took Leia's elbow and turned back toward the makeshift planning room, leaving Jaina and Jag to stand there alone. "Come on, Princess. We've got work to do, and it looks like these lovebirds could use a couple of minutes alone."

Chapter Twenty-four

GUARDING THE OPERATIONS HANGAR DOOR WERE TWO young Jedi Knights whom Kenth Hamner remembered only vaguely, a Bothan male and an Arcona female whose names he did not recall at all. Nonetheless, they knew *him*. The instant they saw him turn the corner and start down the gray kranet-stone corridor, their eyes widened, and the Arcona reached for her comlink.

"You there!" Kenth called, pointing at the female. He used the Force to casually flick her hand away from the comlink, as though he wanted his question to take precedence, then pointed at the heavy blast door behind them. "What's going on inside?"

The pair pivoted around, squaring their shoulders to block his way, but at least they showed the good sense not to reach for their lightsabers. The Bothan cocked his furry head and regarded Kenth with narrowed eyes for a moment, then assumed a wide, assertive stance.

"Shouldn't you be in your quarters, Master Hamner?" he demanded. "We were told you're under confinement."

"I can't imagine who would have told you that. It's utter nonsense," Kenth lied, continuing to approach. The truth was that the other Masters on the Council had "requested" him to remain in his quarters. And they had placed two guards—now unconscious—outside his door to enforce that "request." He stopped a few paces from this pair, then looked over their shoulders toward the hangar door. "What's going on? Are they preparing for launch?"

The two guards did not drop their gazes in doubt, or glance at each other, seeking support for what Kenth knew had to be a difficult decision. They simply stood their ground, stared him in the eye, and did not reply.

"I hope you two understand what's happening in there," Kenth said. "Launching the StealthX wing is an act of high treason."

Unlike Kenth's previous statement, *this* one he believed with his entire heart. It was why, when he had noticed the Force inside the Temple beginning to quiver with urgency and anxiety, he had extended his awareness in the direction of the Operations Hangar and despaired. He had sensed a similar aura of grim resolve too many times in too many places not to recognize what he was feeling: warriors preparing for battle.

And since these were Jedi preparing to do battle against the Galactic Alliance, he had felt obliged to take action. To have remained in confinement while Saba led an Order he loved into combat against a government to which he had pledged loyalty and life would have been a betrayal—not only of the Jedi and the Alliance, but of himself.

When the two Jedi Knights continued to glower at him without responding, Kenth realized he would have to press the issue. He turned to the Arcona. She was small for her species, short enough so that the top of her flat, broad head barely reached Kenth's chin. Her eyes were clear and green, indicating that she had so far avoided the salt addiction that was the great weakness of her species. Most notably, there was something gentle in her leathery features, and that made Kenth think she would be the easier of the two to lull into carelessness.

"I asked a question, Jedi," he said. "Do you understand that, even by standing guard here, you are committing high treason against the Galactic Alliance?"

The Arcona studied him in silence, and it was the Bothan who said, "Razelle, Master. *Vaala* Razelle."

Kenth furrowed his brow. "Vaala Razelle?"

"My name, Master," the Arcona—Vaala—explained. "You didn't seem to know it."

"I'm sorry, Jedi Razelle," Hamner replied. "There are hundreds of Jedi Knights in the Order. It's very difficult to recognize you all."

Vaala nodded, but she did not move. Neither did the Bothan.

"And *your* name?" Kenth asked, turning to the Bothan.

"Bwua'tu," the young male replied. "Yantahar Bwua'tu."

"Bwua'tu?" Kenth began to have a sinking feeling. Nek Bwua'tu hadn't mentioned having any Jedi family members when he'd contacted Kenth to suggest a deal. Of course, Nek would have been worried about drawing unfavorable attention to any relative of his—but it would certainly explain why he had been so eager to avoid bloodshed between the Order and the GA military. "Any relation to the admiral?"

Yantahar nodded. "Yes."

Kenth waited a moment for an explanation that was not forthcoming, then decided against asking for one. Yantahar was either offended that he had needed to ask or suspicious of Kenth's motives; either way, Kenth would not improve the situation by lingering on his mistake.

"Well, I'm very sorry about what happened to the admiral," he said. "The entire Alliance is hoping he recovers soon."

Yantahar's expression finally softened a little. "Maybe not the *entire* Alliance, but thank you."

Kenth nodded, then put some authority into his voice. "I know how the admiral would feel about treason. How about *you,* Jedi Bwua'tu?"

Yantahar shrugged. "There are hundreds of Sith running loose in the galaxy, and Chief Daala is preventing us from going to meet them." He glanced over at Vaala, his first sign of uncertainty. "We have no choice."

"Son, we *always* have a choice." Kenth turned his gaze on Vaala, then continued, "And the time has come for you and Jedi Razelle to make yours. Will you stand aside so I can stop this?"

Vaala was quick to shake her head. "I'm sorry, Master Hamner," she said. "You should return to your quarters now."

Kenth let his chin drop and spoke in a soft, sighing whisper. "That's *Grand* Master."

Vaala cocked her head, turning a recessed ear toward him. "Sorry, sir, I didn't . . . Yant, watch—!"

The warning came to a startled end as Kenth used the Force to pull their lightsabers from their belt hooks. He sent both weapons spinning high into the air, managing to depress the activation switch and slide the safety glide up on Yantahar's. As the sapphire blade crackled to life, both Jedi pivoted away, extending their hands to summon their weapons back into their grasp.

And that was when Kenth stepped between the pair. He struck Yantahar at the base of the jaw with a side hammerfist and simultaneously jabbed a one-knuckle punch into the delicate sensory nub between Vaala's eyes. Both Jedi collapsed, unconscious before they hit the floor. Kenth was not quite quick enough to catch their lightsabers before they landed, but he did deactivate Yantahar's before the weapon clattered to the floor beside the Bothan's leg.

Kenth quickly collected both weapons, removed their power cells, and returned them to their owners' belts. It had been all too easy to catch the pair off-guard and incapacitate them—as it had the pair stationed outside his quarters. Once he resumed his post in the Grand

Master's office, he would need to speak to the combat instructors about the shortcomings in their curriculum. He dragged both Jedi into a nearby fabrication shop and hit them with a Force shock to be sure they would remain unconscious for a time. Then he returned to the hangar and slipped in through the access hatch.

Inside, the hangar deck was crowded with StealthX squadrons, all neatly arranged in their own arrow-shaped combat groups and surrounded by bustling teams of support crew. With the exception of the squadron leaders, the pilots were already in their vac suits and with their starfighters, either seated in the cockpits running system checks or walking around their craft doing visual inspections. Kenth could see that the strike force included the Order's most experienced pilots, with Lowbacca, Izal Waz, Wonetun, and many other Jedi Knights who had fought in the war against the Yuuzhan Vong assigned to craft in the second-in-command slot.

Conspicuously missing was Jaina Solo, whose skill in starfighter combat was second only to that of Luke Skywalker himself. To Kenth's surprise, Raynar Thul was preparing to launch. The position of his StealthX with one of the squadrons near the rear of the hangar suggested that he had not been given any command responsibilities. Even so, that Thul was present at all indicated that either Saba was putting too much confidence in his recovery, or she was desperate for combat-qualified pilots.

As Kenth contemplated which, Thul's scarified head suddenly tipped to one side, as though he were listening to something on his shoulder, and he slowly turned toward the doorway. Kenth retreated into the shadows and drew his Force aura in tight, but Thul's gaze slid in his direction and lingered on the area for a moment. Finally, a tight little smile creased the Jedi Knight's burn-scarred lips, then he dipped his chin in recognition and turned back to his inspection. Heart pounding, Kenth forced himself to remain still until Thul seemed completely occupied, then slipped along the wall searching for Saba and the other Masters.

He found them—most of them—on a large observation balcony twenty meters above. They were gathered along the safety rail, watching the preparations below, pointing and gesturing at the StealthXs as they discussed last-minute strategies. To Kenth's surprise, only four Masters—Kyp Durron, Kyle Katarn, Octa Ramis, and Barratk'l—had donned the distinctive StealthX flight suits. Absent were Corran Horn and both Solusars, the latter no doubt because they were on Ossus with their students.

Everyone else, including Saba, continued to wear their customary robes . . . which could only mean that after the launch, they intended to remain on Coruscant to defend the Temple. With Saba in charge, Kenth had no doubt what form the defense would take. It would be aggressive and cunning, designed to keep Daala and her allies off-balance until they could be incapacitated and rendered *forever harmless,* as the Barabels liked to say.

In other words, killed.

Half expecting a hundred Jedi Knights to turn toward him with every breath he took, Kenth remained in the shadows, slipping along the edge of the hangar until he reached a series of vertical conveyance pipes. He tested each pipe until he found one cool enough to grasp, then braced his feet on the wall and began to ascend. The back side was slick with dust and mold, but he did not use the Force to make the climb easier. With so many Jedi nearby, there was a danger of even a small disturbance being noticed, and his nerves had already been set on edge. Though Kenth felt certain he had been spotted by Thul, he had no idea what to make of it. Did Thul's silence indicate that Kenth had an ally among the Jedi? Or had it been a simple decision to avoid becoming involved in the Masters' power struggle?

There was just no way to know. Thul was a strange man, a Jedi Knight who seemed to see farther than most—but who kept his own counsel and usually appeared to be more amused by the affairs of the Jedi than involved with them.

Kenth reached the support level of the hangar, where a network of supply lines, ventilation ducts, and service cranes hung thirty meters above the maintenance decks. He worked his way out toward the balcony that Saba and the Masters were on, his heart pounding in his ears despite the Jedi breathing techniques he was using to keep himself calm. What he would do when he reached the balcony, he did not know. On the one hand, his best chance of disrupting the launch and preventing the entire Jedi Order from committing a terrible treason lay in taking Saba by surprise and rendering her *forever harmless* before she or anyone else realized what was happening. But he was not sure how the other Masters would react to such a cold-blooded attack, whether they would make allowances for the necessity of taking a ferocious warrior like Saba by surprise, or whether they would consider it a ruthless assassination and turn on him themselves.

After a couple of minutes of very careful, very quiet creeping, Kenth found himself about a meter behind Saba and seven meters above her head. He couldn't make out what she was saying, just that she was hissing commands and questions, and the Masters were answering in subservient tones. If he had had any doubts before, it was clear now who was leading the mutiny . . . and whom he needed to remove if he wished to resume command and prevent the tragedy he saw unfolding in front of him.

But Kenth had not been out of the military for so long that he had forgotten the value of intelligence. It would not be enough to eliminate the traitor. He had to know who was with her, and who was reluctant—he had to know whom he needed to fear after Saba was gone.

Kenth opened himself up to the Force, attuning his ears to its ripples and using it to amplify the voices below. Saba's dorsal ridge instantly rose, and she cocked her scaly head, turning a recessed ear up toward the catwalk where Kenth was hiding. Aware of just how keen her predator's senses were, he held his breath and used a meditation technique to calm his pounding heart. Even then, Saba's head remained cocked, the corner of one eye turned up toward the support level.

Kenth was beginning to think he had lost the element of surprise when Cilghal's gurgling voice began to sound in his ears. ". . . and Mirax are returning to the Temple, and the Solos report the extraction team is ready to proceed."

Extraction team. That could only mean Saba had convinced the Council to strike on multiple fronts at once, sending a team to recover the Horn kids during the confusion of the StealthX launch. It was a smart tactical move, of course . . . and just the kind of thing that would convince Daala the Jedi were going into open rebellion.

"Good," Saba said, thumping her tail in approval. "And the tournament?"

"Booster is expecting Senator Treen to board within the hour," Cilghal reported. "Once she does, they'll be ready to start. The other players are aboard already."

"Ask Captain Terrik to keep us informed. Our timing must be perfect." Saba turned to Barratk'l and asked, "You have made contact with Jedis Saar and Arelis?"

Barratk'l nodded, then rumbled, "My team will rendezvous with them in Arari."

Saba thumped her tail again. "Then may the Force be with you," she said. "Eight Jedi against worldz—this one wishes it could be more."

"Eight must do," Barratk'l assured her. "The Sith are our first concern. But eight Jedi will be enough to offer hope to the slaves. And, with hope, the slaves will free themselves."

"Yes," Saba said. "The Jedi are counting on that."

Kenth could not believe what he was hearing. Not only had Saba convinced the Council to commit high treason and sponsor a prison break, she was also sending a team of Jedi to spark rebellions along the entire galactic rim. And she had recruited Booster Terrik to . . . do what? Organize a celebrity sabacc tournament?

Clearly, the Barabel had to be stopped . . . at any cost.

Saba turned to the Masters in vac suits. "It seemz all is in order. Perhapz you should return to your squadronz."

Cilghal raised a hand-fin to stop them, and for an instant Kenth thought that maybe Saba had not duped the *entire* Council into following her. But then the Mon Calamari spoke, and he realized that matters had deteriorated even further than he thought—the entire Galactic Alliance was *already* beginning to dissolve.

"There is one more development we should consider," Cilghal said. "Head of State Fel has informed the Solos that the Empire is no longer interested in joining a Galactic Alliance led by Natasi Daala."

Kenth saw the jaws of several Masters drop, and his own surprise was such that he let it ripple out into the Force for a full second before he realized he had slipped. He quickly reined in his emotions, but Saba's dorsal ridge was already raised. She turned her head so that one eye was staring into the shadows where Kenth lay hiding, and he knew that he had just lost all hope of taking her by surprise and ending this thing quickly.

"What happened?" Octa Ramis asked. "Why is Fel backing out?"

"Never mind what happened," Kyle interrupted. "What we need to know is whether *Daala* knows yet?"

"If not, she will soon," Cilghal replied. "The *Pellaeon* is preparing to break orbit, and that will not go unnoticed for long."

"Especially not when Head of State Fel returnz to it," Saba said, not turning her head away.

A broad smile came to Kyp's lips. "Any idea why Jag thought the *Solos* needed to know his plans?"

Octa Ramis's heavy brow rose. "Are you suggesting he was offering to coordinate with us?"

"Not *coordinate,*" Kyle said. "That would be interfering in another government's internal affairs. But he was *informing* us."

"Exactly," Kyp said, nodding. "So that we can coordinate with him. When Daala realizes that the Empire is withdrawing from negotiations, she's going to be *very* distracted."

"And that will happen *when?*" Saba asked, finally turning her gaze from Kenth's hiding place. "Did Head of State Fel say when he was departing?"

Cilghal raised a webbed finger and spoke briefly into her comlink, then listened for a moment and looked back to Saba.

"Head of State Fel told them that the *Pellaeon* was *already* preparing to break orbit," she reported. "Leia thinks the Graser Building was his last stop before going to the spaceport."

"So Daala will learn he is leaving *how* soon?" Saba asked. "Fifteen minutes?"

"She *has* to know already," Kyp said. "A Star Destroyer preparing to break orbit isn't subtle, and Jag's pilots are probably prepping his shuttle for departure."

Saba fell silent for a moment, then said, "If Head of State Fel knew where to find the Solos, then he knowz what they are preparing to do—and perhapz what *we* are preparing to do here. He was telling them when to go."

Kyp, Kyle, and the rest of the Masters nodded.

Saba turned toward the hangar floor and surveyed the StealthXs, her forked tongue flicking at the air. Finally, she said, "Ask Captain Terrik to start the tournament at once. And comm the Solos. We go in ten minutes."

Cilghal looked to the other Masters, and Kenth watched in growing horror as, one by one, they nodded agreement. Never before had he felt so shocked, so sad, so alone . . . and so determined. He snatched his lightsaber off his belt, then rose to his feet and took two quick steps, placing himself on the catwalk directly above Saba.

"I'm sorry," he called down. "But I can't let you do that."

Chapter Twenty-five

BEYOND THE BRIDGE OF THE AGING STAR DESTROYER *ERrant Venture* floated the scintillating immensity of the planet Coruscant. It was the brightest jewel of the galactic Core, the hungry heart through which coursed all the blessings and curses of a vast interstellar civilization. And somewhere down there among all those lights hung Booster Terrik's grandchildren, frozen in carbonite and held hostage to an ex-Imperial's insatiable lust for power. Booster had come to free them, and free them he would—even if it meant crashing his Star Destroyer into Chief Daala's offices with every last guest still aboard.

Booster heard a pair of small boots approaching and turned to see a beak-faced Ishi Tib female crossing the deck toward him, her short eyestalks swiveling left and right as she inspected duty stations. Dressed in tight trousers and a bright, puff-sleeved blouse, Lyari looked more like a holostar pirate than the first officer of the galaxy's largest casino ship, and that suited Booster just fine. He liked to remind his patrons they were taking a ride on the wild side, that when they boarded the *Errant Venture* anything could happen—and it usually did.

With Lyari was the latest—and only uninvited—guest, a nondescript human of average height dressed in a conservative business tunic and trousers. Had his collar-length brown hair not been so immaculately trimmed and in place, Booster would have made him for a spy trying to look inconspicuous and unmemorable. Instead he looked exactly like the government bureaucrat he was—a man who was out of his element aboard a den of wickedness like the *Errant Venture,* and way out of his depth gambling with the likes of Drikl Lecersen and Fost Bramsin.

Lyari stopped at Booster's side and made the man squirm by slipping a talon-fingered hand around his triceps. "I present Wynn Dorvan, chief of staff to Chief of State Daala." Her voice was more liquid and purring than usual, a sign that she recognized the value of the catch she had produced. "He's interested in the tournament."

Booster chomped on the stub of his cigar and studied Dorvan out of one eye. "That so, Wynn?" He used the side of his hand to pop the chief of staff lightly in the shoulder, then asked, "You don't mind if I call you Wynn, do you, Wynn?"

Dorvan's face remained placid, his expression unreadable. "It's your ship, Captain Terrik. While I'm aboard, you have every right to call me whatever you wish."

"I suppose I do." Booster pulled a cigar from his pocket and offered it to Dorvan. "Nobody calls me Captain around here. I'm Booster."

"Very well, Booster." Dorvan eyed the cigar warily, then waved it off. "Thank you, but . . . well, whatever it is you do with those, I *don't.*"

"No?" Booster returned the cigar to his pocket, growing more curious every moment about Dorvan's real reason for approaching him. "Sorry Lando didn't send you an invite to our little charity tournament—"

"A top prize of fifty million credits is *not* a little tournament," Dorvan interrupted. "It's enough to attract every serious player on the planet—and you know it, Booster."

Booster shrugged. "So you're a serious player?"

"I'd like to think so, yes," Dorvan replied.

"Then how come we haven't heard of you before?" Lyari asked. "As a sabacc player, I mean."

"Probably the same reason no one learned that the Tendrando Arms Celebrity Sabacc Charity Challenge would be hosted aboard the *Errant Venture* until *after* they paid their million credits," Dorvan replied. "Sometimes a high profile can work against you."

Booster chuckled and spread his hands. "Well, we all have to work with what we are."

Dorvan nodded. "We do, but even with Lando's name attached to the tournament, the *Venture* was nearly denied orbit. You're just lucky General Jaxton was invited."

"What makes you think that was luck?" Booster bragged. "Besides, the entry fees were nonrefundable. Trust me, Merratt Jaxton wasn't the only one pulling strings at Orbital Control."

"But we don't have *your* money yet," Lyari observed, clearly as suspicious of Dorvan's arrival as Booster. "And you brought your own shuttle. If we have such a 'high profile,' why are *you* looking for an invitation?"

"Because Lando Calrissian is too wealthy to involve himself in something untoward, and the *Errant Venture* has a reputation for running a clean game," Dorvan said. "Whatever else may be going on here, I see every reason to believe that the tournament will be an honest one, and I have some very good uses for fifty million credits."

"Assuming you win," Booster reminded him.

"I always assume I *will*," Dorvan replied smoothly. "Do you have a seat available or not?"

"I'll have Lyari check."

Booster nodded toward the comlink in the Ishi Tib's sleeve pocket. Dorvan was such a valuable addition to his guest list that he would have made a seat available even if there hadn't been one. But when he went into something, he liked to know all the angles, and something smelled wrong about Dorvan's claim. Wynn Dorvan was one name he would *not* have expected Han Solo to leave off the invite list.

Booster was still pondering the problem when he felt the large red eyes of his Duros communications officer watching him. He glanced over and found her holding one finger on the MUTE button on her console and the other to the speaker bud in her recessed ear. When she noticed Booster watching her, she signed off and turned to face the command deck, then shot a frown in Dorvan's direction to indicate she needed to talk privately.

Booster excused himself and stepped over to the communications station. "We have a problem?"

The Duros shook her head. "Just a change of plans," she said. "Our dirtside friends want us to start the tournament *now.*"

Booster cocked a bushy gray brow. The tournament wasn't even scheduled to begin for another quarter hour, and just a few minutes earlier Saba had instructed him to hold the start until the last stragglers were aboard.

"Do they know Senator Treen is still running late?"

The comm officer nodded. "I reminded them. They want us to start anyway."

Booster resisted the urge to tug at his beard, but could not quite keep himself from glancing back at Wynn Dorvan. Something important had clearly changed on the ground, and he could not help thinking that it had something to do with his unexpected rival. But who would send the Alliance chief of staff to sabotage a Star Destroyer? Or even to spy on it? Something just wasn't adding up.

"Booster, shall I acknowledge?"

Booster nodded. "I think we'd better, Saliah. These

aren't the kind of friends we want steamed at us." This last part he added loudly enough for Dorvan to hear, just in case the bureaucrat didn't *already* know who their real friends on the ground were. "Then tell Lando to start the tournament *now,* and have Eloa wire Senator Treen's entry fee back to her."

"On it," Saliah confirmed.

No sooner had Booster returned to Dorvan's side than the bureaucrat asked, "Does that mean you have a seat available?"

"I suppose it does," Booster replied, still playing hard to get, "if you've got the entry fee."

"Of course." Dorvan pulled a certified bank voucher from inside his tunic and passed it over. "I know what you were thinking, Booster, but I assure you—I'm not in the habit of asking for bribes."

Booster inspected the voucher. "A million credits," he said, nodding. "That's a big entry fee for a public servant."

Dorvan nodded. "I *told* you, Booster. I know how to play sabacc."

"I guess maybe you do," Booster said, chuckling. He passed the voucher over to Lyari. "Let Lando know that Wynn will be taking Senator Treen's seat, then have someone take him down to the tournament."

"Sure." Lyari spoke into her comlink, then looked back to Dorvan. "The tournament just started. By the time we get you down there, you'll have missed the first dozen hands or so. It's not too late to withdraw, if you find that objectionable."

"You wouldn't have my money if I did." Dorvan turned to Booster, then asked, "May I ask, just *who* are these partners of yours?"

"You can *ask*." Booster motioned for Lyari to get Dorvan off the bridge—then realized that maybe Dorvan's unexpected arrival was no more than the lucky break it appeared to be, what his grandkids liked to call *the will of the Force*. He raised his hand to stop Lyari, then said, "Wynn, how about staying on the bridge for a bit? There's something I want you to see."

Dorvan scowled. "What about the tournament?"

"It's a three-day tournament," Lyari reminded him. "Do you think ten minutes at the beginning will make a difference?"

"And we'll refund ten percent of your entry fee," Booster added. "You won't want to miss this, trust me."

Dorvan sighed, then reached into his pocket and stroked something—probably the chitlik he was rumored to keep as a pet.

"Ten minutes," he said. "After that, I want to be at the table."

"Deal." Booster made a scribbling motion, instructing Lyari to get a voucher, then turned to his Bith navigation officer. "Bring us about, Ratt. You know where we're going."

"Copy, Booster," Ratt replied. "Setting a course for Orbital Mirror Baker Six Tango."

"Good," Booster said. "Marfen, bring batteries eight, ten, and twelve online."

"Batteries eight, ten, and twelve charging and acquiring targets," Marfen, the Brubb weapons officer, confirmed. "Ready to attack in twenty seconds."

"*Attack?*" Dorvan must have been made of sterner stuff than he looked, for his voice was calm and his face empty of surprise. "A climate-control mirror?"

"Didn't I *say* you wouldn't want to miss this?" Booster replied. "Marfen, put the target on display."

The blinding-bright image of a silver, double-paneled mirror appeared on the giant vid display at the front of the bridge. To Booster, it looked a little bit like a Chadra-

Fan's head, with a tiny round ball flanked by two squarish, oversized ears. He knew that each mirror was more than ten square kilometers in area, but that only made it more difficult for Booster to get a sense of scale.

"Orbital Control is demanding to know why we're drifting out of assigned coordinates," Saliah reported. "They're threatening to fine us."

This drew a hearty chuckle from the entire bridge crew.

"Then I guess we'd better get our money's worth," Booster said. "Fire at will, Marfen."

"Copy that," the Brubb replied. "Fi—"

The rest was drowned out by a loud cheer as half a dozen turbolaser beams lanced out and vaporized the thin mirror panels instantly, leaving only twin clouds of roiling flame and fume in their place.

"That was several million credits' worth of Alliance property you just destroyed." Dorvan did not seem nearly as shocked as he should have, and Booster began to have the unhappy feeling that Daala's chief of state had known *exactly* what he was walking into—and done it anyway. "But at least you missed the control hub. You could have killed someone."

"There's always next time," Booster replied. "Ratt, set a course for target two."

"Target *two*?" Dorvan echoed. "I don't know what you expect this destruction to accomplish, but I assure you, it *won't* secure anyone's release. Chief Daala is very determined."

"So am *I*," Booster growled. He grabbed Dorvan by the arm and marched him toward Saliah's comm console. "I've been worried sick about Valin and Jysella, and I'm tired of it. I'm going to keep blasting until my grandkids are free, and if I run out of mirrors before that happens, I'll start on the habitation stations."

Dorvan shook his head. "You haven't thought this through," he said. "The entire Sixth Fleet is in orbit. They'll blast you to bits before you reach the third target."

"Not *me,* Wynn," Booster said, smiling. "*Us.* You, me, Fost Bramsin, Drikl Lecersen, Merratt Jaxton, and ninety-six other very important Coruscanti."

Dorvan's brow rose. "You're holding us hostage?"

"I'm hosting a sabacc tournament," Booster replied, putting some iron in his voice. "And the invitation *did* say 'no early departure.'"

Dorvan shook his head. "You'll never get away with this," he said. "Our security teams—"

"Are no longer a problem," the weapons officer, Marfen, said. "You *have* heard of coma gas, right?"

A series of images appeared on the bridge display, showing several staging areas near the tournament floor. Each of the salons was filled with unconscious bodyguards, many of them already disarmed and bound. Booster was glad to see that Marfen had selected only views with no visible Jedi Knights; he didn't want Dorvan to see the full extent of their plan—at least not yet.

"You might want to explain the situation to your boss." Booster took a mike off Saliah's comm console. "Let her know who we've got aboard. We'll even send her a list, if she wants."

"This is outrageous and foolish," Dorvan said. He was either a great sabacc player or a terrible liar, because his voice remained even and his face expressionless. "You do understand that Chief Daala will *never* negotiate for hostages, don't you?"

"Try her," Booster said. "She might surprise you."

Saliah opened a channel and looked up. "What's Daala's comm code?"

When Dorvan hesitated, Booster said, "Just the one message, then you can go down to the tournament." He took the cigar stub out of his mouth and smiled. "Once you're at the sabacc table, you'll hardly know you're a hostage at all."

Chapter Twenty-six

THE CHALLENGER HAD CHOSEN HIS GROUND WELL. Standing on a catwalk nearly eight meters above Saba's head, he had the advantage of height, and of a safety rail that would serve as a defensive barrier. But to her keen senses, he appeared ill prepared to force a confrontation. When he spoke, his tone was sharp and tense instead of low and confident. His movements were jerky instead of graceful and strong, and the bitterness of his distress lingered on her tongue every time she tested the air. Most of all, her reptilian eyes could see his fear in the infrared glow of his torso and head, in the way his body was holding its blood and heat in its most vital areas. Kenth Hamner did not want to be there. He was frightened and uncertain of himself, and he had spent the last ten minutes stalking Saba without gathering the courage to strike.

That was no way to come after a longtail.

". . . Jedi Order has served galactic civilization since its founding," Hamner was saying. "If you do this, you'll be severing a tradition that goes back twenty-five thousand years!"

"We're serving civilization by saving it," Kyp Durron replied.

Kyp was standing with the other pilots about two meters behind Saba, within easy distance of the narrow metal staircase that descended to the hangar floor. Even if Hamner *tried* to prevent him and the others from joining their squadrons, Saba was in a good position to intervene.

"This wasn't Saba's decision alone," Kyp continued. "The whole Council agreed."

"*I* didn't agree," Hamner shot back. "And *I* am still the acting Grand Master."

Octa Ramis glared up at him. "No. You lost the Council's confidence when you didn't take us into *yours*."

"You were wrong," Kyle Katarn agreed. "You should have told us about the deal with Bwua'tu."

"Why keep us in the dark?" Kyp demanded. "I'll tell you why—because you knew we'd never go along."

"Because it was not *your* decision to make," Hamner retorted. "*I'm* the one Master Skywalker appointed to take his place while he's away."

"Only you are the one Daala agreed to, yes?" Barratk'l growled. "Have you never wondered why that was?"

Hamner's body tensed, and for a moment it seemed he was about to leap down on the fanged tower of fur that was a Yuzzem. Instead his expression turned hurt and angry, and his disappointment rippled through the Force.

"This is not what I expected of you, Barratk'l," Hamner replied. "Had I realized how little value you place on loyalty, I would never have suggested you for the Council."

"Had you told me you wanted loyalty to *you* above the Order, I would not have agreed." Barratk'l checked her chrono, then turned to the other vac-suited Masters. "Eight minutes to launch, and prep takes five. We must go."

"Yes." Saba motioned them toward the stairs, but kept her gaze fixed on Hamner. "This one will finish matterz here."

But the Masters did not start down the stairs immediately. Instead, Kyle Katarn cast one last look up at the catwalk.

"Kenth, it doesn't have to be like this," he said. "We all know how much stress you've been under, but you should never have tried to carry it all on your own. That's why we have a Council."

As Kyle spoke, Hamner's hand came up, and Saba felt the Force flowing to him in a rush. Thinking he had finally gathered the courage to challenge her, she raised her own hand to counterattack—and was astonished to hear not the echoing boom of a Force blast, but the spine-chilling screech of twisting metal. Saba checked her own attack, then glanced back toward the stairs and found a pair of twisted safety rails ending over empty air.

The staircase hit the hangar deck with a deafening clang that drew all eyes toward the Masters, and Saba realized with a heavy heart that Hamner was not going to make this easy on himself. He intended to mount his challenge in full view of the entire Order—a foolish decision that would only heighten his humiliation when he failed to win back his dominance.

"No!" Hamner pointed at the vac-suited Masters and used the Force to send his voice booming across the hangar. "You will *not* lead the Jedi Order into treason! I forbid it!"

The Force erupted into a vortex of confusion and astonishment. A sudden stillness fell over the hangar as all eyes turned toward the observation balcony, and the first wisps of doubt began to seep into the auras of the beings below as Jedi Knights and support staff alike began to wonder whom they should obey. Saba sighed, then caught the gaze of Kyp Durron and pointed to the far end of the balcony, where a second staircase descended to the hangar floor.

"Go," Saba said. "This one will see to Master Hamner."

Kyp nodded, but did not start across the balcony. "Saba, remember that he's one of us. Don't do anything you don't have—"

"This one *knowz* how to fight without killing," Saba interrupted. As she spoke, Hamner continued to bellow about treason, urging the Jedi Knights and support staff to follow the law instead of misguided orders. She looked back toward the catwalk. "But two longtailz in a pod is too many. It causes . . . disharmony."

Saba raised a hand toward the catwalk and began to pull with the Force. A three-meter section of metal twisted and snapped, then came clanging down almost atop her head. Expecting her rival to come with it, feet and fists flying, she gathered herself to spring into a melee.

But Hamner was not there.

Instead, Saba saw him a dozen meters away, barely visible through the catwalk's durasteel grating as he somersaulted along the next section. No longer bellowing about treason, he seemed content to simply keep moving, and as she watched he rolled to his feet and continued out of sight at a Force-enhanced sprint.

"Master Hamner is fleeing?" Saba asked, confused. "He is giving up so easily?"

"Not fleeing," Cilghal replied. She pointed a finned hand toward the heavy blast doors that covered the hangar exit. "Changing tactics."

Saba cocked her head, eyeing the network of catwalks above, and understood. "The *shenbit*!" She turned and sprang onto the balcony's safety rail, then Force-sprang onto the broken catwalk six meters above. "The shenbit *licker*!"

The jump would have been easy for any angry Barabel, and for a Barabel with the Force it was little more than a step. Saba landed three paces down the catwalk, already racing into the maze of equipment and dark empty spaces at a full sprint.

The blast doors had been dropped when the Solos discovered the first Mandalorian scouts watching the Temple, and they had been left down ever since. If Hamner reached the mag-lev generators before the doors were retracted, it would be a simple matter for him to cut their power supplies and trap the entire StealthX wing—maybe not forever, but long enough to prevent a timely launch.

By now, the Solos would be infiltrating the detention center. Daala would be distracted by the news that the *Pellaeon* was preparing to break orbit. Within minutes, the entire Sixth Fleet would be moving to intercept Booster Terrik's marauding Star Destroyer, and the *Errant Venture* would be forced to escape into hyperspace. If the Jedi wanted their StealthXs to escape Coruscant without a fight, the wing had to launch on time. Saba checked her chrono—they had seven minutes.

Everything depended on that one thing. If the timing failed, Luke and Ben would be left to fight Abeloth and the Sith alone—and that Saba could not allow.

She reached the first junction in the catwalks and turned toward the blast doors. The air this high in the hangar was dusty, dark, and hot. There were pipes, ducts, and crane rails everywhere she looked, but Hamner was nowhere to be seen. Saba felt like she was chasing him through the canopy of a durasteel jungle, and she knew it was good terrain for an ambush. She checked her chrono again. Six minutes. Hamner had six minutes until the blast doors opened—and six minutes gave him plenty of time for an ambush.

It did not matter. Saba had sparred Hamner many times, and he was not the fighter she was. She reached out to him in the Force, searching for his presence, sharing with him her hunger to close and fight, the heat in her blood that the chase was bringing.

Then Saba tested the air again and tasted the sour

tang of human fear. She felt an emptiness in the Force, a dozen meters ahead and off to the left, and she knew Hamner was trying to hide from her, drawing his aura in tight so she would not feel his panic and his fear. She saw an intersection ahead and heard a boot heel scuff across the durasteel gratework. She turned the corner, already reaching for him in the Force, and found . . . nothing.

A prickle of danger sense raced up Saba's spine, but she already knew what was coming, and already she was whirling to meet it.

Too late.

The stately figure of Kenth Hamner stood opposite her, in the gloom beyond the intersection, one hand raised toward her chest, his dark eyes filled with cold fury. Saba brought her hand up, lashing out in the Force and trying to knock him off-balance, but it was no good. Hamner had fooled her, and now he had the drop on her. As she unleashed her attack, his slammed her in the chest, lifted her off her feet and hurled her into the safety railing, driving her up and over, flipping her backward so that she found herself staring down at a StealthX squadron fifty meters below. Their canopies were closed, and the air was already shimmering with the heat of their engines.

Less than five minutes to launch. Maybe a lot less.

Saba used the Force to press herself to the safety railing as she dropped. When the cold durasteel began to slide along her tail, she curled the tip and caught herself, and her momentum brought her swinging backward. She reached up and latched on to the catwalk with both hands, locking her talons through the middle of the grate, and she told herself that Hamner had not really intended to kill her—that had she not caught *herself,* he would have reached out with the Force and prevented a fellow Master from plummeting to her death.

Even when she heard Hamner's boots ringing down the catwalk, five or six meters away, Saba refused to believe he had meant to kill her. A leadership challenge was one thing, but to actually *slay* a rival . . . no Jedi would do such a thing. Recalling how Hamner had used misdirection to ambush her early, Saba sissed at her foolishness.

"Good one, Kenth," she said. "Very tricky."

Saba extended herself under the catwalk, locking her talons around the opposite edge, then swung up on the other side, slipping under the rail and rolling to her feet in a fighting crouch.

Hamner was nowhere to be seen.

"Not funny," she growled. "Not funny at all."

Saba raced in the direction of the footfalls, but in the maze of dark steel she quickly lost track of Hamner's route. She checked her chrono. Only four minutes to launch. On the hangar floor, the two squadrons she could see were sealed up tight. Their R9 units were strobing green, and the support crews were unhooking hoses and moving utility carts toward the deck perimeter.

Saba searched for Hamner in the Force. This time, the only presence she could feel along the catwalks was Cilghal's, about a hundred meters away and moving cautiously but calmly as she searched the far side of the maze. Saba hissed in frustration, then started toward the front of the hangar. There were two doors and therefore two mag-lev generators, and Hamner would have to cut *both* power feeds if he wanted to trap the StealthXs. Otherwise, flight control would simply open one blast door, and the squadrons would stream out in single file instead of launching in formation.

So all Saba really needed to do was save one door. If the Force was with her, she would pick the right one and catch Hamner before he did any damage. If not, Daala and Starfighter Command would have three minutes instead of thirty seconds to react. The last squadron or two might find themselves fighting to escape Daala's grasp. But even so, nearly fifty Jedi in StealthXs would escape to join Luke in the fight against Abeloth and the Sith.

Saba reached the front of the hangar with three minutes left before launch. The turadium blast doors were already riding on their mag-lev tracks, their lustrous surfaces shimmering with the reflections of colored signal lamps. A deep roar was building inside the hangar as the StealthXs ramped up their ion engines, preparing for a hot launch.

Saba leaned over the safety railing, peering down at the inside corner of the nearest blast door. From such a height, the mag-lev generator was not at all impressive, a danger-yellow drum about as tall as a Wookiee and surrounded by a transparisteel safety wall. The power feed was entirely nondescript, a gray plasteel conduit tube about as large as a male human's arm that ran up the wall adjacent to the blast door and disappeared into a junction box in the ceiling.

Seeing no sign of Hamner anywhere near the first conduit, Saba reached out for Cilghal and found her back near the observation balcony. This puzzled her for a moment, until she remembered that the quickest way down from the catwalks was via that balcony. Had the Mon Calamari left it unguarded, it would have been a simple matter for their quarry to double back, drop down to the flight deck, and simply walk to the mag-lev generators.

Relieved that Cilghal had thought to cover that route, Saba turned to inspect the second power feed. It was hidden by the far edge of the door, and the turadium was more than two meters thick—enough to hide her quarry, had he already jumped across. Wondering if she still had a chance to save both doors, she started down the catwalk, shuffling sideways so she could keep watch over the door she had just checked. There was no use trying to save the second door if she let Hamner sneak behind her and take the first.

Saba had just reached the midpoint seam—where the doors came together in a magnetic seal stronger than the turadium itself—when a pair of hawk-bats suddenly dropped out of the superstructure above. The din inside the hangar had grown so loud that it was impossible to hear their shrill cries. But she could feel in the Force that they were more angry than frightened, and the way they kept circling back into the darkness suggested they were trying to protect a nest somewhere up on the girder.

Saba ran her gaze along the upper edge of the girder and realized her mistake even *before* she spotted a shadowy figure running toward the doors. Hamner didn't intend to cut the power feeds. He was going for the relay box that controlled the magnetic seal between the blast doors. She raised a hand and used the Force to jerk him off the girder.

If Hamner cried out as he fell, his voice was lost in the general roar of the StealthX engines. But when he looked in Saba's direction, his mouth was gaping in rage, his arms flailing and his eyes filled with betrayal. Determined not to kill him, Saba stepped closer to the safety rail and caught him with the Force, then pulled him toward the catwalk. Toward *her.*

Hamner's hand dropped to his side, and as Saba floated him over the rail half a second later, he had his lightsaber in hand and ignited. She hurled him into the catwalk, slamming him into the durasteel grate facedown, then snatched her own weapon and was standing above him as he looked up. His nose was gashed, crooked, and pouring blood.

Saba ignited her own blade. "Kenth, stop," she yelled,

trying to make herself heard above the roar of the engines. "If we continue, you will only get . . ."

Saba felt her shin scales go flat and barely lowered her blade in time to keep Kenth from cutting her off at the knees. He was only trying to drive her back . . . she was sure of that. Instead of taking an easy counterstrike at his head, she rolled her wrist and sent his blade flipping away, then stepped forward to stomp on an elbow that was suddenly no longer there.

Hamner was rolling toward the edge of the catwalk, turning up on his side with his top arm extended toward his tumbling lightsaber and his lower arm coming around to club her behind the legs. Saba tried to escape by stepping forward. He was too quick, landing a Force-enchanced blow that buckled her knees and would have sent her crashing down on her back . . . had she not had a tail with which to catch herself.

But Saba did have a tail, and so Kenth's attack merely dropped her to her knees at his side. She lashed out, more by instinct than will, barely remembering to retract her claws before she planted her free hand in Hamner's chest. She pushed hard, pinning him against a safety rail support post.

"*Enough!*" she bellowed. "This one is losing patience."

Hamner glared back at her, eyes burning with self-righteous fury. He snarled something Saba could not hear over the roaring of StealthXs, something so filled with hatred it turned his Force aura sour and cold. Suddenly Saba understood how badly she had misjudged the situation. This was no dominance fight. Hamner had one desire: prevent the Jedi from launching their StealthXs. And to achieve that goal, he was very willing to kill.

The fire in Hamner's eyes changed to ice. Saba brought her guard up and blocked the blade flashing toward her neck. She countered with an elbow, trying to catch him below the ear, but her angle was poor and his jaw snapped instead. His eyes went wide, rolled back, and for an instant Saba thought she might have knocked him unconscious despite the miss.

She should have known better. Kenth Hamner was a Jedi Master, and Jedi Masters did not fall victim to their own pain. She felt Hamner's palm striking the center of her chest. Her breath left in an anguished gasp, and she found herself tumbling down the catwalk, using the Force to keep herself between the safety rails as Hamner tried to Force-hurl her over the side.

A dozen somersaults later, Saba finally clamped on to a passing support post and brought herself to a halt. Hamner continued to attack with the Force, banging her up and down, trying to break her grasp and send her flying over the rail. After a couple of seconds, Saba felt an opening to her right, and she realized she was at an intersection. She angled a leg into the corner, braced her feet against the far corner post, and wedged herself into the opening.

A blue strobe began to blink above the blast doors, flashing the one-minute warning. Time was running out fast, and Hamner decided to gamble on a quick kill. Still using the Force to push at Saba, he came charging down the catwalk, his lightsaber weaving a basket of green light as he tried to camouflage the attack pattern he would use.

It did not matter to Saba. All she had to do was keep him busy for the next fifty seconds, then the StealthXs would be launched and reinforcements on their way to Luke and Ben. She waited until Hamner had drawn within two meters, then hooked her foot around the post she had braced it against and released the one she had in her hand.

Hamner's Force push sent her sliding, pivoting around her foot to face the opposite direction . . . and bringing her heavy tail around. She swept it across the catwalk behind her, catching Hamner in the ankles and knocking him off his feet.

Saba stopped sliding. She sprang up instantly, already spinning around to claim the extra fighting space in the intersection.

Hamner had the same idea, and for a moment they stood to either side of the gap, their lightsabers sparking and flashing as they tried to drive each other back. During the first flurry Hamner did a good job of keeping Saba off-balance, varying speed attacks with subtle counters and streetwise knee attacks, which he had always been too gentlemanly to employ during their practice matches. Saba relied on the Barabel power attacks he had never learned to stop, hammering at his guard hard and fast, coming back time and again in an effort to wear him out before she had to kill him.

Finally, Hamner was too slow bringing his guard up after a brutal overhand slash. Saba leapt in to finish it, flipping her lightsaber around for a backhand pommel strike that would surely have knocked him unconscious—had he not been dropping to his haunches and swinging up at her rib cage. She saved herself only by Force-flipping over his head and coming down two meters away, and even then it was only her precautionary tail sweep that stalled his pursuit and saved her life.

Saba spun around to find Kenth firmly in control of the intersection. He used the extra space like the master swordsman he was, launching attacks against either side at will, repeatedly pivoting back and forth so that she would have to face him square-on instead of presenting a flank defense. Under normal circumstances, she would simply have retreated down the catwalk, forcing him to either follow or let her go.

But these were not normal circumstances. If Saba retreated, if she let up for even a second, Hamner would lock his lightsaber blade on and Force-hurl it into the relay box. She had to keep the pressure on, to keep him so busy defending himself he had no chance to attack the blast doors' control mechanism. And so she continued to fight at a disadvantage, expending most of her energy defending herself, but launching a kick or a Force shove or even a threatening slash any time Hamner gave her the chance.

The warning strobe began to flash more rapidly, and Hamner's gaze slid toward the blast doors. Thirty seconds. Saba took advantage of the distraction to launch an all-out power assault, pummeling her quarry with Force shoves and two-handed slashes, kicking at his legs and . . . finally . . . rocking him back on his heels.

Hamner gave ground, struggling to regain the initiative, letting Saba in so close that soon the only weapon he had left was his head.

So he used that, slamming his brow into her armored throat.

Saba stumbled back, sissing not because the strange lump in her throat made it difficult to breathe—though it did—but because she could not believe what Hamner had just done.

"A head butt?" she gasped, grinning despite herself. "Are you *joking*?"

Apparently, Hamner was not. As Saba stumbled back, he pushed after her, following so close she could barely bring her elbows to bear. After two steps, she gave up and tried another tactic, bringing a knee up into her attacker's groin so hard it lifted him off his feet.

And that was when Saba smelled something acrid and familiar. She glanced down to find the emitter nozzle of Hamner's lightsaber pressed to her abdomen just below her rib cage, his thumb still on the activation switch and a gray column of vaporized keratin rising between their bodies.

"Stang," Saba gasped. She tumbled backward, her in-

sides exploding in fiery pain, her vision already starting to narrow. "*Good one.*"

When Hamner deactivated his lightsaber and tried to step free, Saba realized he still had time to sabotage the relay box. She tried to pull him down with her, but her strength was gone, and he pulled free effortlessly. So she took the only option available and helped him along, giving him the strongest Force shove she could manage.

Hamner went flying into the safety rail, both arms flailing and badly off-balance. Still, it looked like he would catch himself and recover—until his lightsaber touched the top rail and burned through in a bright flash. The durasteel did not bend far beneath his weight, only a few centimeters at most.

But it was enough.

Hamner lost his battle against momentum and gravity and tumbled over the rail, arms wheeling and mouth gaping in surprise. Saba was already rolling toward the edge of the catwalk, her insides burning like lava as she reached out with her hand and with the Force.

It was with the Force that she caught him, of course.

She could feel him about twenty meters below, his fear and surprise hanging in the Force like an ice fog, still and white and tranquil as the morning after the storm. Saba peered over the edge and saw him about twenty meters below, upside down and—like any good Jedi—still holding his lightsaber. She reached out to him in the Force, assuring him she would not let him drop, that whatever their differences they were still Jedi Masters and would one day soon return to being friends.

Hamner twisted around until he could look up and meet her gaze. There was no longer anger in his steely eyes, only sadness and forgiveness . . . and unyielding resolve. Saba's heart started to climb toward her throat. With no hope of making herself heard above the roaring of the impatient StealthXs, she reached out in the Force, begging her lost friend to see that he was beaten, to surrender to the will of the other Masters and not make her choose between him and the Skywalkers—between his life and her duty.

But Jedi do not surrender, and they never give up. Hamner locked his lightsaber blade on, then looked away from Saba and sent it spinning up toward the relay box.

"No, Kenth!" Even Saba could not hear the pain—the anguish—in her voice. "No!"

Saba watched the lightsaber spin upward long enough to be certain it was being directed through the Force, then reluctantly reached for it in the Force—and found herself fighting for control. The struggle continued for a span of perhaps three heartbeats, then Hamner smashed into the deck below, and the lightsaber was hers. She sent it tumbling down into a turadium blast door, and finally the strobe light stopped blinking.

Launch.

Chapter Twenty-seven

WITH ITS DROOPING WINGS AND S-SHAPED LANDING struts, the craft hanging above the rolling waters looked more like a seabird than a troop shuttle. It was coming in low and slow, swinging past the Fallanassi's hidden island so tightly that it might have been a clargull returning to its nest on the distant white cliffs. But Luke knew better than to doubt what he was seeing. He could sense the Balance tipping toward darkness, he could feel the Force shuddering with uncertainty and despair.

Something terrible had just happened on Coruscant. Luke had felt it through the Force, a wave of sorrow so sharp and feral it had sent a physical jolt through his entire body. The aftershocks were still coming as others learned of the event—ripples of grief and disbelief and guilt that left Luke feeling worried and forlorn. There had been a death on Coruscant, a loss so profound it had rocked the entire Jedi Order. Exactly who was gone or how, it was impossible to know . . . but it *did* seem clear that Luke could no longer count on reinforcements.

Not that it mattered. The Sith were coming *now,* and Luke had only a single Jedi Knight—Ben—to stand at his side. With the fate of the Jedi and their own lives hanging by a thread, the Skywalkers had run out of time, and whether they stood or ran, the outcome looked the same. Abeloth was free, the Lost Tribe was on the loose, and all that stood between them and the rest of the galaxy were a Jedi Master and his son.

This time, Luke did not know if it would be enough.

Turning his back to the sea and the white-cliffed island, Luke crossed the beach to the tree-filled ravine where he had hidden the *Jade Shadow* beneath a camouflage net. The precaution had kept any Pydyrians from coming to investigate, but he knew better than to think it could hide them from the Fallanassi *or* the Sith. Akanah would know where he was by the disturbance his presence caused in the White Current, and the Sith had only to reach out to Vestara to locate them.

Luke ducked under the netting—which he covered with fresh boughs every day—and ascended the boarding ramp into the *Shadow.* He found Ben slumped in the salon, his glazed eyes fixed on an old episode of *Starjaxx* playing on the holovid. His pale face was covered in blue blisters and weeping sores, and his unkempt hair had not been washed in a week. Luke felt guilty for not showing Ben how to see through the Fallanassi illusion, but Vestara had proven much easier to control after she discovered the rips in their hazard suits and started to believe that she and Ben were infected, and Luke doubted that she would have continued to believe in the illusion if *she* was the only one who seemed to be getting ill. She had already asked several times why he didn't seem sick, and "I'm a Jedi Master" was starting to wear thin as a convincing reply.

"Where's Vestara?" Luke asked.

Ben raised a lethargic arm and pointed aft. "In her cabin. I don't know how long she has left, Dad. She's pretty sick."

"Good," Luke said, starting toward forward. "Come with me."

"Okay." Ben braced his hands on the edge of the

couch and pushed himself more or less upright. "But, I mean, she's *dying*. Aren't you being kind of harsh?"

"*Not* what I meant." Luke jerked his thumb toward the flight deck. "Come on. I'll explain as we fire up."

If Ben did not exactly leap up, he at least made it to his feet. "Fire up? Dad, we can't break quarantine. If we take this disease off Pydyr—"

"We won't, son, I promise you that." Luke's voice had softened, for he could not help feeling proud of Ben's selflessness in the face of his own death. "But we've got trouble coming, and I want us ready—"

"Trouble?" The question came from the back of the salon, where Vestara had appeared still belting her robe. Like Ben, she was covered in blisters and sores, and she looked as though it had taken all her strength simply to rise and dress herself. "I *thought* I felt something."

"I think we both know what you felt," Luke said, not bothering to hide his irritation. "Come with us."

Vestara remained where she was. "Master Skywalker, I have no idea—"

"I said *come,*" Luke interrupted, dropping his hand to his blaster. "If I need to ask again, I'm going to do it with a stun bolt."

Vestara's eyes widened. "No problem."

Luke led the way to the flight deck. Through the camouflage netting, he could make out a large shape low on the horizon, but no more. He motioned Ben to the pilot's chair, then activated the copilot's tactical display. Immediately the designator code for a CSA *Kondo*-class assault shuttle appeared ahead of the *Jade Shadow,* crossing in front of it and descending to land.

"It looks like they want to make a ground assault," Luke observed. He turned to Vestara. "They seem to want to recover you alive, Vestara. They must think you're a pretty good spy."

"If you believe that, Master Skywalker, you don't

know Sith as well as you think you do." Vestara frowned at the tactical display, then began to radiate alarm and fear into the Force, no doubt trying to warn her fellow Sith against approaching the *Shadow* without a hazard suit. "If they want me alive, it's so they can punish me for my betrayal."

"It seems to me that *Ben* is the one who should be punishing your betrayals," Luke said. When Vestara's eyes filled with alarm rather than confusion, he knew he had guessed right about how the Sith had followed them to Pydyr so quickly. "You can keep trying to warn them off if you like, but it *does* give the lie to your words."

Vestara's Force aura abruptly drew in on itself, shrinking to the point where Luke could not sense it without trying. He nodded and waved her into the copilot's seat.

"Buckle up, fold your hands in your lap, and don't move." Luke turned to his son. "Ben, get the ship ready to fly—and do *not* let Vestara out of your sight. If she so much as fidgets—"

"She's dead," Ben said, tapping his lightsaber. "I learned my lesson last time."

"Let's hope so," Luke said, turning toward the back of the flight deck. "We're in enough trouble already."

Before he could depart, Ben asked, "Uh, Dad? Aren't you forgetting something?"

"You'll know what to do when the time comes," Luke replied, knowing that Ben was asking to be filled in on a plan that did not yet exist. "Just be ready—and don't hesitate. Everything depends on that, son—and I *do* mean everything."

Luke went to the aft cargo hold, where he paused to remove a combat vest and two different styles of blaster rifle from the weapons locker. Having already examined the equipment once to make certain Abeloth had not sabotaged it while in possession of the ship, he contented himself with a quick functions check, then secured the locker again and debarked through the loading hatch.

Reverberations from events on Coruscant were still coming to him through the Force, and he was beginning to sense that the death was something the Masters regarded as sad but inevitable. He wanted to reach out to them individually, to see if he could learn more, but he resisted. The Sith would feel the attempt as clearly as he had felt Vestara trying to warn them off, and no good would come of alerting them to the trouble on Coruscant. Instead Luke drew his Force presence in tight, then slipped out from beneath the camouflage netting and raced up the slope to an observation post he had scouted earlier, a siltstone outcropping with a small overhang at the base.

By the time Luke had crawled into his hiding place, the shuttle was resting on its struts at the mouth of the ravine, no more than a hundred meters in front of the *Shadow*. Its rear ramp was just settling into the golden sand, but there was no sign of the Sith assault team that Luke had expected to see pouring out of the vessel. He quickly pulled a thermal detonator off his combat vest and set the timer to three seconds, but stopped shy of arming it. The Force was still and expectant, like the sea before a storm, and until he had a better idea of what was coming, he did not want to be the one who touched things off.

Instead of an assault team, a pair of Sith appeared on the ramp, descending slowly, their arms extended and in plain view. Both wore combat-black hazard suits, but even from a hundred meters away Luke could tell that the one in front had the slender build and fluid grace of a Keshiri Sith. The one in the rear had one sleeve folded up where his arm had been amputated at the elbow. Unless he missed his guess, he was looking at Sarasu Taalon and Gavar Khai.

Luke set the thermal detonator aside and aimed his

longblaster at the lead figure, then peered through the sniperscope at the purple visage that *probably* belonged Sarasu Taalon. He could not be certain because the slender face had grown gaunt and twisted, with brows that hooked sharply upward at the outer ends and cheekbones that protruded so prominently they looked like knuckles. The lips had grown bloated and cracked, and the mouth seemed twisted into a permanent grimace of pain.

But it was the eyes that troubled Luke most. They had turned as dark as wells, and shining up from the bottom were a pair of tiny light points, as bright and silver as stars.

Luke's stomach grew cold and heavy. He pulled away from the sniperscope and gazed down at the two beings with his naked eye, trying to decide whether they might not be a Fallanassi illusion after all. Living beings simply did not change into other kinds of beings. True, there were any number of medical conditions that might cause someone's bones to grow knobby, or his lips to swell. A wasting disease or prolonged bout of hunger might cause a face to grow gaunt and eyebrows to take a different shape. There were even conditions and parasites that could turn hair into something that looked more like worms.

But those eyes . . . eyes simply did not turn into pinpoints of silver light.

Luke peered into the sniperscope again and found himself looking into a slightly less grotesque version of the face he had glimpsed a moment before. The cheeks were no longer quite so knobby, the lips merely swollen and cracked. And the eyes, he saw now, had merely changed color. The irises and sclera had turned as black as the pupils, creating the appearance of emptiness where there was simply darkness.

But the silver pinpoints remained.

Had they flickered or shifted as Taalon moved his

head, they might have been no more than reflections of the Pydyrian sun. But they remained steady, shining out from the darkness of the High Lord's soul, and Luke knew why the Force was so full of portent that morning, why he could feel the Balance shifting toward shadow.

Taalon had been in the Pool of Knowledge, and that changed everything.

As Luke was contemplating this, Taalon reached the bottom of the ramp and stopped. He stared out to sea for a long time, and Luke began to worry that the Sith was actually *seeing* the white cliffs of the distant temple island—that despite the hazard suits the High Lord and his followers were wearing, Taalon had somehow learned the secret of seeing through Fallanassi illusions. Finally, the Sith turned back to the beach and studied the sand, either gathering his courage or biting back his pain. Then, after a moment, he raised his head and looked directly into the sniper scope.

Come now, Master Skywalker. Taalon's voice reached Luke more inside his mind than in his ears—a simple enough Force trick, but nonetheless one that sent a chill down Luke's back. *There will be time enough for that after we talk.*

Luke replied in a normal speaking voice. "You expect me to come down?"

Well, you haven't blasted me yet, Taalon countered.

Luke pressed the trigger and held it down—then felt his jaw drop as bolts began to ricochet off the High Lord's palm. It wasn't the deflection of blasterfire with a bare hand that shocked him—he had fought plenty of Sith capable of *that* trick. What amazed Luke was the speed with which Taalon had moved. In the nanosecond it had taken the first bolt to cross the distance between them, the High Lord's hand had risen to deflect it, traveling so fast that the appendage had literally seemed to disappear from one place and reappear in another.

After tolerating the volley for a couple of seconds, Taalon grew weary of defending himself and crooked a finger. Luke tightened his grasp on the longblaster, expecting to feel it being ripped from his hands through the Force. Instead he found himself sliding out of his hiding place and tumbling through the air as he dropped toward the beach.

Luke tossed the longblaster aside and snatched his lightsaber, then quickly used the Force to right himself before he reached the beach. But Taalon did not hurl him into the sand, or even attempt to send him flying into Gavar Khai's scarlet blade. He merely dropped Luke to the ground at a distance of five meters, then motioned for Khai to put his weapon away.

"For now, Master Skywalker, we have no need to kill each other." Taalon waved a suited arm at the shuttle behind him, where a large company of Sith warriors stood waiting in full hazard suits. "You *can't* succeed, and I'm willing to postpone your death until you are no longer of use."

"Very generous," Luke replied. "But what makes you think I would *want* to be of use to you?"

"Your son's life, of course." The hazard-suit vocabulator gave Taalon's voice a droning quality. "If you do what I ask, he will leave Pydyr alive."

"Provided Vestara is released in exchange," Khai added.

Luke didn't believe them for a moment, of course. But at least the negotiations would allow him to stall and learn something more about what was happening to Taalon . . . and how powerful the High Lord had actually become.

Luke glanced over at Khai. "Vestara has recovered from her beating, but I'm afraid she and Ben have both fallen ill with the plague." He looked back to Taalon, then said, "Assuming Ben survives, I might be interested in your offer."

"*Survives?*" Khai's vocabulator buzzed with his rage. "Have you not been caring for them *both*?"

Before Luke could reply, Taalon flicked a hand, demanding Khai's silence. "I have no time to wait for your son to recover. I must find Abeloth *now.*"

Even from inside his helmet, Taalon's voice sounded more pleading than demanding, and Luke realized that the High Lord's desperation had nothing to do with Abeloth and everything to do with his pain. Taalon needed to understand what was happening to him, and there was only one being in the galaxy who could tell him.

Luke cocked his brow, feigning surprise, then looked out to sea, directly toward the Fallanassi's hidden island. "And you really need me to show you where she is?"

"Assuming the trouble is worth your son's life," Taalon said. He turned and followed Luke's gaze, but showed no sign that he saw anything except the gray rolling sea. "And, of course, assuming you actually know where to find her."

Luke smiled. He was beginning to see how he was going to defeat the Sith.

"I'm afraid I'm going to have to disappoint you." Luke activated his lightsaber and started forward. "We may as well get started."

A couple of dozen Sith warriors began to surge down the shuttle's boarding ramp, and Gavar Khai activated his own weapon and stepped forward to meet him.

Taalon's hand went up immediately. "Hold."

Khai and the others stopped in their tracks, and Luke knew he had read the situation correctly. Han always said the only time to bluff was when the other guy couldn't afford to call, and it was growing clear that Sarasu Taalon had a problem far worse than Luke's. Deciding to press his advantage, he took another step forward.

Taalon retreated and raised a hand.

"I understand your suspicions, Master Skywalker," he

said. "But this time, I *do* intend to kill Abeloth. I have seen what she can do, and I'm no more eager to see her loose in the galaxy than you are."

Luke shook his head. "No," he said. "You don't understand what's happening to you, and Abeloth is the only one who knows. She's the only one who can tell you what you're becoming."

Taalon let his chin drop. "There are some . . . *things* . . . that trouble me, Master Skywalker."

He was silent for a moment, and when he raised his head again, his lavender face had become a withered caricature of itself, a puckered leather bag with a gray-lipped gash for a mouth and two silver suns shining from the bottomless sockets of its eyes.

"Help me find Abeloth," Taalon said. "And after she tells me what I'm becoming, I *will* kill her. I swear it."

Chapter Twenty-eight

A PILLAR OF WHITE STONE RISING THREE HUNDRED METERS out of a rolling gray sea, the island beyond the *Jade Shadow*'s forward canopy was as beautiful as it was awe inspiring. A wreath of dancing sea foam lapped at its base and a thin band of green foliage crowned the summit, and already the distant specks of seabirds could be seen wheeling before its white cliffs. And yet, when Luke glanced into the mirrpanel in the cockpit canopy, he saw Sarasu Taalon slumped in the copilot's seat, still scanning the distant horizon for a destination that lay right in front of him.

Perhaps Luke's odds were not so bad after all.

Taalon met Luke's gaze in the mirrpanel. Like the fifty Sith warriors riding in back with Ben and Vestara, he was still wearing his hazard suit. All Luke could see of the High Lord was a face that grew more haggard and alien by the moment, with sunken oval eyes and thin lavender flesh stretched tight over bones as knobby as knuckles.

"I know what you are planning, Master Skywalker." Taalon's vocabulator gave the words a wispy, almost whispered quality. "And it won't work."

"It's the thermal detonator, isn't it?" Luke asked. A thermal detonator was the last thing on his mind, but he had already learned to avoid thinking about his plans in Taalon's presence. The High Lord had developed some very impressive powers since his dip in the Pool of Knowledge. "I was wondering if I'd have time for that."

Taalon studied Luke for a moment, then said darkly, "Remember your son, Master Skywalker. The instant you betray me, he dies."

"Now I *know* you're lying," Luke said. "According to my plan, Ben will be long gone when I betray you."

"We all have our dreams, Jedi." Taalon shifted his gaze out the canopy again, then asked, "How long before we reach the Fallanassi's home?"

Luke glanced forward again, where the Fallanassi island loomed just a few kilometers away. "It should be coming into view anytime now." He didn't think Taalon could see through the illusion that hid the island, but it was time to be sure. "Why don't you bring up a tactical readout and see what they're sending to meet us?"

"The Fallanassi are pacifists, are they not?" Taalon asked. "What *could* they send against us?"

"Being a pacifist isn't the same as being helpless," Luke replied. "The Fallanassi have many defenses."

Taalon reached over and fumbled with the screen controls, his gloved hands obviously causing him some trouble.

"You may as well take off those gloves," Luke said. "Your hazard suit isn't going to protect you anyway."

"Liar!" exclaimed Gavar Khai, who was seated in the navigator's seat next to Taalon. "You're trying to infect us."

Luke smirked into the mirrpanel. "Do you see *me* wearing a hazard suit?" he asked. "What Ben and Vestara have—what you *already* have—is the Weeping Pox. Hazard suits can't stop it. It spreads through the Force."

"Then why aren't you sick?" Taalon asked.

Luke arched his brows in feigned concern, then asked, "The Sith don't have health meditation?" He did his best to look as though this were a pleasant discovery.

"That explains why Vestara is doing so poorly compared with Ben."

Khai's eyes flashed in alarm. "And you didn't *teach* her?"

Luke shrugged. "I thought she knew," he said. "It's such a basic technique for us."

"*Liar!*" Khai leaned forward. "If *she* dies, then your son—"

"Saber Khai!" Taalon raised a gloved hand for silence. "Skywalker is only playing on your fear. If he can convince us that we are *already* infected, we will removed our suits and become *truly* infected."

Luke shrugged. "So, keep your suits on." Despite his nonchalance, a cold lump had formed in Luke's stomach. Even without knowing the true nature of the "disease," Taalon had almost guessed his intention. "We'll know the truth soon enough."

Khai's eyes hardened, and he glared down at the back of Luke's head. "High Lord Taalon knows the truth *now.*"

Luke allowed himself a smile. Khai's tone was a little *too* insistent. The Saber was getting nervous, which meant Luke had successfully planted the seeds of doubt. With time, those seeds would blossom into a full-blown illusion. And once blue blisters started to appear inside Khai's suit, the rest of the Sith would believe they were infected, too.

Finally, Taalon pressed the right combination of keys. The tactical readout appeared on the primary displays of both pilots, with the *Shadow* in the center and the Sith troop shuttle, the *Obuuri,* following close behind.

Their destination stretched across most of the top of the screen, but the lack of reaction behind Luke suggested the island remained hidden from his passengers. Fallanassi illusions worked from the inside, using the White Current to create an impression within the victim's mind so vivid and realistic that his own intellect worked against him to supply the tiniest details—and to conceal anything that might cast doubt on its reality.

After a moment, Taalon shook his head. "I see nothing." He leaned forward and spoke into Luke's ear. "I warn you, if you think you can lead us astray, you are badly—"

Taalon's threat was interrupted by an astonished cry from the navigator's seat. "Lord Taalon!" Khai extended his arm and pointed at the tactical display. "Look!"

Taalon said something harsh in his native language, then asked, "How is that possible?"

Luke glanced down and, just rounding the island, found a familiar designator symbol: SHIP.

"What kind of tactical readout is *this*?" Taalon demanded. "*ship*? What kind of ships? How big? Do they pose a threat?"

"*They?*" Luke asked, puzzled.

"Have you no eyes?" Khai demanded. "The readout shows a whole squadron—and we're flying straight into it!"

"Oh, *those* ships," Luke said. The display showed only one designator symbol, so the "squadron" was obviously another Fallanassi illusion. "Aren't they yours?"

"*Ours?*" Taalon asked.

Luke pointed at the symbol on his screen. "That's not just *any* ship," he explained. "It's *Ship*—the meditation sphere. Until now, we didn't realize you had a whole fleet of them. So we've just been using Ship's name as its designator symbol."

Luke continued toward the island on a straight course, wondering how long it would take Taalon to admit that the illusory vessels weren't his. The more desperate the Sith were to project a strength greater than they possessed, the more likely it was that they were actually very weak, and that would be valuable information to have. Even so, Luke was ready to put the *Shadow* into an evasive dive at the first tingle of danger sense. The range of most spacecraft weapons was greatly diminished in atmosphere, but Ship remained enough of a mystery that it was impossible to know how soon it might open fire.

The dark speck of a distant vessel appeared on the horizon, about a kilometer to one side of the island, and began to grow rapidly as it closed with the *Shadow.* Luke kept his thumb poised over the targeting pad on the pilot's yoke, but he stopped short of arming the concussion missiles—or even designating Ship as a primary target. Both actions would trigger confirmation messages that his passengers were likely to notice.

When Taalon still refused to admit the illusory vessels were not his, Luke said, "Have your squadron fall in behind the *Obuuri.* It will be easier if everybody follows the *Shadow* in."

"Easier for you, perhaps—and for anyone targeting them," Taalon replied. "*I* will decide how to deploy my squadron, Master Skywalker."

By the time the High Lord had finished speaking, Ship had swelled to the size of a thumbnail and was probably close enough to open fire. Either Taalon actually *believed* that he controlled the squadron of Ships, or he was more afraid of appearing weak than he was of dying. Either way, it was time to call the High Lord's bluff.

"In that case, would you mind asking the squadron to swing about?" Luke asked. "We're entering combat range, and I don't like having all those plasma lances pointed my way."

"Plasma lances?" Taalon asked, obviously bewildered.

Luke lowered his voice in suspicion. "You haven't heard about the plasma lances?" He armed the concussion missiles and designated Ship as the primary target, then caught Taalon's eye in the mirrpanel. "How can you be in command of meditation spheres and not . . . oh, you *aren't*!"

Taalon's bewilderment turned to a knowing smirk. "Nice try, Master Skywalker, but there *are* no such things as plasma lances," he said. "I assure you, I am in *complete* command of Ship and all its mates."

The conviction in the High Lord's voice suggested he truly believed what he was saying—and Luke had a sinking feeling he knew why.

"How did you and Saber Khai escape Abeloth's planet?" Luke asked. "Aboard Ship?"

"Of course," Taalon replied. "I commanded Ship to come to me."

"And Ship limped you out of the Maw," Luke guessed. "Then you brought Ship to Pydyr in a frigate hangar bay . . . *back* to Abeloth."

Taalon's voice grew less confident. "We brought Ship with us, yes," he confirmed. "But it remains under *my* control, not Abeloth's. And right now, Ship is telling me to return to shore and call for reinforcements. There's a large force ahead waiting to ambush us."

"A *Fallanassi* force?" Luke let out a burst of laughter. "For a Sith, you're awfully naïve."

"Ship is not lying to me, Master Skywalker." Taalon's voice assumed a note of urgency—perhaps because he was experiencing a tingle of danger sense similar to the one Luke felt. "Turn—"

The second half of Taalon's command vanished into the screech of proximity alarms. Luke thumbed the firing button on the pilot's yoke, then felt two soft thumps as a pair of concussion missiles shot from their launching tubes. In the same instant a trio of smoke lines streaked toward them from Ship's direction. Streaks of color fanned across the sky as the *Obuuri* sprayed cannon fire at the squadron of illusory meditation spheres. Luke spun the *Shadow* into a barrel roll, dropping to within a few meters of the rolling waves—then continued toward the island.

The smoke lines bent toward them.

Ben's voice came over the intercom speaker. "Uh, Dad? You *do* see all those meditation spheres, right? The ones you're going to fly straight under?"

"Yeah, Ben . . . I see 'em." It was not exactly true, but Luke *could* see the one craft that mattered—Ship. "Don't worry."

"Who's worried?"

Ben's reply was followed by a muffled *I am!* from Vestara, and a chorus of agreement from the other Sith packed into the main cabin.

"We were just wondering if you wanted us to *do* anything," Ben continued.

"Thanks," Luke said. The smoke lines continued to curl toward the *Shadow.* "But we have it under control up here."

"Under control?" Gavar Khai cried. "We are outnumbered six to one!"

"But we've got you and . . . Taalon," Luke said, craning his neck to look through the top of the canopy. At the leading point of each smoke line appeared a tiny ball of orange flame, most likely a friction fire caused by one of the Force-hurled stones Ship sometimes used as missiles. "How about giving those rocks a Force nudge?"

"Which ones?" Taalon gasped. "There must be fifty!"

"Hold on." Luke turned the *Shadow* directly toward the three real missiles, and the tiny fireballs instantly swelled to the size of Wookiee heads. *"Those."*

"Are you *mad*?"

Despite Taalon's surprised outcry, the three fireballs veered sharply to the left and vanished. Luke would have liked to check the tactical readout to see what had become of Ship, but a curtain of white cliff loomed ahead. At the velocity they were traveling, it was impossible to guess the distance. But they were getting *close. Obuuri* cannon bolts were already starting to blast sprays of powdery stone from the island's sheer face.

Luke knew he would never have a better opportunity to lead the Sith into a trap, but with Taalon nearby the only plan that stood a chance of success was no plan. He simply had to act and react.

More cannon bolts began to end their flight in a starburst of superheated stone. Luke hazarded a check of the tactical readout and saw no sign of Ship, only the *Obuuri* jinking about in an effort to avoid illusory missiles.

By the time Luke lifted his gaze, the *Obuuri*'s cannon bolts were exploding into the cliff face a mere second after flashing past the *Shadow.* Luke pulled the pilot's yoke back and felt the star yacht's nose snap upward.

"Are you mad?" Taalon cried.

The *Shadow*'s nose dropped again, and they continued toward the cliff. Luke's heart jumped into his throat. Realizing he had to give the High Lord some reason to pull up *other* than an island he could not see, Luke pointed at the line of exploding cannon bolts.

"Barrier . . . field!" He could barely choke out the words, for the *Ubuuri*'s bolts were erupting against the cliff barely a heartbeat after they streaked past. "Look at the cannon—"

Their nose rose so fast they nearly went into a loop. Luke eased the yoke forward, and the *Shadow* climbed toward the azure sky, running parallel to the cliff—then began to buck and shudder as a shock wave hit them from behind. He fought to regain control for a moment, then glanced at the tactical display and saw the *Obuuri*'s designator symbol vanishing into the bright red circle of a heat blossom.

"Where did *that* barrier field come from?" Taalon demanded. "Why doesn't the tactical display show it?"

"Maybe it's some kind of Force wall," Khai suggested.

"It must be something like that," Luke replied. "What happened to Ship? Did we get it?"

"Our missiles were diverted," Khai said. "But how do you know you were firing at Ship instead of some other sphere?"

"Just a feeling."

"I think you have *many* feelings you haven't been sharing," Taalon said, his voice cold with suspicion. "Feelings that might have saved the *Obuuri*, had you shared them earlier."

"Sorry, I was kind of busy," Luke said. "Next time, maybe you should trust me to fly my own ship."

"Not likely, Master Skywalker," Taalon said. "In fact, I don't trust you now. We will run for shore and call for reinforcements."

Luke shook his head. "And give the Fallanassi more time to prepare?" Outside the canopy, the green-fringed rim of the cliff flashed past, and then the *Shadow* was climbing into an empty sky. "If you do that, it won't matter *how* many Sith you bring."

"The decision is not yours," Taalon said. "You will return to shore, or Ben will dieooooaaagh!"

Taalon's threat broke into an outcry as Luke dropped their nose and reduced thrust, decelerating so sharply that he was thrown against his crash harness. Even so, the *Shadow* was halfway across the island before they were traveling slow enough to see that the surface lay smothered beneath club moss and tree ferns. One edge of the cliff was cut by the fungus-filled fissure of an old stairwell, which ascended to the top of the plateau and became a mossy channel meandering toward a distant cluster of hummocks. As the *Shadow* continued forward, the hummocks began to take the form of cone-shaped huts and long gathering halls with half-barrel roofs. Atop the largest hall, a column of yellow fumes was leaking into the air through a bare patch of stacked stone.

"*This* is the home of the Fallanassi?" Khai asked. Clearly, he was now able to see the island as plainly as Luke was. "It looks like Abeloth's planet in the Maw!"

"At least we know we're in the right place." Luke continued to decelerate, at the same time trying to decide how he could confirm that his passengers were seeing the same island he was—rather than a slightly different illusion. "What are those mounds at the other end of the island?"

"Their *village,* obviously." Taalon's voice filled with menace. "If you trick me again, Skywalker, Ben will be the first to die."

"Not if *you* are," Luke replied. "Tell your warriors to ready themselves."

"Sith are *always* ready," Khai replied. "You are not going to remind us that the Fallanassi are pacifists?"

"No," Luke said. "I've given you warning enough."

Khai's brows arched with curiosity, but they were already approaching the village, and Luke used the excuse to break eye contact without elaborating. He landed in a mossy area that appeared to be the village circle, in front of the large hall that was leaking the yellow fumes.

The *Shadow* was still settling onto her struts when a soft informational chirp announced that the boarding ramp had been lowered. By the time Luke had popped the release on his crash harness, Sith warriors were already racing out to establish a defensive perimeter. Unlike Jedi warriors, who would have had their blasters in hand and ready to fire under such circumstances, the Sabers acted as though their mere presence was enough to prevent an attack.

Leaving the *Shadow*'s systems on READY-STANDBY, Luke rose and followed Taalon and Khai out into the square. Save for a briny hint of sea, the village smelled much the same as had Abeloth's planet, musty and fetid. And it was not just the air that reeked. The Force was sour with anguish and fear. Luke could feel it swirling past, nettling his body all over as it flowed toward the large gathering hall.

"Blast!" Ben croaked, joining Luke and the others. "What *is* that?"

It was Vestara who answered. "Power." Like Ben, she still appeared exhausted and sick. "Raw power."

Ben looked at her, his brow cocked in doubt. *"Power?"*

"Yes, Ben." A hungry smile came to her cracked lips. "You know how it works. Pain leads to fear. Fear leads to anger."

"Anger leads to the dark side," Luke finished.

He turned toward the gathering hall, wondering if the fear starting to gnaw at him could possibly have merit. Could Abeloth be *feeding* on the anguish and fear around her? Could she actually be turning those dark emotions into dark side power?

Luke's musings came to an end when the Fallanassi began to emerge from their huts. Dressed in simple shifts belted at the waist, they were all female and mostly human, and in their haggard faces Luke saw the same anguish and fear he felt in the Force. Despite the deliberate menace being projected by the Sith, a gray-haired woman with worried eyes and a long, blade-thin nose set her gaze on Luke. She led forward half a dozen companions who looked to be of a similar age.

"Do you know her?" Taalon asked.

"No," Luke said. "But that's almost certainly their circle of elders. You should let them approach."

Though Taalon issued no orders that Luke could hear, a pair of Sith stepped aside and allowed the Fallanassi inside their perimeter. The gray-haired woman came straight to Luke. Ignoring Taalon and Khai, she fixed him with an angry gaze.

"Akanah *said* you would betray us."

"I haven't betrayed you . . ." Luke paused, waiting for

the woman's name to rise to the top of her mind, then continued, ". . . Eliya. It's obvious that your community here was *already* in trouble. But I doubt you understand the true nature of that danger. I've come to help you."

"By bringing *them* into our home?" Eliya waved an angry hand at Taalon. "You expect us to heal *Sith*?"

"The danger you face now is far worse than . . . Sith," Luke replied. He was so taken aback by the vehemence in her voice that he nearly missed the cue she had fed him—the Fallanassi already *had* a plan for dealing with the Sith. All he needed to do was keep Taalon from discovering it. "And I need them *alive* to help you."

Eliya studied Luke for a moment, then shook her head in disgust. "Even *you* don't believe they're going to keep their promise." She sighed heavily, then turned to Taalon. "But the Creed gives us no choice in whom we help. Take off those ridiculous suits, and we'll see about saving you."

"*Saving* us?" Taalon asked.

"From the White Plague," one of Eliya's companions supplied. She motioned to Ben and Vestara. "You two come with me. We need to get some jigog salve on those sores right away."

Taalon's hand rose. "Hold."

He turned and studied Luke for a time, no doubt calling on whatever powers of insight had been bestowed on him by his dip in the Pool of Knowledge. It was a helpless feeling, knowing that an enemy could foretell his plans simply by looking at him—but it was also an important tidbit of information, indicating as it did that Taalon actually had to *contemplate* the situation to foresee what would happen.

After a moment, Taalon said to Luke, "You called it the Weeping Pox."

It was Eliya who answered. "The White Plague is known by many—"

Taalon lashed out so quickly that Luke saw nothing but the back of his gloved hand striking Eliya's face. She went down instantly, landing at his feet with blood pouring from a split cheek.

"There is no disease," he announced. "The White Plague is a Fallanassi trick."

Eliya's eyes grew wide with surprise and disbelief, but she shook her head and began, "Believe what you wish, Sith. But it will be your death—"

"Eliya, *don't,*" Luke interrupted. If she continued to lie, Taalon would only make an example of her. "I know this is hard to believe, but the Fallanassi really *will* be better off if you just cooperate."

"We are here to find Abeloth," Taalon said. He looked toward the gathering hall. "Where is she? In there?"

Eliya shot an angry scowl at Luke, then shook her head. "No. Not any longer," she said. "She left—"

"You will see Abeloth soon enough," a familiar voice called.

Luke turned and found Akanah standing in the door of the gathering hall. Her hair was hanging loose and waving about her shoulders, as though caught by a breeze that was not blowing, and there was a darkness in her eyes that seemed to rise from the depths of time itself. Her gaze shifted from Taalon to Luke, and she smiled, revealing a mouthful of small sharp teeth.

"You shouldn't have come," she said. "Really, you shouldn't have."

Chapter Twenty-nine

THE MORNING SUNLIGHT WAS BOUNCING OFF THE DURA-crete wall, aggravating an already splitting headache and making it even more difficult to see through fogged goggles. Somewhere ahead—more than four hundred meters above the nearest pedway and two full kilometers of traffic-choked skylane above the actual planetary surface—was an expansion joint in need of inspection. To Han, it was just a dusky line running through a blurry gray radiance, a convenient excuse to be floating next to Detention Center 81. He shuffled along the repulsorlift-equipped scaffold—a *hoverscaf*—to the seam, then ran his gloved fingers up its length. When he felt a ribbon of sticky slime, he selected an electric slug-paddle from his tool belt and ran it up the trail until he hit something soft.

Instantly the silica slug flattened itself across the expansion joint. Han hit the trigger, electrifying the paddle blade. The slug curled into a ball, and half a second later it was killed and simultaneously captured by a barbed skewer that shot from the handle. Han quickly turned and thrust the body into the incineration vat in the middle of the hoverscaf, but he was not quick enough to prevent its spiracles from releasing a noxious yellow fume that seeped past the respirator mask's imperfect seal. The stuff smelled like boiling tar poured into a nexu's litterbox. His eyes watered, making it even more difficult to see, and his stomach threatened to empty its contents into his respirator mask.

Han stumbled to the back of the hoverscaf and pulled down his goggles and respirator, then braced his hands on the safety rail and stared down into the traffic-choked lane below. Why he had *ever* let Taryn Zel talk him into impersonating an exterminator, he had no idea.

Except, of course, that it had been the only way to get a rescue team close to the building. Given the short timetable and the facility's stepped-up security, it had quickly grown apparent that trying to sneak a squad of impostors inside was out of the question. Then R2-D2 had discovered that the schematics on record with the Coruscant Building Authority—*and* the Planetary Fire Suppression Office—were inconsistent with modern engineering practices, and Zekk had quickly realized that someone in GAS had taken the precaution of filing false plans for the facility. In the end, with no reliable intelligence except the precise spatial coordinates at which the tracking bugs had gone silent, the Solos had settled for the most basic of all plans: blast their way inside, find the Horn kids, and get out.

A respirator-muffled voice sounded from the other end of the hoverscaf. "Who said it was break time?"

Han looked over at his scaffold partner. With his identity hidden behind his exterminator's uniform—yellow hard hat, goggles, respirator, and white jumpsuit bearing the logo RUNKIL REMEDIATION—only the fellow's two-meter height and the wisps of black hair brushing his collar identified him as Jaina's old mission partner and ex-sort-of-boyfriend, Zekk.

"Hey, I'm only human," Han complained. Unlike Zekk and the rest of the Jedi on the "extermination" team, Han could not call on the Force to keep his goggles clear and his gorge from rising. He had only his stubbornness and a lifetime of hard living to get him through the next few minutes of pretending—and for the first time in a long time, he was worried it might not be enough. "If Runkil doesn't want us taking breaks, they should spring for droids."

"Droids won't *do* this work," Zekk joked. He glanced past Han's shoulder, then added, "Now you've done it. The boss lady is headed our way."

Han glanced up to see Taryn Zel zipping toward them on her little boss-floater. Like everyone else on the rescue team, she was dressed in a white jumpsuit bearing the logo RUNKIL REMEDIATION on the breast pocket. Instead of the hard hat and other protective gear, she wore a white supervisor's cap with a bright red bill that clashed badly with her auburn hair.

"Sick again, old man?" she called. "Maybe you should stop going out on work nights."

Han shot her a watery-eyed glower that was only half acting. Taryn was the only member of the rescue team whose face was unlikely to be in the GAS recognition files, so she had been the natural choice to enter the reception area and present a forged work order to the desk guards. Of course, that also meant she got to play the extermination crew's boss and take the easy job flitting around barking orders while everyone else scraped silica-eating parasites off the exterior of Detention Center 81.

"Going out the night before isn't my problem, boss," Han replied loudly. "It's listening to you harp all day that turns my stomach."

It was impossible to say whether the flash that came to Taryn's eyes was one of anger or amusement. But as she swung her boss-floater around next to Han and Zekk's hoverscaf, she was careful to position it so that her body was between them and the nearest cam bubble.

"I don't know why corporate makes me keep you on, you old foghead," Taryn said loudly. "The foam crew is about to catch you."

She pointed ten meters up the wall, where Leia and Jaina were also disguised as Runkil exterminators. They were moving their hoverscaf across the building, coating the duracrete in a thin blanket of foam that, when it evaporated, would leave behind a residual layer of parasite-killing poison. In the meantime, however, the foam was obscuring the cam bubbles that dotted the building and making it impossible for the guards inside to keep tabs on the extermination crew on the exterior.

"It's not my fault they're skipping windowsills," Han groused.

He glanced down and saw that Natua Wan and Seff Hellin were already hovering in front of their go-point on level 1910. Their foam crew, consisting of Yaqeel Saav'etu and Kunor Bann, was just coating the last cam bubble between the two levels where the rescue team would enter the building. All four were formerly psychotic Jedi Knights whom Daala had wanted to freeze in carbonite along with the Horn kids, and Han delighted in knowing that Daala would recognize that the Council had chosen the rescue team to send a message: the Jedi were through being pushed around.

"Your foam crew isn't skipping *anything,* old man," Taryn said. As she spoke, Leia and Jaina descended behind her and coated the last cam bubble in foam. For the next hour, the guards in the detention center control room would be blind to what the extermination crew was doing. Whether the cam bubbles also had audio capabilities was anybody's guess, so the rescue team had to stay in character—at least until they started blowing things up. "If you can't keep up—"

"I can keep up." Han pointed at the cam bubble behind Taryn and nodded. Once the bubbles were obscured, the plan called for the rescue team to enter in two squads, Squad Saav'etu on level 1910 where Jysella's tracking bug had gone silent, and Squad Solo on level 1913 where Valin's had gone silent. "Don't you worry about that."

Leia's foam nozzle began to sputter, and Jaina brought their hoverscaf down behind Taryn.

"Hey, boss," Leia said. "I'm out of foam."

Taryn smiled and winked at Zekk, then turned to face Leia. "Already? What are you doing with that stuff? Drinking it?"

"Oh yeah, boss—by the liter," Leia retorted. "You want it done fast or do you want it done without overspray? I don't do both."

"All right, don't get snappy," Taryn replied. "I'll call the supply van."

It was the ready signal. Taryn activated her comlink and ordered Turi Altamik to bring the "supply van" around. As she spoke, Han and the rest of the rescue team were tearing off their goggles and respirators and removing weapons and equipment vests from the hoverscaf tool bins. By the time the Turi arrived, Han was outfitted with his blaster belt, a vestful of assorted grenades, a hands-free comlink, and a T-21 repeating blaster set to STUN. Zekk and the rest of the Jedi were traveling a little lighter, with only their lightsabers, a couple of grenades apiece, hands-free comlinks, blaster pistols—also set to STUN—and the standard assortment of Jedi equipment that always seemed useless until the instant it was needed.

Taryn waved the "supply van" alongside Han's hoverscaf. Actually a Cygnus-7 armored transport vehicle, it had been disguised by overlaying a set of artificial body panels bearing the colors and logo of Runkil exterminators. The panels, of course, could be jettisoned at the push of a button, and the power train had been augmented with enough quadfeeds and thrust-boosters to give an Aratech BeamStreak a good race.

A side panel swished open to reveal C-3PO and R2-D2 standing in the doorway. "Oh, there you are, Cap—"

R2-D2 interrupted with a sharp tweet.

"Who are you calling a crossed circuit?" C-3PO retorted. "Of course I know we're undercover."

R2-D2 whistled an angry reply.

"Come on, you two." Holding the repeating blaster in one hand, Han lifted the access gate in the rear safety rail. A narrow boarding ramp shot out from the Cygnus-7, bridging the half-meter distance between its side door and the hoverscaf. "We don't have all day!"

R2-D2 rolled onto the ramp and was across in a second, but C-3PO took one look at the traffic-choked chasm below and activated his self-preservation routines.

"Are you quite sure that my presence is required?" he asked. "My gyroservers have been sticking—"

"Quit stalling," Han ordered. He pointed at the foam-covered cam bubble, then held a finger to his lips. "You've got vibration detectors to calibrate."

"Very well." C-3PO put a tentative foot onto the ramp, wobbled, and raised both arms for balance. "But if I should happen to slip, please tell Princess—"

"No one's slipping."

Han leaned over the safety rail and grabbed the droid's arm, guiding him forward—until the simultaneous crackle of two thermal detonators roared behind him. C-3PO raised his arms to shield his photoreceptors from the flash and nearly pulled Han halfway over the rail. Han raised a knee and managed to catch the rail between his thigh and waist, leaving them both hanging over a kilometer and a half of whirring nothingness. C-3PO's arms began to wag wildly, threatening to rip free of Han's grasp or break his hold on the safety rail and send them both plummeting down into the skylane.

"Threepio, stop that!" Han ordered. "Are you *trying* to get us killed?"

"Of course not, sir," C-3PO replied. He lowered his arms at exactly the wrong moment, and Han found himself struggling to keep the droid from falling *toward* him. "Droids can't *be* killed—only destroyed."

Han dropped the blaster onto the hoverscaf and grabbed for the safety rail, but he was already starting to fall backward.

"Oh, dear!" C-3PO cried, now leaning away. "You seem to be pulling me off the *rraaaggh*!"

A fierce pang of agony shot up Han's arm as the droid's weight banged it down on the safety rail. The joint started to hyperextend, then Han felt himself rising and starting to flip over the rail after C-3PO.

"Hold on!" Zekk yelled.

"Hold on?" Han cried, trying not to think about all the things that were going to tear as soon as the droid's weight snapped his elbow straight. "Are you crazy?"

But Han's arm never reached full extension. Instead he felt himself sinking into the velvet hand of the Force. He looked over to find Zekk gesturing in his direction, floating him and C-3PO over the safety rail back onto the hoverscaf. Their feet had barely touched the deck before C-3PO was in front of Han, arms spread wide.

"Captain Solo, you just risked your life to prevent my untimely destruction," he said. "Could you be suffering some manner of cognitive malfunction?"

"Obviously," Han growled. "And—"

"Can we get on with the rescue?" Zekk interrupted. He retrieved the repeating blaster from the deck and passed it to Han, then glanced up the detention center wall. "After those detonators, they know we're here."

Han nodded, glared at C-3PO, then slipped the blaster's strap over his shoulder and looked up in time to see Jaina and Leia disappearing through a still-smoking breach in the detention center wall. The five-meter hole was perfectly round and clean, with sharp edges and a total lack of rubble—which was why thermal detonators were the favorite tool of demolition crews and urban assault squads alike. Han glanced down to check on Squad Saav'etu and saw an identical breach on the 1910 level, with Seff Hellin and Kunor Bann already inside the building and Natua Wan and Yaqeel Saav'etu just leaping off their hoverscaf into the hole. Like Jaina and Leia, their lightsabers remained unactivated—a sign that the detention center guards had not yet arrived to mount a defense.

By the time Han looked away, Zekk was already moving their own hoverscaf up toward the breach. As they rose, Han saw that the bowl-shaped hole had actually exposed part of the level below their target level. Through the narrow gap, he could see down into a long corridor lined by sealed transparisteel doors. Standing behind most of the doors were beings dressed in fluorescent orange detainee uniforms. They appeared to be of many different species—there were a lot of Arcona, Askajians, and humans. Some looked shocked, others menacing. None appeared friendly.

The hoverscaf stopped in front of level 1913. Zekk quickly leapt across the two-and-a-half-meter gap into the building, landing in a corridor similar to the one below. Beyond him, Leia and Jaina were already racing toward a sealed security door, lightsabers in hand but not yet activated. Zekk spun around and used the Force to lift the droids into the passage, then turned to Han.

"You want a lift?"

Han eyed the distance to the edge of the corridor floor and silently thanked Zekk for making it sound like the offer was optional. He nodded. "You'd have made a great son-in-law, kid."

"Too late," Taryn called up. She was inside the Cygnus-7 now, preparing to take her new position as the escape-vehicle gunner. "Finders keepers."

Zekk rolled his eyes, but smiled at her. "Don't worry,

Taryn," he said. "After Relephon, I'm not changing *anything.*"

"What happened on Relephon?" Han asked.

Zekk's swarthy complexion brightened to brilliant crimson. "Sorry." He let the sentence trail off and looked away for a moment, then extended a hand toward Han. "State secret."

Han's stomach grew heavy as he suddenly floated into the air and started across the gap. He glanced back at Taryn, who was standing in the doorway of the Cygnus-7 strapping on a pair of big DL-51 blaster pistols, and thought better of pressing for details.

Zekk set him down, then pointed toward the end of the corridor, where Leia and Jaina were already using their lightsabers to cut through the durasteel security door. "The data socket is up there, Artoo. Let's go."

Zekk took the lead, ignoring the muted clamor of hammering fists and yelling prisoners that followed them down the corridor. Han brought up the rear, keeping watch as C-3PO and R2-D2 advanced ahead of him. As they moved, he set his blaster to FULL and started blasting cam bubbles. Each time he destroyed one, a muffled cheer rose from the inmates in nearby cells.

The prisoners seemed to be males of many different species. Their cells were more or less uniform, though there was often a roost or a nest instead of a bed. Occasionally, the air was tinged brown or green, suggesting a nonstandard atmosphere.

Han and the droids had almost reached the security door when a faint hissing sounded from the ventilation ducts. He pulled the breath mask off his equipment harness and slipped the elastic keeper straps over his head.

"Gas!" He pulled the mask down and opened the air feed, then activated his throat mike. "Squad Saav'etu, watch yourselves. We've got gas up here."

"Down here, too," Yaqeel replied. "They're reacting quicker than we expected."

"Affirmative," Turi confirmed from Cygnus-7. "We've got three pursuit speeders coming our way."

"Stang, that was fast," Han said. "Can you outrun—"

"No need," Taryn replied. The screech of a discharging ion cannon sounded from outside. "There are only three. I can hold them off!"

"For how long?" Han asked.

"Don't worry," Taryn said. "We'll be here when you need a ride."

The rumble of a distant explosion sounded outside.

"That's fine, Taryn," Leia broke in. "Just remember, we're trying to keep deaths to a *minimum*."

"It wasn't *me*," Taryn retorted, speaking over the squeal of her ion cannon. "One of those speeders fired a concussion missile."

Leia cringed behind her breath mask, and Han knew what she was thinking. They were trying to avoid unnecessary casualties—and not only because they wanted to minimize bad press. The conflict between Daala and the Jedi was already out of hand; if it started to cause *civilian* casualties, it would be a stain on the honor of both sides.

"*And?*" Leia asked. She was stooped over, dragging her lightsaber blade through the last section of security door to meet Jaina's. "Did they kill anyone?"

"Hard to say," Taryn replied. "They took out a pedbridge." The next screech was followed almost instantly by the roar of a nearby explosion. "And . . . that time they got a news sled."

"A news sled?" Han's chest tightened. "Not Doran and Bandy?"

"No, a *real* news sled." It was Turi Altamik's voice that said this. "*Sort* of real, anyway. It was ROKS."

Han caught Leia's eye and shrugged. "At least *we're* not the ones killing people."

Leia merely glanced up. *"So?"*

"Yeah."

After all their years fighting side by side, Han knew by that one word what Leia meant—it didn't matter *who* was doing the killing. The Jedi had started this fight, so they bore the ultimate responsibility if civilian lives were lost.

"Turi, you and Taryn better make a run for it," Han said. "Maybe you can draw them off to someplace a little less populated."

"And leave you guys behind?" Taryn objected. "Think again—"

"Taryn!" Zekk interrupted. "This is what backup plans are for."

Even as Zekk spoke, the Cygnus-7 was roaring away, its nose dropping as it dived for the sheltering confines of the undercity. With any luck, Turi would be able to lose her pursuers in the murky labyrinth, then swing back around to pick them up when they had Valin and Jysella in hand. If not, there was always the HoloNews van that Doran Tainer and Bandy Geffer were operating.

A trio of armored wedges streaked past the breach in hot pursuit of the Cygnus-7, sirens shrieking and emergency strobes flashing, then vanished from sight. With the screeching of the ion cannon gone, the din in the corridor faded to the muted roar of prisoners thumping on their cell doors and bellowing for freedom. Given all of the threats and foul language Han heard, he wasn't even *half* tempted to help them out.

The droning of the lightsabers finally snapped to an end, and Han turned to see Jaina using the Force to hold the security door upright. R2-D2 was already plugged into the data socket below the control panel on the wall, blinking and chirping merrily as he sliced into the facility's main computer.

Han turned to C-3PO. "How long before Artoo finds a schematic for us?"

"Any moment, Captain. I believe—"

R2-D2 cut him off with a sharp whistle.

"That's impossible, Artoo," C-3PO retorted. "Your processor is no match for a supercooled Xyn Tachyon Twelve. Stop that at once!"

"*Threepio!*" Han interrupted. "How long until we have that schematic?"

"It should be on your datapads now," C-3PO replied, turning to Han. "And Artoo is attempting to outwit Xyn and override the storage bunker's security program. He's going to give himself a circuit melt."

R2-D2 tweedled sharply.

C-3PO looked back toward R2-D2. "Well, why didn't you *tell* us?" he demanded. "Don't you think they would want to *know* you already have the bunker open?"

"*Open?*"

Han snatched the datapad off Leia's equipment belt. The display contained a three-dimensional schematic labeled DETENTION CENTER 81 LEVELS 1910–1915. The rescue team's locations were not depicted, but with two red dots indicating the breaches in the outer wall, their position was pretty easy to estimate. It appeared that Squad Solo, at least, had reached a bulkhead about a quarter of the way across the building. On the other side of the wall was a huge, multi-level atrium ringed with access balconies serving the detention corridors on each level. In the center of the atrium stood the storage bunker to which C-3PO had referred, a large freestanding vault with hatches high on its walls. From the schematic, at least, there appeared to be no easy way of accessing the hatches.

Han showed the display to his companions, then activated his throat mike. "Squad Saav'etu, do you guys have the schematic on your datapad yet?"

"Affirmative," came Yaqeel's raspy-voiced reply. "We're just inside the security door, waiting for the signal."

"Artoo has the hatches on that vault open," Han reported. "He thinks that's where Valin and Jysella are being held."

R2-D2 gave an affirmative chirp, then added a tweedle.

"Artoo notes that both Horns are indeed listed on the bunker inventory," C-3PO reported. As he spoke, R2-D2 continued to tweedle. "He's trying to deactivate the neutralizer field so he can use the tracking bugs to confirm their exact location. Unfortunately, Xyn is arguing about the proper protocols."

"Keep trying," Han said to R2-D2. "And while you're at it, maybe Xyn can tell us if there are any guards on—"

"There *are*," Jaina said. "About fifty, coming in from all sides."

"*Fifty* . . . is that all? They must be trying to make this easy." Han had been living with Jedi too long to bother asking how Jaina knew the number of guards or whether she was sure. He simply raised three fingers, then asked Yaqeel, "Ready, Squad Saav'etu?"

When Yaqeel responded with a comm click, Han lowered all three fingers.

"Go!"

Jaina waved her hand to the side, and the human-sized rectangle she and Leia had cut from the security door popped free and went tumbling down the length of the balcony. A chorus of startled voices cried out in alarm, then the dull *thung* of durasteel on plastoid rang out from around the corner. In the next instant, the open doorway erupted into a storm of flashing bolts, and the lightsabers of both Solo women snapped to life.

"Going right, Mom!" Jaina called.

"Going left!" Leia confirmed.

They stepped through the door together, their blades weaving baskets of color as they batted blaster bolts back toward their sources. Zekk went next, moving forward to deflect fire from two squads of guards positioned high above in the corners on the opposite side of the atrium.

"Han, grenades!" Zekk called back through the door. "Three-second fuses."

Han let his repeating blaster dangle by its sling and pulled a stun grenade off his equipment vest. He quickly set the timer, then tried not to shake as he moved into throwing position on the other side of the door. Surrounded as he was by three *very* experienced Jedi Knights, he knew there wasn't much chance of a bolt getting through—but there were dozens of bolts coming their way every second, and not even Leia was perfect. Seeing that Zekk was taking fire from two different directions, Han positioned himself a little to the side and tossed the first grenade over the rail.

"Zekk, yours!"

Zekk switched to a single-handed grip and pivoted sideways, allowing half a dozen bolts to slip past his twirling blade as he pointed at the grenade. He flicked his finger toward the opposite side of the atrium, and the grenade flew into the corner on the right and exploded with a detonation as blinding as it was deafening. The guards went down at once, most of them completely unconscious, but a few covering their ears or eyes and rolling around in agony.

Han already had the next grenade ready. Since he was facing Jaina's side of the balcony, he called her name and tossed it over her shoulder. She did not even need to switch to a single-handed grip. She simply fixed her gaze on the wall of guards lined up across the balcony in front of her, and the stun grenade flew toward them as though launched by a rocket. The sergeant saw it coming and managed to raise a hand to point before it detonated in the midst of his squad, leaving them motionless and piled atop one another.

Han turned and tossed the third grenade past Leia's flank. She allowed it to hit the deck grating, then sent it bouncing down the balcony toward a squad of guards who—having the benefit of seeing what had become of their fellows—wisely gave up the fight and simply turned to flee. The detonation caught half of them anyway. Some continued to flee, stumbling down the balcony with their hands pressed to their ears, and some dropped in their tracks and began to writhe about on the deck grating. Those who had been lucky enough to escape unscathed simply continued to run.

Han started to reach for another stun grenade, but Zekk said, "Save it. We've convinced them."

Han looked up to see the last group of guards withdrawing from view. He was about to check the status of Squad Saav'etu when he heard a sporadic clatter in the atrium. Being careful not to invite sniper fire by leaning over the rail, he peered out and saw a steady shower of blaster rifles dropping to the atrium floor. Jaina and Leia quickly began to add to the rain of weaponry, using the Force to hurl every GAS weapon in sight over the safety rail.

"Looks like we're good to go," Han observed. He glanced at the hatches hanging open on the side of the storage bunker. They were a good twenty meters away, and between ten and twenty meters above the atrium floor. "Question is, how do we get *there*? That's a big jump—even for a Jedi."

No sooner had Han asked the question than a happy

tweedle sounded in the corridor behind them. A moment later, a panel beneath one of the hatches slid open. It was followed by another one on Squad Saav'etu's level, and a pair of long catwalk bridges began to extend toward each access balcony.

"Artoo wonders if the bridges might help?" C-3PO translated.

"Yeah, good thinking," Han said. He poked his head back into the cell corridor and looked down at R2-D2. "Think you can lock down access to the atrium around the bunker?"

R2-D2 replied with a long series of tweets and chirps.

"Artoo has convinced Xyn that you are rioting inmates attempting to take control of the detention center," C-3PO translated. "The entire cellblock has been isolated. And the signal neutralizer has been deactivated to prevent you from using the storage bunker to evade surveillance. But I must say, I don't think isolating the cellblock is a very good idea, Captain Solo. Now we're locked inside with dozens of angry guards—and I'm quite certain that a few of them remain conscious."

As C-3PO spoke, a flurry of blasterfire erupted from below, down in the atrium. Han spun around in time to see Yaqeel Saav'etu's furry-headed form somersaulting through the air toward the still-extending catwalk, her amber lightsaber tracing a yellow cocoon around her as she deflected incoming blaster bolts. The sniper fire was answered by a volley of stun bolts from her companions, and by the time she landed the GAS guards had fallen silent. Jaina went next, her feet barely touching the safety rail as she bounded off it and Force-jumped onto the upper catwalk.

"You might have that backward, Threepio," Han said, turning back to the droid. "It's *those* poor noobs who are stuck in here . . ."

Han let the sentence trail off as the squeal of scraping metal rang out from the far end of corridor, sixty meters distant. He looked up and, through the hole by which the team had entered the building, saw one end of the hoverscaf tipping upward. A second later the blunt round nose of a GAS troopsled slid into view.

Han activated his throat mike. "Trouble!" He pulled a thermal detonator off his vest. "We've got armor out—"

The muted *shriek-crack* of cannon bolts began to reverberate up from below, and the air grew acrid with the fumes of molten metal. Han set the detonator fuse to three seconds and, with his free hand, reached into the corridor.

"Out of the way!" He grabbed C-3PO by the wrist and pulled him out of the corridor. "Run for it!"

"Run? I'm afraid my servomotors aren't made for—"

C-3PO's foot caught on the bottom edge of the doorway, and his objection came to a crashing end. At the other end of the corridor, the troopsled had shoved the hoverscaf completely out of the way, bringing the forward canopy and the driver's hatch into view. A couple of meters above the hatch hung the tip of a blaster cannon, already turning toward the corridor. Han planted a foot in the middle of C-3PO's back and squared off in front of the doorway.

"You, too, Artoo!" Han used a full-windup underhand pitch to sling the detonator down the corridor and, with his free hand, waved the little astromech toward him. "Let's go!"

R2-D2 retracted his interface arm and whirred toward Han. In the corridor behind the droid, the detonator dropped twenty meters short—and continued to bounce toward the troopsled.

The front edge of the cannon turret came into view, and the barrel continued to swing toward Han. Unsure whether he was actually strong enough to *lift* an astromech droid over the lip in the doorway, Han stooped down to grab R2-D2.

"Hey!" he called over his shoulder. "How about a little—"

The corridor erupted into a screaming flash of heat.

An instant later Han found himself rolling off C-3PO onto the balcony's deck grating. His ears were ringing and his eyes were filled with dancing spots, and his arms were empty.

A white glow flared inside the corridor, and Han heard a distant crackle that had to be the thermal detonator going off. He rolled to his knees and spun around to see Zekk pressed to the wall on the opposite side of the doorway. C-3PO was between them, pushing himself to his hands and knees, and R2-D2 was nowhere to be seen.

Expecting another volley of cannon bolts at any instant, Han grabbed C-3PO with both hands and spun away from the doorway, dragging the droid down beside him.

"Stay down!"

C-3PO clattered to the grating beside Han. "Very well," he said. "May I inquire why?"

"No," Han said, realizing by the lack of cannon bolts that he had overreacted. He glanced back toward the door and found Zekk cautiously peering around the corner into the corridor. "Is he . . . is he gone?"

Zekk nodded and stepped fully in front of the doorway. "You got him. Nice throw."

"I *meant* Artoo," Han said, standing. "Is he . . . you know?"

"Artoo is gone?" C-3PO scrambled to his feet with surprising grace and clanged past Han into the doorway. "They *melted* Artoo?"

A sharp whistle sounded from the atrium behind him. Han turned and was relieved to see R2-D2 racing across the catwalk bridge toward the storage bunker. The rear half the droid's outer shell was scorched and pocked with melt-circles, but any damage he had suffered had certainly not affected his mobility functions.

At the other end of the catwalk, Leia and Jaina were kneeling in the bunker's open hatch, ready to provide covering fire. Fifteen meters below them, Kunor Bann was standing guard for Squad Saav'etu—which meant Yaqeel and Natua were already inside the storage bunker looking for the Horn kids. Seff, he knew, would be on the balcony three levels below, protecting the route through which Squad Saav'etu had entered the facility. Judging by the lack of cannon fire down there, he had also been successful in taking out the vehicle attacking them.

"Artoo, what are you doing out *there*?" C-3PO inquired. "You were stationed at the data interface."

R2-D2 replied with an irate tweedle, then extended a third tread and bumped over the hatch threshold, entering the bunker.

"There's no need to take that tone with me," C-3PO called after the astromech. "*Of course* I'm happy to see you in one piece!"

Han turned to Zekk, then hitched a thumb at the corridor. "Maybe it would be better if we had a *Jedi* keeping an eye on things outside. My throwing arm is good, but—"

"It's not the Force," Zekk finished. He flipped his palm up and turned his fingers toward Han. Two of Han's last three thermal detonators rose off the equipment vest and floated into the Jedi's grasp. "Be fast."

"Will do." Han waved C-3PO toward the bridge, then activated his throat mike. "How's it going in the bunker? Have you found those carbonite pods?"

"You could say that," Yaqeel replied. "I guess."

"You *guess*?" Han replied. "You do know what a carbonite pod looks like, right? Big black rectangle with a face in it? Mouth frozen mid-scream?"

"Han, just get over here," Leia said. "You're not going to believe this."

"Okay," Han said. When he turned to the catwalk, he saw that he'd have to open the gate for C-3PO—apparently, everyone else had just gone over. "On our way. Cover us."

"Copy that," Jaina said. "But run."

"Run?" C-3PO said. "As I tried to explain to Captain Solo, my servomotors are not equipped to noooooo!"

C-3PO's objection ended in the droid equivalent of a scream when Natua Wan appeared next to Jaina and used the Force to bring him flying toward the bunker. Han pulled the repeating blaster off his shoulder and raced after the droid in a crouching sprint. Even before the snipers opened fire, Jaina began to pick them off, silencing two with a series of quick shots.

Han turned his T-21 in the direction Jaina *wasn't* shooting and, forgetting he had not switched the power level back to STUN, began to lay his own suppression fire. By the time he reached the storage bunker, the steady stream of high-power bolts had triggered the automatic fire-suppression systems. The ceiling nozzles began to pour retardant foam into the atrium.

"Nice trick," Jaina said, speaking from behind her breath mask. She and Natua stepped aside to let Han race through the hatch. "Is that supposed to be camouflage or something?"

"Hey, if the Balmorran infantry can use smoke curtains," Han said, flipping the T-21's power level to STUN, "I can use a foam screen."

Jaina rolled her eyes. "Whatever you say, Dad."

Han shot her a smug wink, then turned to survey the interior of the storage bunker . . . and felt his jaw drop.

He was standing inside a huge refrigerated cylinder, on one of more than a dozen circular balconies. Hanging along the walls on each level were several hundred carbonite pods, each connected to a power supply and a monitoring station by a shielded cable.

"*Bloah!*" Han cursed. "We're gonna need more transport!"

"Captain Solo, there's no way we can take everyone in here," Natua said. The Falleen was probably exuding calming pheromones, but if so, they had no effect through Han's face mask. "And even if we could, there's no way to know whether we *should.*"

Han frowned at her. "Of *course* we should!" He could not help thinking of his own experiences in carbonite, of the frozen eternity of fear and the terrible anguish of awakening. "Do you have *any* idea what it's like to be frozen in carbonite?"

"Han, all Natua is saying is that we can't help them all *now,*" Leia said, stepping to his side. "We came to get Valin and Jysella. And it's going to take more time than we hoped just to find them. This place is huge."

"No kidding," Han said. "Who *are* all these guys?"

Natua shrugged. "Political prisoners? Troublemaker inmates?"

"Daala's old buddies?" Han offered.

"That's as good a guess as any," Leia replied. "All we know for sure is that psychotic Jedi aren't the only ones Daala has been storing in carbonite."

"Assuming it *is* Daala," Jaina said. "This could be something Colonel Retk is doing on his own. It has a certain Yaka sensibility."

"Yeah," Han said. "It's sure sick."

He began to count, first the number of pods hanging along a ten-meter length of wall, then the number of balconies inside the storage bunker. By the time he finished and came up with an estimated number of pods, he felt nauseated.

"Over four thousand," he said. "Even if we only spend a second looking at each one, it could take us . . ."

Han started the calculations, and for once he was grateful when C-3PO jumped in with an answer.

"Eighteen point three minutes," the droid supplied. "That figure assumes that there are four people searching, and that they spend no more than five seconds with each level change."

Natua turned toward the nearest set of stairs. "I'll start at the top."

Han caught her shoulder and shook his head. "Hold on," he said. "We don't have eighteen minutes. We don't even have a quarter of that."

Natua's face scales darkened. "We *aren't* going to give up." Her tone made it clear that she was issuing a proclamation, not asking a question. "Not after we've come this far."

"Of course not," Han said. He turned to R2-D2. "You, start recording. We want the layout, the interfaces, and as many pod faces as you can capture. When we get back to the Temple, the Council is going to want to know who all these people are, and anything you can give them will help."

R2-D2 gave an obedient chirp and spun toward the nearest pod.

"Pardon me, Captain Solo," C-3PO said. "But wouldn't it be better to find a dataport and have Artoo simply ask Xyn for the Jedi Horns' location?"

"No time for that," Han said. "If it were that easy, Artoo would have done it already."

"Then how are we going to find the Horns?" C-3PO asked.

"*We're* not," Han replied. "You are."

"Me?"

"Sure," Han said. "The signal neutralizer is off, and we know those transmitters Mirax planted are in here *somewhere.*"

"Of course!" Leia shot Han one of those admiring smiles that always made his day. "See-Threepio has a full-spectrum receiver."

"That's true," C-3PO said. "But I fail to see how that's going to help me find the Horns. They won't be calling us on their comlinks."

"No, but those tracking bugs are," Jaina said. "Taryn said they disguise their microbursts as background radiation, remember?"

"Right," Han said, turning back to C-3PO. "So do a full-spectrum scan and—"

"There!" C-3PO extended an arm and nearly swept Natua off her feet as he lurched to the safety rail. "Just one level below us. I recognize the signal from our planning session."

"Good job!" Han slapped C-3PO on the back and—ignoring the droid's protest—turned to Natua and Leia. "Why don't you two help Yaqeel and Seff bring up the pods. Jaina and I will get started on the extraction strategy."

Instead of running for the stairs, Leia and Natua simply leapt off the balcony, grabbing the safety rail with one hand and using it swing themselves onto the level below. Han returned to the hatch and knelt beside Jaina, then removed the last of the stun grenades from his vest and arrayed them on the floor. He still had the single thermal detonator that Zekk had left him.

"Now comes the fun part." He peered out into atrium, which looked like it had been hit with a blizzard of flame retardant. "Do you know where the snipers are?"

"Sure." Jaina waved her hand in an arc, indicating the upper balconies lining the atrium wall opposite them. "Pretty much everywhere."

"So we're not going to have trouble hitting them, huh?"

"I doubt it." She looked over and said, "You know, Dad, this wouldn't worry me so much if you were a Jedi Master."

Han smiled. "Don't worry, kid," he said. "I've got my luck—and it's gotten me this far, hasn't it?"

Jaina smiled back. "I suppose it has." She kissed him on the cheek, then reached over and flipped his repeating blaster's power setting back to FULL. "Just in case, though, let's give them a reason to keep their heads down."

Han barely heard this last part because his attention was fixed on her hand. Actually, it was fixed on her ring finger, where he had just noticed that a very familiar, very expensive engagement band had reappeared.

"Hey, where'd that come from?" he asked. "I thought you told Jag to toss that in the lake?"

Jaina blushed and looked away. "I never told him that."

"Something like that," Han said. "So what gives?"

"Nothing, Dad," she said. "Don't read too much into it, okay? We're not sure what it means ourselves yet. I'll tell you later."

"But it means *something*?" Han pressed. "This is the real reason he tracked us down before he went back to the *Pellaeon*, right?"

"Dad!" Jaina said. "Don't you have an escape to organize?"

"Piece of cake." Han activated his throat mike. "Zekk, how's it looking outside?"

"We're *definitely* going to be on the holo tonight," Zekk said. "There are about a dozen newsvans filming me as we speak. I see BAU, HNE, HoloNews, and . . . a *lot* more, Captain."

Translation: Zekk was worried about eavesdroppers, but Doran and Bandy—in the MSHoloNews van—were in pickup position.

"Okay," Han said. "What about our ride?"

"The Cygnus-7 is having trouble getting back to us," he said. "Their communications have been compromised, and every time they try to circle back to the detention center, they run into more GAS sleds. They think they've got twenty or thirty trying to box them in already."

Translation: Turi and Taryn were deliberately allowing their communications to be monitored, trying to draw off as many GAS pursuit vehicles as possible.

"*Stang!*" Han said, pretending to be dismayed. He knew better than to think their comlinks' Jedi encryption had been broken, but Zekk's caution made it sound as though he were relaying their transmissions directly to the Cygnus-7—for the sole purpose of misleading GAS, of course. "We can't get out of here without that Cygnus-Seven. Tell them to report in . . ."

Han glanced back and saw Leia leading Yaqeel and the other two Jedi toward him at a sprint. Between them, floating on tiny repulsorlift engines, were two carbonite pods bearing the terror-stricken faces of Valin and Jysella Horn.

"Two minutes," Han said into his throat mike. "If the Cygni can't shake free by then, we'll head for the undercity and try to escape on foot."

Translation: We'll be at the pickup point in two minutes. Make sure Doran and Bandy are waiting.

"The *undercity*?" Zekk replied. "On *foot*?"

"In two minutes, that may be our only way out," Han said. "It's better than rotting in a GAS prison cell . . . right, Kunor?"

Kunor's surprised voice sounded over Han's earpiece. "Uh, sure, Captain Solo." Across the atrium, Kunor's white-clothed figure began to race along the access balcony toward a stairway that would take him up to Zekk's level. "If you want to make a run for it, I'm with you."

Translation: I'm on my way up to the extraction point.

"Okay, then I'll start a count." Zekk sounded truly terrified—which was how Han knew he was acting. The only thing Zekk feared was the dark side, and he had even faced *that* down a couple of times. "We'll talk in two minutes."

Translation: Get yourself over here. The ride leaves on time.

As Leia and the others approached, Han stood and laid out his plan in less than ten seconds.

When he was finished, Jaina asked, "Dad, are you *sure* you should be one of the ones pulling the pods? Without the Force, you'll be vulnerable enough."

"That's why I'm going last. By the time I start across, there won't *be* anyone left shooting." Han checked his chrono. "Enough talk. Just remember, *don't* stop for anything. Get to the extraction point, get aboard, and get going."

He nodded to Natua and Seff, who immediately ignited their lightsabers and charged onto the catwalk. A storm of colored bolts rained down on them from the balconies. Instead of leaping into an acrobatic routine, the two Jedi remained on foot, intentionally drawing fire, their blades weaving glowing spheres of color about their heads as they batted bolts aside.

Han and the two Solo women made good use of the tactic. Han armed stun grenades and tossed them out into the atrium, and Leia or Jaina immediately sent them flying at the guards who had revealed their positions by attacking. By the time the two Jedi Knights were halfway across the bridge, the blasterfire had faded to a drizzle.

Han tapped Jaina on the shoulder. "You and Yaqeel are next. Go."

Jaina tossed her blaster aside and launched herself from the hatch, snatching her lightsaber off her belt and activating it in mid-stride. Unlike Natua and Seff, she merely held the blade at a high guard, flicking it back and forth almost leisurely whenever one of the remaining snipers gathered enough courage to take a shot—and risk the flurry of bolts that Han and Leia sent flying back at him.

As soon as Jaina had advanced four meters onto the bridge, Yaqeel ushered R2-D2 and C-3PO through the hatch and started to herd them across. Despite C-3PO's predictions of doom and certain destruction, the sniper fire dwindled to nothing after Yaqeel batted aside a single bolt.

When the droids reached the halfway point on the bridge, Han let his repeating blaster dangle from its shoulder strap and rose. He shot a smirk across at Leia, then turned toward the carbonite pods hovering on their repulsorlifts.

"See? Nothing to it."

A deafening chorus of clangs reverberated through the storage bunker as all of its hatches slammed shut simultaneously. Han spun back around to find Leia sitting on the deck grating, her hands braced behind her and her mouth hanging agape. She was staring dead ahead, where an oily durasteel panel now blocked their only escape route.

Leia slowly turned a pair of angry brown eyes in his direction. "You just *had* to say it."

"It's not my fault!" Han said, stabbing a finger against a button on the control panel. When the hatch remained closed, he added, "Artoo didn't say anything about Xyn changing her mind!"

"My guess is someone helped her," Leia said. She rose

and stepped over to examine the hatch. "That's a turadium shield alloy. It's going take *forever* to cut through it."

"Yeah, well, we don't *have* forever." Han checked his chrono. "We've got sixty seconds."

Leia's brow furrowed. "You don't think they would leave without . . ." She let the sentence trail off, then shook her head. "Forget it. They don't have a choice."

Han nodded. "That newsvan doesn't have armor *or* weaponry," he said. "They *have* to take off without us—or get shot down."

"I'll let them know." Leia activated her throat mike, then frowned. "But not with this thing. The signal neutralizer is back on. We've lost the comlink."

Her eyes grew distant and unfocused as she reached out in the Force—most likely to Jaina, with whom she had the strongest connection. Han took the chance to glance around the bunker, searching for any means of escape Xyn might have overlooked. It was eerily silent inside the bunker, and only dimly lit. The blinking status lights on all those thousands of carbonite pods made him think of a Coruscant skylane at dusk. The temperature was not uncomfortable yet, but he knew it was cold enough to cause hypothermia within a few hours.

Failing to see any obvious means of escape, Han pulled the datapad from his vest pocket and rechecked the schematic R2-D2 had provided earlier. It took only a moment to find what he needed. He looked up into the top of the bunker, which curved into a vaguely conical dome about thirty meters overhead.

Han turned the schematic toward Leia and pointed toward the bullet-shaped peak. "This thing sticks up through the roof. I remember seeing that when we set up the hoverscafs."

"Me, too," Leia said. "So?"

He tapped a small globe hanging from his equipment vest. "So I've still got a thermal detonator."

"Okay . . ." Leia's eyes began to brighten, but she did not seem quite on board yet. "And *then*?"

"Then we're out on the roof," Han said. He grabbed Valin's pod and started to float it toward the nearest stairway. "Where the GAS boys don't expect to see us."

Leia cocked her head. "Well, it's better than staying trapped in here. I'll keep reaching out to Jaina and see if I can get across the idea that we're going up."

She grabbed Jysella's pod and floated it after Han, and together they began to climb as fast as possible. They spotted a cargo lift almost immediately, but didn't use it for fear of betraying their plan. Besides, with Leia using the Force to pull the pods up the stairwells, the ascent wasn't too strenuous. After a couple of minutes, they were standing on the uppermost balcony looking up into the pointed dome.

Han pulled the thermal detonator off his vest, then tried to gauge the distance between them and the apex. "That ought to be far enough above us that we're clear of the blast, right?"

Leia studied the dome for a moment, then nodded. "I think so, and if we're wrong . . ."

The sound of hatches opening rang out below. GAS guards in full riot gear began flooding into the bunker, and a moment later blaster bolts began to scream upward.

"That was fast," Han observed. He and Leia pressed themselves against the wall, then he set the detonator fuse for three seconds and asked, "Ready?"

When Leia nodded, he tossed the detonator toward the dome and started to count seconds aloud.

Leia extended a hand, catching it in the Force—and several guards cried out, *"Detonator!"*

The blaster fire stopped as the guards dived for the nearest exits. Leia flicked her hand upward, and the thermal detonator flew into the apex of the dome.

"Three!" Han warned.

Both Solos closed their eyes and turned toward the wall. Even so, the flash was so bright that it made Han's head pound. He felt a wave of heat so searing that he feared they had misjudged the distance to the apex.

A tremendous crackle rang through the bunker, then the heat and the light faded as quickly as they had come. Han stood frozen for several heartbeats, just to make sure he *was* actually alive, then finally let his breath out.

"Hey, we made it!" He opened his eyes and turned to hug Leia . . . and nearly stepped off a half-disintegrated balcony. "*Leia?*"

She wasn't there. And neither were the Horns.

More than half of the balcony had been caught in the blast radius and was simply gone. But that still left a good half a meter of durasteel upon which Leia *could* have been standing—and *should* have.

"Leia!"

Han dropped to his knees and peered over the white-hot edge of the balcony, expecting—*hoping*—to see her hanging from a balcony below.

There was no one there. No one but about four thousand very quiet carbonite prisoners.

"*Leiaaaagghh?*" The call was half question and half wail, a scream unlike any Han had unleashed before. "Leiaaaaa!"

Han?

Leia's voice came to him as much within his mind as in his ears, and he imagined she was reaching out to him through the Force, trying to touch him one last time before she was gone . . . forever. The tears welled in his eyes.

Then she called out to him again. *"Han!"*

He looked up, his eyes so watery that he could see nothing but a blue smear where the detonator had disintegrated the roof. "Leia?"

"Han!" she called. "Will you get moving, already? They're waiting for us!"

"Waiting?"

Han stood and turned toward the voice, growing more confused. There was no way Zekk and Jaina and the others in the newsvan were on the roof—even if they *had* disobeyed orders, GAS would have shot them down. And he could not imagine who else might be waiting with Leia, except all of their beloved ones who had gone before . . . so, was *he* dead, too?

Han looked up again. He could barely make out a female form kneeling at the edge of the detonator hole—*Leia's* form. Behind her loomed the bulky shape of a Cyngus-7 armored transport.

"Leia! You're . . ." He caught himself, not wanting to act like a total fool in front of the woman he loved. "You're out already?"

"Han, I've *been* out for five seconds—and the Horns have been out for a couple!" When the sound of running boots began to rumble up from the depths of the bunker, Leia frowned and asked, "What's wrong? Did you hit your head or something?"

"Uh, yeah." Han wiped his eyes on a sleeve. "Sorry, I must have."

"What's the holdup?" demanded a familiar Hapan voice. A moment later Taryn Zel appeared next to Leia and began to pour blasterfire down through the hole. Behind her, the screech of the Cygnus-7's ion cannon began to shred the air. "Let's get moving, Solo!"

A steady stream of blasterfire began to fly up from below, ricocheting around the upper ring of the bunker and vanishing into the sky above. Han pulled his blaster off his shoulder, glanced up to see Leia already extending a hand in his direction, and began to return fire as she rocketed him out of the bunker straight into the open cargo bay of the Cygnus-7.

Leia and Taryn dived in on top of him, and an instant later Turi had the supercharged transport slipping over the edge of the detention center and streaking downward. Han and the two women tumbled down against the forward bulkhead of the cargo bay and lay there in a tangle atop the cargo pods, trying to catch their breath and still their pounding hearts. Finally, the Cygnus-7 entered the concealing gloom of the undercity and leveled out.

"There." Han snaked an arm around Leia's shoulder and planted a big kiss on her lips, then pulled back and gave her one of his crooked smiles. "Didn't I *say* this was going to be easy?"

Chapter Thirty

TAHIRI, IT SEEMED, WAS NO LONGER NEWS. FOR THE FIRST time since her trial had opened, the spectator area of the Ninth Hall of Justice sat nearly empty. As word had spread of the *Errant Venture*'s attack on Coruscant's climate-control mirrors that morning, half the reporters in attendance had drifted out of the room and not returned. When news had arrived of the StealthX launch, the rest had departed, and by the time the *Venture* had escaped into hyperspace, even casual observers were leaving. Now, with Daala making noises about martial law and the whole planet waiting to see if she would attempt to storm the Jedi Temple again, the only beings still in the courtroom were those directly involved with the trial.

And that, according to Sardonne Sardon, was a problem. With Eramuth Bwua'tu ambling back and forth in front of the witness stand, seeming to fumble about in search of a defense while actually preparing to demolish the prosecution's most damaging witness, the galactic media was nowhere to be seen. The momentum of the trial was about to swing toward the defense, and no one was going to see it. In the court of public opinion, Lieutenant Pagorski's claim that the defendant had violated a direct order would be allowed to stand. Tahiri would continue to be regarded as a renegade Jedi who had murdered a legendary commander, and—of course—potential clients would not see on live HoloNet how quickly Sardonne Sardon had reversed the course of the trial.

Which was fine with Tahiri.

All she wanted was the truth brought to light. And the *truth* was that Caedus *had* instructed her to kill Pellaeon if it was necessary to secure the Empire's military cooperation. Tahiri had followed those orders exactly. Whether that had been an act of war or a murder was for the jury to determine. She just wanted them to make that determination based on facts.

Bwua'tu's pacing carried him back in front of the witness stand, where he paused to scowl at Lieutenant Pagorski. "So you're telling me that *Bloodfin* Security had *all* compartments on the vessel under surveillance?"

"Yes, sir," Pagorski replied. As before, she was in full Imperial dress uniform, white jacket with epaulets over a gray shirt buttoned to the throat. "All compartments except the admiral's refresher. That was what we were told."

"I see," Bwua'tu said.

The trap had been Sardon's idea, but even she had recognized that opposing counsel would see it coming if she tried to lay the groundwork in her own meticulous, orderly style. That was just one of the reasons Tahiri was glad that Bwua'tu hadn't been allowed to resign in protest when she had insisted on adding Sardon to the defense team. Together, they were a great pair, Bwua'tu's experience and style a perfect complement to Sardon's intellect and organization. With them working together, she didn't see how she could lose.

"And *that's* how you knew that my client was present at this *supposed* conference aboard the *Bloodfin* before the Battle of Fondor?" Bwua'tu asked, weaving another strand in his web. "You saw her in the conference compartment with the Admirals Niathal and Pellaeon and Colonel Solo?"

"Not quite, Counselor," Pagorski said. "No one but FinSec sees those vids. I was told of her presence afterward, by a FinSec officer."

Bwua'tu cocked a furry brow in feigned astonishment. "It was the habit of the *Bloodfin*'s security team to gossip about what they observed on their surveillance vids?"

"Not normally," Pagorski replied. "I happened to be close with a FinSec officer."

"So you're saying this was pillow talk?"

"That's not what I said," Pagorski replied.

"But it could be characterized that way?"

Pagorski blushed, then reluctantly nodded. "It could. We were very close."

"*Were?*" Bwua'tu asked. "Then your relationship has ended?"

"Not in the way you're suggesting," Pagorski replied. "My friend was killed during the mutiny."

"Oh dear. I'm sorry to hear that." Bwua'tu's ears drooped in sympathy. "I take it you were in love?"

"We were."

Sardon leaned close to Tahiri. "This is artistry," she whispered. "I only wish we hadn't lost the news crews. Then the entire galaxy would have seen who the *real* victim is here."

Tahiri cringed. "I'm no victim."

"Of course not." Sardon patted her shoulder. "You were a soldier, following orders."

In front of the witness stand, Bwua'tu paused. With his chin slightly lowered and his shoulders hanging slack, it looked as though he were giving the witness a moment to compose herself. What he was really doing, Tahiri suspected, was drawing the jury's attention to her emotional state, making certain that they were closely watching her reaction to what he said next.

"And your friend?" Bwua'tu asked. "That would have been . . . Commander Liyn?"

Pagorski's eyes grew wide. "How did you know *that*?"

Dekkon must have sensed the trap before Pagorski did, for the Chagrian was instantly on his feet, his long lethorns swaying as he objected. "Your Honor, I fail to see what Lieutenant Pagorski's personal life has to do with these—"

"It goes to credibility," Bwua'tu interrupted. "I'm simply trying to establish the reason the witness has been lying to this court."

"*Lying*, Counselor?" Judge Zudan asked. She peered down from her bench, the tiny scales on her Falleen face deepening to a somber scarlet. "That's a very serious allegation in my court."

"And one I fully intend to prove." Bwua'tu turned back to Pagorski. "Unless the witness wishes to recant her earlier testimony now? After all, memory sometimes fails us *all*."

"My memory is excellent, Counselor," Pagorski replied icily. "Colonel Solo instructed Lieutenant Veila *not* to kill Admiral Pellaeon. Of that, I'm certain."

"I see," Bwua'tu said. "And might that certainty be because you hold Lieutenant Veila responsible for your lover's death?"

Pagorski narrowed her eyes. "It would not."

"Oh." A sardonic smile came to Bwua'tu's muzzle. "Just checking."

A juror—the Askajian—let out a snort of amusement, which instantly drew an outraged "*Your Honor!*" from Sul Dekkon and a stern glare from Judge Zudan. Bwua'tu used the opportunity to return to the witness table, where he made an elaborate show of opening a plastoid box and withdrawing a high-capacity military-grade datachip. He carried it over to the jury box and carefully displayed it, making certain that each of the occupants saw the crest of the Imperial Navy stamped on the outside of the case.

The datachip was Sardon's accomplishment. After listening to Tahiri's account of the killing and the events leading up to it, she had immediately begun to search for ways to expose Pagorski's lie. A little research had revealed the Imperial obsession with security and surveillance, and from there it had been a short leap of intuition to guess that ship security might have a surveillance vid that would either prove or disprove Pagorski's claim. Sardon had immediately requested, through formal diplomatic channels, any records relating to Tahiri's time aboard the *Bloodfin*. She had received a prompt reply promising to look into the matter and get back to her within two months. A day later, Bwua'tu had supplied the comm codes for Jagged Fel's Chiss assistant, Ashik. Two weeks later, the orginal datachips—not copies or transcripts, but the originals—had arrived via special courier.

When all the jurors had been given a chance to inspect the datachip, Bwua'tu took it to the witness stand and placed it on the railing. "Lieutenant Pagorski, do you know what that is?"

Pagorski barely glanced at the chip. "Where did you get *that*?"

"That will become evident in good time, my dear," Bwua'tu replied. "Until then, you must try to remember that *I* am the one asking questions here. Now, do you know what that is or not, Lieutenant?"

"Of course I do. It's an Imperial Navy high-capacity datachip," she said. "We use them by the thousands in ComInt."

"I'm sure you do." Bwua'tu turned to face the jury. "Can you tell me, Lieutenant, do military datachips like those have any special properties?"

"They do." Pagorski's tone had turned wary, but she clearly realized that refusing to answer the question would only give Bwua'tu an opportunity to make her look foolish. "When tampered with, they self-destruct. They're shielded to withstand damage from heat, cold, water, and electromagnetic pulse. And they can be accessed only with a top-secret passcode."

"A *passcode*?" Bwua'tu did a credible job of sounding surprised. "And who would know this passcode?"

"Only users of each particular datachip," Pagorski replied. "And their direct superiors, of course."

"I see. And would you happen to know the passcode to *this* one, Lieutenant?"

"No."

"How do you know?" Bwua'tu asked. He turned the datachip over, displaying the label etched into the back of the casing. "You haven't even looked at its identification code."

"Very well." Pagorski leaned forward to inspect the datachip, and her eyes went wide. "It's a FinSec surveillance chip!"

Bwua'tu's smile grew predatory. "Thank you, my dear. I was hoping you would be able to identify that for us." He retrieved the datachip and stepped toward Judge Zudan's bench. "For the record, Your Honor, this FinSec datachip was one of many sent to defense counsel in response to a request for all surveillance records relating to Tahiri Veila's presence aboard the *Bloodfin* during the Battle of Fondor."

Before Sul Dekkon could object, Sardon produced a thin sheaf of flimsiplast from a document folder next to her chair and rose. "If I may, Your Honor, these are affidavits from Kthira'shi'ktarloo, personal assistant to Head of State Fel of the Galactic Empire, and a series of Imperial officers. All relate to the nature of this datachip."

She quickly handed one set of affidavits to Sul Dekkon, and another to the bailiff, who passed it up to Judge Zudan.

"They attest to the chain of possession of said datachip," Sardon continued, "and provide assurances that the content has not been altered in any way."

"I take it you wish to enter this datachip into evidence?" Zudan asked.

Sardon nodded. "We do."

Zudan's gaze shifted to the prosecution table. "Does prosecution have any objection?"

"One moment, Your Honor," Dekkon replied. "We'd like to examine the affidavits."

Zudan nodded, and Dekkon and his assistant huddled over the affidavits, whispering and pointing. If Sardon's plan was going to fail, it would be now, Tahiri knew. There were a whole host of technicalities that could be used to challenge the admission of the datachip, and although Sardon had prepared counterarguments for every one, she still put their chances of getting the datachip admitted at roughly 50 percent. Bwua'tu, on the other hand, felt certain it would be admitted, provided their documentation was in order—which was why he had insisted on preparing it personally. After a few minutes, Dekkon nodded to his associates, then rose.

"Your Honor, we *do* have one question."

"Yes?" Zudan replied.

Dekkon turned to Sardon. "How did you *ever* get the Empire to release this material?" he asked. "We've been requesting it for months!"

Sardon narrowed her eyes, obviously searching for the trap.

Bwua'tu merely smiled. "We called Head of State Fel's office, of course," he said. "I'm guessing you tried diplomatic channels?"

Dekkon's face darkened with irritation. "That would be correct." He turned back to the judge. "Everything seems to be in order, Your Honor. But I do reserve the right to have an expert examine the datachip to establish its authenticity."

"Of course." Zudan turned to Bwua'tu. "You may enter the datachip as Exhibit Omega."

Sardon returned to her seat looking more worried than ever, obviously wary of Dekkon's easily capitulation. Bwua'tu merely passed the datachip—Exhibit Omega—to the court's media officer, along with a flimsiplast containing the passcode and a list of files. A wall panel began to glow with backlighting, and the image of a corridor aboard thc *Bloodfin* appeared. A moment later, Tahiri and Caedus entered, approaching from the top of the image, where the narrowness of the corridor suggested a respectable distance.

They were tiny figures moving down a long durasteel tunnel, but the image was clear enough to see that they were talking as they walked. Tahiri had already seen the vid fifty times, gone over it with Sardon and Bwua'tu until she had recalled every word they said during the short stroll. Yet watching it still made her feel cold and hollow, reminded her of how thoroughly she had been under his power, and of all the things she had done in Caedus's name.

Killing Pellaeon had not even been the worst of those acts. When she allowed her mind to drift back to those days, she wondered if she was doing the right thing by even *offering* a defense for her actions. Sometimes only the unflagging support of the Solos—and Leia's stubborn insistence that criminals could not judge themselves—kept her from offering to save the GA the trouble of a trial. Han and Leia had come to regard her as a link to their lost sons, and had she simply given up, she knew they would have been devastated.

The images on the vid panel grew larger as they continued down the corridor, and soon Tahiri's voice became audible. ". . . value can I bring that a remote holocam can't?"

"If Pellaeon interferes with my plan in any way . . ."

Caedus flicked a finger, and both the audio and image disintegrated into static.

"Unfortunately, the surveillance equipment seemed to suffer a glitch at that point," Bwua'tu explained. He turned back Pagorski. "But *you*—or, rather, your friend—heard the entire conversation. Is that not correct?"

"I've already said it is," Pagorski replied.

"And what would you say if I informed you that we had the conversation digitally reconstructed. And that the rest of the exchange is as follows:

"Colonel Solo says, '*then you stop him . . . Do you understand what I'm asking you to do?*'

"Tahiri replies, '*I think so.*'

"Then Colonel Solo continues, '*Some deaths . . . some sacrifices are necessary, however callous they may appear.*' "

Pagorski considered her reply for a moment, no doubt weighing whether such a reconstruction actually existed. It did not, of course—but Pagorski could not be certain of that. Finally, she answered, "I would say that your expert is probably mistaken. And even if he *were* correct, it doesn't change anything *I* heard directly."

"You're referring to the communications intercept you described during your previous testimony, I assume?" Bwua'tu asked. "The intercept in which Colonel Solo allegedly orders Lieutenant Veila *not* to kill Admiral Pellaeon. Wasn't *that* your testimony?"

"Yes. In that intercept, I *did* hear Colonel Solo specifically order the defendant *not* to kill the admiral," Pagorski replied. "That was—that *is*—my testimony."

"Of course." Bwua'tu's long lip curled into a hungry sneer, and he turned to face the jury. "The intercept in which you *did* hear the defendant and Colonel Solo discussing whether to kill the admiral."

Sardon propped her elbows on the table and leaned forward, clearly relishing the way Bwua'tu was leading Pagorski into the trap.

"Very well, Lieutenant. Would you tell the court what you did next?" Bwua'tu asked, still looking at the jury.

Pagorski frowned. *"Next?"*

"Yes. After you heard the defendant discussing whether to assassinate your admiral," Bwua'tu replied. "What did you do? Did you alert the admiral? Report the conversation to FinSec? Mention it to your superior?"

"Oh." Pagorsk settled back into her seat. "Yes, of course."

"Of course what?" Bwua'tu pressed. "Which of those actions did you take?"

Pagorski thought for a moment, then replied, "Well, I did all three, of course."

A ridge appeared down the back of Sardon's robes as her dorsal spines rose in apprehension, but Bwua'tu pressed blithely on.

"All three?" he asked, turning back to the witness stand. "You must have been quite busy, then."

Pagorski nodded. "For a short time."

"I see."

Bwua'tu started back to the defense table. Sardon pushed back in her chair, her face scales bristling in anger now instead of alarm. She wasn't worried that the old Bothan had made a mistake, Tahiri realized, she was upset with what he was doing. When he reached the table and started to open the box from which he had removed the first datachip, Sardon's hand shot out to cover his.

"Eramuth!" she whispered. "What are you doing?"

Bwua'tu's ears were pricked forward in surprise, his snout wrinkled in disapproval. "I assume you know," he whispered. "I'm about to expose Lieutenant Pagorski as a liar."

"What about *Dekkon*?" she demanded, still hissing. "You haven't asked if he coached her testimony."

"Because the prosecution has done nothing improper," Bwua'tu replied. "Sul didn't know she was lying, or he would have fought harder to prevent us from admitting the datachips."

"So?"

Sardon stood and leaned closer to Bwua'tu's ear, giving Tahiri a clear view of both the prosecution table and the jury box. All eyes were on her attorneys, and all eyes looked as disapproving as they did astonished.

"The jury will draw its inferences from the question alone," she said. "Then, after you spring the trap, it will taint the testimony of all the prosecution witnesses."

"Or backfire and convince them that we're pulling a fast one with an altered datachip," Bwua'tu countered. "People are suspicious of the Jedi right now. It's better to play it safe and simply impeach the witness. We do *not* need to smear opposing counsel."

This caused Sardon to draw back. "Are you afraid of him?"

She asked the question loudly enough to raise brows in the jury box, and Tahiri realized the pair were not doing her any good at the moment.

"Uh, *Counselors*!" She leaned forward, sheltering her hand from anyone's view but theirs, and jerked a thumb toward the jury box. "Do you think you're doing me any good here?"

Bwua'tu's ears flattened with embarrassment, and Sardon's face flushed to purple.

"Sorry, my dear," Bwua'tu said. "But I won't go after Sul Dekkon simply because he was duped by his own witness. It's not in your best interest."

Sardon rolled her eyes. "You're playing it safe, Eramuth," she said. "You can't do that against Dekkon. We need to cripple him while we can—because he has a lot more than just Pagorski on his side. He has the facts."

"And *we* have the truth," Bwua'tu retorted.

Before he could say more, Judge Zudan's voice sounded from the bench. "Is the defense counsel ready to proceed?"

Dekkon rose. "If counsel needs a short adjournment—"

"No!"

Bwua'tu and Sardon spoke the word together. Tahiri was relieved to discover they were in agreement about *that* much. Even *she* realized how much of a mistake it would have been to further break the rhythm of the examination.

"The defense thanks the prosecution for its kind offer." Bwua'tu nodded to Dekkon, then turned to address the judge. "And we thank the court for its patience. But there's no need for an adjournment. We're ready to proceed."

"By all means, please do," Zudan ordered.

Bwua'tu nodded, then reached for the box again—only to find Sardon's hand covering it. Bwua'tu showed the tips of his fangs, Sardon extended the tiny claws on her fingertips, and Tahiri began to feel sick to her stomach.

"Please!" Tahiri whispered. Realizing that the choice was ultimately hers alone—and that Sardon was right about the facts of the case being against her—she decided to go for the crippling attack. "Eramuth, just ask Pagorski whether she was coached, okay?"

Bwua'tu's jowls sagged. "You're certain?"

"No," Tahiri admitted. "But this argument has to end, and looking for surveillance vids *was* Sardonne's idea."

Bwua'tu nodded. "It's your choice, my dear."

He removed his hand from the box, then turned away without the second datachip—the one that showed the interior of the *Bloodfin*'s ComInt compartment during the entire Battle of Fondor.

All eyes were on Bwua'tu as he approached the witness stand again, his gaze fixed on the floor and his hands folded behind his back. Once he arrived, he took a moment to look around, as though inspecting the room for the first time, then addressed Pagorski.

"Would you please state your name and occupation for the record?"

Pagorski's brow shot up—along with everybody else's. "Sir?"

"Your name and occupation," Bwua'tu said, growing testy. "We need it for the record."

Pagorski glanced over at the judge, who did her best not to look confused as she said, "The witness will answer."

"Lydea Pagorski," she said. "I'm a junior lieutenant in the Imperial Navy."

The courtroom was too empty for there to be a murmur, but the air grew still with astonishment, and Tahiri could see her own confusion mirrored in the eyes of everyone else in attendance.

"I see," Bwua'tu said. "And in your capacity as a junior lieutenant, you do what, exactly? Fly starfighters?"

Again, Pagorski looked to the judge. This time Zudan raised a hand for the lieutenant to wait, then leaned over the bench and motioned Bwua'tu closer.

"Counsel will approach for a conference."

"*Bloah!*" Sardon whispered. "The old nerf is trying to sabotage us!"

Tahiri shook her head. "No, it has to be something else," she said. "Eramuth wouldn't *do* that."

"*No*? Look at him."

Instead Tahiri looked toward the jury—and was surprised to find them looking not at Bwua'tu, but at her. To a being, their faces were filled with pity and patience, and in their eyes she found no judgment or condemnation, only sympathy and forbearance. And when the Askajian shot her a blubber-lipped smile, Tahiri understood exactly what Bwua'tu was doing.

The old Bothan was taking the blame for the scene that Sardon had caused, making it appear that it had been his senility instead of her ego that had caused the earlier disruption at the defense table.

"I can't believe he would do that," Tahiri said.

"Me either," Sardon said. "It's entirely unprofessional."

Tahiri frowned at Sardon's disapproving tone. It was obvious to her, at least, that Bwua'tu was sacrificing a reputation built up over a lifetime—a *very* long lifetime—to protect his client.

"*What*, exactly, do you find unprofessional?" Tahiri asked.

"*That.*" Sardon gestured toward the judge's bench, where Bwua'tu was doing a very credible job of looking angry and bewildered. "Feigning incapacity so he can withdraw from the case."

Tahiri shook her head. "I don't think that's what he's doing."

"Trust me, it is." Sardon laid a scaly hand on Tahiri's arm, and she felt herself growing serene as the Falleen flooded the air with calming pheromones. "But you have nothing to worry about, my friend. I've been preparing for a big case like this my whole life."

Tahiri nodded. "I can see that." She rose, then said, "Excuse me, Your Honor, but I've come to a difficult decision."

Zudan motioned for Bwua'tu to be silent, then looked to Tahiri. "Yes?"

Tahiri caught Bwua'tu's eye, and was not surprised to see him give her an encouraging nod.

She smiled back at him, then said, "I think I need to dismiss a defense counsel."

A wave of relief flooded Zudan's face. "I'm inclined to agree." The judge's gaze dropped back to Bwua'tu. "*Please* proceed."

"Thank you, Your Honor." Tahiri turned to Sardon, then said, "I'm sorry, Sardonne. You're an excellent attorney, but I think Eramuth works better alone."

Sardon's eyes went wide with shock and outrage. Suddenly Tahiri's serenity of a moment before began to develop a bitter, frightened edge as the Falleen exuded anxiety-producing pheromones in an effort to convince Tahiri that she was making a terrible mistake.

"Sardonne, I suggest you leave this table on your own two feet," Tahiri whispered. "If I have to throw you over the bar, it's going to look bad for a both of us."

Sardon's eyes narrowed in anger, but she retrieved her datapad and stood. "You *do* understand that you're throwing your life away?" she hissed. "That old fool doesn't understand the first thing about operating in a modern courtroom."

Without awaiting a reply, she marched into the spectator area and out of the room.

When Tahiri turned forward again, it was to find Judge Zudan staring down at her in disbelief. "I hope the defendant fired the right counsel."

"I think I did," Tahiri replied. She fished the second datachip out of the box on the table and held it out for Bwua'tu. "And very soon, everyone else will think so, too."

Bwua'tu smiled broadly, then retrieved the datachip, entered it properly into evidence, and presented it to the court's media officers. Within a few minutes, the jury was watching a vid of Lieutenant Pagorski sitting at her duty station. Bwua'tu pointed out the time stamp in the corner, verifying that the vid had been recorded during the period Pagorski claimed to have intercepted the converstion regarding Admiral Pellaeon.

Then he allowed the vid to play without comment—the entire thirty-two minutes of it. Not once did any hint of alarm come to Pagorski's face. And though she spoke to her superior twice, neither time did either of them show any concern or take any visible measures to warn Pellaeon's staff or FinSec that the admiral might be in danger. In fact, the only thing it *did* show was Pagorski sitting at her duty station, not doing any of things she had claimed.

When the vid finally came to an end, Bwua'tu strolled up to the witness stand and laid the remote control on the rail. "Now, Lieutenant Pagorski, would you care to show the court exactly *when* it was that you intercepted this order to my client?"

Pagorski stared at the remote blankly for a moment, then reluctantly picked it up. "I—I can't recall . . . exactly," she said. "It might have been toward the beginning."

To Tahiri's surprise, it was Sul Dekkon who spoke next.

"I highly doubt that." The Chagrian rose and bowed first to Tahiri, then to Bwua'tu, and finally to the judge. "Your Honor, I would like to apologize to the defendant and opposing counsel for my obvious error in judgment in presenting this witness."

Bwua'tu tipped his head in acknowledgment. "Apology accepted, Counsel."

"Thank you. That's very gracious of you." Dekkon inclined his head to show his sincerity, then turned to the bailiff. "And second, as an officer of this court, I request the immediate remand of the witness."

"*What?*" Pagorski cried. "You can't do that! I'm an Imperial officer!"

"Who bore false witness in a murder trial," Dekkon replied, barely restraining his obvious anger. "In the Galactic Alliance, that is a serious crime, Lieutenant—and you can be sure that Tahiri Veila will be testifying at *your* trial."

Chapter Thirty-one

THE COUNCIL CHAMBER HOLOPROJECTOR WAS ORIENTED toward the chair at the head of the speaking circle. That chair now sat vacant; Saba remained in her customary seat, in the middle of one side. She had not done this because it forced Chief of State Daala to converse with a turned head—though that was the effect. Nor had she chosen this location to suggest to Daala that Kenth Hamner was merely absent instead of dead—though she intended to do just that. She had not even chosen this seat because it made it easier to hide her own injuries by presenting her profile to the holocams—though she hoped that would work.

No. Saba had chosen her customary seat because she was not worthy of the Grand Master's chair. She had slain Kenth Hamner in a dominance fight, and good longtails did not make such mistakes. They knew how to control without killing, to lead without biting away the parts that made a pack strong. Now the Order was missing a worthy Master, the young ones had lost a wise teacher, and Saba would have no chance to repair a friendship that had meant much to her in the past. And all of that was her failure.

The hologram in the center of the circle flickered, then finally stabilized as Daala stopped searching for Kenth and fixed her gaze on Saba.

"I was expecting to speak with Grand Master Hamner," Daala announced. The life-sized hologram revealed the toll recent events had taken on the Chief of State. Her face looked haggard; her eyes were red and the skin below them sagged with exhaustion. "Fetch him at once."

"Grand Master Hamner is not available," Saba replied evenly. "You may speak to this one."

Daala shook her head. "No," she said. "You *will* fetch Hamner at once. After what the Jedi have done today, you are on the verge of open warfare with the entire Galactic Alliance military."

"The *entire* military?" Saba let out a derisive siss. "This one does not believe you."

"What *you* believe doesn't matter," Daala said. "Where is Master Hamner?"

"Unavailable."

As Saba spoke, a door on the far side of the Council Chamber slid open. Corran Horn entered the room with Cilghal close on his heels and strode toward the speaking circle. As soon as they were close enough to see Daala's hologram hovering over the projector pad, they stopped and remained outside the cam angle.

"Very well, then," Daala said. "Assemble the rest of the Council."

Knowing that Daala would notice even the slightest flicker of her eyes toward Corran and Cilghal, Saba was careful to keep her gaze fixed on the hologram. Instead, she touched both of them through the Force, just a gentle nudge to see if they wished to assume their seats. When both shook their heads, Saba leaned closer to the holoprojector.

"The rest of the Council is not available," she said. "If you wish to speak to the Jedi, speak to this one."

Daala's eyes narrowed. "Where are they?" she demanded. "What are you planning *now*?"

"The Jedi have executed their planz, Chief Daala,"

Saba replied. "Now the question is this: what are *your* planz?"

"You would be wise to assume the worst, Master Sebatyne," Daala replied. "You leave me no other choice."

"There is alwayz a choice, Chief Daala." Saba sat back in her chair and placed her hands on the armrests. "This time, the choice is yourz. If it is a fight you wish, the Jedi will oblige you—in that much, at least."

Daala's expression hardened to ice. "Am I to take that as a threat, Master Sebatyne? Don't waste your breath. The Jedi might *take* hostages, but they would never kill a hundred beings in cold blood. Even *I* don't believe that."

Saba started to deny that the sabacc players were hostages, but she stopped when Corran Horn gave her a Force nudge and stepped into the camera range.

"Chief Daala, did you believe the Jedi would join forces with the Sith?" Corran asked. Instead of slipping into his seat at the end of the speaking circle, he crossed in front of the cam and came to stand at Saba's side. "There are many, many things you don't know about the Jedi Order. *You* would be wise to keep that in mind."

"Master Horn, I remind you that I am the Galactic Alliance Chief of State," Daala replied coolly. "Threatening me is an act of treason."

"Who is threatening?" Saba broke into a fit of sissing. "Chief Daala, that is too funny. We are long beyond *threatening*, are we not?"

The color drained from Daala's cheeks, but that was the only sign of fear she betrayed. "Yes, Master Sebatyne, I suppose we are."

"Good." Saba leaned forward and stared into the cam lens, deliberately making her image as menacing as possible. "This one is glad we understand each other. Much will depend on it."

Then Cilghal stepped into cam range. "The *hostages*,

as you call them, will return in three days, when their sabacc tournament has come to an end." She crossed the speaking circle and came to stand opposite Corran, so that she and Corran were flanking Saba. "Let us hope they will not find a city in ruins."

"I agree, Master Cilghal," Daala replied. Her white-sleeved arm rose, signaling an assistant to end the transmission. "One can always hope."

The hologram vanished, leaving Saba and her companions to stare at the swirls of color fading on the projection pad. They remained silent for a moment, each taking the time to form his or her own impression of Daala's words without being influenced by the others. Saba was not sure what to make of the Chief-of-State's reaction, whether the call had simply been a ploy to find out what was happening inside the Jedi Temple, a diversion, or a last-ditch attempt to avoid an all-out battle. All she knew for certain was that Daala had been frustrated by her inability to speak to Kenth Hamner—and it seemed safe to assume that her frustration had left her somewhat off-balance.

Finally, when they had all looked up, Corran said, "*That* certainly went well."

Saba cocked her head around so she could look up at him. "You are joking, yes?"

Corran shook his head. "I am joking, no. We rocked Daala back on her heels today," he said. "We launched the StealthX wing without a fight, we recovered Valin and Jysella—"

"Your young are here now?" Saba asked.

"Not yet," Corran said. "But they're aboard the Cygnus-Seven and on their way."

"On their way is not here," Saba said. "This one will not stop worrying until they are with us."

"Me either," Corran said. "But they're with the Solos. That's the next best thing."

"It is very good," Cilghal agreed. "But I don't agree

that the conversation with Daala went well. She's afraid of us now, and fear breeds danger."

"True," Corran replied. "But it also breeds caution, and we gave her plenty of reason to be cautious—and to think we're ready to dish out more. Everything we've tried has worked. Now she has to be wondering what *else* we have up our sleeves."

Saba nodded. "No one expectz the shenbit to stop biting until the prey is devoured," she said. "Daala will want to take care, and care takes time."

"So does politics," Corran added. "The *Errant Venture* also got away clean with a hundred of Coruscant's social elite. That's going to put a *lot* of pressure on Daala to avoid a fight until *after* they're scheduled to be back. If she tries to move before then, she risks losing her power base."

"That's true as long as everyone understands that our, um, *guests* on the *Venture* are safe," Cilghal replied. "I suggest we ask Lando to transmit live updates of the tournament. If the public sees sabacc players playing sabacc, Daala will find it difficult to do anything that might put them in danger."

"And it will show that they are not hostages," Saba replied. "Perhapz we should ask Booster to offer them the option to leave?"

"Are you crazy?" Corran asked. "No one's going to leave with a hundred million credits in play."

"*Exactly,*" Cilghal said. "I like it."

"We are in agreement, then," Saba said. "But when the tournament endz—Daala will come for us, will she not?"

"Oh yeah," Corran said, nodding. "One way or another, she'll be coming. After the ruckus she made about the Jedi being a danger to the government, she can't let us win. If she does, she's done as Chief of State."

"Then she is done either way," Saba said, "because the Jedi are not going to lose this fight."

Saba braced her hands on the chair arms and pushed herself to her feet. Her knees nearly buckled with the waves of agony that rolled through her battered body, but pain was nothing, only information that a Jedi could chose to examine or to ignore. She ignored it.

"We should ask the Solusarz to join us," Saba said. "The Masterz—those who are available—should name a leader to guide us through the next few dayz."

"What's wrong?" Cilghal asked. She took Saba's elbow, which was how one checked for a pulse on a Barabel. "Aren't you feeling strong enough?"

"This one is strong," Saba said, puzzled. "But she has killed another Jedi. She must present herself to judgment."

"*Judgment?*" Corran asked. "By whom?"

"By the leader." Saba curled a lip, flashing a bit of fang. "Sometimes it seemz like you have rockz in your nest, Master Horn."

Corran's brow rose. "*Does* it?" He looked to Cilghal, then asked, "I don't know, Master Cilghal. The Masters Solusar are busy running evacuation drills. Do you think we really need to disturb them?"

Cilghal thought for a moment, then shook her head. "Under the circumstances, no. I think we all know who the temporary leader should be."

Corran nodded. "Agreed."

Saba waited for them to say a name—but when they merely turned to look at her, she began to have a guilty, uneasy feeling in both of her stomachs.

"No," she said. "It is wrong. This one cannot take the place of a longtail she has killed."

"I'm afraid you don't have a choice," Cilghal said. "We're going to need a warrior leading the Order, and that's not me."

"And I'm too filled with anger and thoughts of vengeance," Corran said. "If I take lead against Daala, I'll walk us all into the dark side."

Saba shook her head stubbornly. "It isn't right."

"But it *is* necessary," Cilghal said. "You started this, Saba. You're the one Daala fears. You *must* do this—for the good of the Order."

Saba let her muzzle drop. She had hoped to escape this burden, to avoid being elevated by her mistake. But the Force was not so forgiving. Every act was a link in the chain of consequence, and she had been a fool to think that she could avoid the taint of the decision she had made in the hangar—to think that she could allow a Jedi to drop to his death and not find herself walking the line between the dark side and the light.

"Saba, we need you to say yes," Corran said. "We'll sort out the rest after it's done, when the Order is safe and the Sith are defeated—"

"When Daala is gone," Saba finished. She pointed at the chair at the head of the circle. "This one will do this until Grand Master Skywalker is sitting in that chair again. But when he is, this one *will* be judged."

Corran nodded. "Fair enough. Now, tell us how we're going to keep this thing from turning Coruscant into a battlefield."

Saba looked over at him. "There is only one way to do that, Master Horn," she said. "We must remove Daala from office."

Chapter Thirty-two

A TRIO OF *KONDO*-CLASS SHUTTLES HAD BEEN TRACING vapor trails across the sky for the last half hour, searching in vain for an island located almost directly below them. Meanwhile, the small group of Sith warriors who were actually *in* the village, searching for Abeloth, were outnumbered six to one by Fallanassi adepts. Sarasu Taalon had grown so weak that he was swaying on his feet, and he looked more unsteady by the moment. So why the High Lord continued to believe he controlled the situation, Luke could not imagine.

"So Abeloth came to the Fallanassi for protection, and you expect me to believe you have no idea *why*?" Taalon demanded.

Taalon was standing in what had once been a stone courtyard but was now a moss-covered ring. Across from him, just beyond lightsaber's reach, floated a cross-legged woman. She *looked* like Akanah, but Luke had begun to fear she was actually their quarry, Abeloth. The transformation might have been mere illusion, or it might have been complete replication, or it could even have been an actual transference of mind and spirit. Luke had no clue. He was certain of only one thing. If he wanted to destroy Abeloth for good, he needed to discover which.

"That is not what I told you," Akanah said, replying to Taalon. "I *said* we don't know who she is."

Anger smoldered in Taalaon's weary eyes. "Your answers are honest, yet they reveal nothing." He stepped closer, and Akanah floated back. "I tire of this game."

Akanah turned her palms up in a gesture of helplessness. "You are not here at our invitation. I see no reason to care how you feel."

"Then perhaps Saber Khai should give you one."

Taalon nodded to Khai, who now wore dark robes, having removed his bulky hazard suit when Taalon declared the Weeping Pox a Fallanassi deception. Luke could tell by Khai's tense body language—and by that of the rest of the Sith, who had also switched to robes—that the act had been one of faith rather than belief. The Fallanassi illusion was still working on them, using their own minds to make them feel sick and prove Taalon's mistake.

Khai extended his hand toward the edge of the circle, where dozens of Fallanassi Adepts stood watching the confrontation, and the gray-haired elder whom Taalon had struck earlier began to move forward, her toes dragging and digging small furrows into the moss. Worried about what might happen next, Luke let his hand edge toward the lightsaber hanging from his belt. He stepped away from Taalon and Khai, buying room to maneuver, and felt a Force nudge from the edge of the circle.

He glanced in that direction and found his son standing with one hand on his lightsaber, body angled to keep an eye on Luke and Vestara both. The girl appeared just as ready, standing well out of striking range, her body angle a mirror of Ben's. Despite all the violence and death both teenagers had seen in their brief lives, Luke hated that they would see what was about to happen. The battle—if it could be called that—was bound to be more slaughter than fight, and there was a strong possibility both of their fathers would fall. He would have given anything to spare them that, but some things were beyond the abilities of even a Jedi Grand Master.

By the time Luke had returned his attention to the circle, Gavar Khai was using the Force to hold the elder—Eliya—before him. The cheek that Taalon had struck earlier was swollen and blue, her jaw obviously shattered. But as Khai pressed his unignited lightsaber against her thigh, the old woman showed no sign of fear.

Luke stepped forward. "This will accomplish nothing," he said. "If you think the Fallanassi can be threatened with violence—"

"This matter is no concern of yours, Jedi," Eliya said. "You have done enough harm to us already."

Taalon smiled at her bravery, then turned to Akanah. "You will tell me why Abeloth came to the Fallanassi for protection *at once,*" he said, "or this old woman will suffer for your stubbornness."

"Tell him nothing, Lady," Eliya said, turning from Luke to Akanah. "These sewer eels don't deserve your—"

"There is no harm in telling him this much, Sister." As she spoke, Akanah kept her gaze fixed on Taalon. "Abeloth returned to the Fallanassi because she *is* Fallanassi."

"*What?*" It was Ben who blurted this. "How is that possible? Abeloth has been locked in the Maw for twenty-five *thousand* years!"

Akanah's gaze slid toward him. "The Fallanassi are older than that, Ben Skywalker," she said. "They are older than the Jedi, older than the Sith, as old as civilization itself."

Taalon narrowed his eyes at her claim, then turned to Luke and raised a questioning brow. "Can that be true?"

"I suppose it *could,*" Luke replied, daring to hope Taalon might not find it necessary to torture Eliya. If Akanah—or Abeloth—was willing to reveal something of the Fallanassi's history in order to spare Eliya, perhaps she would reveal something else: Abeloth's hiding place. "But I'm more interested in whether Abeloth was *always* Fallanassi. Or did she join more recently?"

A sly smile crossed Akanah's lips. "The answer would tell you whether she is still here," she said. "And *that* I won't reveal."

"You *will* in time," Taalon said.

The High Lord nodded to Khai, who activated his lightsaber. The emitter was still pressed to Eliya's thigh, and the crackle of the activating blade could barely be heard over the woman's scream. The smell of burning flesh filled the air, then her thigh buckled, and she pitched forward into Khai's chest. He stepped back, allowing her to drop the rest of the way onto his blade, and her voice fell abruptly silent.

The *snap-sizzle* of igniting lightsabers sounded throughout the village as the Sith search party—no doubt alerted to the possibility of trouble through the Force—activated their weapons. But if Taalon truly believed the Fallanassi response would come in the form of physical violence, he had learned nothing during his hour of attempting to intimidate them. Luke placed a hand on his own weapon, but did not activate it—or even remove it from his belt. He wasn't ready for a fight with Taalon and his men, so he had to be careful not to provoke them. Abeloth, after all, was his first target.

Akanah merely floated a little higher, placing herself above Taalon, and said, "You think you can intimidate *me?*"

As she spoke, Gavar Khai's gaze dropped to Eliya's cleaved body, and his eyes widened with horror. He brought his blade up and began to slash at the air, pivoting and dodging as though he were in combat. Twice, he cringed as though he had taken a blow. Each time, a deep, anguished sigh gusted from his mouth, and his movements grew less confident and energetic. He began to flinch more quickly and started to retreat, his motions becoming awkward and slow, his posture stooped and elderly.

Finally, Khai simply turned his back on the corpse

and, screaming, began to totter away. Had his daughter not flicked a hand in his direction and buckled his knees with a Force blast, he might have kept going until he had left the village—and perhaps even the island. As it was, he simply covered his head and lay on the ground wailing—an embarrassment that caused his daughter to render him unconscious with a second Force blast.

Taalon flicked a finger toward Akanah, drawing her back down to eye level. "I will turn the whole Fallanassi order into ghosts, if you like."

"I assure you," Akanah said, "that won't be necessary."

Before Taalon could reply, Sith all over the village began to scream and hack at the air. Sometimes they hit Fallanassi, sometimes they hit a tree fern or a fungus-covered hut, occasionally they even hit one another—but most of the time they struck nothing at all. Still, they universally began to cringe and wince as though taking blows, and within seconds they began to retreat into defensive squares that did nothing at all to diminish their panic.

Luke glanced over at Ben and was relieved to see that Akanah had spared his son—and Vestara—from her illusion. He signaled them to come and stand with him and Taalon, who also seemed to be free of the deception. Then he withdrew his presence from the White Current, just far enough to see the illusion to which the Sith were reacting.

It appeared the Sith were being swarmed by translucent green figures. These phantasms had ghastly, distorted faces and thin tentacles lashing from their fingertips, and every couple of seconds one of them would belch a cloud of brown vapor into the face of a warrior. The victim would age a dozen years in a heartbeat, the face wrinkling and the posture growing more stooped.

But it was the tentacles that were the most gruesome. They would shoot out from the ghost's fingertips to lodge themselves in the eyeballs or nostrils or ears of an intruder. What looked like thumb-sized drops of dark Force energy would pulse down the tentacles, and with each globule, the phantasm seemed to grow a bit more solid and real looking.

As the ghosts grew more opaque, they stopped belching brown fumes and started to spew flame. Before long, there appeared to be wildfires springing up everywhere, driving the Sith toward the edges of the village, screaming and stumbling just as Gavar Khai had done. Within seconds, the fastest Sith had reached a low stone wall that separated part of the village from a thousand-meter plunge to the sea.

When Luke saw the first warrior vault over the wall and drop screaming out of sight, all doubt about the woman before him vanished. No Adept of the White Current would have used her art to kill any being so casually.

Luke immersed himself within the Current again. The scene before him changed from horror to simple madness, with the Fallanassi standing pressed against their huts while the Sith flailed at empty air and rolled in the moss, trying to smother flames that did not exist. Whether the Adepts were contributing to the illusion or just standing aside while Abeloth alone tormented the intruders, Luke could not say. But it seemed clear to him that the Fallanassi were under Abeloth's influence, or they never would have permitted the White Current to be defiled in this way.

After a few moments watching the madness, Taalon seemed to gather his courage. He snapped his lightsaber off his belt and pointed it at the woman floating before him. "You will end this, *now.*"

Abeloth merely smiled. "I *could.*" She drifted out of his reach and turned toward the large gathering hall where she had first appeared. "Or I could explain what's happening to you."

Taalon's expression changed from exhaustion to rapture. He glanced in the direction of his maddened followers, but Luke knew the choice he would make, even before the High Lord looked away again. Apparently, so did Abeloth, because she started toward the gathering hall without awaiting his reply.

"The choice is yours," she said. "But make it quickly. You don't have much time."

That was all it took to send Taalon scurrying after her.

Luke waited until the High Lord had moved out of earshot, then turned to Ben. "We need to secure the *Shadow.* Take Vestara and—"

"Don't even say it. The *Shadow* is locked up tighter than Daala's smile." Ben waved his lightsaber toward the gathering hall. "I'm *not* letting you go in there without me."

"And there's no way you're leaving *me* out here—with Ben or without him." Vestara turned a hand toward her now unconscious father, and he rose off the ground and started to float toward them. "Look around, Master Skywalker. I think we're safer with you and Lord Taalon."

Luke thought for a moment, then nodded. Given the madness in the village, if Ben and Vestara tried to board the *Shadow* now, they would find themselves fighting off crazed Sith. And even if they made it safely aboard and obeyed an order to leave the island, they would find themselves at the mercy of the three *Kondo*-class shuttles overhead. For days, he had been hoping the Jedi reinforcements would arrive in time to help. Now it was clear: He and Ben were on their own.

"Okay," he said. "But no heroics in there. I'm still trying to figure this thing out. I'll *tell* you when I want you to do something."

Ben glanced over at Vestara, who nodded, and then he

said, "Sure thing, Dad. Just don't get yourself killed, and we'll do fine."

They started after Abeloth and Taalon, stepping into a stream of dark side energy so thick it felt sticky. Luke recalled the miasma of fear and anguish he had sensed when they debarked the *Shadow,* and he knew Vestara had been right: it was raw power. He was feeling pure dark side energy, and it was being generated by the fear and suffering caused by the "plague" gripping Pydyr. And Abeloth was gathering that power to herself, no doubt calling on it to heal from the wounds she had received in the Maw.

They entered the hall, a gloomy post-and-beam chamber with a vaulted ceiling, swirling in shadow and smoke. At the far end was a sunken stage, ringed by several tiers of recessed seating. Rising from the stage pit was a red glow, shimmering with a heat so ferocious that it brought sweat beads to Luke's face even ten meters away. At the edge of the pit stood Abeloth and Taalon, Abeloth glaring across the room at Luke.

"I don't recall inviting *you.*"

"I wanted to check on you, Akanah." Luke signaled Ben and Vestara to wait by the door and started forward. He knew he wasn't fooling Abeloth—that she would be aware of his suspicions regarding her true identity. But his only chance to get close enough to strike was to convince her that she was a step ahead of him—that she was manipulating *him* into position. "By the look of that pit, it's a good thing I did."

"And what makes you think that is not how it *should* look?" Abeloth did not move away as Luke approached, and he saw that the stage floor had actually split. The interior of the crevice was too bright to peer into, but he had heard enough blurping magma in his time to recognize the sound rising from the fissure. "It's not as if you have been here before, Luke Skywalker."

"We *both* know this isn't how a Fallanassi meditation hall should look." Luke *knew* he was talking to Abeloth, not Akanah. But how did *she* know he had never been here before? Had she stolen Akanah's memories along with her appearance? Did she have them *all*? That would make her even more dangerous—and Luke even more vulnerable. "Tell me what's going on here, Akanah. Fallanassi don't use the Current to kill."

"*Wialu* did, at the Battle of N'zoth," Abeloth reminded him. "And you are the one who asked her to do it. A pattern is emerging, don't you think?"

Luke shrugged, though inside him a cold lump of fear had started to form. Only a hundred people in the galaxy knew what had happened at the Battle of N'zoth, where he had persuaded the Fallanassi leader, Wialu, to help the New Republic win a desperate fight. And Abeloth *wasn't* one of those hundred people.

"I didn't ask you to kill anyone this time," Luke said, stopping beside her, on the side opposite Taalon.

"No, but it is the Jedi who make it necessary. Because of your nephew, the Current has changed." Out of the corner of her eye, Abeloth caught Taalon's gaze—and held it. "Because of what Jacen Solo did, the Throne of Balance will be claimed by a usurper."

"A *usurper*?" Taalon asked.

Luke uttered a silent curse. It was difficult to guess how much Abeloth knew about his visions of the throne—but however much that was, even mentioning it in Taalon's presence posed a danger to Allana.

When Abeloth did not respond to his question, Taalon asked another. "Are you speaking of the Jedi queen?"

Abeloth pretended not to hear, returning her gaze to Luke. "Because of Jacen Solo, the Fallanassi must do *whatever* is necessary to restore the Current to the proper flow," she said. "Wherever Jedi tread, Master Skywalker, mayhem follows. If the Fallanassi must set right your mistakes, the burden for our actions does not fall on us."

"Only the killer is a criminal, not his executioner," Taalon agreed. "Tell me about this usurper."

Abeloth finally acknowledged his question, lifting one brow in his direction. "Is that a request, or an order?"

"An offer," Taalon said smoothly. "Name this Jedi queen, and you shall have whatever the Sith can offer."

"She's toying with you. This queen and her Throne of Balance are just another illusion," Luke said quickly. Abeloth's effort to set them against each other was a good sign, suggesting she lacked the strength to battle them outright. Unfortunately, it was also a good tactic, as Luke could not permit *any* Sith to know Allana's true identity and leave the hall alive. "Akanah told you herself that Abeloth was a Fallanassi. You can't believe in her trickery."

Abeloth smirked at Luke, then turned back to Taalon. "You have bathed in the Pool of Knowledge," she said to the Sith. "Trust what you see."

"Good advice, if you're a master of illusions," Luke said sarcastically. He looked past Abeloth to Taalon. "She's trying to play us against each other. You *do* see that?"

"Do you think a High Lord would be unaware of that, Master Skywalker?" Taalon kept his gaze fixed on Abeloth. "Whether it works will depend on what she is offering."

Abeloth circled around to Taalon's far side, placing the High Lord between herself and Luke. "Sarasu Taalon, I will teach you what you are becoming." She was purring these words into his ear, just loud enough for Luke to hear, even over the bubbling of the magma. "And when you understand *that,* you will not need *me* to learn the identity of the Jedi queen. You will *know* it."

Taalon fixed his gaze on Luke and said nothing, and a cold shudder raced up Luke's spine. The High Lord had made his choice, leaving the Skywalkers outnumbered and outpowered against him *and* Abeloth. And there was no way to save Ben except win.

Luke used the Force to touch Ben with a sense of danger, then put on an innocent act and began to peer into the corners of the hall.

"All right, Abeloth. What did you do with Akanah?" Luke asked. He stepped away from the speaking pit on the pretext of going to look for her. "Did you trade bodies with her, like you did with Dyon Stadd?"

But Taalon knew the true reason Luke was moving, and the High Lord was not about to let himself be pinned against the pit. In the blink of an eye he had his lightsaber in hand and was moving to cut off his Jedi foe . . . which was exactly what Luke expected.

Luke grabbed Taalon in the Force and sent him sailing toward the door in a high arc. The *snap-hiss* of an igniting lightsaber confirmed that Ben understood what Luke intended. By the time Luke had his own weapon in hand, his son was Force-leaping into combat, his blue blade tracing an arc that an exhausted and weakened Taalon would be hard-pressed to avoid.

Thinking they might win this battle after all, Luke thumbed his own blade to life and spun to attack Abeloth—and that, of course, was when the crackle of Force lightning rang out from the door, where Vestara was standing. Ben cried out in surprise and anguish, then two distinct thuds sounded behind Luke, his son slamming into one wall and Taalon into another. A terrific *pop* echoed across the hall, and Taalon bellowed in pain.

Luke was already on Abeloth, launching a vicious thrust kick. She took it like a durasteel wall, then her arm flew up to rake at his eyes. Luke was ready, and his blade burned through the limb as though it were nutripaste.

"Luke!" The cry came in Akanah's voice, the terror unmistakable. "Don't! It's *me*! Akanah!"

Luke knew better than to believe her, even for a heartbeat. He continued his swing, sweeping the blade across at thigh level, and felt it slice into a leg. Abeloth shrieked in a dozen voices and spun away, falling toward the tiers of sunken seating. He used a Force nudge to send her arcing toward the cleft in the stage floor and lost sight of her against the glow of the magma.

Desperate to know what had become of Ben, Luke reached out in the Force and felt the frightened, groggy presence of someone who had taken a head-shaking blow. He turned and found his son trapped against a wall, defending himself from Vestara's fierce attack, an unrefined high–low–low–high pattern, which Ben was blocking only because of his strength in the Force and the reflexes drilled into him by thousands of hours of practice.

Luke flicked a finger in Vestara's direction and sent her tumbling toward Taalon, who was limping across the floor toward Ben, one knee buckling every time he placed weight on it. Had the High Lord been at his best, he would simply have redirected the girl straight into Luke. Weakened as he was by his injury and his ongoing transformation, he barely managed to Force-jump over her—and that left him vulnerable.

Luke raised his lightsaber and grasped the Sith in the Force, intending to bring him tumbling into an ignited blade . . . then felt something catch him across the ankles. He had no time to be astonished, barely even the nanosecond required to realize Abeloth had survived her fall into the cleft. He merely felt his feet shoot away and found himself dropping face-first.

Luke tucked his chin and managed to flip to his back before he hit the stone floor. Abeloth was on top of him, her flesh blistered and smoking, her remaining leg entwining *both* of his, her remaining arm wrapped around the back of his neck. She drove the still-sizzling stump of her amputated arm into his throat, catching him square in the voice box and pressing hard. The cartilage began to give. He pushed back with the Force, reinforcing his larynx and trying to throw her off.

It was no good. Abeloth had a dozen times the Force strength Luke had, and he could do no more than keep her from crushing his throat. He tried to bring his knee up and found his legs incapable of moving. She straightened her leg, forcing his knee to bend against the joint, and something gave with a muted *pop*. He slammed a Force-enhanced knuckle strike into her side and heard three ribs snap . . . and remained entangled. She dug her nails into the root of his ear, then twisted, and his head erupted in pain. He slipped his deactivated lightsaber between their bodies and jammed the blade emitter against her stomach. He thumbed the activation slide and saw the blade shoot out the other side.

Still Abeloth held on, clinging to him like a self-tightening cargo cable. It seemed impossible to shake her, and Luke knew that he had to. To fail was to die, and take Ben with him. He reached out with the Force, grabbing for anything that might help him, anything to give him a second or a centimeter to counterattack.

Half a dozen loose cushions rose from the seating tiers and bounced harmlessly past. He continued to reach, felt something heavy and liquid rising from the stage floor, and a glob of molten heat arced onto them, splashing across Abeloth's back and spattering off the floor, driving tiny pinpricks of anguish into Luke's arm and face where it hit him.

A hundred-voiced wail erupted from Abeloth's mouth, shrill and loud and inhuman. Plumes of greasy smoke shot from her back, and the smell of charred flesh grew sickening in the air. The heat of the magma burned through Abeloth's body to sear him, and he heard organs sizzling inside her chest. Any normal being would have been dead by now. But Abeloth seemed to live in the Force as much as she did in a physical body, and now she was using the Force to animate a body that should have been in its death throes.

Finally, the pressure on Luke's throat eased—not much, but enough to draw breath. It made him hope he might survive . . . at least fight a few moments more. He continued to reach with the Force, now going higher toward the ceiling vault, and caught hold of one of the long crossbeams that held the roof in place.

Luke pulled, trying to open a little space so he could gain his feet and fight, and they both began to rise.

Abeloth pulled in the opposite direction, and they dropped back to the floor. Luke opened himself more fully to the Force, using his love for Ben and his lost wife and the entire Jedi Order to draw it into him. The foul miasma of dark side energy, still swirling into Abeloth, seeped into him, filling him with greasy nausea. But the light side *rushed* in, flowing in from all sides, pouring through him like fire. A golden glow began to rise from his skin—cells literally bursting with the power of the Force—and Luke felt them both start upward again. Abeloth countered, hissing in anger, and they hovered a hand span above the floor.

A tremendous crack echoed down from the vaulted ceiling. They dropped again, hitting so hard that Luke's breath left in a groan. Abeloth slammed down atop him, her single leg still wrapped around his, the stump of her arm driving harder into his throat. Something crunched in his larynx. His breath came in shallow, wheezy gasps, and the crushing hand of panic began to clench at his heart.

Then a two-meter length of beam came plummeting out of the darkness and caught Abeloth across the back. The impact compressed his chest until he thought it would split. Then her leg went slack, her stump slipped from Luke's throat, and she fell motionless, her face pressed against his, cheek-to-cheek.

Luke planted his feet flat on the floor and bridged, trying to throw her off. The effort rolled waves of agony up his rib cage, and Abeloth's leg and hips slid to one side, limp and loose. But the rest of her remained on top of him, pinned in place by the heavy beam. Guessing that her spine had been crushed, he pressed his lightsaber's blade emitter against her flank. Akanah's voice sounded in his ear.

"Luke, forgive me," she whispered. "I didn't . . . I didn't understand."

A shudder raced through her body, then her head rose, and in the depths of her eyes shone a pair of tiny silver specks. Her hair assumed a golden cast and tented around Luke's face, forming a private world where there was only them, and her lips broadened into a full-lipped mouth so large it stretched ear-to-ear.

The mouth opened, revealing a row of slender fangs, and started to descend toward his throat. Luke thumbed his lightsaber switch and dragged the hissing blade up the length of her body. She gave a long gasp of anguish, then the silver light faded from her eyes, and her head cracked down on the stone next to his.

A pang of sorrow shot through Luke. Abeloth had taken over Akanah's body, but Akanah had fought through with those final words to ease his conscience. He knew that he still didn't fully understand Abeloth's power, but he was too frightened for his son to spend time thinking about it now. Ben was still locked in battle against Taalon and Vestara, and judging by the fear radiating from his son's Force aura, the fight was going badly. Luke used the Force to push aside the heavy beam, then *tried* to spring up . . . and nearly collapsed as his injuries blossomed into crippling pain. The act of breathing was like choking on a rock, his knee felt catchy and swollen, and there was a crushing in his chest that made him wonder if the beam had smashed his sternum.

He found Ben near the door of the hall, somersaulting through the smoky air, his blade tracing a sapphire helix as he tumbled away from Taalon toward Vestara. Vestara, for her part, was crouched to spring, dancing back and forth as she looked for a chance to dart past and rejoin the High Lord. Knowing that he would not last through a prolonged, strenuous battle, Luke used the Force to grab the beam and send it spinning toward Taalon.

It appeared the attack would take the Sith entirely unawares—until he suddenly pivoted, bringing his lightsaber up to cleave the beam in half. One end tumbled past harmlessly.

The other slammed Taalon between the shoulder blades. Rather than absorb the full impact, the High Lord let it launch him into a diving roll. Luke swept his hand in the Sith's direction, using the Force to accelerate the tumble and send him crashing into the far wall.

Hoping to leap in and finish his enemy, Luke gathered his legs to spring. His knee caved, nearly sending him to the floor. Rather than damage the joint any further—and arrive unable to stand—he lurched after Taalon, calling on the Force to stabilize the injury.

As he staggered forward, Luke glanced over to check on Ben—then found himself gritting his teeth in frustration. His son had slipped into an attack pattern more suitable for disarming than killing. Clearly, he was more confident of Luke's victory than he should have been—or still too enamored of Vestara to see how dangerous it was to show her mercy.

Before he could shout an order to take her down, a new arrival stepped into the hall. At first, Luke could see little more than a figure silhouetted in the doorway. With

Abeloth destroyed, he feared the Sith were coming to their senses and rushing to Taalon's aid.

But this figure was wearing the sleeveless robe of a Fallanassi Adept, and as she strode into the hall, her high cheeks and full-lipped mouth became more obvious. By the time her aquiline nose and gray eyes grew recognizable, Luke could not believe what he was seeing.

"Callista?"

The woman smiled, showing a mouthful of small sharp teeth, and continued toward him. "You *could* say that."

The blood in Luke's veins ran cold. Callista had been one of his early loves, a former Jedi Knight who had lost her ability to touch the Force and, discontented, drifted out of his life. The last time he had seen her had been in the Maw, when she had revealed herself to be one of the untold victims whom Abeloth had absorbed into her own being.

As the figure drew closer, the mostly healed scars of their previous battle began to grow visible—burn medallions left by Sith Force lightning and the pale gash lines left by lightsabers. *This* Abeloth, Luke realized, was using the same body he and the Sith had fought in the Maw.

And yet, the woman Luke had just slain had *also* been Abeloth. There could be no other explanation for the power she had wielded. They were *both* Abeloth.

Luke began to lose heart. He did not think he had the strength to kill her . . . *again.* And if he was lucky enough to succeed, how many times would she return? Not wanting to be trapped near the stage pit, he limped toward the front of the hall.

"How many bodies *do* you have?" he asked.

"More than you can kill." The Callista-eyes shone, perhaps in delight at the fear she was causing Luke, and she began to advance. "I promise you that."

As she moved, a ripple ran through her, and she became the hideous, tentacle-armed creature they had fought in the Maw, tall and vaguely human, with a long cascade of yellow hair and tiny sunken eyes with silver, pinpoint pupils. Luke raised a hand, hitting her with a blast of Force energy whose only effect was to hold her back for half a second as she took her next step.

Luke felt a sudden shiver of danger sense, and dived away a mere heartbeat ahead of a dancing fork of Force lightning. Realizing that Abeloth's change of form had been an attempt to distract him more than frighten him, he spun to counterattack against Taalon—then Abeloth was on his back, her tentacles twined about his neck and limbs almost before he felt them. She pulled hard, bending back his limbs until his elbows ached, prying the lightsaber from his hand and squeezing his already injured throat until his vision began to narrow.

Taalon staggered up, so exhausted and sickened by his condition that he could not be bothered to run. He stepped to Luke's side and, without ceremony or hesitation, pressed the blade emitter of his unignited lightsaber to Luke's flank.

But Abeloth spun away, and Taalon's blade crackled to life without injuring Luke.

"No," Abeloth said. "First, you must do something for *me*."

Luke glanced over to find Taalon frowning in confusion.

"Skywalker has already killed one of your bodies," the High Lord said. "Are you sure you want to give him a chance at a second?"

"I *want* what you offered." Abeloth started toward the back of the hall, where her other body—Akanah—lay at the edge of the glowing stage pit. "I want you to make Luke Skywalker suffer as *we* have suffered."

Taalon's lavender face transformed from an expression of bewilderment to one of understanding, and he looked toward the front of the hall, where the drone-and-crack of clashing lightsabers had assumed a new urgency as Vestara attempted to keep Ben from disengaging and going to his father's aid.

Luke reached for his son in the Force, urging him to flee.

Abeloth's hot breath hissed into his ear. "There *is* no escape, Luke." She was speaking in Callista's voice, with an edge so cold and vengeful it made his stomach sink. "Not for you . . . not for your son."

Abeloth carried him to the edge of the pit, where Akanah's burned and broken body lay, her back grotesquely crushed. Deciding to try again, Luke used the Force to reach into the vault overhead and . . . Abeloth's tentacles tightened around his throat. He felt himself falling, and in his dream he heard the roaring clatter of a collapsing roof.

But it was only a dream, and he continued to fall . . . deeper . . . deeper . . . deeee . . .

Chapter Thirty-three

WHEN LUKE AWAKENED, HE WAS STILL UPRIGHT, STILL wheezing, and still locked in Abeloth's grasp. Taalon stood a couple of meters away, on the adjacent side of the sunken stage. At his feet lay Ben, caught in a crackling net of Force energy and writhing in pain. Behind him stood Vestara, looking exhausted, battered, and—to Luke's surprise—more than a little frightened and sad. Even Gavar Khai had been brought to the edge of the pit, though he remained unconscious and moaning in his Fallanassi-induced nightmares.

"You are weak because you have not been feeding," Abeloth was saying to Taalon. "Mortals need to feed, do they not?"

"Of course." There was impatience in Taalon's reply, but even more, there was fear. "But I haven't been able to keep food down since I fell into the Pool of Knowledge. Its water must have been poisonous."

"And your healers cannot find the toxin?"

Taalon shook his head. "They've run every test known to us."

As they spoke, Luke's eyes were sweeping the area, searching for some way to escape that did not involve using the Force to spray them all with magma. But he was also listening, because if he and Ben survived—and he was determined they *would*—anything Abeloth told

Taalon about what he was becoming might be a clue to destroying *her*.

When Abeloth did not reply, Taalon continued, "They've found nothing."

"Why do you think that is?" Abeloth asked. "You have bathed in the Pool of Knowledge, my child. Is it that you remain *truly* ignorant of the answer? Or that you are afraid to know it?"

Taalon's brow furrowed, and a look of comprehension and horror slowly came to his eyes. "I . . . I . . ." He looked over at Abeloth, his lavender face now so pale it was almost alabaster, then asked, *"How?"*

The tentacle around Luke's throat tightened, and his vision began to narrow again.

"First, your promise," Abeloth said. "Luke betrayed us, and for that, he must pay."

"As you wish," Taalon said.

The High Lord glanced down at Ben, still writhing at his feet. The Force net began to contract, and Ben's eyes widened in surprise. For a moment, he seemed more confused by what was happening than alarmed by it. Then his flesh began to bulge between strands, and his surprise changed to fear as it dawned on him that the net was just going to keep contracting, that the thin lines of energy would soon start cutting into his flesh and slowly . . . painfully . . . chop him into tiny squares of meat and bone.

Luke could not bear the thought of Ben dying such a horrid and anguished death, but he knew he had very little chance of preventing it. The instant he tried to call on the Force, Abeloth would tighten her tentacle again, and he would drop into darkness. The cold tide of despair began to rise inside him, threatening to engulf him, and he felt a shudder of delight ripple through Abeloth's tentacles. She was feeding on his fear, just as she was feeding on the fear of the plague-stricken Pydyrians—

using it to fuel her dark side power, to heal the terrible wounds she had suffered when Luke killed the other two bodies.

Thin lines of blood began to appear as the strands bit into Ben's flesh. The first hint of pain appeared in his expression, but he made a point of catching Luke's eye.

"Don't . . . worry." He spoke through clenched teeth, obviously fighting to keep his voice from breaking. "I have a . . . *plan.*"

The statement was so ludicrous and unexpected that Luke would have burst out laughing . . . had he not been sick with fear. Still, he did not show his terror to Ben—he did not want that to be the last thing his son ever saw. So he rasped a few words past the pain in his throat. "I hope it's a good one."

Ben smiled. "Don't worry, Dad." He flicked his eyes toward his shoulder, but Luke did not see anything useful there—only Vestara, standing a pace behind Ben looking entirely remorseless. "It *is.*"

Taalon chuckled darkly. "Oh, really? Then I must finish this quickly." He looked over at Abeloth and smiled. "Before young Skywalker escapes and kills us both."

"No." Abeloth stepped over to Taalon, standing so close their shoulders touched. "We aren't done with him."

One of Abeloth's tentacles slithered up Taalon's chest. His eyes widened, and his head drew back involuntarily. The tentacle continued to rise, pushing its tip between his lips—and then it began to pulse. Taalon's expression changed from repulsion to surprise to hunger, and he leaned forward and began to suckle.

"Stang!" Ben gasped, making a sour face. "Just kill me *now.*"

Again, Ben's eyes flicked toward his shoulder, and Luke realized with a sinking feeling that it *was* Vestara to whom his son was attempting to draw attention.

Luke couldn't believe it. Here they were, both nearly helpless and on the verge of death, and his son was counting on a Sith girl to save them—a Sith girl who had betrayed them both half a dozen times already. Had he been able to, Luke would have shaken his head in despair. Ben had been raised better than that.

As Taalon continued to drink, he began to look less weary and haggard by the moment. His pupils contracted to tiny pinpoints of light, and Luke realized with a shudder that *this* would have been his destiny, had he allowed the Mind Walkers to convince him to drink from the Fountain of Power—or bathe in the Pool of Knowledge. There were horrors in the galaxy that transcended all the glories of galactic civilization, evils that had existed before the founding of the first city—and that would remain after the razing of the last.

Taalon glanced down at Ben. The thin lines of blood swelled into rivers as the Force net tightened. Ben's eyes rolled back, and he hissed between his teeth. Taalon grasped the tentacle and began to drink more greedily.

"Fear will make you strong," Abeloth said, encouraging him. "Fear is the food of gods. Drink deeply and you—"

Luke reached for the ceiling in the Force and—hoping Abeloth would be distracted enough for him to succeed—pulled.

But the tentacle tightened. His vision darkened. His knees buckled, his hearing faded, and he felt himself falling again.

Luke continued to pull.

The floor started to vibrate beneath a clattering avalanche of roofing tiles and cross-supports. Something flat and hard broke over Luke's shoulder and something long and light glanced off his head, then the tentacle around his throat slackened and the distinctive sizzle of a Keshiri lightsaber filled his ears.

Luke tried to spin away . . . and found himself still entangled in Abeloth's tentacles. But his vision was returning, and he saw the cascade of tiles and cross-supports as it continued unabated, pummeling him, Abeloth, and everyone else.

He could also see about half a meter of crimson blade protruding from Taalon's chest, slicing left, then right as the wielder made certain of a kill. To his astonishment, when the blade came free and the High Lord's lifeless body tumbled away, the hand holding the hilt belonged to Vestara.

In the next instant, the girl went cartwheeling across the room. The blow had been so quick that Luke did not even realize Vestara had been struck until Abeloth's tentacle retracted and began to twine itself around his forearm.

By then, it was too late for Abeloth to recover. The Force net had sizzled away with Taalon's death, and Ben's blood-sheeted form was already leaping in to attack. He ducked a lightning-fast tentacle slash, then spun into an ankle-high heel-kick that had Abeloth's feet flying off the floor before she could coil the tentacle for another strike.

Luke and Abeloth landed hard, with Luke purposely slamming his head back into her face. In the next heartbeat he drove his elbows into her ribs. The blows clearly stunned her, for suddenly he had room to fight. He grabbed the tentacle around his throat and rolled, turning away from his son so she would be forced to release her choke hold—or present her back to Ben.

Abeloth released Luke. He rolled to his feet coughing and staggering, his chest aching and his knee trembling with pain.

But Abeloth was advancing on his son now, lashing high and low. When Ben extended a hand to summon Taalon's lightsaber, her tentacle caught his wrist before it arrived, and she spun him into her grasp.

So Luke extended *his* hand, summoning the weapon

into his grasp and stepping in to attack in the same instant. As the blade crackled to life, it was already descending toward her collarbone.

Abeloth would not be killed so easily. She spun around, swinging Ben like a club. It was all Luke could do to shift his strike and cleave through her shoulder instead of his son's head, and even then Ben's swinging hips caught him under the arms, and Abeloth sent them both tumbling toward the fiery cleft in the stage pit.

Luke caught his son in one arm and grabbed for the front wall with the Force. They came down on the first seating tier, more or less on their feet, and facing Abeloth.

If she had ever been anything but a monster, she did not look it now. Her eyes were blazing pits of silver fire, her wide mouth a gaping cave of fangs. The tentacles on her remaining shoulder were lashing around her in a wild tempest that was either a defensive pattern or an expression of immortal fury, and she was surrounded by a knee-high ring of shimmering Force energy that seemed to be pouring from her wound.

Luke slapped a hand against his belt and found, as he had expected, that his lightsaber was somewhere else. Without looking away from Abeloth, he asked, "Ben, do you know where your lightsaber is?"

"Uh . . . yeah."

"Not on you?"

"Taalon took it," Ben replied. "You?"

"No idea." Luke passed the one lightsaber they had—Taalon's—to his son. "Wait for my signal."

"As if I'm going anywhere without you."

They began to edge apart, forcing Abeloth to divide her attention. To Luke's relief, she seemed no more eager to re-engage than they were—at least not yet. Even *with* the gruesome wound, Luke knew she would be replenishing her strength much faster than any human could . . . even a *Jedi* human.

The Skywalkers had put about five meters between them when a Sith lightsaber crackled to life on the far side of the stage. Luke cursed under his breath and hazarded a glance in that direction, anticipating another last-moment betrayal. Instead, he found Vestara tossing her lightsaber in his direction.

"Go!" she yelled.

The girl was already swinging both hands toward Abeloth and unleashing a dancing fork of Force lightning. Swallowing his surprise, Luke extended his hand to summon her lightsaber and sprang forward as best he could on his injured knee.

It was like hitting a wall of solid Force energy. One moment, he was hurling himself forward, reaching out to coordinate with Ben. The next, he was standing motionless, head spinning and ears ringing, watching Abeloth stumbling out the front door of the hall.

Luke managed to remain standing for the handful of seconds it took to be certain that she wasn't returning—that, once again, they had wounded her severely enough to make her flee. Then his knee collapsed, dropping him to the floor in pain.

Ben was at his side at once, pulling the medkit from his belt. "Dad! Are you okay?"

"I'll live." Luke eyed his son's blood-soaked form. At the very least, Ben was going to need a kilo of bacta salve and two liters of plasma. "How about you? Anything feel bad?"

"None of it feels *good,*" Ben replied. "But it's just a flesh wound. Well, okay, a *lot* of flesh wounds, but it's still only flesh wounds."

Luke heard a groggy groan on the other side of the stage and realized that Gavar Khai was slowly returning to consciousness—a sign, perhaps, that the Fallanassi were no longer under Abeloth's control. He glanced toward the door, wondering what had become of the Sith outside, and extended a hand for Ben to help him up.

"Let's get going," Luke said. "We should hurry, if we want to make it back to the *Shadow* in one piece."

"I think you can forget *that* idea," Vestara said, joining them. She stopped well outside of lightsaber range, then added, "Considering that you would have to escape Sith custody first."

Ben's head snapped around. "*Custody?*"

Vestara waved her hand toward the door. "You *are* badly outnumbered, in case you've forgotten." She extended her hand. "It would be best if you handed your weapons over now. We don't want any misunderstandings when I take you outside."

Luke sighed and turned to Ben. "Some plan." As he spoke, he was reaching out to Gavar Khai in the Force, trying to draw the Sith's semiconscious attention to their conversation. "Tricking Sith girl into killing High Lord . . . good work. Letting Sith girl betray you *again* . . . not so good."

"Ben didn't *trick* me," Vestara objected. "It had to be done."

"Because you couldn't bear to see me tortured?" Ben's tone was light and unconcerned, a sure sign he understood what Luke was trying to do. "I *knew* you were falling for—"

"Don't be ridiculous," Vestara interrupted. "Anyone could see what had to be done. Abeloth was making a pet of Lord Taalon. That wasn't going to do the Sith any more good than you Jedi."

"*Vestara?*" Gavar Khai cried. He rose and, fumbling for his lightsaber, started around the stage area toward them. "*You* killed High Lord Taalon?"

Vestara exhaled sharply. "Ah *criik*!" She looked toward the ceiling and let her eyes roll back, thinking—or, perhaps, wishing a slow death on *both* Skywalkers—then shot Luke a glare and raised a hand toward Gavar Khai. "This is just a dream, Father. Go back to sleep."

She hit her father with a Force blast and sent him tumbling into a wall. When he came to a rest in a limp heap, Vestara watched long enough to make sure he was still breathing, then lowered her hand and dropped her gaze in thought.

"So what's it going to be, Ves?" Ben asked, flashing her a grin cocky enough to do his uncle Han proud. "Stick around for Sith justice . . . kill your own father . . . or help the Skywalker boys escape?"

Vestara exhaled hard, then pulled a pair of familiar-looking lightsabers from her robe pockets and faced the Skywalkers.

"You couldn't have just knocked me over the head?" She passed the weapons back to their rightful owners, then narrowed her eyes at Ben. "And if you think I did any of that for *you,* think again. It's the last time I *ever* save a Jedi."

Chapter Thirty-four

BEN AND HIS FATHER AND VESTARA WERE STILL FIFTY meters from the *Shadow* when dazed Sith began to drift back into the village circle. With battered faces and torn robes, most of them looked as if they had been in a cantina brawl rather than fleeing illusory ghosts. But there were a few serious injuries, compound fractures and caved-in faces typical of high-impact collisions or long falls. To a being, they had the unfocused, saucer-eyed gazes of trauma victims, and they were so wary and jumpy that it was not unusual to hear the crackle of crossing lightsabers whenever two of them encountered each other unexpectedly.

"This is bad," Vestara said. "They're coming to their senses."

"Just act casual," Ben said. "We'll be fine, as long as we don't draw attention to ourselves."

"That's right," Luke agreed. He had one hand resting on Ben's shoulder, steadying himself. "They don't realize Taalon is dead yet, so they have no reason to think anything is out of the ordinary here."

There was a calm confidence in Luke's voice that suggested he was experiencing the same waves of reassurance that kept rolling over Ben. Someone they knew was using the Force to encourage them, trying to tell them that help was on the way. The touch was not familiar enough for Ben to recognize, though he suspected his father knew *ex-*

actly who was reaching out to them—and how far away they were. Ben just hoped it wasn't another Fallanassi illusion.

Luke's knee gave way again, and Ben sucked air through his teeth as his father's hand clamped down on his semi-diced shoulder. But he didn't complain—he was far too grateful to have a father there to hold on to him.

"Just keep walking," Luke urged. "We're almost there."

"*Almost* is the problem," Vestara replied. Nearly two dozen Sith had entered the circle now, and a few dazed eyes were beginning to swing in the Skywalkers' direction. "They're never going to let us board without Taalon or my father. It might be better to duck out of sight and hope they get distracted when they find Lord Taalon's body."

"We can't wait," Luke said. He pointed his chin toward the far corner of the island, where Ship's red-veined globe was just starting to climb for the sky. "Abeloth is leaving—that's why the Fallanassi have stopped killing intruders."

Vestara frowned. "So?"

"So, we still have a chance of tracking her," Luke replied.

"And that's a *good* thing?" Vestara ran an appraising eye over both Skywalkers, then said, "You two are a long way from fighting form, and if you think I'm going after her alone—"

"Hardly," Luke interrupted. The trio had closed to within thirty meters of the *Shadow,* but a lean Keshiri Sith with deep purple eyes and alabaster hair was starting in their direction—and motioning for others to follow. "We just have to finish this."

Vestara looked at him as though he were crazy. "*Why?*" she asked. "Say you *do* manage kill Abeloth . . . again. So what?"

"Dad, Vestara kind of has a point about that," Ben said. He could think of only one reason a badly wounded

Abeloth would flee her Fallanassi protectors, and it *wasn't* because she expected the Skywalkers to return to fighting shape before she did. She had to be worried about fighting someone else—maybe a whole bunch of someone elses. "Killing Abeloth doesn't accomplish much."

"It keeps her weak," Luke countered. "And *that* protects the Shelter Jedi."

The observation struck Ben like a blaster bolt. Like his father and everyone else, Ben had attributed the Jedi Knights' recovery to the death of Abeloth's first body. But after discovering she was still alive, it had never occurred to him to ask why those Jedi were still sane. The answer, of course, was probably just what his father had suggested—after the destruction of her first body, she had been too weak to reach out to the Shelter Jedi. But if she ever regained her strength, she would certainly do so again—especially if she could use them against the Order.

As of now, the Skywalkers were the only ones in position to track her. His father had shed more than enough blood to use a Dathomiri blood trail against Abeloth. But if that didn't work, they would have to track her by analyzing her hyperspace jumps—and to do that, they needed to be close enough to record them.

Chest filling with pride at his father's endurance and foresight, Ben glanced over and asked, "We're going to be doing this for a while, aren't we?"

Luke smiled and nodded. "I'm afraid so, son." He turned to Vestara. "Are you up to this? You could still take your chances with the friends-and-family plan."

Vestara's brow rose. "You'd let me remain with them?"

"Whatever your reasons, you saved Ben's life in there," Luke replied. "I think I can give you a break . . . just this once."

Vestara considered the offer for nearly a dozen steps,

then tipped her head and looked over at Luke. "Is this a test, Master Skywalker?"

Ben was asking himself the same question, because the last thing his father would want was Vestara repeating what she had overheard about the Jedi queen. Though, now that he thought about it, Abeloth hadn't revealed anything Taalon hadn't known already—she'd merely confirmed that a Jedi queen was destined to claim a throne the Sith coveted themselves.

"If I accept your offer of release," Vestara continued, "how quickly will I find myself dead?"

Luke chuckled. "That's not my style," he said. "You're free to stay behind, if you want to take your chances with the Sith. But if you come with us, it can't be as a prisoner. We're going to have enough trouble without worrying about you. So if you stay with us, it needs to be because you want to."

Ben began to wonder if his father might have suffered a concussion during the fight. "Uh, Dad, you know it wasn't *us* she was trying to save when she killed Taalon, right?" he asked. "She was just trying to keep Abeloth from making him her tentacle cleaner—then using him to take control of the Sith."

"That's *not* a bad thing, Ben." As Luke spoke, he kept his gaze on Vestara. "And neither was sparing the galaxy another of Abeloth's kind."

As Luke spoke, the purple-eyed Keshiri started across the circle on an interception vector, with a dozen more Sith following close behind. Vestara watched them for a moment, then lowered her chin.

"Thank you for giving me a choice, Master Skywalker." Her voice was so soft that Ben could barely hear it. "But killing so far above my station will make me a target for many years—if I survive the initial retaliations. I think I'm better off with you than with my own people."

Ben's heart began to dance a little bit—he didn't *trust*

Vestara, but he was beginning to think he might have a real chance of turning her to the light side.

"So you're still coming with us?" he asked, grinning.

Vestara sighed in exasperation. "It *doesn't* mean I have fallen for you, Ben Skywalker." Giving him no chance to reply, she nodded at the approaching band. "And now, perhaps the time has come to make a run for the *Shadow.*"

Before Ben could remind her of his father's injured leg, Luke said, "We're fine. Running will start a fight, and a fight will cost us even more time."

"You Jedi, are you *all* mad?" Vestara whispered.

Ben was about to side with her—until he noticed the speaker bud in the Keshiri's ear. The Sith was speaking into a throat mike as he walked and casting uneasy glances toward the sky, and the Force was fairly sizzling with his panic.

"Master Skywalker, running is our *only* chance," Vestara pressed. "We're outnumbered—badly."

"We're not." Ben glanced skyward. He didn't see any sign of help yet, but he knew he wouldn't—not until the moment it arrived. "Trust me on that."

"*Trust* you?" Vestara retorted. "You *are* mad."

Before Ben could explain, the band of Sith spread across their path. The purple-eyed leader stepped forward and glared down at Vestara. "I need to speak to High Lord Taalon. Where is he?"

Vestara shrugged. "I am sorry, Master Vhool, I don't—"

"You'll find Lord Taalon in the hall," Luke interrupted, waving an arm toward the door behind them. "Along with Gavar Khai. We had quite a fight with Abeloth in there."

The Keshiri's eyes widened. "Is Lord Taalon well?"

"About as well as can be expected, considering," Ben supplied. He gestured toward the *Shadow.* "It's my dad and me who need the medbay. Do you mind?"

"That will have to wait." The Keshiri—Master Vhool—turned to Vestara. "You can operate their vessel?"

Vestara's brow shot up. "I will need their help to get inside."

Ben could see by the way Vhool's eyes narrowed that the last thing he wanted was the two Jedi within earshot of a comm station—which only made sense, if what Ben suspected was true: that help was on its way.

"It's not that hard, Vestara," Ben said. He reached out to the *Shadow,* using the Force to release the lock hidden inside the boarding hatch. "Just palm the control pad. It'll open."

Vhool studied Ben for a moment, then said, "Your cooperation has just saved your life, Jedi."

Ben shrugged. "Hey, we're still on the same side in this thing," he said. "Aren't we?"

"Of course." Vhool's tone was cool, but Ben could tell that his act had bought them a little time. The Sith turned back to Vestara. "Prepare the craft for departure. We will be leaving as soon as I return with your father and High Lord Taalon."

Vestara could not keep her eyes from widening, but her tone remained cool. "As you command, Master Vhool." She glanced back at Ben. "Is there anything I should know about cold-firing procedures?"

"Just one thing." Ben grinned. "You wouldn't want to leave without us."

Vestara suppressed a smile that Ben couldn't read, then nodded curtly at Vhool. "That will depend on the wishes of High Lord Taalon, of course."

She hurried ahead to the *Shadow* and palmed the control pad. As the hatch opened, Vhool turned back to Luke. "You and your son will await High Lord Taalon's pleasure here."

He sent three of his escorts to round up the rest of the

Sith on the island, then ordered the others to wait with Ben and Luke.

"Treat them as allies as long as they behave like allies," he said. "But if they do anything suspicious—"

"Why would we do that?" Luke interrupted. "Is something wrong?"

"Nothing that concerns you." Vhool could not prevent his eyes from drifting skyward as he spoke. "We Sith are merely cautious by nature."

The Keshiri turned toward the gathering hall, and a moment later the *Shadow*'s repulsorlift engines whined to life. Ben half expected to see the star yacht rising off its struts as Vestara made her escape alone.

Instead a hatch cover beneath the nose slid open. Several of the Sith guarding Luke and Ben turned toward the sound, then scowled in confusion when a retractable blaster cannon dropped from the opening.

"*Whoops*—she did it again." Ben rolled his eyes and tried to sound casual. "Wrong button."

This seemed to reassure the Sith—until a flash brightened the sky. Ben glanced up to find a silver globe of radiance almost directly overhead—then a second and a third globe appeared, all contracting with the distinctive reverse flare of a detonating proton torpedo. A flurry of secondary explosions followed, filling a section of sky with roiling blossoms of fire. Smoke trails and flashing bolts of color began to spiral down through the atmosphere, pieces of disintegrating starships and starfighters bringing their dogfights dirtside.

The SteathXs had arrived—and not a moment too soon.

Ben glanced over at his father, looking for the cue that said it was time to grab for his lightsaber. But Luke Skywalker's eyes were fixed on the skies, looking worried and sad and weary. Ben thought for a moment that the battle was going poorly for the Jedi, that the Grand

Master was sensing the pain and fear of his dying Jedi Knights.

Then another series of flashes erupted, a little off to their right, and Ben realized his father wasn't looking toward the battle at all. He was concentrating on their quarry, no doubt trying to get a fix on Abeloth and Ship—and some idea of where they would be headed. Two StealthXs appeared in the sky, swooping downward in pursuit of half a dozen outdated Javelins. Cannon bolts began to stream from the StealthXs, and the first two Javelins were plummeting seaward when an alarmed voice cried out from the gathering hall.

"Stop Vestara Khai!" Vhool's boots began to pound across the circle toward the *Shadow.* "She killed—"

Ben did not hear the rest of the accusation. He felt Vestara touching him through the Force, and he suddenly had a strong urge to duck. Pulling his father along, he dived for the ground and pressed himself as flat as possible. A heartbeat later a volley of cannon bolts screeched past, barely centimeters above his back, and filled the air with a spray of blood and charred Sith flesh.

By the time the cannon fire stopped a second later, both Skywalkers had their lightsabers in hand. Luke sprang up first, igniting his blade and crossing the last fifty meters to the *Shadow* in a series of one-legged Force bounds. Ben was a step behind, covering their backs and trying not to look as he passed over the charred remains of their guards.

The *Shadow* was already rising off her struts when they jumped onto the boarding ramp. Ben had to use the Force to stick himself to its surface as Vestara swung the vessel around and streaked away from the island. His father took him by the arm and pulled him the rest of the way aboard, then let out a sigh of relief and hit the control pad to seal the hatch.

"That's *twice,*" Luke observed.

Ben nodded, knowing that his father was referring to the number of times Vestara had saved their lives, then smiled. "She can deny it all she likes," he said. "But she's *absolutely* fallen for me."

Before Luke could object, Vestara's voice came over the intercom.

"How about a little help up here?" she said. "I don't know the passcodes—and there's some noob on the comm who wants to talk to Master Skywalker *now*."

"On our way," Luke replied.

He started to wag a cautionary finger at Ben, then simply sighed and led the way forward.

They reached the flight deck just as the *Shadow* was slipping free of the atmosphere. Space to their starboard was laced with the colored streaks and blossoming fireballs of a starship battle. A quick glance at the copilot's tactical display revealed that the Jedi had the fight well in hand; half a dozen Sith frigates were already blinking red for DISABLED, and the rest were turning to withdraw. To port, silhouetted against the silvery glow of the moon Drewwa, was the bright red wedge of an old Imperial II Star Destroyer.

"*Stang!*" Ben gasped. "That looks like the *Errant Venture*!"

"It *is*," Vestara confirmed. "And he's threatening to blast us back to atoms unless I put your father on the comm *now*."

Vestara thumbed a toggle on the control yoke, and the familiar voice of Lando Calrissian came over the cockpit speakers.

"Luke, old buddy, that had better be you," he said. "Booster is firing up his turbolaser batteries."

"It's me." Luke slipped into the copilot's seat and transmitted an authentication code, then asked, "What in the blazes are *you* doing here?"

"Hosting a sabacc tournament," Lando replied. "And

when you come aboard, you're not going to believe who's winning."

"I'm afraid you'll have to tell us now." Luke motioned Ben toward the navigator's seat, then added in a meaningful tone, "Abeloth's still out there, and we have to stay on her trail."

"Are you *spacesick*?"

As Lando spoke, Ben slipped into the navigator's seat and brought up the tactical display, then initiated a search for Ship's profile.

"From the intercepts we've been hearing, you've had a rough few weeks," Lando continued. "It sounds like you *both* need some quality time in a bacta tank."

"We do," Luke said. "But we can't lose Abeloth, and right now that means *I* have to stay on her trail. She's been trying to recruit Force-users to guard her, and if that happens . . ."

Luke let the statement trail off, and Lando filled in the rest. "Right . . . she'll make the Yuuzhan Vong look like a bunch of second-rate party crashers. But you've got backup now. Stay in touch, and we'll catch up."

"Thanks," Luke said.

Ship's designator code appeared on the tactical display. It was just swinging around the far side of Almania. As soon as Ship escaped the planet's gravity well, it would jump to hyperspace. Ben leaned across the flight deck and pointed at his father's tactical display.

"Listen, we've got a fix on Ship," Luke said. "We're going to need to cut this short. You've got about thirty seconds to fill me in."

"Copy," Lando said. "There are a couple of things you should know. First, the Horn kids are on their way back to the Temple."

Luke's brow rose. "Daala released them?"

"Not exactly," Lando replied. "Han and Leia gave her a little help. Second, Kenth Hamner is dead."

The last news struck Ben like a stun bolt, but Luke merely closed his eyes and nodded. "I sensed something like that."

"I don't want to go into it over the comm."

"That's fine," Luke said. "I'll find out later. Can I assume that we're using the *Errant Venture* as a StealthX mother ship because . . . Daala *isn't* cooperating?"

"You could say that," Lando replied. "In fact, you could shout it."

Luke cringed. "I see." The immense blue disk of the planet Almania began to creep across the canopy as Vestara swung the *Shadow* after Ship, and he said, "We've got ten seconds, Lando. I'll contact the Temple again as soon as possible. Anything else?"

"One bit of good news," Lando said. "It looks like Wynn Dorvan may be considering early retirement."

"*Retirement?*" Ben and Luke asked the question simultaneously.

"That's right," Lando said. "He made the final table, and he's the hands-down favorite to win the first Tendrando Arms Celebrity Sabacc Charity Challenge."

Chapter Thirty-five

LEIA FOUND HER ALONE IN THE APEX OF THE TEMPLE, standing like a statue as she looked out over a Coruscant already twinkling in the evening gloom. The Barabel held her hands clasped tightly behind her back, as though she feared what they might do if she allowed them to hang free. Her shoulders were rising and falling in time to breathing so heavy and steady that it was audible on the far side of the cupola. Wary of intruding on a Master's meditations—even if she *had* been ordered to report—Leia stopped just inside the entrance and waited for a summons that was only heartbeats in coming.

"Let there be no ceremony between *us*, Jedi Solo." Though Saba continued to gaze out the viewport as she spoke, her voice seemed to rise from Leia's shoulder. "We have been friendz too long, this one and you."

"Yes, we have," Leia said, crossing to the Barabel's side. "But part of being friends is knowing when one shouldn't intrude."

"That is so?" Saba turned to face her, and Leia saw that the Barabel's narrow eyes were rimmed in red. "There are times when humanz do not cherish the companionship of close ones?"

"Sometimes," Leia said, watching Saba's face carefully. "Such as when we're crying. Sometimes we want to be alone then."

Saba showed the tips of her fangs, creating what seemed to be a sad grin. "You think Barabelz cry, Jedi Solo?"

"Maybe not," Leia said, not quite sure whether she had offended Saba or amused her. "But I *can* feel it in the Force when you have a heavy heart."

Saba let her chin drop. "Yes, today this one has a heart like a stone." Her chin remained against her chest, but she lifted her eyes to look at Leia. "You have heard about Grand Master Hamner?"

Leia nodded. "Yes, I'm sorry that had to happen," she said. "It wasn't your fault."

"Then whose fault was it, Jedi Solo?" Saba asked, cocking her head. "It was *this* one who chose to let him fall."

"And Kenth is the one who forced you to make that choice," Leia reminded her. "If you hadn't, Luke and Ben would be prisoners of the Sith right now—or worse. And the Jedi would have no way to find Abeloth. You made the right choice."

Saba shrugged and looked out the transparisteel again. "Master Skywalker would have found a better choice."

"Luke wasn't there, Master," Leia said. "No one will ever know what he would have done differently. Perhaps he wouldn't have tried as hard as you did to save Kenth's life."

"He wouldn't have *had* to, Jedi Solo. That is the difference." She unclasped her hands and laid one across Leia's back, an unusual gesture of intimacy for a Barabel. "Grand Master Hamner will require a funeral, like Mara had?"

"Yes, I suppose he will," Leia said.

"This one does not understand such thingz," she said. "You will help her organize it?"

"I think that would be best," Leia agreed. During her apprenticeship to become a Jedi Knight, she had spent enough time with Barabels to understand that, being responsible for Kenth's death, Saba would feel duty-bound to give him his death rites. "Leave that to me—you're going to be busy enough with Daala."

Saba's hand, so large it stretched across Leia's entire back, tensed. "Yes, Chief Daala is too quiet. She is preparing something big."

A knot of tension formed in Leia's stomach. This was the bad part about all the Order's successes. Daala was going to respond—she *had* to, and the less the Jedi heard about it, the more likely that response was to be something lethal and outrageous.

"And the Jedi have *no* idea what Daala is planning?" Leia asked.

Saba shook her head. "Not yet. This one is working on it."

"In that case, have you given any thought to evacuating the Temple?" Leia replied. "The more clustered we remain—"

She was interrupted by the tremendous thump of Saba's tail against the floor. "Abandon the nest?" she hissed, whirling on Leia. "Did this one train a *snekket*?"

Knowing better than to cringe away from a Barabel, Leia leaned back toward Saba and put some durasteel into her voice. "You know better than that, Master," she said. "But it's a tactical mistake to keep us bunched up inside. All it would take is one baradium missile to wipe out fifty percent of the Jedi Order."

"Daala would *do* that?" Saba's scales were lying flat against her cheeks—a sure sign that she felt threatened. "She would use a baradium missile on *Coruscant*?"

"We don't *know* what Daala would do—that's the point," Leia replied. "She's certainly done worse things in the past."

Saba's gaze grew thoughtful, and she leaned away from Leia. "You are right, Jedi Solo. We mustn't let her strike first, not with the . . . with our Temple at risk." She turned back toward the window, her heavy brow lowered in thought. "Thank you, Jedi Solo. You have been helpful."

Leia recognized a dismissal when she heard one, but she made no move to leave. "Master Sebatyne, I didn't mean to imply we should—"

"This one *knowz* what you mean," Saba said. "And she has no intention of attacking Daala *first.*"

"But you're not going to let *her* attack first, either?" Leia clarified. "If she tries, the Jedi will stop her?"

"No," Saba clarified. "The Jedi will be quicker."

Leia was silent for a moment, contemplating the simple elegance of Barabel diplomacy: don't start the fight—*win* it.

"That's a very fine line to walk," Leia said. "To an outsider, it may not seem like there's a line at all."

"That is why *we* are Jedi and they are not," Saba replied. "Because we are accustomed to fine lines."

Realizing she had made her point, Leia inclined her head. "Very well, Master. Please let me know if I can be of assistance."

Saba dismissed her with a nod, but as Leia turned to go, she added, "There *is* one thing, Jedi Solo. Has Head of State Fel broken orbit yet?"

"I don't believe so," Leia added. "Jaina was hoping to speak with him before he left."

Saba nodded. "Good. Ask Jaina to suggest to Head of State Fel that he should remain awhile longer."

"If you like. May I ask why?"

Saba cocked her head and studied Leia out of one eye. "This one thinkz you *know* why, Jedi Solo."

"I suppose I do," Leia said, nodding. It wasn't a question of *if* Daala was going to attack, but how quickly—and in all probability, that meant Jag's reasons for withdrawing from the negotiations were soon going to be a thing of the past. "I'll ask Jaina to convince him to stick around for a few days."

Leia waited until Saba dismissed her again, then stepped outside into the corridor, where Han was pacing back and forth, waiting. He took her arm and started toward the lift tube, obviously worried about being late.

"So?" he asked. "How was Saba?"

"Not good," Leia admitted. "Maybe even a little scary. She's not handling the Kenth thing very well."

"Who is?" Han asked. "Even I'm feeling guilty about some of the things I said to him."

"It's more than just guilt—she seems to think it's a failure of leadership." They reached the lift tube and stepped inside, then Leia continued, "I'm not sure I fully understand. It might be a Barabel thing."

"Then I'm sure you *don't* understand," Han said. "Nobody understands Barabels except Barabels. It's too bad Tesar and the others aren't here. Maybe they could do something."

"That *would* be nice," Leia agreed. "But she didn't say anything about them—"

"And it's dangerous to ask—I know," Han said. "Any guesses what they're up to?"

Leia shook her head. "Not really. Saba hinted that she has someone keeping an eye on Daala. That might be them."

Han scratched his jawline for a moment, then nodded. "Makes sense," he said. "Barabels are pretty good at thinning out vermin."

"Han! That's terrible."

"Yeah, but it's true," he countered. "Am I right?"

Leia smiled. "You're right," she admitted. The lift stopped, and they stopped out onto the infirmary level. "Speaking of missing offspring—"

"Just talked to her," Han said, waving his comlink. "She and Barv have been off exploring. They're on their way."

Leia frowned. "*Exploring?*"

"Relax, will you? Allana's a kid—she's got to have some fun," Han said. "Besides, they're still in the Temple . . . *somewhere.*"

"I don't like it," Leia said. "Not while we're having all this trouble with Daala."

"Okay, I'll talk to her," Han said. "But don't worry, she's on her way. She's not going to want to miss *this.*"

"Bloah!" Allana kicked the hatch, then stepped back and nearly tripped over her pet nexu, Anji. She braced a hand on the wall and caught herself, then wiped the hair out of her eyes—inadvertently smearing her brow with grease, dust, and a whole bunch of other stuff she really didn't want to think about. "Someone welded this one closed, too!"

Anji began to scratch at the base of the door, and a soft rumble sounded behind Allana—a deep voice suggesting in its native Ramoan that maybe little girls shouldn't use words like *bloah.* Allana spun around and shone her glow rod up into the big green face of her best friend, Bazel Warv.

"I'm not a little girl, Barv," she said. "I'm a famous xenoarchaeologist exploring a twenty-five-thousand-year-old temple."

Bazel rumbled again, offering the opinion that smart women like famous xenoarchaeologists probably didn't use words like *bloah,* either.

"Probably not," Allana admitted. "At least not when someone's listening."

She consulted her datapad again, then swung the glow rod back and checked the hatch number.

"But that door isn't supposed to be secured like this. You'd better use your lightsaber to cut it open."

Allana ran the glow rod along one edge of the hatch, illuminating the silvery smears of two welds. Bazel shook his head and said the welds looked fresh, which meant someone had probably sealed the hatch for good reason.

"Then why didn't they enter it on the Temple maintenance log?"

Allana held the datapad above her head for the huge Ramoan to inspect. He peered at it for a moment, then suggested that whoever had done the work had just forgotten to file a report.

Allana sighed and lowered the datapad. "Look, Barv, it's going to take an hour to go back around. That means *I'll* be in trouble and *you* won't be there when they let Valin and Jysella out of carbonite."

When Bazel didn't have anything to say to that, Allana looked up from the corner of her eye and added, "And you *do* want to be there, don't you? I mean, while everyone else got to break into the detention center, you were stuck watching me and Anji—"

Bazel interrupted, informing her that guarding her and Anji was the most important job in the whole plan. Leia and Taryn had told him that three times—*each*.

"Yeah, sure," Allana said. "But you and Yaqeel are part of the *Unit*. That means you've *got* to be there, right?"

Bazel sighed, then used a big hand to pull her behind him, asked her to hold Anji, and ignited his lightsaber. Two minutes later, the hatch was open, and the most awful odor Allana had ever smelled was coming from inside. Anji, of course, bounded straight through the opening.

"Stang!" Allana gasped. "What *is* that poodoo?"

This time, Bazel did not complain about her language. He simply shook his head and asked if she wanted to go around *now*.

Allana considered this a moment, then checked her chrono. "Can't," she said. "We're already gonna be late."

Bazel was afraid of that. He switched on his own glow rod, then took a deep breath and stepped through the hatchway into a small, hot, humid chamber. He paused a moment, checking the place with the Force, then informed Allana that there was someone inside.

"Who?" She stepped around his massive thigh and, shining her glow rod ahead of her, led the way forward. *"Hello?"*

Something sissed ahead, then clattered, and Anji gave an inquisitive mewl. A moment later, Allana's glow rod fell on a wall of tiny rodent bones as tall as she was. She could tell that they were rodent bones because a lot of the little bodies still had their heads, and a few had pieces of fur. Anji was eating one.

Allana stopped in her tracks. Without turning around, she asked softly, "Barv . . . do you see *that*?"

He asked if she meant the nest.

"The *nest*?" she repeated. "That can't be a . . ."

Allana let her sentence trail off as the bones began to clatter and rustle in front of her. Anji gave a startled yowl and sprang away. Allana backed up—and ran straight into Bazel's boulder-sized knee. A moment later four big scaly heads popped out of the bones, glaring at her with slit-pupiled eyes. Anji hissed and went to hide behind Bazel.

"Tesar?" Allana gasped. *"Dordi?"*

"And Wilyem and Zal," Zal added.

"Amelia?" Tesar sounded as surprised as Allana was. He glared at Bazel, then demanded, "How did you *find* us?"

Bazel started into a long, nervous explanation about trying to teach Allana how to read building schematics by exploring the sub-basements of the Temple.

Allana waved him silent, then said simply, "We didn't mean to. We were just exploring."

"Exxxploring?" Tesar hissed. "Our hunting groundz?"

"You didn't tell anyone they were *yours,*" Allana objected. "You just disappeared."

As she spoke, Tesar and the other three Barabels slithered out of the nest, leaving several small cavities through which Allana glimpsed a clutch of large spotted orbs.

"Hey, those are *eggs*!" Allana looked up at Tesar, then asked, "Did *you* guys lay them?"

It was clearly the wrong thing to ask. In the blink of an eye, three of the Barabels had their lightsabers ignited and stood surrounding her and Bazel—who had the good sense to keep his own blade deactivated. The fourth, Zal, had Anji by the scruff of her neck, ignoring the infuriated nexu's clawless attempts to rake apart the arm that was holding her.

"*Now* you have done it!" Dordi informed her.

Allana looked from Tesar to Dordi, but a Barabel was pretty much a Barabel—the females looked just as ferocious as the males. "Uh . . . is there any chance that what I did is a . . . *good* thing?"

"Maybe." Wilyem thumped his tail, scattering tiny rodent bones everywhere. "It dependz how you look at it."

Bazel rumbled a question, asking what Wilyem meant by that. But the Barabels did not understand Ramoan, so they just narrowed their eyes and looked like they might be thinking about eating him.

Allana turned back to Tesar. "Depends on how I look at *what*, exactly?"

"Spending the next two monthz down here," Tesar informed her. "Now that you have seen the nest—"

"*And* the eggz," Zal reminded him.

"And the eggz," Tesar added, "you must stay for the hatch."

Allana's heart clawed its way into her throat. "Two *months*?" she gasped. "We *can't*. Mom will kill me!"

"Better Jedi Solo than *this* one," Wilyem said darkly.

"And at least you will have two good monthz before you die," Dordi agreed. "It will be fun. We can hunt."

Allana frowned and tapped the chrono on her datapad. "You don't understand. Barv and I are supposed to be in the infirmary in fifteen minutes."

Tesar took the datapad and tossed into the nest. "This one is sorry," he said. "You're going to be late."

Barv rumbled an ominous Ramoan warning, swearing on his ancestors' tusks that he was going to be there when Valin and Jysella awakened.

The Barabels, of course, ignored the sacred vow—which was a big mistake. A heartbeat later, there were lightsabers popping and sizzling, then Barv tossed a Barabel out the hatch behind him, and things started to get ugly.

Allana drew a big breath, then called on the Force the way her mother had taught her the last time they had rendezvoused on Shedu Maad.

"Hey!" she yelled.

Five sets of startled eyes turned to look at her. When a quick check with the glow rod revealed that no one was missing any actual *limbs,* Allana stepped into the middle of the group and looked up at them.

"We can work this out."

The Barabels looked doubtful and Bazel grumbled that he *wasn't* going to miss the thawing, but when Allana locked gazes with Tesar, the Barabel reluctantly thumped his newly shortened tail against the filthy permacrete.

"*How?*" he asked.

"You're just worried that Barv and I will tell someone about your nest, right?" she asked. "Because you have to *know* we're not going to sneak down here to try to eat your eggs."

The Barabels exchanged glances, studied Bazel doubtfully for a moment, then finally seemed to come to a decision.

"Nobody is going to eat our eggz," Wilyem declared.

He shot a warning glare at Bazel. "This one will be here to make sure that never happenz."

"That's what I thought," Allana said. When a queen sees progress, she must be quick to build on it—that's what her mother always said about sponsoring negotiations. "So we've just got the secret to deal with. What if we trade?"

"Trade?" Dordi asked. "Trade *what*?"

"Secrets," Allana replied. "I'll tell you guys a big secret. That way, Barv and I will *never* say anything about your nest to anyone—because then you could tell everyone *my* secret."

The Barabels glanced at one another for a moment, then Zal said, "This is a very *big* secret? As big as our nest?"

Allana smiled. "Trust me, it *is*. If you ever reveal it, I'm dead."

"Dead?" Tesar repeated.

"*Really* dead," Allana said. "Within a year, for sure."

The Barabels didn't even have to look at one another. They simply nodded, and Dordi said, "Dead is big enough."

"Good." Allana turned to Bazel. "Barv, are you in?"

Bazel swore on his ancestors' tusks that he would never reveal anything he learned in that room, even to himself. The Barabels seemed to get the general idea and nodded.

"Okay, then, here goes." Allana knew this was the biggest risk she had ever taken, but her grandpa always said that when the table looked right, you couldn't be afraid to shove in all your chips and hope. "My name *isn't* Amelia, and I'm *not* really a war orphan—at least not in the usual way . . ."

She explained her situation to the Barabels in its entirety, telling them that she was really the daughter of Jacen Solo and Queen Mother Tenel Ka.

A few minutes later, she, Bazel, and Anji were riding a lift tube up to the Jedi Temple's infirmary level. They all smelled like something a dianoga had spit up, and Allana was fairly certain that they would both end up being thoroughly disinfected before they made it off the level. She just hoped she would be able to stall long enough to see Valin and Jysell Horn emerge from carbonite.

As they ascended, Bazel asked if her name *really* wasn't Amelia?

"No, Barv, I told you—it's Allana Solo," she said. "But you can *never* tell anyone. You have to call me Amelia."

He promised that he would, then asked whether the Solos knew her secret.

"Of course *they* know," she said. "They're part of it."

Bazel wanted to know if he could tell them.

"*Barv!*" she said. "*No one*! You can't even tell *Yaqeel*—not about *anything* that happened down there!"

Down where? Bazel asked.

Allana punched him in the knee, then the lift opened and they stepped out onto the infirmary level. There was already a small group gathered in a room at the end of the corridor, with Master Horn and his wife, Mirax, standing opposite each other, each next to a hovergurney bearing the carbonite pods with their frozen children. Master Cilghal and her assistant Tekli were standing between the two pods, already fiddling with the controls. Allana's grandparents were waiting at the edges of the room, their eyes brimming with tears of joy and hope.

At the foot of one of the pods stood Yaqeel, whose sensitive Bothan nose began to wrinkle and twitch as Allana, Anji, and Bazel drew near. For a moment, it looked as though Yaqeel was going to make some sort of wisecrack about the way they smelled, or at least ask where they had been. But Yaqeel simply took Bazel's hand and drew him over to stand beside her.

Allana took Anji and went to stand between her grandparents, who merely pressed in close and did not even *think* to ask why she smelled so bad. Han even mussed her dirty hair.

"Glad you made it, kid."

Allana looked up and spotted a tear on his cheek. She smiled and looked back to the Horns. "Me, too."

Cilghal and Tekli pressed something on the pods, and a high-pitched whine started to rise from them. The black carbonite casing began to melt away from the bodies of Jysella and Valin Horn, and Allana felt a sudden wave of joy rippling through the Force.

"Me, too," she repeated, in a voice so soft no one heard.

Read on for an excerpt from
Star Wars: Fate of the Jedi: Conviction
by Aaron Allston
Published by Del Rey Books

CORUSCANT, JEDI TEMPLE
INFIRMARY LEVEL

THE MEDICAL READOUT BOARD ON THE CARBONITE POD flickered, then went dark, announcing that the young man just being thawed from suspended animation—Valin Horn, Jedi Knight—was dead.

Master Cilghal, preeminent physician of the Jedi Order, felt a jolt of alarm ripple through the Force. It was not her own alarm. The emotion was the natural reaction of all those gathered to see Valin and his sister Jysella rescued from an unfair, unwarranted sentence imposed not by a court of justice but by Galactic Alliance Chief of State Daala herself. Had they some to see these Jedi Knights freed and instead become witness to a tragedy?

But what Cilghal *didn't* feel in the Force was the winking out of a life. Valin was still there, a diminished but intact presence in the Force.

She waved at the assembly, a calming motion. "Be still." She did not need to exert herself through the Force. Most of those present were Jedi Masters and Jedi Knights who respected her authority. Not one of them was easily panicked, not even the little girl beside Han and Leia.

Standing between Valin's and Jysella's gurneys with her assistant Tekli, Cilghal concentrated on the young man lying to her right. His body still gleamed with a trace of dark fluid: all that remained of the melted carbonite that had imprisoned him. He was as still as the dead. Cilghal pressed her huge, webbed hand against his throat to check his pulse. She found it, shallow but steady.

The readout board flickered again and the lights came up in all their colors, strong, the pulse monitor flickering with Valin's heartbeat, the encephaloscan beginning to jitter with its measurements of Valin's brain activity.

Tekli, a Chadra-Fan, her diminutive size and glossy fur coat giving her the aspect of a plush toy instead of an experienced Jedi Knight and physician, spun away from Valin's gurney and toward the one beside it. On it lay Jysella Horn, slight of build, also gleaming a bit with unevaporated carbonite residue. Tekli put one palm against Jysella's forehead and pressed the fingers of her other hand across Jysella's wrist.

Cilghal nodded. Computerized monitors might fail, but the Force sense of a trained Jedi would not, at least not under these conditions.

Tekli glanced back at Cilghal and gave a brisk nod. All was well.

The pulse under Cilghal's hand began to strengthen and quicken. Also good, also normal.

Cilghal moved around the head of the gurney and stood on the far side of the apparatus, a step back from Valin. When he awoke, his vision would be clouded, and perhaps his judgment as well. It would not do for him to wake with a large form standing over him, gripping his throat. Violence might result.

She caught the attention of Corran and Mirax, parents of the two patients. "That was merely an electronic glitch." Cilghal tried to make her tones reassuring, knowing her effort was not likely to succeed—Mon Calamari voices, suited to their larger-than-human frames, were resonant and even gravelly, an evolutionary adaptation that allowed them to be heard at greater distances in their native underwater environments. Unfortunately, they tended to sound harsh and even menacing to human ears. But she had to try. "They are fine."

Corran, wearing green Jedi robes that matched the color of his eyes, heaved a sigh of relief. His wife, Mirax, dressed in a stylish jumpsuit in blacks and blues, smiled uncertainly as she asked, "What caused it?"

Cilghal offered a humanlike shrug. "I'll put the monitors in for evaluation once your children are checked out as stable. I suspect these monitors haven't been tested or serviced since Valin and Jysella were frozen." There, that was a well-delivered lie, dismissing the monitor's odd behavior as irrelevant.

Valin stirred. Cilghal glanced down at him. The Knight's eyes fluttered open and tried to fix on her, but seemed to have difficulty focusing.

Cilghal looked down at him. "Valin? Can you hear me?"

"I . . . I . . ." Valin's voice was weak, watery.

"Don't speak. Just nod."

He did.

"You've been—"

She was interrupted by a stage-whispered notification from Tekli: "Jysella is awake."

Cilghal adjusted her angle so she could address both siblings. "You've been in carbonite suspension for some time. You will feel cold, shaky, and disoriented. This is all normal. You are among friends. Do you understand me?"

Valin nodded again. Jysella's "yes" was faint, but stronger and more controlled than Cilghal had expected.

"Your parents are here. I'll allow them to speak to you in a moment. The Solos are here, as well." *And little Amelia and her pet Anji, both of whom smell like they've been rolling in seafood shells left rotting for a week.* Cilghal had to blink over that fact. The child should have received a thorough disinfecting before being allowed in this chamber. Come to think of it, Barv also reeked. Where could a youngling and even a Jedi Knight go in the clean, austere Temple and end up smelling like that?

She set the question aside. "Bazel Warv is here, and Yaqeel Saav'etu, your friends. They can answer many questions about an ailment that afflicted the two of you just prior to your freezing."

Jysella looked around, barely raising her head, her attention sliding across the faces of friends and loved ones, and then she looked at Valin. He must have felt her attention; he looked back. A thought, the sort of instant communication that only siblings can understand, passed between then. Then the two of them relaxed.

Jysella looked again at her parents. "Mom?"

At Cilghal's nod, Mirax and Corran came forward, crowding into the gap between the gurneys. Tekli moved out of their way, circling around the head of Valin's bed to rejoin Cilghal. She craned her neck to look up at the Mon Cal. "All signs good."

Cilghal nodded. She turned to the others in the room. "All but the immediate family, please withdraw to the waiting area."

And they did, exiting with words of encouragement and welcome.

In moments only the Horns and the medics remained with Valin and Jysella. Cilghal took a few steps to the nurse's station and its bank of monitoring screens, giving its more elaborate readouts a look . . . or pretending to. Tekli found a mist dispenser and sprayed its clean-smelling contents around the chamber, driving away reminders of Amelia's, Anji's, and Barv's recent presence. Then she rejoined her superior.

If Cilghal's predictions were correct, Valin and Jysella would be reaching full cognizance right about now, if they had not already. And if the madness that had caused them to be subjected to carbonite freezing were still in effect, their voices would be raised in moments with accusations: "What have you done with my *real* mother, my *real* father?"

That was the insanity that had visited them, the manifestation of the dark-side effect of their connection with the monster known as Abeloth. But recently, Abeloth's power over the "mad Jedi" had been broken. They had all returned to normal—all but these young Horns, their recovery delayed by their suspended state.

Valin's voice was raised in a complaint, but it was not an accusation of treachery and deceit. "I can't stop shaking."

"It's normal." His father sounded confident. "Han went through it years ago. He said it took him quite a while to warm up. This gurney is radiating a lot of heat, though. You'll be warm enough before you know it." He frowned. "He also said his eyesight was gone right after he woke. How is it that you're seeing so well?"

"We're not." That was Jysella, raising her arms above her to stretch, an experiment that caused her to wince with muscle pangs. "I'm seeing mostly with the Force."

Valin nodded. "Me, too."

Cilghal and Tekli exchanged a glance. That was a relief. The conversation was idle chat, and would soon turn to minute discussions of who had been up to what while Valin and Jysella slept. All was well.

Unless . . . Cilghal still had one more test to run.

She raised her voice to catch the attention of all the Horns. "Excuse me. I must interrupt. We have to let the monitors get several minutes of uninterrupted data, and all this talking is interfering. I must ask you two to withdraw for a while."

Mirax gave her an exasperated look. "After all the time we've waited—"

Tekli held up a hand to forestall her. "After all that time, you can afford to indulge in a few minutes of quiet relief with your husband." She made a shooing motion with her hands. "Out."

Grudgingly, the older Horns withdrew. They'd be joining the others in the waiting area.

From a cabinet, Cilghal took a pair of self-heating blankets. She approached the gurneys and spread one blanket over each patient. "Tekli and I need to make some log entries about your recovery. Josat will be here in a moment—ah." As if on cue, and it was indeed on cue, a teenage Jedi apprentice, cheerful and maddeningly energetic, entered the chamber. Red-haired, lean with a teen's overactive metabolism, he offered Cilghal and Tekli a minimally acceptable respectful nod and immediately moved over to the nurse's station monitor to familiarize himself with his two charges.

Cilghal finished adjusting Jysella's blanket. "If you need anything, Josat can provide it, and if he is not here, say 'Nurse' and the comm router will put you in contact with the floor nurse."

Jysella glanced over at her brother. "I have just been tucked in by a large fish."

He smiled, and when he spoke, there was amusement in his voice. "Maybe you're hallucinating."

The waiting room was a long chamber decorated with plants from a dozen worlds and a wall-side fountain shaped to simulate a waterfall on the planet Alderaan, destroyed so long ago. The air here was fresher than that in the infirmary chambers, smelling of oxygen from the plants, mist from the waterfall—

Fresher in most ways, fouler in others. Leia turned to Allana and crossed her arms. "Sweetie . . ."

"I know, I know." The child did not sound at all child-like, but she hugged her pet nexu to her with what looked like a need for reassurance. "We smell bad."

"What did you get into?"

Allana's shrug was uncommunicative. "I don't know."

Leia glanced at Barv, but the Ramoan Jedi Knight, big and green with ferocious tusks, avoided her eye.

Well, of course he didn't want to explain. He'd been entrusted with watching over Allana, and he'd failed to keep her out of mischief. This was the sort of humbling experience young Jedi needed to have from time to time.

Han leaned into the conversation, but his attention was on his wife, not his granddaughter. "Garbage Compactor Three Two Six Three Eight Two Seven."

Leia scowled at him. "Oh, shut up."

Han grinned and there was a bit of mockery in the expression. He switched his attention to Allana. "Sweetie, I can remember when your grandma smelled just like that. And unlike you, she was rude and ungrateful, too."

"Han—"

"Go get cleaned up, and sanisteam Anji if you can, while your grandma and I discuss the impossibility of keeping children—or teenage princesses—clean."

"Yes, Grandpa." Allana scurried while the scurrying was good. She didn't have to look back to detect the glare Leia was visiting on Han.

Cilghal and Tekli walked toward an office at the far end of the hall from the Horns' chamber, just short of the waiting room.

Cilghal had Josat's script timed and running in her head. Het would now be moving around the Horns' chamber, humming to himself, cautioning Valin and Jysella not to move or talk—the monitors needed stillness to do this evaluation—but *he* could talk, fortunately, for it was impossible for him to keep quiet, or so his family said . . .

Tekli interrupted the holodrama in Cilghal's head. "So, what *did* cause the pod monitor to fail?"

"Maybe what I said. And maybe it was a spike of the ability Valin manifested when he went mad."

"The one that blanked out the encephaloscan?"

"Yes. He was probably using the technique when he was frozen. The monitor failure would have been the last bit of that usage."

"Hmm." Tekli didn't comment. She didn't need to: Cilghal knew what she was thinking. Retention of that scanner-blanking ability was not an indication that Valin retained the madness, as well, but neither physician liked mysteries.

When the two of them entered their office, the main monitor on the wall was already tuned to a hidden holocam view of the Horns' chamber. They could see Josat indeed bustling among the cabinets, assembling a tray full of beverages, receptacles for medicines, blood samples, swabs.

Tekli heaved a sigh. "So far, so good."

Cilghal offered a noncommittal rumble. "Time will tell."

Josat moved to Valin and then Jysella, offering drinks. His voice was crisp over the monitor speakers. "We gave you the farthest room from the turbolifts and offices and waiting room. Much quieter here. If there's an emergency, though, it's safer to head to the stairs instead of the turbolifts. Right next door, take a left when you leave this chamber, it's the door straight ahead, you can find it in pitch darkness. That can be important. I never used to pay attention to things like that, but since I started studying nursing, I have to know these things. Jedi Tekli will make me run laps if I ever don't know where the emergency exits are from any of my stations. Were your Masters always assigning you exercise when you messed up? Don't answer, the monitors need quiet."

Cilghal blinked, pleased. "He worked that in very well."

"About the punishment?"

"About the stairs."

"I know."

Cilghal sighed. "Mammalian humor. Deliberate misinterpretation."

"Tends to drive a Master crazy, doesn't it?"

Josat now stood beside Valin's gurney, his lightsaber swaying on his belt within Valin's easy reach. The apprentice eyed one of the wall monitors. "Slow progress on your evaluation. No matter. Nobody will come back to bother you until it's run its course. Half an hour at least, I'm guessing."

Cilghal nodded. "The last of the bait. He is not a bad actor." Under ideal circumstances, Valin or Jysella might feel a trace of deceit from him through the Force, but now, still suffering a little from the aftereffects of carbonite freezing, they were unlikely to.

They were, however, likely to add up four important details. First, they were in a room at the end of the corridor, away from most visitors and medical personnel. Second, they were next to stairs that would allow them to reach any level of the Temple while bypassing well-traveled turbolifts. Third, they had half an hour before their absence would be noticed. And fourth, they had ready access to a lightsaber.

If they were still mad, and merely concealing the fact, could they resist the bait?

But neither Horn made a grab for the lightsaber.

If they had done so—well, it wouldn't have been too damaging. The lightsaber would not have ignited. Switching it on, or having Cilghal or Tekli press a button on the comlinks they carried, would cause the false lightsaber to emit a powerful stunning gas. The Horns would have been felled without violence, never having even reached the corridor. Josat would have been felled as well, but it would have been easier on him than being thrashed by two experienced Knights.

But, clearly, escape was not a priority for them. Which meant that they, too, were sane. Cured.

Valin had felt nothing but warmth and relief from his parents—

From the man and woman *masquerading* as his parents.

As he lay listening to Josat's endless, maddening blather, Valin forced himself to remain calm. Any distress might send a signal through the Force to his captors, a signal that their deception had been detected.

And perhaps, *perhaps,* the man and woman who wore the faces of Corran and Mirax Horn didn't even know that they were imposters.

What a horrible thought. Perhaps they were clones, implanted with memories that caused them to believe, in their heart of hearts, that they were the real Corran and Mirax. What would happen to them when the truth was revealed? Would they be killed by their secret masters? Were they even now implanted with strategically-placed explosives that would end their lives when they were no longer useful?

Valin clamped down on that thought, suppressing it.

Again Josat came near, chattering about his studies, about politics, about the best mopping techniques for apprentices assigned to clean Temple corridors. Again his lightsaber swung invitingly just within Valin's reach.

But, no. He and Jysella needed to know much more than they did now if they were to stage a successful escape. They needed to be rested, informed, and somewhere other than deep in the enemy-occupied Jedi Temple before they struck out on their own.

So he looked at his sister and offered her a smile full of reassurance. That emotion, at least, was real. In all the universe, the one person he knew to be true was Jysella. He'd known it from the moment they had reached for each other in the Force. Dazed, barely conscious, dreading what they would find, they had still connected, and they knew they were not alone.

She smiled back at him, an expression he felt more than saw.

They had each other, and for now, that was enough.

A GALAXY ON THE BRINK OF DESTRUCTION THREE HUNDRED YEARS AFTER THE EVENTS OF *KNIGHTS OF THE OLD REPUBLIC*!

STAR WARS

THE OLD REPUBLIC

A NEW SERIES BASED ON THE HIGHLY ANTICIPATED MULTIPLAYER ONLINE GAME FROM BIOWARE AND LUCASARTS!

ROB CHESTNEY ALEX SANCHEZ MICHAEL ATIYEH

AVAILABLE AT YOUR LOCAL COMICS SHOP

To find a comics shop in your area, call 1-888-266-4226

For more information or to order direct visit darkhorse.com or call 1-800-862-0052

IN A GALAXY DIVIDED
YOU MUST CHOOSE A SIDE

CREATE YOUR OWN EPIC STORY
IN THIS HIGHLY ANTICIPATED
MULTI-PLAYER ONLINE VIDEOGAME

YOUR SAGA BEGINS AT
WWW.STARWARSTHEOLDREPUBLIC.COM

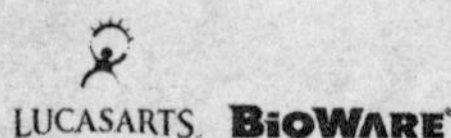

LucasArts and the LucasArts logo are registered trademarks of Lucasfilm Ltd. © 2010 Lucasfilm Entertainment Company Ltd. or Lucasfilm Ltd. & ® or TM as indicated. All rights reserved. BioWare and the BioWare logo are trademarks or registered trademarks of EA International (Studio and Publishing) Ltd.

EXPLORE THE WORLDS OF DEL REY AND SPECTRA.

Get the news about your favorite authors.
Read excerpts from hot new titles.
Follow our author and editor blogs.
Connect and chat with other readers.

Visit us on the web:
www.Suvudu.com

Like us on Facebook:
www.Facebook.com/DelReySpectra

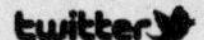

Follow us on Twitter:
@DelReySpectra

For mobile updates:
Text DELREY to 72636.
Two messages monthly. Standard message rates apply.

SPECTRA

DEL REY SPECTRA